Lola looked at Drew, really looked at him.

If she'd seen him on the streets of New York, she wouldn't have looked twice. He didn't have a smile that charmed or a wardrobe that said he had great taste. He'd never barge through a crowd as if he owned Wall Street or cut in front of her at the corner Starbucks because he was late for a meeting.

But there was a reason he was the sheriff. He was steady and reliable, the opposite of her dead husband.

"Lola." Drew's voice had grown soft. His gaze on her face softer still. "Let this go. Nothing good can come of it."

"All I have to do is find the woman these things belong to and—"

"This is a small town, and people aren't going to like you poking around trying to identify who Randy knew... *personally*."

She made a sound of disgust. "You understand where I'm coming from. You might even be sympathetic that I've been hurt. But there's one thing you don't know." And here, she hardened her voice along with her resolve. "I'm going to find this woman and [illegible]."

Can't Hurry Love

MELINDA
CURTIS

FOREVER
New York Boston

Forever
Hachette Book Group
1290 Avenue of the Americas, New York, NY 10104
read-forever.com
twitter.com/readforeverpub

First Edition: March 2020

Forever is an imprint of Grand Central Publishing. The Forever name and logo are trademarks of Hachette Book Group, Inc.

ISBN: 978-1-5387-3341-7 (mass market), 978-1-5387-3342-4 (ebook)

Printed in the United States of America

OPM

10 9 8 7 6 5 4 3 2 1

To Mom, who always believed that
laughter was the best medicine.

Acknowledgments

First off, a huge thank-you to Alex Logan, my editor at Forever. You believed in the heart and humor of this book and, with a gentle hand, made it infinitely better. Thanks also to the rest of the staff at Grand Central Publishing—editorial, art, production, sales, publicity, and marketing—for gearing up for a great series launch. Big hug to my agent, Pamela Hopkins, who listens to my story ideas and somehow manages to come up with a strategic marketing plan (plus she knows how to interpret legalese).

A big thanks to my family, starting with my college-sweetheart husband, who didn't blink an eye when I said I wanted to change careers and write romance—okay, maybe he blinked but then he said, "Go for it"—and continuing with my kids, who hand-sell my books to everyone they meet. A special thanks to my son Colby, who has a knack for adding unusual twists to plots. Thanks to my brothers, who've been sideline cheerleaders, especially through the passing of our parents. As anyone who has lost someone important in their life knows, it takes time to get your sea legs back after a broken heart.

Writers tend to collect a tribe of friends. I've been blessed to have some really great ones who encourage me, challenge me, and support me. Thanks much to Cari Lynn Webb, Anna J. Stewart, and Jane Ann Krentz. Special shout-out to Brenda Novak and a twenty-plus-year friendship. Big thank-you to the rest of my professional team—Sheri Brooks at Purple Papaya, Nancy Berland, and the staff at Writerspace. Your support gives me time to write.

And finally, thanks to my readers, bloggers, and reviewers, who spend time with me and the characters I create. I hope Lola and Drew find a place in your heart. I know they found one in mine.

Prologue

♥

Mims Turner sucked at poker.

She hadn't always but it seemed like she hadn't won in months. She was always betting on the wrong hand or folding when she should call. Just once, she'd like to win. And if Mims could win only once, she'd like it to be today.

"I'll see your five." Mims tossed a stack of five pennies in the pot, followed by a second set. "And raise you five."

"Ditto," Clarice shouted, having predictably left her hearing aids at home. Her pennies bounced into the center of Mims's card table.

"Now we're all in." Bitsy's words rang with finish-line finality. She thought she was going to win. Again.

Just this once…

Mims ground her teeth. She was an outdoorswoman. She was president of the Sunshine Valley Widows Club, a group of thirty women who raised money for causes that benefited the small town of Sunshine, Colorado. She considered herself unflappable. She should be able to master a game of cards. It was just that lately, Mims's entire life was off. She couldn't always make the point she wanted to, and sometimes she lost track of what she was saying midsentence. It was like going through menopause all over again!

She glanced at her opponents. Clarice was a free spirit. She considered bras too establishment. But she knew how to work the hand she was dealt. And Bitsy? Bitsy looked like her ancestors had come over on the *Mayflower* and settled in Boston. And yet she played cards as if she'd grown up in Vegas.

The trio made up the board of the Widows Club. Privately, Mims, Clarice, and Bitsy liked to call themselves the Sunshine Valley Matchmakers Club. With every Widows Club fund-raiser, they gave Cupid a little help, a nudge to someone they felt was ready and worthy of love. Whoever won this hand would win the pot of pennies *and* the right to choose whom the group nudged next.

Mims's cards stuck to her slightly damp palms. Two red kings, two red aces, a two of hearts. All that red had to mean something. It had to mean Mims could break her losing streak!

"I like Edith Archer," Mims blurted, unable to hide her agenda any longer.

"You haven't won." Clarice's loud voice reverberated in Mims's cozy parlor.

Bitsy's black velvet hair bow trembled above her bobbed blond hair. "Edith is old."

"We're all old." If seventy was old, Mims was ancient. "Edith is widowed, which means she gets priority." That was a rule.

"You can't touch Edith." Clarice harrumphed. "She's been widowed less than three months." That was another rule. They didn't begin matching widows or accepting them into the general membership until they'd been bereaved at least half a year. Although the club offered a shoulder to cry on, they were primarily an organization dedicated to good works.

"I like Lola." There was something in Bitsy's normally gentle tone that wasn't so gentle. "Lola's a widow. And she's not even thirty."

"Bitsy's got a point," Clarice said, still using her outdoor voice.

Normally Mims would agree that a younger widow needed more help getting back on her feet, but instead she said, "You should have seen Edith at church last Sunday." Her short gray hair had looked as if she'd stuck her finger in a light socket. "When Charlie died, she fell apart." And kept falling.

Not that Mims hadn't been coming apart at the seams too. Charlie had been Mims's first love. He may have chosen Edith more than half a century ago, but when Mims had become a widow, Charlie had become her emotional rock, unbeknownst to Edith. When Charlie had died, it had been like losing Mims's husband all over again.

Mims resented having to share Charlie with Edith, even in death. She'd do anything to keep her rival out of the Widows Club. This was her last chance. "Edith needs a man, or she'll do something she'll regret."

"Mims has a point too." Clarice considered her hand.

"She'll have to back it up by winning." Bitsy showed

her cards. "Two pair." Two black kings and two black aces—yin to Mims's yang.

Impossible. Mims couldn't breathe. She spread her cards on the table with cold fingers.

"Well, I'll be," Clarice murmured. She glanced at her cards and then laid them facedown. "It's a tie."

Bitsy looked like she'd missed one of her grandchildren's birthdays. "We've never had a tie before."

"We need a rule to cover ties," Mims said. Such as *In case of a tie, the person who's won the least is the winner*.

Before Mims proposed her rule, Clarice came up with one of her own.

"This is a sign." A slow grin worked its way across Clarice's thin, leathery face. "I propose we match both Edith and Lola."

She didn't need to ask Mims twice. "I second."

They both turned to Bitsy, who was staring at her cards as if she were a puzzled fortune-teller.

"Just one question," Bitsy said finally, her gaze landing squarely on Mims. "Is either one of them ready for love?"

Chapter One

♥

If Lola Williams had known Randy would be unable to honor his wedding vows…

If Lola had known Randy would toss aside her love like he did his dirty laundry…

If Lola had known Randy was untrustworthy, unfaithful, and untrue…

She would've returned to New York City before his wedding ring left a tan mark on her finger. But after one year of marriage and one year of widowhood, New York was out of reach, lost to her, a log at the bottom of a fast-burning fire.

Because of Randy.

Because of Randy, Lola was no longer doing hair and makeup for celebrities on Broadway. She was doing hair and makeup for the elderly at the Sunshine Valley Retirement Home and for the dead at the Eternal Rest Mortuary.

She might have salvaged her career on Broadway if she hadn't believed theirs was the forever kind of union. But she was a dreamer. After Randy's fatal car crash, she'd decided their love needed a grand gesture of mourning—*a year's worth*—tying up the loose ends of his life bit by bit, until the only thing left to do was go through his clothes and his side of the closet on the anniversary of his death. Only then had she learned her husband had been sleeping around.

Sitting in her driveway, Lola tossed another pair of Randy's tighty-whities on the bonfire.

She should move her folding chair back from the small blaze before it singed her eyebrows more completely than the afternoon's revelation had made ashes of her heart. Those ashes clogged her lungs, deadened her limbs, and numbed her brain until she couldn't do anything besides bend slightly, reach for another pair of undies, and toss them on the fire.

Cars passed by. And slowed.

Drivers stared. And scowled.

Across the street, Mrs. Everly's mauve curtains twitched.

The familiar burn of being an outsider—*Worse! That gal from New York City*—made Lola wish she'd used Randy's fifty-year-old bottle of whiskey to light the fire instead of nail polish remover. A swig of spirits might have given her the courage to do more than send answering glowers at passersby.

Couldn't they see she was devastated? Couldn't they see she'd hit rock bottom?

A dented and dinged white Subaru wagon parked at the curb. The governing board of the Widows Club looked at her with interest. Lola sank deeper into the creaky webbing of her folding chair.

Yesterday, she'd been thinking that joining the Widows Club and remaining single until her dying day would be the crowning achievement of her bereavement. Today, she was thinking twenty-nine was too young to join a group of widows.

The first widow to the sidewalk was Clarice Rogers. She wielded her hickory walking stick as if it were a gentleman's cane. Trend-wise, Clarice had never moved beyond the 1970s—not in hairstyle, not in fashion, not in the use of sunscreen. Her long gray braids made her thin, sun-damaged face look even longer. Her lime-green geometric blouse had been in and out of style at least five times in the past five decades.

Bitsy Whitlock's black patent loafers gracefully touched the pavement next. If Clarice was clinging to the seventies, Bitsy was an eighties girl. Her dyed blond hair was held back neatly with a big black velvet bow. Pearls adorned her ears and rimmed the crew neck of her turquoise sweater, which was held up by linebacker shoulder pads.

Rounding out the Widows Club board was Mims Turner, the driver of the Subaru and their president. She wasn't stuck in any specific era. She looked like everyone's grandmother with her short gray curls and navy *I ♥ My Grandkids* T-shirt. It was the neon-orange hunting vest with utility pockets that gave away the fact that she packed heat in her pink pleather purse.

The three conferred before walking to the edge of Lola's driveway, stopping a safe distance from the cinders of her life.

"Lola, dear." Mims straightened her orange hunting

vest and waved a hand toward Randy's smoldering underpants. "What's this all about?"

Was it too much to hope that building a fire in her driveway made Lola a poor candidate for the Widows Club? "I found condoms in Randy's dresser. The receipt for them was dated two weeks before he died."

"Lola, dear." Mims made sympathetic noises. "Don't throw them out. I believe condoms have a three-year shelf life."

The horror of that statement coming out of grandmotherly Mims's mouth temporarily silenced Lola.

She reached for another pair of Hanes, wishing she hadn't waited a year to clean out Randy's side of the closet. She was such a romantic fool. And she'd been one since she was nine.

Back then, at the urging of her grandmother, Lola had started a scrapbook of dreams—a flowered and rainbowed blueprint of how her life should be. Land a job doing hair and makeup on Broadway by age twenty-seven (she'd done it by twenty-five), fall in love with her one true love by age twenty-eight (she'd met Randy on her twenty-seventh birthday), have a whirlwind romance and fairy-tale wedding by age twenty-nine (she'd been ahead of the game, marrying Randy mere weeks after they met), and have babies by age thirty (her only failure).

Who was she kidding? It was all a failure. Lola should have brought the scrapbook out to burn.

"You don't understand. We'd been trying to get pregnant for six months before Randy's accident," Lola said in a voice as hard as the metal coffin Judge Harper had special ordered last week. She didn't use that tone because she was annoyed at being misunderstood by the widows (well, maybe a little), but because she'd cut off her dreams of being a makeup artist / hair stylist to the stars to be with Randy, and because she'd cut back on caffeine and wine to increase her odds of having his baby. And all the while, Randy hadn't been cutting back on anything! "It was a large box of condoms, and it was nearly empty." Thirty used from a box of forty. *In two weeks!*

Lola felt sucker punched.

"You think he was..." Clutching her pearls, Bitsy drew a dramatic breath. "*Cheating*?"

The word cut through the white smoke in the air and the ashes in Lola's stomach. It cut and cut and cut until Lola thought she might flutter like ribbons into the flames.

Was she really so gullible? Was she really the woman who'd had no clue her husband was unfaithful?

Lola blew out a breath and admitted the truth. *She was.*

A mournful, wounded sound collected in Lola's throat. She swallowed it back and gripped the fake-wood chair handles.

Just then the sheriff's car pulled to the curb, lights flashing.

"Thank heavens," Bitsy murmured.

Wearing his crisp brown-and-tan uniform and a stern expression, Sheriff Drew Taylor arrived with a fire extinguisher. He rented the run-down farmhouse Randy had inherited from his grandmother and was everything Lola's husband hadn't been—terse, tall, and trustworthy. Sure, he didn't have Randy's blond-haired, blue-eyed, all-American good looks. Drew had short walnut-brown hair, a bump on the bridge of his nose, and a small nick above his right cheekbone. But he had the steady eyes and reserved smile you appreciated in an officer of the law.

Drew planted his boots on the pavement. "Ladies."

That one word. It said, *Peace will ensue.*

Lola shifted in her chair, not ready to be peaceful.

Now Drew…Drew would never cheat on his wife (for the record, she'd left him *and* their daughter). He'd probably never cheated on anything in his entire life.

"I'll give you thirty seconds to explain why there's a fire here, or I'm going to have to take somebody in." His gaze bypassed the Widows Club and landed on Lola.

It landed with a brown-eyed howdy-do that rocked Lola against her chair. It landed and made her think about empty seats across the dining room table, of shared laughter, shared pillows, and shared nachos. All the things she missed about marriage.

When Lola didn't explain herself, the sheriff quirked a dark eyebrow. "Twenty-five seconds."

Mrs. Everly's mauve curtains twitched again.

Howdy-do aside, Lola didn't want to take a ride with the sheriff. "My husband did his own laundry," Lola said, as if Drew should understand what that meant. "He bleached all the evidence out of his shorts."

Without so much as a *Come again?* the sheriff flipped the safety tab on the fire extinguisher.

And yet he didn't immediately put out the fire. His gaze connected squarely with Lola's.

For the second time that day, Lola felt sucker punched.

Drew knew.

He knew Randy was a cheater. And if the sheriff knew, everyone in town knew.

Well... Her gaze drifted to the governing board of the Widows Club.

Maybe not everyone.

Lola tossed the last pair of briefs on the flames and went inside.

If Drew wanted to arrest her, he'd have to come and get her.

And give her some answers while he was at it.

* * *

Females plus fire often equaled trouble.

When Sheriff Drew Taylor arrived on the scene, he'd done a three-point inspection of the female with the fire—no weapons, no tears, nothing out of the ordinary in Lola Williams's appearance. In short, this wasn't shaping up to be trouble.

Drew knew all about women and trouble. He was a single dad to a precocious six-year-old girl and the big brother to four younger sisters. When Drew was ten, his dad had seen the pink writing on the wall and hit the road, sentencing his son to a life of hair bows, chatterboxes, and long bathroom queues.

Granted, that made Drew qualified to raise a little girl alone but experience told him a woman's appearance was sometimes more important than her outward expressions of emotion. When his sisters had sunk into Woe-Is-Me mode, they'd called for pizza and raided Drew's dresser for his old sweatpants. The healing power of an elastic waistband and a pepperoni pie was amazing. When his sisters had reached Watch-Out-World mode, they'd donned their female battle gear (tight-fitting clothes, man-hunter makeup) and cut down anything in their path, including cheating boyfriends, backstabbing girlfriends, and well-meaning brothers.

Contrary to what Florence in dispatch had reported, there wasn't a wild woman setting fire to the neighborhood on Skyview Drive. Lola hadn't been dressed to wallow or wound. Her makeup had been as natural as her sun-kissed brown hair. In shorts and a pink tank top, she'd been dressed to wash her car or work in the garden, not eat her way through a pizza or confront her dead husband's lover with a weapon.

Drew aimed a chemical stream at the small flames in Lola's driveway, vowing that Becky wouldn't fall in love until she was thirty. By then, he'd be fifty-five and ready to sit back and enjoy being a grandpa. He wouldn't have to worry about the women in his life—Becky, his sisters, his ex-wife.

My ex-wife...

Drew gripped the fire extinguisher as if it were an empty, crushable beer can.

He looked around. The widows watched him in patient silence. A gentle breeze rustled bright-green leaves on trees up and down Skyview Drive. Two houses down, Joni Russell watered the daisies in her window boxes. This was Sunshine. Quiet, sleepy Sunshine.

Keeping the peace in Sunshine was easy compared to keeping the peace in Afghanistan, New York, or a household with four sisters. Shoot, worry about his siblings had kept him up more nights than worry about his own kid. The twins were finishing college over in Boulder, occasionally running out of money, occasionally posting heart-stopping activities on social media. Eileen was twenty-seven and worked at the local animal shelter. She had a habit of bringing home strays she couldn't handle. The last stray had two legs and a southern accent. And then there was Priscilla, who was about Lola's age. She was newly divorced and pushing the boundaries of her newly found freedom, acting more like the twins than a woman of twenty-nine.

Sometimes Drew wanted to arrest his sisters for their own good. The absolute last thing he needed was to add Lola Williams to his Watch-Over list, which was already filled with his mother, his four sisters, and his daughter.

He exhaled and changed his grip on the fire extinguisher.

"Drew Taylor." Mims gave him a stern look she'd perfected while running the elementary school cafeteria. "You are *not* going to arrest Lola."

Having no intention of reading his landlord her rights, Drew set the safety on the extinguisher.

"She didn't hurt anyone." That came from Bitsy, the protector of the underdog. She'd recently retired from working in customer service at a cable company's call center in Greeley, where rumor had it she'd comped irate customers more free services than were listed in the coupon book the high school band sold every year.

"We're here to take Lola under our wing." Clarice shook her walking stick at him, tottering only slightly on those two new knees she'd gotten six months earlier. "What that girl needs is a life, not a police record."

"Oh." As in *Oh no*. Drew had a sudden burst of sympathy for Lola.

The Sunshine Valley Widows Club did good work, but most of its members were old and set in their small-town ways. For local charities, they held fund-raisers as traditional as bake sales and as politically incorrect as kissing booths at the fair. Tonight, the Widows Club was holding a bachelorette auction at Shaw's Bar & Grill. Clearly, they were looking for another woman to auction off.

They wanted to auction Lola off tonight? If Lola wasn't allowed a little time to come to terms with Randy's infidelity, she'd reach Watch-Out-World mode. And then Drew would need more than a fire extinguisher to control the damage. "Give Lola some space, and I won't arrest her."

"It's her time," Mims said with all the practicality of a woman announcing her car was due for an oil change. "We've given her an extra six months."

"Being widowed," Clarice tsk-tsked, "it can be lonely."

"Loneliness can fester," Bitsy said in that soothing voice of hers.

"And then widows start acting odd." Mims pointed toward the pile of driveway ashes.

Loneliness had nothing to do with Lola acting odd. It was the realization that Randy wasn't the man she'd thought he was.

Six years ago, Drew had seen that same shell-shocked expression on his ex-wife's face. That was the last time he'd seen Jane. He would bet his ex hadn't worn that expression when she'd called him this morning. Nope. He would bet he was the one who'd looked like the rug had been yanked out from under him. Jane hadn't seen Becky since she was three months old and suddenly wanted joint custody? It was enough to T-bone a man.

Frustration crowded its way into his lungs and up his throat until he had to focus on something else to breathe easier—the ashes in the driveway, the sturdy oak door, Lola.

Compared to Jane, Lola was no trouble. Sure, a few people in town considered her stuck-up because she was from New York City, and others couldn't understand how she could do hair and makeup on corpses. There was talk she'd swindled Randy's mother financially after his death, and some folks, like Lola's neighbor Ramona Everly, took that as a personal affront. And despite all that, it probably didn't help that Lola didn't try to blend in. She didn't wear traditional cowboy boots. She didn't have a four-wheel drive. And she rooted for the New York Giants!

But once Lola got over the shock of the truth, she'd be fine. There were guys in town who'd ask her out because she was a looker and didn't have kids. She had roots here now—real estate, two jobs. She'd find her footing and get back on track.

A red SUV parked across the street. Avery Blackstone got out. She was dressed for this evening's auction in high-heeled boots, black leggings, and a shiny low-cut black blouse. She and her family were some of the few Ute tribe members who didn't live on the nearby reservation, and if Drew hadn't gone to school with her, he might have been in awe of her beauty.

Avery nodded to Drew. "Florence called me."

Drew made a mental note to thank his dispatcher for contacting Lola's best friend.

"Just in time." Mims took Avery by the arm and led her to the ashes. "Lola needs you. She burned Randy's drawers."

Avery hesitated, as silent and solemn as if she'd just joined a graveside vigil. Finally, she asked, "Randy's dresser drawers?"

"No. His..." Clarice ran a hand down one of her gray braids and then pointed briefly downward. "His *underthings*."

"He was cheating on Lola before he died," Bitsy said in a hushed tone. "Can you believe it?"

Avery's heavily made-up, dark eyes widened. "No."

Drew could believe it. The farmhouse he rented from Randy and Lola had a separate two-car garage at the back of the property with an apartment above it. The garage, which wasn't included in Drew's rent, had access to a road down by the South Platte River. Until Randy died, Drew had often been awakened by Randy's truck rumbling in from the back and a text: Do Not Disturb. Randy's truck was always gone by morning, leaving Drew wrestling with his conscience. He didn't consider cheating to be the answer to a bad marriage. But what could he do? No laws he upheld had been broken. And the one time he'd tried to hint at the truth to Lola, she'd thought he was hitting on her.

"Thanks for stopping by, Avery." Drew opened his car door. He had two more calls to answer and needed to move along. But first, he fixed the widows with a stern stare. "Lola needs friends right now much more than she needs to be auctioned off by the Widows Club for a dinner date."

"You're meddling." Mims's broad-faced grin looked innocent on first glance. It was only upon closer inspection that her steely determination could be seen in the tight lines radiating from her mouth. "The only way we'll agree to letting Lola skip the fund-raiser, Sheriff, is if you agree to show up tonight."

"It's Saturday, Mims." Drew glanced toward Lola's front window. The curtains were closed. "And your event is at the only bar in town. Of course I'll be there."

Besides, Becky was sleeping over at her best friend's house, and given Jane's demand for custody, Drew could use a drink.

Chapter Two

♥

"Huddle up, gals." Mims drew Bitsy and Clarice close on the sidewalk as the sheriff drove away. "Haven't I been saying for years the sheriff is like a peach just waiting to ripen?"

Clarice and Bitsy nodded.

"Did you see the way Drew looked at Lola?" Mims lowered her voice in case one of Lola's front windows was open.

"Yes," Clarice said brightly. "And he didn't arrest her."

"He's ready for love," Bitsy said slowly.

"But she's not ripe," Clarice added with a toss of a silver braid. "Or ready."

"Lola's a caution," Mims agreed, ready to put their efforts with Lola on hold so the group could devote all their energy to finding Edith a man. "Now, Edith—"

"Lola's in shock." Bitsy had a determined gleam in her eyes, holding to her poker pick. "It's not a deal breaker. Did you see that look Drew gave her? It smoked nearly as much as the fire."

Mims's cell phone rang. She dug it from her hunting-vest pocket and read the display. "It's Susie Taylor." Drew's mom.

"It's a sign." Clarice pounded her walking stick on the sidewalk, grinning. "You know how I love signs."

"Let's not get carried away with those signs of yours," Bitsy cautioned in a soft voice. "You said a tie was a sign. And before that your sign had us trying to convince Wendy Adams that Harlen Martinez was *the one* for her."

That had been a disaster.

Hoping their efforts with Edith would be more successful, Mims answered her phone.

* * *

After the bonfire, Lola expected the knock on her door.

She just didn't expect Avery to be the knocker.

"Randy was unfaithful?" Avery wrapped her arms around Lola and squeezed like she could put the pieces of Lola's life back together by sheer force of will. "Who was he sleeping with?"

"No idea." Lola peeked past the cascade of Avery's black silken hair to the empty curb. "No Widows Club? No sheriff?"

"Forget them." Avery backed away from Lola just enough to study her face. "How badly is your heart broken?"

As the horror of betrayal and the fear of being arrested—or finagled into the Widows Club—burned out, Lola's legs crumpled like charred logs. She would've fallen if not for Avery, who propped her up and hustled her to the brown leather couch.

It wasn't the first time Avery had come to Lola's rescue. That was how they'd met. Lola had been working on her first postmortem client at the mortuary, holding the heebie-jeebies at bay until she'd realized Mrs. Baumgart needed her nose hairs tweezed and she'd removed more than nose hair. She'd rushed out back and lost her breakfast in the trash, only to be found by Avery. She managed the movie theater, which shared an alley with the mortuary. She'd taken Lola into the theater office and given her a ginger ale and a pep talk about surviving in small towns.

Lola could use another pep talk about now.

"Tell me what you know." Avery eyed Randy's wet bar.

Lola collapsed sideways on a couch cushion as she recapped what she'd discovered.

In the ensuing silence, Lola's gaze found their wedding picture on the wall. Her hair had been perfect. Her dress Vera Wang. She should have recognized the zit on her forehead as an omen. "I thought Randy loved me."

Avery poked around the bar, grabbing hold of Randy's unopened fifty-year-old bottle of whiskey. "He gave you a ring and his name."

"And uprooted me from New York." Lola wanted to curl into a tight ball and cry. But what good would that do? Randy would still be dead, still have been unfaithful, and she'd still be surrounded by his things.

His things.

She jolted upright. The deer head mounted above the redbrick fireplace. The branded beer mirror over the living room bar. The leather couch. The familiar decorations of the updated small Craftsman that had given her comfort after Randy's death. They were... It was...

"I'm living in Randy's bachelor pad." A chill crept over Lola. "I need to redecorate." Not move. Because Randy had taken out second mortgages on both houses, and his life insurance had gone to his mother. If Lola left now, she'd leave with nothing but debt.

"Haven't I been telling you to redecorate for months?" Avery handed Lola a full shot glass. Randy's expensive whiskey sat open on the bar.

Lola hesitated before accepting the shot. She wasn't a drinker, and Randy had been saving that bottle.

"Yes, I opened the whiskey Randy paid five hundred dollars for." Avery filled her glass to the rim, drinking it without so much as a wince.

"But—"

Avery narrowed her expertly lined eyes. "Is Randy going to complain?"

"No."

"Would you rather the other woman drank it?"

"*No!*" It took Lola two burning swallows to get it all down. The whiskey didn't fill the hole in her heart or the wound to her pride but it did give her a false jolt of courage. "Who was it, Avery? Who is the other woman?"

"I don't know." Her friend shrugged, staring at the bottom of her shot glass. "Does it matter?"

"*Yes!*" The need to know pressed a panic button

inside of Lola, one she'd had no idea had been factory installed. "Why wasn't I good enough for him?" Lola pressed a hand over her eyes and groaned. Despite her best efforts to the contrary, she was turning into her mother. Her slightly dramatic, slightly eccentric, slightly foolish mother, who'd often wailed the very same question during the first few months after Lola's dad had left them.

"Forget about Randy. You're coming to Shaw's with me tonight." Avery made her second whiskey disappear in one smooth swallow. "You could use a therapy session with a good bottle of wine."

"Shaw's doesn't have good wine." It had Widows Club fund-raisers. "Did Mims put you up to this?"

"No, but it's been a long time since you left this man cave." Avery sat next to her and poured them both another drink. "You need a new man."

"I need to get rid of my old man first." Lola downed the whiskey. It didn't burn any less than the first time. Trust Randy to buy crappy, expensive liquor. But it served a purpose. She stood on steadier legs. "Randy goes. Starting now." Lola marched toward the stairs.

On the second floor, Lola made it past another wedding picture and the king-size bed without choking up. She entered the walk-in closet, which was bigger than most bedrooms, big enough for two floor-to-ceiling shoe racks and two dressers. But not big enough to hide the truth of Randy's infidelity.

"Is that your dream book?" Avery rushed to Lola's dresser. She flipped open the stained pink fabric scrapbook of Lola's youth. "Look at these autographed playbills. And hairstyles. And swatches of lace. And..." She cooed. "That is the sweetest baby nursery I've ever seen."

And it would never be Lola's. "My mother told me when I was nine..." Right after Lola's dad announced he'd gotten his mistress pregnant. "There are no happily-ever-afters." She'd been right. Lola reached for the scrapbook, which held crushed dreams and broken promises. "That's going in the trash."

Avery cradled the book to her chest. "You aren't giving up on your dreams just because Randy was a jerk. I still believe in Prince Charming. And you should too."

Lola's eyes misted. More than half the scrapbook was filled with aspirations of family and love. Those seemed as out of reach as her abandoned career doing hair and makeup on Broadway. She had no reason to keep the scrapbook, except...

Nana's dear face came to mind, her bright-blue eye shadow and rosy blush framed by a steel-gray beehive. She'd sat at the kitchen table with Lola, cutting out pictures from *Playbill* and *People* and recounting Grandpa's courtship.

"My grandmother used to say true love is home, and home is where dreams are made." Lola took the dream book and put it back on the dresser. Someday, she'd make new dreams. "Can you box up Randy's shoes? I'll finish the dresser." And then all she'd have left was the shelf above it.

Lola sat on the carpeted floor and opened the bottom drawer. Mistake. The sweatshirts smelled of Randy.

She used to love the clean way he smelled, as if he'd just showered and put on a set of freshly laundered clothes. Had his obsession with the shower and the laundry been a necessity to hide his lying lifestyle? Of course it had.

"I'm ready for another drink now." Lola started to stand.

"You've got to earn it first." Avery planted a hand on Lola's shoulder and pressed her back down. "Or I'll never get to Shaw's by five thirty."

"I hate that you're right." Lola emptied the bottom drawer of Randy's sweatshirts. And then it was on to the drawers with Randy's shorts: cargo (including a pair he'd worn on their honeymoon on the Gulf Coast), basketball (he'd played on the men's team in Greeley on Thursdays), padded bike shorts (for that spin class he'd attended in Greeley on Monday nights).

Basketball? Spin class? And what about those late nights when he'd claimed to be at Shaw's with the guys?

Questions, suspicions, and doubts filled Lola's chest, causing more congestion than rush hour traffic in Times Square, making it hard to breathe. She couldn't be sure of anything anymore.

Randy's T-shirt drawer was next. Lola had to rise to her knees to empty it. The *Playboy* T-shirt he'd worn the day they'd met. Denver sports teams. Blue shirts advertising his business—*Your Second Husband Handyman Service*. A small white plastic bag from Valley Drug Store was stuffed in the back. Inside was a pair of dangly silver earrings that momentarily blinded

Lola to infidelity and had her stepping back into the fantasy of a perfect marriage.

"Randy was always buying me little gifts and then forgetting to give them to me. I'd come across bags like this in the glove box of his car, out in the garage with his tools, and..." The earrings slipped through her fingers. They were clip-ons. Lola had pierced ears. She had to face the truth. None of those hidden gifts had been meant for her. "I hate him."

"Attagirl." Avery shoved Randy's shoes into a box as if she couldn't get rid of them fast enough.

The top drawer of the dresser was clear, having harbored Randy's briefs and the condom box, which now sat on the floor in the corner. On top of the dresser was the teak box where Randy used to put his wallet and the love notes she'd written him. Lola opened it but other than the keys to the farmhouse they rented to Drew, there was nothing inside. She'd removed the paper trail of their romance soon after his death. The love letters were in a kitchen drawer downstairs. Sometimes she read them with her morning coffee.

Her stomach churned at her romantic naivete.

Avery finished with Randy's shoes, took one look at Lola, and hugged her again. "Let's forget about Shaw's and the bachelorette auction. Let's go to the theater. We can sit in the projection room, watch movies, and eat buckets of popcorn." A privilege they regularly indulged in since her family owned the theater.

Broken Lola, the woman who'd believed in true love, wanted to put on a pair of baggy sweats, order pizza, and hide away from the world. Angry Lola, the woman who was discovering she had too much in common with her mother, wanted to flush every photo of Randy down the toilet, put on her sexiest dress, and paint the town red. But there was another Lola inside, one who was strong and scrappy and a survivor.

"No. I'm finishing this." There was nothing more Randy could do to hurt her.

Lola stood on a footstool and reached for the last of Randy's things on the dusty top shelf. She handed Avery yearbooks, the small safe containing Randy's handgun, and then a bulky brown leather duffel.

"It's heavy." Avery dropped the duffel to the floor. "Can I open it?" Not waiting for Lola's approval, she knelt beside it, releasing the zipper.

"What is it this time?" Lola didn't want to look. "A supply of perfume? Chocolates? Lingerie for his lover?" Was it too much to hope that he'd monogrammed something personal for the other woman? At least then she'd have a clue about his mistress's identity.

"Holy cow." Avery sat back on her heels. "It's a pair of adult blow-up dolls."

"A pair? His and hers?" Had she thought Randy couldn't shock her anymore? Whiskey swirled up Lola's throat. With effort, she swallowed it back down.

"He had an adventurous side." Avery opened the bag wider, revealing a box with a man's and a woman's cartoony faces. "Who knew?"

"Not me." Lola's words, like her spirits, were meek and beaten.

"Hey, it's never been opened." Avery squeezed Lola's

hand. "He could have bought it for you two to play with. You should be flattered."

"I'm horrified." Lola stared at the plastic faces, which looked drawn on with big markers. The smiley-face buttons at Walmart had more character.

"Well, maybe..." Avery opened the bag completely. "Maybe he ordered the wrong thing. These don't have parts."

"P-p-parts?"

"You know." Avery glanced up. "Boy parts. Girl parts."

"I had no idea life-size dolls came fully equipped," Lola said weakly.

"These are definitely cheap," Avery said, suddenly a sex-toy expert. "He could have gotten them as a wedding gift and been waiting to give them to someone else."

"Randy wasn't the regifting type." Trouble was, Lola didn't know anymore what type of man she'd married. "I'll take that drink now."

Avery nodded. "I think you've earned it."

Chapter Three

♥

Drew's next stop after putting out Lola's fire was Gigi Nelson's place.

The octogenarian called at least once a week to report something. This time it was a rabid rodent in her backyard. If Drew had to guess, the rodent was a raccoon, wasn't rabid, and would most likely be gone by the time he arrived. Not that it mattered. Gigi would have coffee ready. She was lonely, and those in the sheriff's office, Drew included, didn't mind a quiet coffee break with fresh-from-the-oven cookies.

But today…

His past had risen up to bite him in the butt.

"You said we could move to Nashville." Six years ago, Jane's words had been wooden. "You said marriage wouldn't change anything."

"But something else has." Drew held Becky closer but her precious, swaddled body couldn't thaw the ice forming around his heart.

"You said you'd support my dreams." Jane had stared at Drew as if he'd just stepped off the express elevator from Hades and she didn't recognize the loathsome demon he'd become.

"That was before we got pregnant." An accident. "Before Becky was born." Before he'd become a dad and they'd become a family. "Between my shifts as a sheriff and your gigs on the road, we need a support group." His mother. His sisters. Her parents. "We wouldn't have that in Nashville. Think about Becky." He angled her cherubic face in Jane's direction. "We can't move now."

Jane had looked away.

And she had never looked back. She'd filed for divorce that morning, signed over custody of Becky by noon, and left for Nashville before sundown.

Drew flexed his fingers on the steering wheel. He needed mind-numbing action today so he wouldn't think about Jane. A quick search online after her call had found a startling statistic: more often than not, absentee moms won the right to visitation and partial custody. What did that mean for Becky? Would she go to school half the year here and the other half in Nashville?

Not if Drew could help it.

A skateboarder flew off the curb in front of the cruiser, narrowly avoiding being run down.

Drew slammed on his brakes, shoved the car in park, and hopped out just as another skateboarder did the same thing. "Boys! Do you have a death wish?"

As one, the Bodine brothers, identical twins, stepped on the back ends of their boards and came to quick, noisy stops. The tall, lanky teens had shaggy brown hair that hung in their eyes and smiles that had charmed them into—and out of—trouble for most of their sixteen years.

"I had plenty of time to get across." That had to be Steve. He was the more cynical twin.

Phillip slugged Steve's shoulder. "Arrest him. He was going to skate in the town square."

"Way to go, loser." Steve slugged him back, but they were both grinning like idiots. "Now neither one of us can skate there."

Because it was against a recently passed town ordinance.

Victor Yates drove his feedstore truck slowly around Drew's cruiser, giving the Bodines a hard look before giving Drew one of equal intensity. He was on the Sunshine Town Council (had been for decades), had authored the skateboarding ordinance (among other fun-killing laws), and had the demeanor of a man with serious constipation issues (he cut no one a break). None of which endeared him to the town's youth or Drew. Didn't help that he was Jane's father.

"Now what are we supposed to do?" Phillip rubbed his shoulder.

As one, they turned to Drew, waiting for him to make a suggestion.

Drew could think of lots of places they could skate—the old boat launch at Kismet Lake, the courtyard at the Methodist church, the loading platforms at the idle grain mill. None of which were legal either, but all of them tended to be deserted on Saturdays. Drew had been hoping the teens would outgrow their affection for skateboarding over the winter and go back to bull riding. No such luck. But the day was clear, and there was nothing going on in town to distract them. If they were going to skate, he'd rather they did it where no one would complain. "Try the grain mill."

Whooping, they hopped on their skateboards and set off.

"Be careful," Drew called after them, most likely too late.

A white Subaru wagon pulled up next to Drew, blocking the traffic going the other way.

Flashing that determined smile of hers, Mims leaned over the steering wheel so she could see Drew through the open passenger window. "Sheriff, we just heard from your mother that you're looking for a good child-custody lawyer."

Kudos to Mom for holding out four hours with the news.

Drew kept his voice carefully neutral. "Do you have a recommendation?" There were only two law firms in town, each run by one of Judge Harper's sons.

"We do." Clarice smoothed a gray braid over her shoulder and said in complete seriousness, "You should get married."

Drew clutched the cruiser's doorframe.

"No judge will take Becky away from her married, upstanding father," Bitsy added from the back seat.

A truck turned onto Main Street and headed toward the Subaru.

"Not for a woman whose only claim to stability for six years has been a post office box." Mims gave the slowing truck a finger—her index finger—as if to say, *Just a minute.*

"And we have the perfect woman for you," Bitsy said in that soothing voice of hers.

Drew wasn't soothed.

"We called Wendy Adams," Mims said in a rush, causing Bitsy to frown. "She's interested."

"Bring cash to the auction tonight." Clarice jabbed a finger in his direction. "And don't be late."

The approaching truck honked. The widows promised to see Drew later and drove out of the way, leaving him standing in the middle of Main Street.

Get married?

Get real.

Except, a small voice in his head whispered, *it makes sense on paper. To protect Becky.*

Drew shook his head, sliding behind the wheel and putting the car in drive. It didn't matter that he'd been thinking about putting himself back in the dating scene now that Becky was older. If he'd learned anything from Lola and Randy, it was that whirlwind romance did not make for a happy, stable marriage. When he got married again, it'd be to someone who'd be a great mother for Becky. Someone generous and kind. Someone predictable and stable. Someone who'd value their marriage vows and who loved Sunshine and never wanted to leave. Someone like…

Wendy Adams.

Wendy was a secretary at the elementary school, taught Sunday school to tots, was a member of the quilting club, and had never drunk herself under the table at Shaw's. She was a few years younger than Drew and a Sunshine native. And okay, she was pretty, a petite blonde with subtle curves and a soft voice. She didn't dress as if she were going to a New York City nightclub, but she didn't dress like a nun either.

His cell phone rang through the cruiser's console.

"Dad, Daddy, Papa, Padre!"

His daughter's enthusiastic greeting always made Drew smile. "What is it, honey?"

"Granny says we're getting married." Becky giggled and giggled and giggled some more, as if she were being mauled by a small, overly affectionate puppy.

"Granny is jumping the gun." Drew clenched his jaw, turning down Gigi's street. "Put her on the phone, honey."

"Granny Susie!" Becky's cowboy boots clumped on hardwood. "Granny! Daddy's on the phone." And then her voice dropped to a whisper. "Don't tell her I called you."

"Hello? Drew?" When Susie Taylor came on the line, she sounded innocent. Too innocent. Which usually meant his mother was guilty of more than she was willing to admit. "What's up?"

"Marriage? Am I not the only one of your children who's provided you with a grandchild?"

"Oh, but Drew—"

"And what did I say the last time you set me up on a blind date?"

"Oh, but Drew, I haven't—"

"I said give it time." He parked in front of Gigi's white picket fence. "I said give Becky and me both time."

"Ah," his mom said, lowering her voice. "You saw Mims."

"After *you* called her. Yes. And then Becky told me I was getting married."

"Well, that exploded in my face pretty quickly, didn't it?" His mom sighed. "I called Mims because her grandson went through a custody battle last year. I wanted some advice for you. Mims mentioned how Carl's being engaged helped him in court. And then she suggested the bachelorette auction."

Drew closed his eyes. "*And*..." There had to be more.

"And Wendy Adams. She mentioned how Wendy Adams would be perfect for you." His mom's tone took a defensive turn. "If you know these things, why do you interrogate me?"

"Because cops love confessions." Not that it made him feel any better about the situation. Drew opened his eyes to face his next call.

Gigi had the front door open. She was thin and frail and made a really good pot of coffee. If she'd been fifty years younger, he might have considered marrying her.

"I'm sorry." His mother didn't sound apologetic. "Becky overheard me on the phone with Mims so I tried to make a joke of it."

"I'll get a good lawyer." If not one of the Harpers, then someone in Greeley.

"Yes, but could you keep an open mind about Wendy?" His mom wasn't going to let this go easily. "Jane has always been very determined once she makes up her mind."

"I'm hanging up now." Because his mother was starting to make sense.

Chapter Four

♥

After his shift, Drew dropped Becky off at Mia Hampton's house with her sleeping bag and a pizza and then arrived at Shaw's Bar & Grill, hungry and tired.

Besides Lola's bonfire, Gigi's raccoon search, and checking on the Bodine boys at the mill, Drew had impounded a rooster named Marvin (no livestock allowed in city limits), settled a dispute at the retirement home (between two siblings vying for their father's affection and bank account), and investigated reports of gunfire near the high school (traced to Bob Lumley's backfiring '57 Chevy). That was nearly triple the number of calls he responded to on an average day.

Drew blamed it on spring-thaw madness, which in Sunshine was like a full moon, only it lingered for weeks instead of one night. It was May, and suddenly the temps were creeping up to seventy. That change in temperature put folks on edge. By June, things would settle back to normal. Hopefully, Jane's custody demand would disappear just as quickly.

Shaw's had a big stage and a dance floor on one end,

balanced on the other side by padded booths and large wooden tables around a well-used pool table. In the middle was a long, narrow bar with seats on both sides. There were license plates on the walls instead of photos or mirrors. Old saddles were mounted on the rafters. And on Saturday nights, the shells from free peanuts littered the floor. It was *man-vana*.

Drew settled in at the bar and ordered a beer, contemplating his options pertaining to Wendy. He'd told his staff he was showing up to make sure things at the auction didn't get out of hand. It was one of the town's favorite spectacles, resulting in more drunk and disorderly arrests than at the county fair. Last year, Paul Gregory had a few too many daiquiris with the date he'd won at auction, and boot-scootin'-boogied across the bar. Topless.

Drew studied the crowd. It was the typical auction mix of women dressed for date night and cleaned-up cowhands from ranches up and down the valley. He couldn't spot a petite blonde, perhaps because there were so many cowboy hats. It seemed like every yahoo within a fifty-mile radius was sardined on the dance floor.

Noah Shaw slid a tall, frosty beer and a bowl of peanuts in front of Drew. His family had owned Shaw's for three generations. The big man had never met a stranger, at least not one who paid their bar tab. "You bidding tonight?"

"I haven't decided." It wouldn't hurt to test the waters with Wendy if she decided to participate. Drew took a sip of his beer and then started shelling peanuts.

"This is a first." Noah leaned on the bar. "Which woman finally caught your eye?"

Before Drew could answer, Mims took the stage with all the command of a general in front of her troops. She'd traded in her hunting vest and boots in favor of a blue dress and white sandals. "Thank you all for showing up to the Date Night Auction to benefit the Sunshine Valley Boys & Girls Club. The bachelorettes for auction tonight—"

Hoots, whistles, and hollers erupted. The horde sounded like over-sugared, deep-voiced children who'd been told it was time to open Christmas presents.

"—will be available for prescreening for the next few minutes on and around the stage. Ladies, we're still taking names if you want to join in on the fun." Mims stared down at the crowd. "Gentlemen, as a reminder, bidding starts at one hundred dollars. This is a cash-only event. Any man who sets foot on the stage makes an immediate purchase. Winning bidders also pay for dinner and drinks afterward."

Was he really thinking about bidding on Wendy? Drew shelled a peanut, shifting in his seat. His wallet was fatter than usual in his back pocket, considering he'd withdrawn $400 in cash from the ATM. If that wasn't intent to bid, he didn't know what was.

The noise was nearly deafening. Drew craned his neck to see the women who'd agreed to this mad dating game but he had yet to see Wendy. He had too much pride to push through the crowd and confirm her presence.

A few minutes later, the auction started with Tiffany

Winslow, who'd been in the same grade as Drew's sister Eileen. Tiff worked as a checker at the pharmacy and sold for $250.

Daisy Newbury went next. She worked at the convenience store and sold for $200 to a cowboy Drew didn't recognize.

If Wendy hadn't come, Drew would've bet he'd be in bed early tonight without anyone in one of his jail cells. The crowd was noisy but behaving.

His sisters were not.

Priscilla claimed the stool next to him. "Wish me luck, Bro. I'm going on the auction block. All I need to do is track down Clarice and the sign-up sheet." Priscilla worked at a bank and normally dressed conservatively with little makeup. Tonight, her eyes were lined like Gigi's imaginary raccoon, and her fire-engine-red blouse plunged alarmingly.

Drew nearly choked on a peanut. "You aren't going up there looking like…like *that*." Like she wanted a man to value her physical assets more than her personality. "You're practically thirty, not twenty-three. Noah, sell me a Shaw's T-shirt. Extra large."

"Forget the T-shirt, Noah." Pris sniffed. "And I'm size medium, not XL."

"Whatever it takes to cover you up." Drew couldn't bring himself to look directly at his sister.

"You're such a prude." Pris blew a kiss to someone across the room. "Now I know why Eileen isn't talking to you right now. Tyrell was a total hottie, and you had no right to run him out of town."

"I didn't run him out of town," Drew said through

clenched teeth, thinking about Eileen's latest stray. "He stole Eileen's SUV and was arrested in Denver."

"Only because you reported the SUV stolen. Eileen said he had her permission."

"Only to drive to the drug store in town, not to Denver." Drew gripped his beer glass so tight that he thought it might shatter.

"Anyway, landing the right guy takes time and the right bait." Pris bumped her shoulder against Drew's. "Tonight is going to be awesome because I'm feeling wonderful."

Wonderful. It was a word the Taylors used to tell each other they were okay.

"Tone it down a notch." Or ten. Anything less than wonderful. Drew took a deep drink from his beer.

After his father had left and his mom had taken on two jobs, Drew had needed a system to determine which sister needed help and what kind of support she needed. *Woe-Is-Me* meant someone needed alone time. *Watch-Out-World* meant he needed to give a brief lecture and then hunker down somewhere safe until the storm was over. And *Wonderful*? *Wonderful* meant everything was normal, no intervention needed.

"I heard Jason Petrie is here." Pris craned her head around him, leaning every which way, scoping out the crowd gathered on the dance floor. "I'm not going to catch him with a Shaw's T-shirt."

"You're not going to catch him no matter what you wear. He always bids on Darcy Jones." The bull-riding champion played the field on the circuit but protected his interest in Darcy when he was home. "If you go up there, I can guarantee you that Paul Gregory and his man boobs will bid on you." Drew risked a sideways glance at his sister. "The ink on your divorce papers is barely dry. Enjoy that freedom you wanted so badly. You know you don't need a man to complete you, right?"

"Freedom is overrated." But there was a wrinkle on her brow. "I see other hot cowboys in the crowd. I like cowboys."

Drew ran a hand over his face. He would bet Wendy never had these types of conversations with her older brother.

Noah joined them on his side of the bar. "My money's on Paul. He's waving fifties. But it's a moot point. The widows already closed entries." He caught Drew's eye and mouthed, *You owe me*.

Pris slumped enough to make her red blouse gape in front.

"*Posture! Posture!*" Drew shoved his napkin at her chest.

Pris straightened and tossed his napkin on the floor. "Great. It's Saturday, and I'm dateless. That means my big brother needs to buy me dinner. Nothing fancy. Just a burger and fries here at the bar."

"Have I just been played?" Drew glanced from Noah to Pris.

Indeed he had. They were both laughing.

Before he could bicker and eventually cave in to feeding his sister, he heard Mims announce the next date being offered: "Lola Williams."

Catcalls and hollers of appreciation practically raised the roof.

Lola stepped into the spotlight, wearing a shimmery white cocktail dress and high-heeled white sandals that weren't made for walking. Her long brown hair fell in lustrous waves over her shoulders. She looked like an angel, until you saw the fire in her eyes.

Buy her, a voice in Drew's head said, probably because he valued keeping the peace, and the expression on Lola's face was anything but peaceful.

"I'll tell them about me." Lola grabbed the microphone from Mims. There was a Watch-Out-World edge to her voice. "I'm Randy Williams's wife. He used to run Your Second Husband Handyman Service."

The crowd quieted, either because they were stumped that a woman in the date auction claimed to be married or because they saw the wild look in her blue eyes and weren't sure whether it was a good wild or a bad wild.

Bad. Definitely bad.

Drew swore and hopped off the barstool, pushing his way through the crowd. Passing Paul, who was waving fifties in front of his face like a fan. Passing Jason, who was grinning up at Lola. Passing a cowboy who raised his glass in Lola's direction and spilled beer on Drew's arm.

Drew was only halfway to the stage when Lola said, "Randy's dead, but I want to know who my husband was handy with besides me."

The energy in the crowd shifted from wary to predatory, like a watchful cat who'd spotted an unsuspecting mouse and was preparing to play with it before moving in for the kill.

Lola was oblivious to the target being painted on her. "Randy was handy with another woman. Or maybe another man..." She looked bewildered by this statement, as if she couldn't quite believe it herself.

Had she been drinking? Drew couldn't tell. She didn't slur her words. She hadn't stumbled across the stage.

The men on the dance floor had been drinking. The volume in the peanut gallery increased as ribald comments were tossed about like volleyballs at the beach on a holiday weekend. The crowd's need for spectacle wrapped around Drew's chest and squeezed. He worked harder at reaching the stage, hoping to keep his landlady from starting a riot.

Off to the side, the Widows Club board was in urgent conference. Bitsy looked up and caught sight of Drew. She nudged Mims. When Mims saw him, the apprehension on her face morphed to relief and then, as she took a glance toward Lola, to calculation.

Drew didn't like that look. Especially when he saw Wendy in the wings wearing blue jeans, cowboy boots, and a frilly pink blouse buttoned to her neck.

"Please. I need to know." Lola closed her eyes, as if she didn't really want to know the truth. "Why was my husband unfaithful?"

The crowd drained of energy.

Some of the fight seemed to drain from Lola too.

Mims took advantage and reclaimed the microphone. "We're ready to bid. Remember, Lola isn't your average local. She's from New York City. She does hair and makeup professionally. We'll start the bid at one hundred dollars."

Lola froze, staring above the crowd as if wishing she were above the mess she'd made.

Drew finally reached the stage. From his vantage point, his landlady's legs looked incredibly long. Distractingly long.

With a raucous crowd at his back, Drew couldn't afford to be distracted. "Lola." He reached for her. "Come down."

She was coming down all right. She was coming down from Watch-Out-World mode and sliding into Woe-Is-Me territory. She blinked watery eyes. "Sheriff?"

"How about seventy-five?" Mims didn't seem to be working the crowd as much as she was working Drew. She smiled down at him. "Do I hear fifty?"

Lola's brow furrowed. "I'm being marked down?"

"For God's sake, Mims." Drew hopped onto the stage. "We made a deal." That the widows wouldn't bamboozle Lola into participating.

"Sold!" Mims grinned triumphantly. "For fifty dollars to Sheriff Drew Taylor."

"I didn't bid," Drew snapped. He took Lola's arm and turned her toward the stairs, catching a whiff of alcohol on her breath. He nearly ran into Wendy waiting in the wings. Her gaze dropped to the floor, along with his hopes that she might be his best defense against Jane.

"Rules are rules, Sheriff." Mims tsk-tsked into the microphone. "Fifty dollars is a bargain and for a worthy cause. Please pay the cashier." She gestured toward Clarice. And then she lowered the microphone, raising her voice to be heard above the crowd. "We didn't break our agreement. Lola volunteered." The Widows

Club president glanced toward the bar. "Of course, if you want to be a stickler about it, I could take Priscilla in Lola's place. She looks pretty tonight, and she mentioned she might be ready for some excitement."

No way was Drew letting his sister on that stage. He paid Clarice and led Lola away as the next bachelorette was put on the chopping block.

It was a long walk to their booth. People smiled and shouted congratulations as they passed.

Lola lagged half a step behind Drew, ducking her head to avoid attention.

Drew slowed, eased his grip, and leaned close to her ear. "Are you okay? I can take you home if you like."

Her blue eyes caught his, and she gave him a tentative smile. "I—"

"Hey, Sheriff," Iggy King called from the bar, tipping back his straw cowboy hat. "Way to take advantage of a *fire* sale."

Lola's smile hardened. She quickened her steps, bee-lining to their table and the full flutes of champagne, as determined as his twin sisters to find trouble.

Drew was faster and body-blocked her. "You've had enough."

"I'm just beginning." Lola elbowed Drew out of her way, nothing soft about her now. "This is my date. I call the shots." She flounced onto the bench seat.

Drew scowled. "Technically, I bought you."

"Pity purchases don't count." She flung her sun-kissed brown hair over one shoulder, radiant in her Watch-Out-World indignation.

"It was a rescue." Drew bared his teeth in a smile.

Lola was exactly the kind of woman he and Becky didn't need—obstinate and unpredictable.

"He said, she said." Lola raised her glass. "To the truth." She drained her bubbly and reached for the bottle.

Drew's hand got there first. He parked the champagne on the seat next to him.

The crowd laughed at something Mims said, and the bidding began anew. On Wendy.

"If you don't pour me another glass, I'm going to interrogate you." Lola fixed Drew with a steely-eyed glare worthy of the finest police detectives in New York City. "You weren't surprised when I told you about Randy's laundry habits today. You knew he'd strayed."

"How much have you had to drink?" Drew countered.

"A couple pregame shots. For courage," she added. "Did Randy use your house for his dirty deeds?"

The last thing Lola needed right now was the truth about her husband. If Drew told her there'd been two sets of headlights every few nights, she'd grill each woman at Shaw's who drove a car, including Pris.

Drew's gaze drifted to his sister. When her marriage had begun to crumble a year or more ago, she'd separated from her husband. His mother had let slip once that Pris had found someone new. That relationship hadn't panned out, obviously... Because Randy had died?

Pris laughed at something Noah said and ordered a beer.

Drew shook his head, refusing to believe Pris had been Randy's other woman.

Next to his sister, Iggy stared at Lola as if he were

a bird dog and she were a plump pheasant he'd startled from the brush.

Without meaning to, Drew jutted his chin.

"He *did* cheat at the farmhouse." Lola sat back and raised her voice. "Did Randy host wild parties? Did you double-date with my husband? Did he dance with blow-up dolls?"

Several passing patrons glanced their way.

"Keep it down." Drew took a swig of champagne. "Identifying Randy's lover won't make you feel any better."

"Wanna bet?" But Lola's words lacked fire, and she pressed her eyes closed. When she opened them, she looked at Drew with a vulnerable expression, like the one his sister Eileen got when she lost a stray she'd been trying to save, the one with watery eyes and too much trembling around her mouth. "I just want to know. Was it a long-term affair or something intense and brief that Randy regretted? Did he think I was stupid?" She swiped his glass, raised it to her lips, and then put it back down, untouched. "I have to know." Her voice dropped to a whisper that Drew had to strain to hear. "*Was it real? Did he love me?*"

The helplessness in her voice reached deep inside Drew and took hold.

His annoyance with Lola dissipated, and it wasn't a hardship to meet her tearful gaze, to admire her fragile beauty, to hope she'd find her way past the shock she'd had today. "No one can answer that but Randy."

Chapter Five

♥

"You need to eat." Drew studied Lola as if she were a perp he was considering arresting. "Shots and champagne don't sit well on an empty stomach."

As if on cue, Lola's stomach pitched and threatened to empty. She took a shallow breath and slid Drew's champagne flute back into his space. "You can't distract me from getting answers."

He flashed the detached smile he used when handing over his rent check. "This isn't completely about your empty stomach. I'm hungry." He gestured toward the stage, where the auction was still going on. "And if I'm the only one ordering, Mims will have my hide."

Wendy Adams was sold to Paul Gregory for $400. Drew frowned.

Were Drew and Wendy an item?

The bench seat seemed to roll beneath Lola. She gripped the table. Drew and Wendy didn't matter. The truth about Randy mattered. "You're trying to distract me again."

"I'm not," he said, as stiff as his starched uniform.

Not that Drew was always stiff. In fact, he'd surprised her when he'd escorted her to their table. He'd moved in close, and his warm breath had wafted over her cheek. His offer to take her home had made her feel less the betrayed outcast and more like a woman a man could be interested in, truthful with, loyal to.

"Why did you volunteer for the auction?" Drew leaned forward slightly, brown eyes pinning her as if he were conducting an investigation and she was withholding a key piece of information.

Lola didn't flinch. "I thought it'd be the best way to get the word out."

"What word?"

"That I want to talk to Randy's mistress." Lola watched Drew closely, ready to capture the most minute reaction, anything to tell her what he knew. "Is she here tonight?"

"How would I know?" Oh, he had a good poker face. It was all that starch. "What do you plan to do with this woman when you find her?"

"I told you." She tried to smile, but her cheeks seemed too heavy for her lips to lift. "I want to know if—"

Noah Shaw appeared, bearing two plates. He set a burger in front of Drew and a turkey sandwich and fries in front of Lola. "I know. I'm a mind reader."

Drew stared at his plate. "What? No fries?"

"You need to watch your waistline." Noah turned away but not before flashing a friendly smile at Lola. He was handsome, but Lola felt no howdy-do.

"The next thing he'll be doing"—Drew grumbled in a most un-sheriff-like fashion—"is serving me light beer."

Lola had rarely seen Drew exhibit a sense of humor. It almost made her smile. She tore off a piece of crust and chewed it slowly, allowing Drew to eat a few bites of his meal before resuming her push for information. "Never fear. I'm not out to shoot or stab the other woman. You can tell me who she is."

"I don't know the who or the why." He eyed her fries. "But I wonder if you're asking for proof this woman can't provide. How did you know Randy loved you when he proposed?"

Of all the… "He wouldn't have proposed if he didn't love me!"

At the bar, Iggy glanced their way again. On stage, Avery went up for auction.

Drew considered Lola in that measuring way of his. "Did he get down on one knee with flowers and a ring? Or was it one of those spur-of-the-moment things?"

If Lola could choose one otherworldly ability, it would be shooting daggers from her eyes. She'd take aim at that gold badge on Drew's chest and—

"Ah." Drew stole a fry. "A moment-of-passion proposal."

"It wasn't." Lola couldn't lie. She slumped. "It was."

They'd met in Times Square, literally bumping into each other in a crowd. It had been Randy's first time in New York, and he'd been looking up. Lola had still been grieving over her grandmother's passing a few days before and had been looking down.

After careening into him, she'd staggered to find her balance, and her heel had snapped on the edge of a grate.

Randy had steadied her and then knelt to retrieve her

heel. He'd held it up as if it were a ring and he were proposing.

"Oh, Nana," Lola had breathed, because Nana had always promised Lola a prince and Randy was golden and glowing. "Why now?"

"Bad day?" He'd stood and given her a smile New Yorkers didn't often bestow—a kind smile, an interested smile.

Lola had been horrified to realize she was near tears. Over a shoe. *Over Nana.*

"Hey, don't cry." Randy had hustled her out of the foot traffic and into the doorway of a tourist gift shop, next to a display of green foam Statue of Liberty tiaras. "I'll pay for your shoe. It was my fault."

In her broken shoes, Lola had been off-kilter. "Thanks, but that's not necessary." She'd stared at him a little too long, fighting the feeling that her grandmother somehow had a hand in this meeting.

"It's not necessary." Randy had grinned and gone from handsome to hunky. "But what is necessary is a drink and a sympathetic ear for your problems."

He'd been such a good listener. After that, they'd spent every waking, nonworking moment together for a week.

He'd rolled over in bed one morning and whispered in Lola's ear, "Wouldn't it be great to wake up like this every day?"

She'd squealed her acceptance: "*Yes!*"

Two weeks later, they were married, and she'd moved to Sunshine.

Lola dropped her forehead to the table. "He didn't even propose." Not with the right question.

"Hey, now." Drew patted the table near her head, most likely so he could snatch another fry. "Randy could have backed out at any time."

"Being left at the altar would've been preferable to this." She'd still have a job on Broadway. She'd still have her self-respect.

Drew didn't immediately reply.

Lola lifted her head to look at her dinner partner.

He was chewing. *Chewing!*

"My life is flaming out, and you've got nothing to say? *Nothing?*"

"I'm hungry." Drew didn't flinch from her incredulity. "The food is hot. And you don't want my advice anyway."

Her life was in ruins, and the man who'd bought her for a date—*marked down*—thought it was more important to eat his burger than to offer her sympathy or advice? Lola wanted to kick him in the shins. And she might have if she hadn't been wearing open-toed sandals. As it was, her foot kicked out, completely of its own accord, and brushed Drew's firm thigh.

He stopped chewing. "Are you... Was that..."

"That was an accident." Lola placed both feet solidly on the floor, wishing she could disappear.

There was heat in his gaze. And amusement. "Nervous twitch?"

"Something like that."

"Do you want to know what I think?"

"Not really." Not anymore. She eyed the door.

He waved aside her remark and delivered his opinion in the same tone of voice a doctor used to deliver bad news. "I think Randy loved you."

"Really?" A tiny spark of hope ignited in her chest.

"Yes." He wiped his hands on a napkin and looked her in the eye with that detached cop expression of his when she much preferred howdy-do heat. "I just don't think it was the passionate I'm-gonna-die-without-you kind of love."

The horrible truth of that statement belly flopped in her stomach.

"My grandmother was wrong," Lola said after a moment. Her hopes, her dreams, the scrapbook. She never should've believed Nana. "There are no happily-ever-afters."

Drew stopped tucking a tomato back into his burger. "Don't say that."

"Why not?" There was so much fragile hope in those two quiet words that Lola almost wanted to snatch them back.

Someone bid an exorbitant amount for Avery. Then the bidding stopped, and the auction was called to a close.

"Just...don't say there's no happy endings." Drew had that look men got on their faces when they found themselves unexpectedly talking about feelings with a woman. The same back-against-the-wall look Randy had had on his face the day he'd agreed to marry her. "I'm probably wrong. My sisters claim I know nothing about life. Or love."

There was something about buttoned-up Sheriff Drew Taylor fumbling around in a conversation about love that almost had Lola smiling.

"But maybe..." Drew was fixing his drippy burger and

not paying attention to Lola. "Maybe *you* were the other woman. Maybe you're the one who stole him away."

The anger that had led her to burn Randy's underwear reared its fire-spitting head. "If that were true, wouldn't there be an ex-girlfriend around?" A woman the townspeople liked more than Lola? She lifted her chin and stared down her nose at Drew.

He shrugged. *Shrugged!*

"Sheriff." It was Mims who spoke, but the Widows Club board trailed behind her. "It looks like Lola's ready to go home."

Lola smiled fondly at the widowed sisterhood.

"Come along, hon." Bitsy, whose black dress was vintage eighties A-line with a set of those shoulder pads she was so fond of, gently drew Lola from the booth.

Lola didn't need to be asked twice to leave. She scooted to the edge of the seat. She'd ridden with Avery, who was seated on the other side of the room with a man Lola didn't recognize. Her date was just starting. "Don't you need to stick around for the auction's after-party?" she asked the board.

"Nope." Clarice leaned on the table and raised her voice to be heard over the crowd. "We've collected our money, and now we're taking care of our own."

Edith Archer appeared behind Mims. She looked as unkempt as a doll stuck in the crack of a couch for too long—mussed short gray hair, wrinkled yellow polo and blue jeans, and that sad air of abandonment that Lola had felt all year. "I want to join the Widows Club."

"Not now," Mims said tightly without turning. "It hasn't been six months."

"That's a rule," Clarice shouted as Bitsy pulled Lola free of the booth.

"I don't care." Edith looked as empty as Lola felt. She elbowed her way into the center of the clustered women. "My husband's dead. My dog is dead. And I feel dead. I need something to do."

"I can take Lola home," Drew said wearily. He pushed his plate away, burger unfinished. "Edith needs you ladies."

Before Lola could refuse, Clarice blocked the sheriff with her walking stick. "Now, Sheriff. We don't want Lola to be taken advantage of. You shouldn't kiss on the first date, much less get past the front door."

"All I said was I can drive Lola home." Drew held up his hands in surrender. "No passes were planned. Remember, I didn't even want to buy her."

Lola lifted her chin above her wounded pride. "The Widows Club is driving me home."

"We'll discuss this later, Edith." Mims signaled the rest of them toward the exit. "We're leaving."

"Not without me." Edith was adamant, dogging Mims.

On the way out, Lola stopped by Avery's table to make sure she didn't need saving and to tell her she was going home. Avery didn't look pleased with her date, an attractive man with thick curly hair, but she assured Lola everything was fine.

A few minutes later, Lola was jammed in the back of Clarice's minivan and stuck between Mims and Edith. Clarice drove as if they'd robbed a bank and were in the getaway vehicle, making Lola wish she'd accepted a ride from Drew.

"This is Widows Club business." Mims wielded that I'm-in-control voice like a stock trader on Wall Street. "I'm not sure why you came, Edith."

"I'm a widow." Edith sounded more confident than before, possibly because she hadn't been left behind. "Just because we've had our differences in the past, Mims, doesn't mean you can bar me from the club."

"Differences?" sputtered Mims.

"I won Charlie fair and square fifty years ago." Edith patted Lola's knee and said, sweet as you please, "Lola, did you fill out your Widows Club paperwork? If not, can we do it together?"

Mims growled like a wounded predator.

"I've done no paperwork, but I don't think I should be a member." Which seemed disloyal when the board had been so timely getting Lola out of the bar. "Randy was sleeping around. And before I commit to the Widows Club, I'm going to find out if he loved me."

"Good for you." Edith patted Lola's knee again.

"We encourage forgiveness and moving on," Mims said.

"Forgiveness?" Edith bumped into Lola's shoulder on a sharp turn. "If Charlie had cheated on me, I'd want the slut to hang from her toenails in the town square."

"Really?" Mims jerked sideways in her seat, snarling at Edith. "Is that the advice you'd give a young widow?"

"Yes. I'd want to know all the details." Edith's outraged voice filled the minivan. "I'd go see Madame LeClaire to talk to Charlie from the afterlife and get the truth."

"Dead husbands tell no tales," Mims intoned.

Lola was open to asking the afterlife for answers, seeing as how she was getting so little from the living. "And while I had Randy on a spiritual line, I'd ask him where things went wrong."

"Do *not* take the blame for Randy's actions," Mims said in her commanding voice.

"Now, Mims," Bitsy said from the front passenger seat. "Don't dismiss the healing power of talking to the dead. I find great comfort sitting graveside." She'd been widowed three times and was always as friendly and composed as a saint. "I talk to Jim about financial matters. I talk to Terry about house upkeep. And I talk to Wendell about being lonely." This last revelation was drenched with unmistakable longing.

"What are we talking about?" Clarice asked in her loudest voice.

Bitsy leaned across the front seat divide and shouted, "Visiting our husbands at the cemetery."

"Oh. Sometimes when I visit Fritz's headstone and tell him my problems, I can almost hear him answer back." Clarice sent the tires squealing as she turned the corner onto Skyview Drive.

There was a moment of silence, almost like a silent *amen*, either because all the older widows agreed with Clarice or because Clarice had pulled safely into Lola's ash-strewn driveway.

Mims broke the silence, continuing her offensive but without her previous intensity. "What's past is past. Edith and Lola need to think about their futures."

"I can't lay the past to rest that easily," Edith said in

a loud voice, as if she who spoke the loudest was right. "Some people need more closure than others." She got out of the minivan.

"Amen." Lola tumbled out after her older compatriot, dodging the boxes and trash bags filled with Randy's things. The thrift store was picking them up on Monday.

"Some people," Edith continued, "need the truth to move on."

This sounded like an argument that wasn't going to be solved tonight. "I can take it from here, gang." Lola brushed past Edith toward the front door, fumbling for the house key pinned to her bra strap. She opened her door, stepped inside, and then shut it behind her. The dead bolt struck home, and Lola plastered her back to the wood, listening to the widows bicker as Edith worked her way back to the minivan.

Randy and Candy, the two blow-up dolls, flanked the fireplace. Because they looked so similar, with shapeless, androgynous bodies, she and Avery had dressed them and propped them up before they'd left for Shaw's. In his boxers and wifebeater, Blow-Up Randy looked ready for bed. Candy cleaned up much better. She wore a scarlet cocktail dress Lola no longer fit into, and despite not having any cleavage, she looked like she would've gone for more than fifty dollars at auction.

"That dress looks better on you than me." Lola moved to the bar and poured herself a shot of whiskey. When her stomach protested, she set it down untouched next to Randy's gun safe and turned to face her husband. Or at least his plastic stand-in. "Okay, Randy. Time to come clean. Did you love me?"

Stand-In Randy said nothing, which was probably for the best since he was full of hot air.

Real Randy had been full of it too. Full of compliments like "*Your hair is so fine and soft*" or "*I love it when you wear blue. It's my favorite color.*"

Lola rubbed her temples, moving closer to the fireplace. Her head was starting to pound with hangover intensity.

She longed to hear Randy's voice telling her he loved her and asking for forgiveness.

But she also longed to hear him tell her whether their marriage had been a mistake.

And then she longed to kick him to the curb.

Stand-In Randy said nothing, of course.

She rubbed her temples again.

"*I can almost hear him answer back,*" Clarice had said.

"Fine." She'd go out to the cemetery tomorrow and have a heart-to-heart with Randy.

Blow-Up Randy lost his footing and slid to the carpet, wheezing slightly, as if he'd sprung a small leak.

Lola kicked him toward the door and went to lean on the bar. She had too many unanswered questions and was too wound up to sleep.

Randy's head was turned her way, and he reached for her with one pale, stubby arm as if inviting her to go somewhere. Randy had always been so nice—opening doors, helping her cook, getting her oil changed without asking. He'd never grabbed her arm and yanked her along like Drew had done tonight. He'd never put his hunger before her emotional needs. Or so she'd thought.

"I hate you," she said to her plastic husband. And then louder, "I hate you!"

Unfazed, Randy kept his hand out, as if he wanted her forgiveness.

"We're a long way from the f-word, Buster." But Lola took pity on him. She walked over and propped him up by the door. "I wish you could talk."

Blow-Up Randy wheezed, a shifting of dead air that sounded like a sigh.

Lola stared at his simple, smiling face. "Fine. I'll take you to the cemetery tomorrow." It seemed appropriate to bring him. If Edith was to be believed, it might serve to channel Randy's spirit.

Of course, if she went tomorrow, people would see her with a blow-up doll. They'd be reminded of the bonfire today, small though it'd been, and her meltdown at the auction tonight. People would think she'd lost her marbles when it was exactly the opposite. Lola was afraid she'd found them too late to do her any good.

She didn't want people to talk, but she wanted to bring the life-size symbol of her cheating husband to the cemetery. She'd just have to go when it wasn't crowded.

Except the only time the cemetery was guaranteed to be empty was at night.

"Well, that settles it." Lola grabbed her key ring and Stand-In Randy.

She'd just have to go now.

Chapter Six

♥

"Sheriff, we've got a report of a ghost in the cemetery."

Drew had just sat down on his couch at home and had just started to regret not being able to buy a date with Wendy when the call came in from dispatch.

Flo's deep smoker's voice crackled over the radio, which was still strapped to Drew's shoulder. "Do you want me to send Gary or Emily over to check it out?"

"No." Drew spoke into the radio. "The cemetery is closer to my house." Besides, the farmhouse was too quiet without Becky. Even in sleep, her presence made the place feel lived in. Was this how it would be if Jane won her custody battle? He got to his feet. "I'll go."

"That's what I thought." Flo should've applied for the sheriff's job. She practically ran the department anyway, even though she used a wheelchair and worked from home.

Drew drove his cruiser down a deserted stretch of foggy two-lane highway to the Sunshine Valley Cemetery. The wrought iron gates had been painted a pearly white and were uncharacteristically open.

Drew drove slowly between them. Chances were some local kids were out drinking and egging each other on. He swiveled the cruiser's spotlight around the fog-blanketed cemetery, nearly missing the ghost.

It was Lola.

She wore the same white minidress she'd had on earlier. Her skin glowed like ivory in the spotlight. She had on a pair of black rain boots and was pointing a gun at a body lying on the ground.

Drew's pulse kicked past prank procedure to armed-and-dangerous action.

He threw the cruiser in park and shouted out the open window. "Lola!" He jumped out of the car and drew his firearm. "Drop the gun."

Lola didn't spare him a glance. "Hey, Sheriff." So casual. As if he were dropping off his rent check.

"Put the gun down, Lola." She hadn't just gone over the edge; she'd plunged into dangerous territory. Drew kept her in his gun sights as he moved carefully up the hill. "Put the gun down now."

He was too late. There was something wrong with the person on the ground. Their skin was the yellowish-pink color of the long dead, and they weren't moving.

Maddeningly, the fog obscured the details.

Drew ran up the hill, weapon still drawn, his gaze darting between Lola and her victim. About ten feet away, he realized Lola was aiming at a person with no toes and no pulse. She was aiming at a blow-up doll.

He swore. With relief-fueled gusto.

In a string. With colorful verb use.

And pointed his muzzle to the ground.

"Randy never was one to give a straight answer unless he was cornered." Lola sounded sane and sober, but the gun pointed at the plastic body contradicted that impression.

She'd taken Watch-Out-World to a whole new level.

"Put down the gun." Drew knew better than to trust anyone with a drawn weapon.

"I decline." She spared Drew a glance. "I need a moment alone with my husband. The widows said if I was quiet, I could hear Randy speak."

That did it. Tomorrow he was going to have a heart-to-heart with Mims & Company. Drew took a few steps closer, gauging the distance between them. For the public's safety and his own, he had to disarm Lola, and to do so, he had to keep her talking. "What's Randy saying?"

"Nothing. He's taken his secrets to the grave." Lola shifted her stance and drew a breath, as if preparing to shoot.

Drew wrested her gun away but in the process knocked her down. They tumbled together, rolling several feet downhill until Drew's back slammed into a headstone with a breath-stealing, bruise-making thud.

For several seconds, he didn't move, letting the pain in his back radiate outward. He was aware of the damp earth beneath him, the smell of gardenias and cut grass, and the warm body in his arms.

"Ow." Lola lifted her head to stare at him with blue eyes that were clear and disapproving. "Was that necessary?"

"Yes."

"Why?" She propped herself up on her elbow. Her soft brown hair caressed his neck.

He resisted releasing a gun and grabbing a handful. "Because you wouldn't drop your gun. Because you built a bonfire today." Because she was just as unpredictable and emotional as his sisters. It was official. She'd made it onto his Watch-Over list.

He vowed then and there to call Wendy tomorrow. He needed a sane, conventional woman in Becky's life, one who wasn't a candidate for his Watch-Over list. Watching over could come later.

Lola stood, tugging down her dress.

Suddenly, his arms felt empty, which was as crazy as his entire evening.

Lola marched uphill in the fog. "I'm going to take my gun and my fake husband and go home."

"I'm going to take you in." After the stunts she'd pulled today, who knew what she'd do in the wee hours of the night. Time in a jail cell would do wonders for her perspective and allow him to sleep tonight.

"You're arresting me? On what charge?" Lola put her hands on her hips and stared him down with a haughty glance that pinged something inside Drew's chest.

Drew was too well-trained to be distracted by mere pings. "Drunk and disorderly." He holstered his weapon and checked the chamber in hers.

No bullets. Of course.

"I'm angry, Sheriff. Not drunk. Jeez, a twenty-four-hour grace period should apply to discovering your husband was a slimeball." She kicked the grass, sending her skirt fluttering to tantalizing levels.

"*Disorderly* still applies." Drew moved closer to inspect her victim. She'd dressed Randy the way he deserved, Drew supposed. In his skivvies. "Do you have a permit for this weapon?"

"I'm sure Randy did." She grabbed the doll and tucked it under her arm like a surfboard. "You can't arrest a widow for visiting her husband's grave."

"I can." Blood pounded in his veins the way it did when his sisters did something stupid. Except Lola wasn't one of his sisters. The fact that he kept sneaking looks at her legs proved that point. "Do you want me to add resisting arrest?"

"Seriously?" Lola didn't seem upset. She wasn't violent. She sighed, which was completely unexpected given the doll and the gun and the midnight visit to the cemetery. "Okay, but I'll need to lock up the cemetery and return the key."

"Fair enough." And worthy of his respect. "Where did you leave your car?"

"In the circle by the crypts. I'll get it tomorrow."

It was the most ridiculous arrest of Drew's career.

But he wasn't laughing.

* * *

"*He had it coming.*" Lola crooned a line from *Chicago* to Stand-In Randy, who was propped in the cinder-block corner of her jail cell with a satisfied look on his plastic face, the creep.

Lola's mother had taken her father's leaving hard but she'd never been thrown in the Big House. She'd been caught outside Lola's dad's lover's apartment with binoculars. She'd called Lola's dad's office at night just to listen to his voice on the answering machine. She'd lost more weight than was healthy, bought a push-up bra, and had her nose done. But an arrest record? Nope. Her mom hadn't crossed that line.

Lola lay on a bench, feet doing choreography on the back wall. A black rooster huddled nearby, sleeping.

A door opened. Footsteps scuffled across the linoleum in the hall from the sheriff's office proper.

She repeated the line from *Chicago*, tilting her head backward to see who approached.

It was Drew and Paul Gregory, who was shirtless (not a good look on him) and listing from side to side like an ocean buoy.

"You're in luck, Lola." Drew worked the key in the lock. "Paul needs the jail cell to sober up."

"I don't." Paul bumped his face into the bars and then looked startled to have done so.

"*He had it coming*," Lola sang half under her breath. She rolled to her feet, slipped into her rain boots, and linked arms with Randy, walking him to the cell door as Drew unlocked it.

Paul squinted and pointed at Randy, who was still in his boxers and wifebeater. "And you hauled *me* in for indecent exposure?"

"Drunk and disorderly," Drew deadpanned, stepping back for Lola to exit before escorting Paul to the bench. "Don't disturb Marvin, or he'll crow." It was the same advice he'd given Lola.

"I like a firm mattress," Paul muttered happily,

stretching out on the bench. "And fresh eggs for breakfast."

"That's a rooster." Drew sounded as weary as Lola felt.

Lola hurried down the hall to the door separating the cells from the office proper, only to find it locked.

Drew ambled behind her. "Why is everyone always in a hurry to get out of here?"

Was that humor? The sheriff had lines of fatigue around his brown eyes, lines she was sure matched her own. But there was a hint of a smile on his face, one that contradicted the flat-lipped expression he'd had when he'd brought her in.

"I can't speak for Paul or Marvin, but I want out because the acoustics are better in my shower." Lola followed Drew through the security door and into the main office, eyeing the door a few short steps away and anticipating the air of freedom.

He opened the door to the small station. Two wooden desks and two visitor's chairs. Drew's office was smaller still, about the size of Lola's walk-in closet. There was a faded picture of a man in uniform on one wall and a framed motto on the other: *If dispatch doesn't know where you are, only God can help you.*

Drew hung the cell keys on a hook on the wall. "Maybe the acoustics were bad because you were singing pop, not country." Deadpan sarcasm. No mistaking it this time.

Lola gasped dramatically. "You don't recognize the lyrics from *Chicago*?" At his blank look, she added, "Famous Broadway musical? Made into a movie?"

"I'm not much for musicals of any kind."

"I've gotta get out of here." Meaning out of town. For good. Someplace where they appreciated the theater.

Drew opened the front door and gestured for her to precede him out, as if they were going somewhere together.

Randy's plastic toes dragged Lola to a halt.

She looked about the office. "Don't I need to sign out and get a court date or something?" She wasn't looking forward to court.

Judge Harper meted out the worst punishments. Just last week, he'd given Harlen Martinez, up for drunk and disorderly, a choice—spend thirty days in jail or sit in the town square on a Saturday, holding a sign that read, DRUNKEN TROUBLE. Harlen had opted out of jail and had sat with two cowboys holding their own signs: DRUNKEN STUPID and DRUNKEN FOOLISH.

Lola didn't want to think about what punishment Judge Harper would create for her.

"I didn't book you." Drew rubbed a hand over his face. "I didn't want to fill out any paperwork. I just wanted you to have a chance to cool down."

"I didn't need to cool down." Lola clutched Randy tighter to her side to prevent her from swinging him like a bat at Drew's head. "I needed time alone with my husband."

"And I gave it to you." There was that almost grin again. "Come on—I'll give you a ride home."

Marvin crowed, followed by a girlie shriek from Paul.

"*We* don't need a ride." Lola lifted her chin and clumped past Drew in her boots. Like everything in downtown Sunshine, her home was only a few blocks away. "You should check on your prisoner before he murders Marvin."

"Point taken." Drew leaned against the doorway, chuckling softly as she made her way down the walk. "I won't worry about you. After all, you've got an escort."

That chuckle. It telegraphed another howdy-do, replaying in Lola's head all the way home.

Chapter Seven

♥

When Lola woke up late the next morning, she felt more like herself and less like a woman racing down the rapids without a paddle.

Oh, there was an edge of woman-wronged vulnerability in her veins, like a still-fresh memory of a jolt from a live wire. She was her mother's daughter, after all. And the thought of Randy's betrayal made her angry and turned her stomach, although possibly her gastric upset was due to consuming too much alcohol. But purging Randy from the house had helped.

Gone were the pictures of her husband on her nightstand. Gone were the wedding portraits on the wall. The deer head. The beer signs. The burl-wood clock that didn't work. All gone and stacked in piles in her driveway. And she'd put her wedding ring in her jewelry box.

She may not have gotten answers from visiting Randy's grave, but she felt one step closer to…something. And more determined than ever to uncover the truth, even if it made her the butt of jokes at Shaw's.

It was Sunday, her day off, and a scrunchie kind of day. Lola put her hair in a messy ponytail, applied light makeup, and tugged on a red T-shirt and sky-blue patterned leggings. Her footsteps echoed as she came downstairs.

Two figures were embracing at her front window.

Lola stumbled on the last few steps and clutched the banister. It took her a moment to register the couple as Randy and Candy.

She crossed the living room, shaking her head. Dragging Plastic Randy to the graveyard with a gun. What had she been thinking?

The sheriff should've arrested me.

An image of Drew's half smile came to mind, along with the sound of his deep-throated chuckle. She didn't like the things she was discovering about Sunshine's lawman. Mostly, she didn't like the he-man/she-woman vibe she felt when he was near. How could she suddenly be attracted to a man she'd known for two years?

She adjusted the plastic sinners and opened the curtains wider. The next time she saw the sheriff, she needed to treat him like a stranger on a dark night in New York City. Cross the street, look the other way, move along.

Coffee was the next priority. Then she needed to get her car from the cemetery.

While her cup was brewing, she texted Avery, asking for a ride. And then she stared out the dining room window. Mrs. Everly and Darla Bastion were standing on the sidewalk across the street, ogling Lola's window display as if it were Christmas and she'd set up a blasphemous tree.

By the time Lola finished her coffee, Avery was pulling up in front of the house. She wore a pair of black pants and a maroon polo shirt with the movie theater logo. Her hair hung down her back in a sheet of sleek black. A true friend, Avery glared at the neighbors until they dispersed.

Lola opened the door before Avery could knock.

"Are you still mowing that witch's lawn?" Avery charged in, dark eyes blazing.

"Yes." Randy had mowed Mrs. Everly's lawn for free whenever he'd mowed their lawn. It hadn't seemed right to stop after his death. To avoid an argument with Avery, Lola asked, "How was your date last night?"

"Horrible. My life is ruined." Avery's voice cracked, and she looked as if she couldn't decide if she was going to cry or pick a fight with Mrs. Everly. "The guy who bought me at auction? Frank? He's trying to buy the entire block downtown, including my family's movie theater." She pressed the heels of her hands to her temples and muttered, "Not that my family said a word to me about it." She blew out a breath and dropped her hands to her sides. "If the town council approves, he's going to tear it all down, and I'm going to be out of a job."

"Oh no." Lola rubbed Avery's back. "Is there anything I can do?"

Avery shook her head, staring at Randy and Candy. "Why are Randy's dolls on display?"

"It's modern art." Lola adjusted Randy's hand on Candy's waist. She'd had to deflate him a little to get more bend. It gave him a laid-back swagger.

Avery raised her finely shaped eyebrows. "That kind

of creative expression will get you thrown in the pokey in this town."

"Been there, done that." Lola tried for nonchalance, but she was afraid she might have sounded a little cocky. "The sheriff locked me up last night." Not many women in Sunshine could say that.

Avery perked up. "Did Drew handcuff you first? He seems like the quiet but possibly kinky type." She slid a red strap off Candy's shoulder.

"The sheriff is too starched to have a kink." Lola tamped down memories of half smiles and low chuckles and slid into a pair of black Keds. "After we get my car, do you want to go to Greeley for some shopping therapy?"

"Can't." Avery looked down at her work clothes, her features returning to the doom-and-gloom expression she'd had when she'd arrived. "A Disney movie opened this weekend, and every family in town is coming to the first two matinees. Stacey Wexley called in sick already, which means there was a party hosted by the Bodine twins last night, so she won't be the only teenage no-show." Avery huffed on her way to the door, and no matter how hard Lola tried to lighten the mood, she continued huffing until she dropped Lola off at her car.

When Lola got back home, she sat at the kitchen table, contemplating how to spend the day. By now, the entire town would've heard about her making a spectacle of herself at the bachelorette auction. Mrs. Everly would be telling people about her window display. And Lola could look forward to Drew showing up with her rent check, possibly including a lecture about small-town decorum, because that was the way the sheriff rolled.

Randy and Candy fell to the carpet in a passionate heap.

"Typical." Lola righted the pair and propped them up with dining room chairs on either side. "Why couldn't my husband cheat where Mrs. Everly could see?"

Oh, snap. Where did Randy do the deed?

She had no idea. She'd accused Drew of being party to the debauchery, but that didn't hold up to the light of day, not when Drew had a little girl.

Lola washed out her coffee cup, realized it was from a restaurant she'd never been to in Greeley, and threw it away. A few minutes later, the kitchen was eradicated of shot glasses, mugs, and plastic cups from all the places Randy had frequented.

How much more cleansing of Randy's stuff was she going to have to do? There were a few tools in their garage. And, come to think of it, she'd never gone to the farmhouse. Randy had told her once that he stored things there, both in the garage and in the apartment above it. She'd never been inside.

"Aha!" Lola turned and pointed a finger at Randy and Candy.

The garage at the farmhouse she rented to Drew was located on the back of the property and was accessible by a dirt road along the river.

Lola ran upstairs, snatched the spare keys to the farmhouse buildings, and then ran out the door.

Fifteen minutes later, she parked in front of the two-car, two-story garage. Her sweaty hands shook.

The farmhouse was a hundred feet away. Drew's police cruiser sat close to the house. This was why Drew knew Randy had been unfaithful. He'd had a front-row seat.

There were cobwebs crossing the corners of the big garage doors. But whatever was inside the auto bays wasn't of interest to Lola. She gripped the steering wheel and lifted her gaze to the second-story apartment. She didn't move. Fear of what she'd find kept her glued to her seat.

If her beloved Nana were here, she'd check her teeth for lipstick in the rearview mirror, tug her dress over her knees, and say something like *What's gotta be done has gotta be done.*

Lola gritted her teeth because Randy had done this to her. Cheated. Lied. Made her doubt. Made it necessary to ferret out the truth. She got out of the car and climbed the stairs. When she reached the top, a small wounded noise, like the beginning of a breakdown sob, escaped her lips. She wanted to turn around and drive away. She wanted to erase the past two years.

But turning back time only happened in fairy tales. And if she'd learned anything from Randy's infidelity, it was that fairy tales didn't exist. There was no white knight on a fiery steed, no Prince Charming to wake her with a kiss, no wand-waving fairy godmother to make everything all right. Moving forward, there was, and only would be, Lola.

She inserted the key in the lock and opened the door.

It was dark inside. All the blinds were down. Lola yanked them up, revealing a studio apartment with a small kitchenette and a tiny bathroom. Dust motes floated in the air, as scattered and directionless as Lola.

There was no furniture beyond a brass bed and a woman's black lacquered bureau with a matching mirror on top. It would have all been very boring except the bed was draped in a blue comforter with cream-colored ribbon trim and plump blue satin-covered pillows.

Satin pillowcases. Perfect for avoiding bedhead.

A thick strand of pale hair lay across one of the pillowcases, not as long as Lola's brown hair but too long to have been Randy's.

Here was proof. Randy had a lover. And she was a blonde.

Stomach churning, Lola rushed into the bathroom and vomited. But no amount of heaving could rid her of the taint of failure. She'd vowed not to have a marriage like her mother's, not to be cast aside like last year's fashion. She was the last person this should've happened to. She'd known the signs. How had she been duped?

"Damn you, Randy." She sank to the pink ceramic floor tiles, trembling with defeat.

Big, fluffy black towels hung from the rods in front of her. The same exact towels they had at home. The shower had Randy's favorite bar of soap in the dish. And the toilet paper was double quilted, the brand Randy had insisted she buy even though it was nearly a dollar more than other four-packs. To add insult to injury, the TP was hung under, not over, the dispenser.

That was it. Randy had won. He'd made a mockery of their marriage with his mistress. And Lola had let him override everything about her life, including how she hung her toilet paper.

The first thing Lola was going to do when she got

back home was put the toilet tissue on the roll the right way.

Lola stood and rinsed out her mouth. She stared at herself in the mirror over the sink, trying to work up the courage to face the bed again.

Coward that she was, she opened the medicine cabinet instead. It didn't have anything as incriminating as the other woman's prescription medication. Toenail clippers, dental floss, toothpaste, mouthwash, and a supply of toothbrushes still in their packages. Randy had always been hell-bent on hygiene.

Or hell-bent on disguising the taste and scent of another woman.

Lola's stomach threatened to heave once more.

You have to be a big girl. That's what her mother had told Lola after her dad had left. *You have to forget about dreams and stop crying.*

Lola didn't want to be a big girl. She wanted to go home, crawl in bed, and hug something.

And there was a hard truth. She had nothing to hug.

Lola splashed water on her cheeks and turned to face the main room. A bed and a bureau. What purpose did the bureau serve? Maybe there was something in its drawers to give Lola a clue about who her husband's mistress was. A change of clothes. A receipt from a bar. A photo of the cheating couple.

The front door swung open.

Lola shrieked, bumping into the bathroom doorframe and jarring her shoulder.

But it wasn't Randy's mistress. It was Drew, dressed for his day off in blue jeans, boots, and a blue checked shirt. His police radio was clipped to his shirt pocket. Dark whiskers, dark tousled hair, dark eyes that saw too much.

"Couldn't you knock?" she demanded, swaying like Paul had last night when facing the jail cell.

"Couldn't you leave the past alone?" he replied with a scowl, standing tall and unshaken. He handed her a check.

Lola tucked his rent into her bra strap.

"Go away." She only half meant it. His presence calmed her. She marched across the beige linoleum, clutched the handles to the top bureau drawer, and pulled.

Stubby candles. A battery-powered strobe light. A canister of red rose petals made of silk.

"No pictures, no matchbooks, no love letters," Lola mumbled, swimming her hands through the near-empty drawer with increasing speed.

"Don't do this." Drew caught her wrists and pulled her away from the bureau. "I'll get Gary to come up here and help me move everything out. Don't put yourself through this." His words were measured and calm. His dark eyes lined with concern. The sheriff doing his duty, keeping the peace.

But there were still drawers to go through and answers to find, and Lola could feel her mother's dramatic, foolish, eccentric impulses building inside her like a pressure cooker without a vent. She eased from his hold. "I have to know if what we had was real."

The next drawer was filled with silky lingerie. Black, white, red, pink. Bustiers, thongs, corsets, baby doll gowns. She held up one racy black number. It was see-through.

"Okay. All right. You get the idea." Drew snatched the nightwear away and stuffed it in the drawer. "I know what you're thinking. Just…don't say it."

"My lingerie isn't half as nice as hers," Lola blurted, pathetically envious.

"I told you not to say what you were thinking." Drew placed his hands on Lola's shoulders. They fit, those hands.

Or maybe she was just so lonely that anyone's touch would have comforted her.

He turned her toward the door. "You need to go home."

"To what?" Lola dug in her sneakers and resumed her search.

The two bottom drawers were deep. The first one had a variety of costumes for both men and women. Fireman, black cat, nurse, schoolgirl, Santa.

Oh, Santa.

Lola shook out a crumpled bit of blue polyester. It was a jumpsuit with a halter top, and it loosely resembled a cop uniform. Whoever Randy's mistress had been, she had an overactive imagination. Lola lifted the uniform to Drew's shoulders. "You might be able to squeeze into this. Polyester is very stretchy."

"I'll wear my own pants, thank you." Drew put his hands on hers and gently but firmly pushed them back into her space.

Lola's hands lowered, and she looked at Drew, really looked at him. If she'd seen him on the streets of New York, she wouldn't have looked twice. He didn't have a smile that charmed or a wardrobe that said he had great taste. He'd never barge through a crowd as if he owned Wall Street or cut in front of her at the corner Starbucks because he was late for a meeting.

He could have made a snarky remark about the lingerie (or hers). He could have lost his temper when she'd teased him about wearing the cop costume. There was a reason he was the sheriff. He was steady and reliable, the opposite of her husband.

Nothing had been said during her scrutiny of his face. Lola hurried to fill the void. "Who broke your nose?"

He didn't answer. His gaze dropped to her left hand. "What did you do with your wedding ring?"

Add *observant* to his list of attributes. Randy never would have noticed if Lola had done her hair differently, much less if she'd been wearing his ring.

"Lola." Drew's voice had grown soft. His gaze on her face softer still. "Let this go. Nothing good can come of it."

Deep down inside, tucked away where she kept her fondest memories of Nana, something agreed. Letting it go was the smart, logical thing to do.

But nearer to the surface, Randy's betrayal festered, like a mosquito bite that refused to stop itching. The only way Lola could see to heal was the stinging balm of the truth. She reached for the last drawer.

"Holy shades of gray," Lola muttered, peering inside. "Are those lederhosen?"

Drew bent for a closer look, apparently as curious as she was.

Lola shuddered. "I feel so—"

"Sheltered?"

"No."

"Repressed?"

"No!" Lola hunched over the open drawer, back to wishing Drew would leave. "I liked you better as the stiff and starched sheriff."

"I'm sorry." Drew squared his shoulders and frowned at Lola as if he were considering making an arrest. "I interrupted you. You were saying you feel so..."

Had she hurt his feelings? Now she felt guilty.

"Lacking." Lola sighed. "I feel lacking. I couldn't wear a fake cop uniform or lederhosen without dying of laughter."

The corner of his mouth twitched up, and his shoulders downshifted. "You wouldn't hold up long in an interrogation."

He's teasing me.

Be still my heart.

Said heart fluttered in her chest.

"Sheriff, it's a good thing I haven't committed a crime." Lola forced her gaze back to the drawer, forced herself to focus on what was inside instead of who stood next to her. And then she saw it. "Well, hello." There was a small cedar box beneath all that leather. Trying not to touch anything else, Lola retrieved the box and stared at it, suddenly too numb to move. "My grandmother used to store her love letters in a box like this."

"Aren't you going to open it?" Drew stood close to her shoulder. He smelled of coffee and cotton. Clean, the way Randy used to smell. Familiar. Comforting.

Lola hesitated. "What if there are pictures in here?

Matchbooks from restaurants? Tender notes that say how much he..." *Loved her.*

"What if it's empty?" Drew sounded as if he didn't believe Randy was capable of such sentimentality.

The Randy she'd fallen in love with had been. Lola set the keepsake box on the bureau and lifted the lid.

There were no notes or photographs, just five small items. A dangly ruby earring. A turquoise pendant on a silver chain. A silver beaded bracelet interspersed with tiny copper bells. A near-empty vial of Joy, which was a very expensive perfume. And a blue velvet box stamped with a gold insignia: *Yonkers Jewelry.*

Lola's stomach lurched. "This is my grandmother's pearl ring. I thought I'd lost it after the move to Sunshine."

Nana...

"*Your grandfather was a prince.*" Nana had taken off the pearl ring and slipped it on nine-year-old Lola's finger. It was a simple ring with a fleur-de-lis to either side of the pearl. "*He claimed I was different than other women and therefore I needed a different kind of wedding ring. Someday, this will be yours. Someday, you'll wear it and know that love came before you and love is ahead of you.*"

Standing in Randy's love shack, Lola knew that having her grandmother's ring returned to her would make everything all right—the hurt, the betrayal, the uncertainty. She cradled the velvet box near her heart and opened it slowly.

Her stomach lurched again.

"Huh. No ring." Drew took inventory of the cedar

box's contents, moving each remaining item around with one finger.

What had Randy done with Nana's ring?

Lola swallowed back the sickening feeling that she'd never see the pearl ring again, realizing she'd found what she'd come for. Clues. "None of those other things are mine." She nodded toward the cedar box and raised her gaze to Drew's. "Do you know what that means?"

"I'm a cop. I draw conclusions from evidence all the time." He took the ring case from Lola and put it back among the other items, closing the lid decisively. "Obviously, it means your husband loved Halloween a little too much." His gesture encompassed the bureau. His smile tried to encompass her.

Lola's breath caught. She blamed her awareness of the man next to her on their proximity to the provocative costumes.

"Or he was a cross-dresser and lost a lot of jewelry." Drew's lips twitched up on one side again. "Not that there's anything wrong with that."

He's trying to make this easy on me.

There was no way this could be easy.

Lola shook her head, shaking off the distracting attraction. "What it means is all I have to do is find the woman these things belong to and—"

"I don't want to burst your bubble—"

"But you're going to try." Lola closed the drawers, noting Drew's disappearing smile and finding comfort in the familiar territory of his disapproving expression. "Go ahead."

"This is a small town, and people aren't going to

voluntarily claim their missing personal effects from you." The unflappable sheriff stood before her, stating the situation as he saw it, pointing out risks and predicting downfalls. "People aren't going to like you poking around trying to identify who Randy knew...*personally*."

"I'm not going to stalk women with a gun." Lola glared at him, this man who smelled so good and always seemed to think the worst of her. "By the way, I need my gun back."

"You can have *Randy's* gun"—Drew's jaw hardened—"just as soon as you get a permit for it."

She made a sound of disgust. "You're impossible."

"I'm the law."

"Show some compassion."

"Show some common sense." His annoyance sparked between them like static electricity on a cheap polyester cop uniform. "Bonfires. Public confessions. Blow-up dolls. And now a witch hunt." He looked like he wanted to roll his eyes. "Take a look at what's happening to you."

"What *happened*," she said firmly. "Past tense. And I'm just now finding out about it. I need my twenty-four-hour cool-down period."

He did roll his eyes then. "I give my daughter time-outs when she has meltdowns."

"I won't melt down." She'd done that already. "I just need to find this woman. I just want to know..." She closed her eyes and left the rest of the statement unspoken.

"If he loved you," he finished for her in an understanding voice that was almost as soothing as Bitsy's. "And if you were to blame."

Lola's eyes flew open. Drew had a compassionate look on his face.

"I get it," Drew continued, oblivious to the hypnotic quality of his own voice. "Women always think they could've done something different in the relationship. Better nightclothes, better cooking, better bedroom moves. I've got news for you. When a man strays, it's least likely to be the woman's fault."

"How do you..."

"You forget I have four sisters. I've seen it all." His brown gaze was direct and unflinching. "Bad boyfriends, catty girlfriends, lying husbands—"

"I get the point, Dr. Phil." Lola cut him off but she couldn't seem to look away from his face. Full lips. Strong, stubbled chin. Fine lines around his eyes as if he'd spent too much time in the sun. He wasn't as beautiful as Randy had been, but he was genuine, and that honesty was the un-ignorable howdy-do her libido found irresistible. She forced herself to stare into Drew's eyes and only into his eyes. "You understand where I'm coming from. You might even be sympathetic that I've been hurt. But there's one thing you don't know." And here, she hardened her voice along with her resolve and picked up the cedar box. "I'm going to find this woman and get my answer."

"Lola," he warned.

She tore her gaze away and pushed past him.

"Don't make me arrest you."

"You're welcome to arrest me." She paused in the doorway and stared back at the sheriff, her chin in the air. "*If* I break a law."

Chapter Eight

♥

Lola Williams epitomized spring-thaw madness. She deserved to be on Drew's Watch-Over list.

She deserves to be watched all night. Those legs...

Drew reminded himself he was sheriff and should think about Lola the way he thought about the Bodine twins. He doubted she'd identify Randy's mistress but it was even money whether she'd rattle the cages of folks in town. There was a way you went about things in Sunshine, and Lola wasn't going that way. She was stuck in Watch-Out-World mode, determined to get out in Sunshine and cause trouble.

His phone chimed with a message. It was from Jane.

I'm coming home. For good.

Jane back in town? To stay?

Drew's knees threatened to buckle. He sat on the bed.

Jane, who'd been arrested outside of Nashville for possession of marijuana.

Jane, who'd been arrested in Nashville for indecent exposure during one of her street concerts.

The same Jane who'd tried desperately to find herself at Sunshine High School, being just as likely to show up to class in Goth gear as in a Catholic schoolgirl outfit. The same girl who'd sat mutinously in the back of algebra class, painting her nails and applying coats of slick lipstick, humming choruses of popular songs and occasionally belting out a lyric in that deep, sultry voice of hers. She'd been a problem in every class except band, where she'd learned to play a variety of instruments, and English, where she'd written all her assignments as poems.

Becky will worship her.

Becky would worship Lola too if given the chance. She was at that age when girls latched on to role models.

But Jane. Jeez.

If Jane came home, Becky might grow up to be a rebel, just like her mother. She'd laugh if he suggested college, and drive off after graduation. Maybe not to Nashville. Maybe to LA or Chicago, or worse—New York City.

Drew bolted out the door. He had to find Becky. He had to hold his baby in his arms and cling to her innocence.

And he had to get married to someone safe and predictable.

A few minutes later, Drew was in the police cruiser, speeding toward town, when the car radio squawked.

"Sheriff, on your way to pick up Becky, could you drive by Lola's?" Usually, Flo's husky voice reassured. Not today. Not when she mentioned Lola.

Had Lola found Randy's lover already? "Is she causing trouble?" With that stubborn attitude and those skin-tight leggings, she was built for disturbing his peace.

"Not exactly," Flo said. "Ramona Everly is concerned about something in Lola's window."

As if he didn't have enough to worry about with Jane and her sudden desire to be a mommy. Lola had probably put a sign in her window before she'd left this morning: WANTED. INFORMATION ABOUT MY HUSBAND'S MISTRESS.

She'd probably offered a reward!

Drew hit the cruiser's lights and accelerated. The blood in his veins ran faster than his wheels on the pavement. Lola just couldn't let things go. If Drew held on to grudges the way she did, he'd be locking up everyone in Sunshine.

But he couldn't dwell on Lola for long. He had to defend himself against Jane. He couldn't wait for Monday to call a lawyer. With only two choices in town, he called Rupert Harper while he drove. But his call went to voice mail, and the recording cheerfully explained Rupert was on vacation. A call to Rupert's brother, Oliver, the only other lawyer in town, revealed he was on vacation as well. The day was going from bad to worse.

When Drew pulled up in front of Lola's house a few minutes later, he almost couldn't believe his eyes. He certainly couldn't tear them away.

There was no sign in her window. What was behind the panes was worse than a sign.

A rap on his car door had him jumping. He needed sleep, maybe less caffeine, and certainly less Lola.

Ramona Everly was dressed in her Sunday best, a beige dress that hung off her thin shoulders and low white heels. "That's not right, Sheriff." She pointed a bony finger toward Lola's small home.

The blow-up doll Lola had carried around last night was locked in an embrace with its female counterpart. They were posed at a forty-five-degree angle, as if he'd dipped her during a dance. The female doll wore a red dress. A strap hung off one shoulder. The Randy doll wore a red flowered Hawaiian shirt.

It was just like something Jane would do.

Drew flexed his fingers on the steering wheel.

Lola wasn't home. Her impractical red Fiat wasn't in the driveway, which was filled with boxes and black trash bags, a mounted deer head, and various items of furniture.

"I'll have a talk with her," Drew promised Ramona, turning the cruiser lights off.

"Make sure you do." Ramona clasped her hands piously. "This isn't New York City."

No. It wasn't. No one would look twice at Lola's window in New York City, other than to take a selfie in front of it.

Drew pulled away at a much slower pace, wondering where Lola had gone. Gas? Grocery store? Greeley? He kept his eyes open on the way to pick up his daughter.

Mia Hampton lived in the newer part of town. Houses here were finished in stucco and were cookie-cutter, affordable but lacking the character of the farmhouse or Lola's hundred-year-old Craftsman.

"Dad! Daddy! Papa! Padre! Did you get married?"

Becky bolted down the front walk in red cowboy boots, a Denver Broncos jersey, and a pink tutu. Her fashion choices may have been eclectic, but her long brown hair was in a neat French braid that he'd had no hand in creating. Without waiting for an answer to the question of marriage, Becky shouted, "We had waffles!"

Drew swept Becky into his arms, breathing in the familiar scent of her, enjoying the tight loop of skinny arms around his neck, forgetting about French-braid fails, sisters who might have slept with married men, and the threat of Jane.

"Did you arrest anybody last night, Daddy?" Becky craned her neck to see whether there was anyone in the back of the cruiser. At the shake of his head, she added, "Shoot. Nothing exciting ever happens here."

"You're exciting," Drew argued with a gentle tug on her braid.

It was true. As much as he'd wished for a quiet, sweet daughter who wore pretty dresses and was happy playing jacks and hopscotch, he loved Becky's exuberance. Until today, he'd been convinced that the older Becky got, the more conformist she'd become, especially with Mia as her best friend. Mia was the girl in Becky's class who wore pretty dresses and was enrolled in ballet.

"Let's go." Becky wiggled in his arms.

"You need to thank Ms. Hampton properly." He set her down. He needed to thank Mia's mother too and collect Becky's things.

Becky ran ahead, tutu bouncing with each step. She tossed a smile over her shoulder. "Come on, Daddy."

An image of Lola came to mind, walking her blow-up

husband home, staring back at Drew with a challenge in her eye. What had she been like as a kid? Wilder than Becky, he'd bet. Maybe as wild as Jane.

Drew picked up Becky's sleeping bag and backpack from the porch and thanked the Hamptons for their hospitality, promising a sleepover at his place soon.

Duty done, Becky ran toward the cruiser without looking back. Like any kid, she had a jumble of interests, all of which Drew encouraged. Lately, she'd been talking about wanting to play the guitar or the piano. His mind blended an image of Becky with a childhood memory of Jane. His ex-wife had always had eclectic interests and her own fashion sense. Did that mean there was nothing he could do to keep Becky in Sunshine, where he could ensure she was safe and happy?

He stowed Becky's things in the trunk, trying to reassure himself that his daughter was nothing like Jane.

"Ten-four, Flo." Becky returned the handset to its cradle as Drew leaned in the open driver's door.

"Rebecca Maureen Taylor." Drew used the drill sergeant voice he reserved for Paul when he was drunk and his deputy Gary when he was overzealous in his enforcement of justice. "Are you supposed to use my radio?"

"No, but Flo—" At his hard stare, Becky started again. "*Ms. Carlisle* asked for a status update on your whereabouts. Didn't you hear her?"

He hadn't. He'd turned off his mobile radio when he'd been talking to Lola in the garage apartment. Drew turned on the handset clipped to his shirt, and then pointed to the back seat and Becky's booster. Driving around with his kid in the back seat, where criminals were supposed to sit, probably wouldn't look good in family court, but the cruiser was easier for her to get in and out of than the department's SUV. And it wasn't practical to switch out department vehicles with a personal car when he was on call 24/7.

At this rate, he'd second-guess himself into a mental breakdown. He inhaled deeply, trying to find balance. "Were you a good girl last night?"

"Yes, sir." Becky scampered out the car door and to the back, climbing into her booster behind the driver's seat. "Where are we going, Daddy-O?"

"Home." Drew buckled her in.

"But Daddy, it's Sunday." Becky made her sad eyes, pouting and blinking in the universal language of the hopeful. "Can't we go to the Saddle Horn?"

Drew waited to answer until he was behind the wheel and pulling away. "Didn't you just say you had waffles at the Hamptons'?"

"Waffles, not hot chocolate." Becky found his gaze in the rearview mirror and gave him her sweetest smile.

If Jane hadn't texted, if Drew hadn't been realizing his parental weaknesses, he might have held firm. Instead, he turned down Main Street.

A bright-yellow SUV approached. It had something large inside, something nearly as tall as the cab interior.

Drew raised a hand in greeting as they passed.

The driver, his sister Eileen, didn't turn her head or acknowledge Drew, but her vehicle swerved slightly, as if his gesture startled her.

"You shoulda honked," Becky said. "Aunt Eileen didn't see me. And I waved."

Eileen was still peeved about her so-called boyfriend being arrested for grand theft auto. She'd insisted on dropping the charges and blamed Drew when Tyrell hadn't returned to Sunshine along with her vehicle. That had been weeks ago. Drew needed to clear the air.

Plus do a million other things, like broach the subject of infidelity with Pris and advise Lola to close her drapes and give up the mistress search.

But first, he needed to treat his daughter to hot chocolate, solidifying the father-daughter bond and the hope that Becky would never leave Sunshine.

* * *

If Mims had been Catholic, she might have gone to confession this morning.

Guilt kept trying to weigh her down. Guilt was undoubtedly why Mims felt as if she saw the world differently than Bitsy or Clarice lately. The three women never used to argue about whom to match.

Drat that Edith. She wanted to get revenge on the woman who'd cheated with Charlie. She wanted to hang her up by her toenails! She wouldn't understand that Mims hadn't cheated with Charlie. Not in the biblical sense. She and Hamm, Edith and Charlie. They'd been friends. And friends didn't cheat on friends. Not in Mims's book.

I'm not that kind of woman.

Which was why Mims was convinced confession wouldn't help save her soul. Her conscience would be eased only if she found Edith a new man and got her mind off her loss. And if Edith's enthusiasm for the Widows Club waned while she was in the process of falling in love again, why, that would be a bonus.

So Mims had fidgeted through Pastor Mike's services as he'd talked about loving thy neighbor. (The minister always was a mind reader.) And when he was finally done, she'd headed straight for the Saddle Horn for a board meeting of the Sunshine Valley Matchmakers Club.

The Saddle Horn coffee shop had been in existence since before Mims was born. It was named after a snowy peak that sat high above Sunshine Valley in the Rockies. On Sundays, it served hot chocolate with mile-high whip. You weren't supposed to eat the whipped cream with a spoon. You were supposed to dive in with your face. It was an institution and guaranteed a constant stream of families on Sundays.

Mims pushed through the front door, ringing the bell overhead. Customers looked up, nodding and calling out greetings. She walked past the counter with its red seats and silver swivel stools. Her low heels rang out on the green-and-white checked linoleum until she reached the corner.

She eased her way to the back of the red vinyl circular booth the board always occupied on Sundays. The cushion had an airflow problem. If someone sat down with too much gusto, the rest of the occupants bounced, as if sharing an air mattress. It could be an annoyance, but from the corner booth, the Matchmakers Club could see everyone coming and going.

The moment Mims's purse was tucked on the seat,

Pearl slid a coffee mug in front of her. Pearl was Bitsy's mother and as much a fixture at the Saddle Horn as Sunday-morning hot chocolate. The wiry old waitress would probably die with a coffeepot clutched in one hand and a can of whipped cream in the other.

Bitsy arrived next, sitting so primly the air beneath the cushion barely moved. In no time, Pearl had a small pot with tea steeping and an empty cup before her.

"Thank you, Mama," Bitsy said absently. She wore a pink twinset and a pair of white wool slacks. Her blond bob was held back with a white velvet hair band.

There might have been a time when Mims was envious of Bitsy's slender sophistication but at her age Mims had accepted she'd never be a size eight or be the type to buy clothes that needed the delicate cycle, much less dry cleaning.

"How was your husband?" Mims cradled her still-hot coffee mug.

"Which one?" Bitsy frowned.

Mims paused. When Bitsy visited her husbands' graves, at least one of them had something to say about Bitsy's life or the world at large.

Bitsy stared at the door so intently that Mims looked to see who'd come in. The bell hadn't rung. The door stood closed. No one was on the other side.

"No one talked to me today," Bitsy admitted with a sigh.

"Oh." Mims sat back. The last time that had happened, Bitsy had begun dating someone. Soon after, she'd gotten married, dropping out of the Widows Club for several years.

"*Oh?*" Bitsy echoed, fingering the pearls at her throat. "We need to talk about Lola and Drew."

Mims held up a hand. "I'm going to keep my eye on Drew and Wendy. You can keep looking for someone for Lola if you'd like, but she's not ready."

Bitsy's blue gaze sharpened.

"Sorry I'm late." Clarice took the seat on the other side of Mims with a plop that gave Mims a little air bump. She set her walking stick against the wall and adjusted her hearing aids. In a tribute to her hippie roots, she wore a blue peasant blouse with white embroidered flowers and faded blue jeans. "I was setting out the bird feeders and spilled all my seed. The squirrels are going to get fat."

Pearl appeared with a hot chocolate topped with frothy whipped cream and a stack of napkins.

"When are you going to grow up and give up hot chocolate, Clarice?" Bitsy rarely snapped at anyone. She was friendlier than the doormat at Pastor Mike's office, the one that read, *Hug a stranger and love your fellow man.*

Mims began to seriously worry about her friend.

"Grow up?" Clarice said, unfazed by Bitsy's derision. She tossed her gray braids over her shoulders and bobbed like a bird, pressing her face into the swirl of whipped cream. She straightened and smiled at Bitsy, wearing a lopsided white beard. "I'll give up Saddle Horn hot chocolate when I'm dead."

"I'm guessing that's a long time from now." A familiar sparkle returned to Bitsy's gaze as she said this, easing Mims's concern about losing Bitsy from the Widows Club.

"Dead is a long way off." Clarice wiped away her

melting beard and prepared to start over. "Matchmaker business first?"

"Yes." Mims wasted no time. The second church service of the day would be getting out soon, and the coffee shop would begin to fill, eroding any hope of privacy. "I have some candidates I think would be perfect for Edith."

Clarice dipped her chin in the whip, creating a pointed beard. "Give us the list."

So Mims did. "Bart Umberland. He's divorced and lives alone in a cabin on the mountain." A forty-five-minute drive from Sunshine in good weather.

"The mountain is a deal-breaker." Bitsy poured her tea. "Edith enjoys life in town."

"Agreed." Clarice dabbed her creamy whiskers away with a napkin. "Next."

Drat. Mims's list went downhill from there. "Darryl Woolsey. He's a retired mechanic and can fix anything."

"Hmm." Clarice's gaze grew distant as she considered Darryl. "I heard Edith complain about a persnickety dishwasher last night."

"That won't work either." Bitsy added a dollop of cream to her tea. "Darryl can't get the grease out from under his fingertips, and Edith is a bit OCD."

Mims had been afraid of this. There wasn't a big pool of eligible men over the age of sixty in town.

"Well..." Clarice spun her hot chocolate slowly, examining what was left of the froth the way Mims studied deer tracks in the snow during hunting season. "Maybe we should let Edith into the club."

"No." Mims almost added, *Never*. She fell back

against the banquette, which forced the air in it to either side, giving Clarice and Bitsy a gentle ride on a wave of air. "We have rules in the club for a reason."

Bitsy gave Mims a hard look. "What aren't you telling us?"

"When it comes to the club, we don't keep secrets." Clarice wiped her mouth with a fresh napkin. "That's a board rule."

The need to tell them she and Charlie had been hunting and fishing buddies for more than a decade weighed heavily upon Mims. They'd take it wrong. They'd think…They'd think she was the worst sort of person. When really, she'd done nothing wrong.

Mims drew herself up. "I—"

"I was so excited." Edith plunked down next to Clarice, sending a wave of air around the booth cushion and squishing the air from Mims's lungs. "I rushed out of church without getting into the fellowship line and came in the coffee shop back door." Edith elbowed Clarice deeper into the booth. She wore a pink flowered dress that had seen better days and a smile like a schoolgirl with a full box of valentines. "Get me up to speed. What are we doing?"

Mims felt trapped in the back of the booth.

Pearl set plates down in front of the board. Scrambled egg whites for Bitsy. Hash browns and sausage for Clarice. A western omelet for Mims.

"We're eating?" Edith smiled as if she'd won the annual trout-fishing contest. Which was ridiculous, because she never fished. "Pearl, have Alsace make me a special." Edith grabbed Pearl's apron before the waitress could turn to go. "Only tell Alsace to hold the potatoes, the onions, and the cheese. Oh, and the tomatoes."

Pearl frowned. She was pricklier than a porcupine if people didn't say what they meant. "You want scrambled eggs with bacon."

"Yes." Edith put roll-your-eyes punch into the word. "But the special is two dollars less."

Pearl's steel-gray eyes narrowed.

Mims held her breath with barely contained glee, waiting for Pearl to put Edith in her place.

"*Mama*..." Bitsy saved Edith from certain censure. "Are you coming to my house for Sunday dinner?"

Without turning her head, Pearl angled her narrowed gaze toward her daughter. "Don't I always?" She tugged her apron free of Edith's grip and headed toward the order counter.

"Don't forget my special," Edith sing-songed. She smiled at them all, as clueless as she'd been back in high school to the emotional tone of those around her.

Had Mims been worried Edith would figure out she and Charlie had been pals? She shouldn't have been. Edith couldn't detect a ripple in a still pond.

"Thank you for the reminder about the board meeting, Clarice." Edith beamed at the traitor and her latest whipped cream beard. "I'm ready to serve. Swear me in." Edith looked better today. She'd combed her hair but lines emanating from her eyes hinted at despondency.

"We're discussing the upcoming fashion show benefiting the Holly Scouts," Mims lied, glancing up from sprinkling her omelet with Tabasco to give Clarice a stern look.

What had Clarice thought inviting Edith would accomplish?

"I've always wanted to walk the runway." Edith craned her neck to look around the coffee shop. "Where did Pearl go? I'd like coffee."

Bitsy scooted out of the booth, darted behind the counter, and returned with a cup and a coffeepot. She'd worked at the Saddle Horn through her teenage years, before she'd found higher-paying work at the cable company in Greeley.

"Thank you," Edith said with that all-is-right-with-my-world smile of hers, adding before Bitsy could sit, "and could you get me some creamers? The ones with the flavors, not half-and-half." She aimed that smile at Clarice next. "I guess Bitsy won't be joining us for the meeting, since she's working."

Bitsy frowned, not that Edith noticed. And then Bitsy pivoted gracefully in her black ballet flats to do Edith's bidding.

Mims stabbed her omelet as if it needed a death blow.

"My, but you're particular, Edith." Clarice had demolished her whip. She sighed and slurped hot chocolate from her mug.

"I don't get out much, and when I do, I like to enjoy the good life." Edith gave Clarice's hot chocolate a deprecating glance. "Of course, you wouldn't understand that, living as simply as you do."

Clarice set her mug on the table with a thud. She adjusted her hearing aids as if she couldn't believe she'd just been insulted.

Mims waited for Clarice to snap back but nothing

happened. Nothing. And postmenopausal Mims couldn't think of a thing to say to defend her friend.

Bitsy placed two capsules of French-vanilla creamer in front of Edith and slid gracefully into the booth without so much as a poof of air.

"Thank you." Edith flashed that smile Bitsy's way. She'd perfected the art of getting people to do her bidding. "But I'd like two more creamers. The coffee here is always bitter."

Mims shoved a bite of omelet into her mouth to keep from telling Edith to make do.

Almost without looking, Bitsy's hand darted out and found Pearl's arm as she passed. "Two more flavored creamers, please, Mama."

Pearl gave her daughter a look that seemed to say, *Let me put her out of your misery.*

Again, Mims waited.

Again, she was disappointed when Pearl turned away without comment. Was Mims the only one who challenged Edith?

"Is it too late to sign up to model at the fashion show?" Edith dumped the two creamers in her coffee with too much verve, creating puddles on the sparkly white Formica. "And what about the kissing booth at the county fair? Is it staffed? I was quite the kisser in my day." Her gaze tracked Pearl, but her train of thought was obviously on a different rail. "You know, I have an idea that will revolutionize the pancake breakfast."

The Widows Club board exchanged glances, not that Edith noticed.

"My idea will double the event's income." Edith

always butted in where she didn't belong. "Let's hold a pancake breakfast with kisses from the *cooks*." Who were usually the older widows in the club. "I know you staff the kissing booth with young ladies, but I think we should let some of the more mature gals have a turn at smooching."

Mims choked on her omelet. "Women our age don't—"

"Women our age *do*," Bitsy said sharply, fiddling with her shoulder pads.

Mims tugged at the neckline of her dress, suddenly hot. Maybe she'd swallowed too much Tabasco. Or maybe she wasn't successfully swallowing her anger at the idea of Edith replacing Bitsy on the board if Bitsy remarried.

Mims's game was off. She couldn't juggle everything the way she used to. At this rate, Edith would muscle Mims out of the presidency, and the Matchmakers Club would dissolve, if only because it would be Mims and Clarice, who was a dear but a stickler for the rules, and Edith, who was more than one brick shy of a full chimney.

Life just wasn't fair.

Pearl slammed two creamers in front of Edith. "Are you going to be here every week from now on?"

"No," chorused the three board members.

"I am," said Edith, as hard of hearing as Clarice without her hearing aids.

Chapter Nine

♥

The bell rang over the door of the Saddle Horn, followed by the jubilant ring of Becky's voice. "And then Ms. Hampton said we looked like hookers." Becky glanced up at Drew. "What's a hooker, Daddy?"

The Sunday-morning crowd stopped talking and waited for Drew to answer. Or die of embarrassment.

Drew had too much experience with precocious young women to take the heat for a comment he hadn't made. He met every gaze squarely, softening his glance for Norma Eastlake, whose husband had been killed a few days ago in a car accident. Drew had worked the scene and had had trouble sleeping that night. There was talk around town about needing a light at the intersection but until someone championed the idea, it would only be talk.

Drew shepherded Becky to the counter, near Jason Petrie.

Iggy sat on the other side of Jason, his straw cowboy hat tilted so far back on his head that it looked like a large misplaced halo.

"A hooker is a lady who wears pretty dresses." Drew

didn't bother lowering his voice. The crowd would only strain to hear.

"I won't ever be a hooker, Daddy." Becky hopped on a counter stool and spun, waving to the regulars. "I hate dresses."

Their audience chuckled and returned to the business of eating.

"I love it here," Becky crooned. "I love it, I love it, I love it."

Drew's heart swelled with love. Becky was his girl. She was so like him that she'd never get bitten by the wanderlust that had clamped onto her mother.

The bell rang above the door. As one, the clientele turned to see who was entering next.

Wendy Adams stood in the doorway. She wore a long tan skirt and a blue blouse that was buttoned clear to her neck.

Drew stared at Wendy a little longer, at her short blond hair and pretty face, waiting for something. A spark. A zing. Lust.

He sighed and looked away. So maybe Wendy's hair didn't overload Drew's system the way Lola's legs did, but she was attractive in her own way and came with the benefit of being predictable.

Boring.

That sounded like Lola's voice. He stuffed the thought away.

Wendy took a seat between Becky and Jason, set her Bible on the counter, and smiled at no one in particular. One thing Drew could say about Wendy: the silence and peace she brought with her was a welcome respite.

In the corner booth, Mims and Clarice smiled at Drew with a similar expression, one that said, *We know you're interested. Let's get this show on the road.*

Drew heeded the advice of those all-knowing smiles. "Hey, Wendy." When his daughter didn't immediately take his lead and greet Wendy, Drew nudged her.

"Hey, Ms. Adams," Becky said dutifully as if he'd asked her to unload the dishwasher.

"Hi," Wendy replied, barely above a whisper.

Pearl slid a coffee in front of Drew and a hot chocolate with a mountain of whip in front of Becky. The waitress flicked an assessing glance at Wendy. "What can I get you?"

"Water." Wendy cleared her throat. "And a menu."

The menus were laminated and in front of Wendy on the counter, tucked behind the salt and pepper. Pearl slapped one on the counter and charged away in her white running sneakers.

"I never come in here," Wendy said with a sideways glance and a shy smile in Drew's direction. "My parents didn't allow it when I was growing up."

Her dad, more likely. Howard Adams had a reputation for a short fuse and a conservative outlook on life.

Wendy cleared her throat again. "It's been on my bucket list."

Drew gave a little head shake. Wendy was too young to have a bucket list.

"We come here every Sunday." Becky wobbled her chin from side to side. "Ho ho ho. I'm Santa." Her whipped cream beard listed to the left.

"Oh, honey. Don't make a mess." Wendy grabbed

a handful of napkins from the dispenser and wiped the beard and grin from Becky's face.

Becky crossed her arms and glowered.

"Did I do something wrong?" Wendy looked perplexed.

"No," Drew said quickly.

Becky's glower swiveled in his direction, to which he responded with a look that she undoubtedly knew meant *Behave*.

His daughter glowered at the salt and pepper shakers.

"It's a thing at the Saddle Horn to make whipped cream facial hair on Sundays." Drew gestured toward a booth where the two Yancey girls giggled at each other and their puffy beards.

"I'd forgotten that was a thing." Wendy's lips wavered toward disapproval. "That's so...messy."

Pearl plunked a small ice water in front of Wendy, shook a can of whipped cream, and put a fresh coil of whip on top of Becky's hot chocolate.

Becky tossed her hands in the air. "You're the bestest waitress in the whole wide world, Pearl."

"Tell that to Alsace." The elderly waitress gave Becky a rare grin. "I could use a raise."

The bell tinkled. The coffee shop quieted.

Lola walked in. Her messy ponytail had gotten messier since Drew had seen her at the farmhouse. And yet somehow, she created a spark inside him. A zing. Lust.

It was her legs, he decided. They were world class in length in those leggings. In fact, those leggings should be outlawed in Colorado. They might make male drivers run off the road. Just look at Iggy. He was staring at Lola's legs with a smile splitting his sharp face as if he was imagining—

Lola's gaze bounced into Drew, jarring all rational thought into neutral. Drew was aware of Becky sitting next to him, the clink of a fork on a plate, and Lola's deep blue eyes. But he was in limbo. Waiting. Waiting for Lola to say something to him.

She said nothing. Her chin might have dipped a bit before she moved on to study Wendy, perhaps cataloging whether she was wearing a pearl ring or was missing an earring.

Drew scowled and shook his head, brain working once more. No way was Wendy Randy's lover. Comparatively, Pris was a likelier candidate.

Instead of finding a seat, Lola stood at the cash register and waved a large red thermos. "Bring the pot, Pearl."

"Order up," Alsace called from the kitchen, sliding a plate of scrambled eggs and bacon under the heat lamps.

Talk resumed. Beards were made. Lola pretended to be oblivious to it all. A lock of her light-brown hair curled around one cheek.

Iggy continued to give Lola's legs an appreciative glance. Jason leaned forward to see what had captured his business partner's attention, and grinned.

Drew felt a stab of annoyance. "When you get a minute, Lola..." He caught his landlady's eye. "We need to talk about your front window."

"Is it broken?" Becky tried to lick whip from her

upper lip. "Or is her window dirty? You made me clean windows last summer, and I didn't like it."

Drew swiped his daughter's white mustache but that did nothing to stop her from staring at Lola like she was an exotic animal in the zoo.

Lola pretended great interest in her cell phone.

"She doesn't like to clean windows either. I can tell." Becky dunked her face in the whipped cream, shifted her chin around, and then surfaced. She used her fingers to make the whip on her chin into a point, pivoting her face toward Drew.

"Nice," Drew said.

Becky angled her face toward Wendy, who didn't notice his daughter looking for attention. She was reviewing the menu as seriously as if it listed the features of a new car she was considering.

"Excellent villain." Lola gave Becky two thumbs up.

Becky slid off her stool and ran over to Lola, tutu bouncing. She tilted her face up for inspection.

"I couldn't have made a better bad-stache with real hair." Lola leaned down for a closer look. "And I've made all kinds of beards and mustaches from hair."

Beaming, Becky raised her arms and turned around on her tiptoes, a cowboy-booted, football-jersey-wearing ballerina. She held the pose for Lola. "Did you make bad-staches for dead people?"

The coffee shop quieted again. Even Drew wanted to hear the answer.

Meanwhile, Becky's pointy beard plopped to her tutu.

"Oh, honey. You're making a mess." Wendy held up another handful of napkins and then paused, suddenly uncertain. She blinked at Drew. "You have to wipe them when they drip, right?"

"Sure. Of course." As a kid, he'd thought dripping was half the fun, possibly because the rest of the week he'd had to wipe the noses of four squealing, frustrating girls. Most Sundays, he let Becky drip on herself. But that was before the threat of Jane. Becky needed more decorum and discipline if he was going to retain full custody.

Drew called Becky over, grabbing his own set of napkins.

"Lola." Bitsy called Lola over to the Widows Club table. "We're holding a bake sale Tuesday night benefiting the Little League. We'd love to have you participate."

"Are you sure?" Lola looked as if she'd unexpectedly been chosen to pitch in game seven of the World Series when she'd never pitched in her life. "You've never asked me before."

"*Dad.*" Becky tried to squirm out of reach. "Too hard."

Drew released Becky and wiped his own hands, shamelessly eavesdropping on Lola, same as the rest of the coffee shop patrons.

"I suspect not asking was our loss." Bitsy grabbed on to Lola's hand as if they were dear friends. "Anyone can participate. In fact, Wendy Adams raises the most money every year. There's a prize for that."

Wendy didn't lift her gaze from the menu. "It's my chocolate-apple Bundt cake. It's an old family recipe."

Drew made a sound of agreement. Wendy's superior baking talent wasn't news. Her Bundt cake always sold out.

Lola had been chewing the lipstick from her lips. "I'm not a very good cook."

"With a body like that, who cares how well she bakes?" Iggy whispered to Jason.

Drew scowled at him. He didn't want Becky to hear talk like that.

His daughter scrambled to her knees on her stool just as Pearl topped off her hot chocolate with more whipped cream.

"I'll help you." Bitsy's congenial tone convinced even Drew that Lola could be a success.

Still, Lola hesitated.

"Can we count on you?" Edith asked a second before Mims opened her mouth, presumably to ask the same thing.

Mims frowned.

There were too many cooks in the Widows Club kitchen. Drew bit back a grin. It was about time someone gave Mims a run for her money.

"Okay. If you're sure." Lola turned to go, looking less than excited at the prospect of being included in the bake sale.

She should be happy the widows weren't blackballing her for that window display.

"I don't win *every* year," Wendy said kindly to Lola as she passed. "You can set up next to me if crowds make you nervous."

"That's very kind." Again Lola's gaze swept Wendy speculatively.

Drew pressed his lips together to keep from telling her Wendy wasn't the owner of Randy's jewelry collection. Wendy was the marrying kind. Everybody knew that. Since she'd come in, Iggy hadn't given her more than a cursory glance.

"You be good to Scotty," Pearl said to Lola, exchanging the thermos for Lola's cash.

The coffee shop quieted. Gazes turned to Norma, Scotty's widow, who sat frozen in her booth with her oldest teenage daughter, who had a mug of hot chocolate untouched before her.

"Will do." Lola nodded and left.

"Lola does good work with the dead," Pearl said into the silence. "Always comes in here for coffee before she starts."

Drew hadn't known that. He watched Lola walk across the street in those leggings. No cars screeched to a halt. No men drove their trucks into parked cars. It was a miracle.

When she'd disappeared around the corner, he turned his attention to his coffee cup and protecting his daughter. "Wendy, what are you doing later? Say after three?" Before his daughter could ask what he was doing, Drew added, "There's a new Disney movie out, and I promised Becky we'd go see it today." He'd done no such thing, but at the prospect of going to the movies, Becky remained silent.

"I'd love to." Wendy smiled that gentle smile of hers, the one that said she was no trouble. Ever. "You'll change, of course," she said to Becky.

"Why?" Becky jolted upright, flinging a trail of whip from her chin across the counter. "I have clothes on."

"Because that's what you do when you go places."

Wendy's smile never wavered. "You put on clean clothes and make yourself look presentable."

Drew smiled. Wendy was definitely going to be a good influence on Becky.

Why, she probably knew how to French braid.

Chapter Ten

♥

Lola walked the short block to the Eternal Rest Mortuary.

The past twenty-four hours had been surreal. Randy's betrayal, the Widows Club fund-raiser, and the two sides of Sheriff Drew Taylor.

After she'd left the farmhouse, she'd parked down by the river, letting a few tears fall. There were fewer tears than the day before because she had clues to help her uncover the truth.

She'd scrutinized the contents of Randy's keepsake box, committing each piece to memory, breathing in the scent of the near-empty perfume bottle like a bloodhound.

The river rushed by as fast as the unanswered questions streaming through her head. Why had Randy kept such things? He hadn't saved the ticket stubs from the New York Yankees game they'd attended together. What had Lola meant to him? Why had he taken her pearl ring, and what had he done with it? The pearl ring and her book of dreams were all she had left of Nana, of her promise of true love.

If he'd been alive, she would've slapped him and demanded he move out. But he was dead, and the best she could do was slap the steering wheel.

In the midst of her low, her boss, Augie Bruce, had called to say Scotty Eastlake's body was ready for her services. Never mind that it was Sunday; working on a silent client was just what Lola needed to center herself.

She entered the mortuary through the back door, relieved to have escaped the microscope of the coffee shop. In Sunshine, she was the oddity. Most people didn't understand her. Most people didn't want to try. From the day Augie had hired Lola, she'd been judged on the quality and compassion of her work, not the city she was born in or the way she dressed. She hurried down the back stairs to the basement, entering the preparation room and nearly running into her boss.

"You didn't have to come in on a Sunday." Augie's round features and bald pate were tan from keeping up the grounds. In addition to managing the mortuary gardens and cemetery, he did the embalming, while his wife, Rowena, ran the front office. "I only let you know I'd finished with Scotty so you'd know what you had on your plate on Monday."

"I needed a break." Lola put on plastic gloves and took shallow breaths. The nose-burning scent of embalming fluid still lingered. She opened a small window and then placed a hand on her client's firm shoulder. "Hello, Scotty."

She hadn't known the deceased personally but she

knew of him. It was hard to live in Sunshine and not have heard of most people in town at one point or another. Scotty had been a house painter who'd commuted to Greeley for work. He hadn't seen the semitruck that hit him at the same intersection where Randy had been killed. No, she hadn't known Scotty, but Lola understood him. He wanted to look his best for his final farewell with his family and friends.

"Are you still okay covering for us in a few weeks?" Augie asked. His daughter was graduating from college in Denver.

"Of course." There'd be little to do unless someone died.

"Good. I left you Scotty's file on the counter." Augie shed his gloves but not his compassionate expression. He cared about the people he served in the basement. They were his friends, his neighbors. "The file has photos from his wife and an article the *Sunshine Valley Weekly* did on Scotty two years ago. I put his wedding ring back on, but we haven't received his suit yet. Let me know if you need anything." He left her, closing the door behind him.

Lola stared at Scotty's face—his soft chin and plump cheeks, the spidery lines on his face that told of the head trauma that had killed him. Her nose burned, not from a chemical reaction but from grief. Scotty had many of the same wounds Randy had had. She could see where Augie had built up his nose and forehead. He'd also applied wax to Scotty's fingers, filling in the cuts and scrapes.

A year ago, she'd insisted upon preparing Randy for

his funeral. Lola should have made her husband up like a clown and dressed him in his *Playboy* T-shirt and silk heart boxers.

But this wasn't her philandering husband. This was Scotty Eastlake, who by all accounts had been a devoted husband and father. A man who'd left behind a widow, a woman who'd stare at the ceiling through the long lonely nights ahead and try to imagine a future without her spouse.

Lola ran her hand through Scotty's thinning brown hair. Unlike her living clients, his scalp didn't give beneath her fingers. She leaned closer, gauging his skin tone. He wasn't as tan as Augie, but he'd seen more sun this season than she had. He'd lived his life, while she'd wasted hers on Randy.

Lola scanned Scotty's file. "You pitched in your softball league." Another reason for the tan. "And served overseas. Thank you for your service."

She poured herself a generous cup of coffee and turned on music she thought Scotty would like—classic country. While Lola assembled her supplies, a singer crooned about a sheriff who was too good to be true.

Amen, sister.

There had to be a psychological explanation for the howdy-do the sheriff suddenly inspired in her. She'd felt it only after Randy's indiscretion had come to light. Surely the reason she was out of kilter where Drew was concerned was because she'd been betrayed and he stood for justice.

None of which mattered at the moment. Scotty needed her attention.

"You were a house painter." Lola plugged in the makeup sprayer. "You'll appreciate this."

There was a scuffle outside, a stumbling on the stairs.

"You can't go in there, Mrs. Eastlake." Augie, who never raised his voice, was practically shouting. "I told you your husband would be ready for a private viewing tomorrow."

Naked, scarred, skin translucent, Scotty was in no condition for his grieving widow to see him.

Lola ran out the door and shut it behind her.

Augie stood midstair, his arms locked to either wall. A woman was poised on the stairwell above him. She had red-rimmed eyes and shoulder-length mousy brown hair in need of a good cut and color. She'd been in the coffee shop earlier. Mrs. Eastlake. Lola hadn't known.

When Scotty's wife saw Lola, she sobbed. "He's in there? My Scotty?"

At the door above, a shapely teenage girl with straight brown hair stared at her mother in horror.

This was Scotty's family. Lola was determined they not see him in his current state.

"Mrs. Eastlake." Lola peeled off her plastic gloves and tossed them to the landing behind her. "I'm so glad you're here. I need your advice."

"You need *me*?" Mrs. Eastlake whispered.

"Yes," Lola fibbed. When Randy died, she would've been lost without purpose, which was why Augie had allowed her to do Randy's final preparations.

Above them, the teen's upper lip trembled.

"Let's go to the lobby." Lola kept her tone light. The lobby had a view of the garden out front with its cheerful tulips and the towering, snowy Saddle Horn in the distance. Beauty could sometimes ease grief.

The Eastlakes turned around.

Augie mouthed his thanks as Lola passed.

The lobby was 1950s chic, meaning the Bruces were lucky that mid-century modern was back in style, because the place hadn't been redecorated since the mid-century. Lola sat in a chair with wooden arms and green burlap cushions, inviting Mrs. Eastlake and her daughter to sit on the matching couch. Augie walked to his office, giving them some privacy.

"I'm sorry for your loss." Lola found herself reaching for Mrs. Eastlake's hand the same way Bitsy had reached for hers in the coffee shop earlier. "I lost my husband a year ago."

Mrs. Eastlake gave a brief nod. Her daughter bowed her head, face crumpling into a scowl that couldn't stop tears from falling.

"I didn't tell Scotty I loved him." Mrs. Eastlake squeezed Lola's fingers until bone met bone. "We argued in the morning about me always having to do the housework alone." Her voice echoed through the funeral parlor, amplifying the off-key sound of her pain. "Scotty went off to work, and I didn't say I loved him." She drew a shuddering breath. "I saw you in the coffee shop earlier. I know he's downstairs, and I want to see him. I have to tell him I love him."

Lola understood regrets, but more than anything, she understood the shock of the dead for those unaccustomed to their appearance. Redirection was called for. "How long were you married?"

"Twenty years." Mrs. Eastlake released Lola to clutch a pendant hanging from a gold chain, hidden beneath her blouse. "We went to school together from kindergarten through high school." Her gaze drifted toward the stairs. "Do you think Scotty knew I loved him?"

"He knew," Lola said with certainty. "You can't have been married that long and not know that." You could be married one year and be clueless, but not twenty. No way. "Was your necklace a gift from Scotty?"

Mrs. Eastlake nodded. "He gave it to me a few years ago at Christmas." She lifted the heart-shaped, ruby-studded pendant for Lola to admire and then clasped it again as if afraid she'd lose it. "I told him it was too extravagant. I mean, we were making payments on it until this last holiday. But he said I could pass it down to Aubrey one day, and..." She choked up, releasing the pendant to wrap an arm around her daughter. "And...he said I was worth it."

Her daughter buried her face in Mrs. Eastlake's shoulder. The sound of a country song drifted up to them, barely audible above the girl's sobs.

"Scotty volunteered everywhere." The widow's voice cracked. "He was never home. With all the good works he did, I shouldn't have complained about the dishes." Her expression turned haunted. She looked at Lola but she didn't seem to see her. "I need to apologize."

"And you will." Lola wished Scotty's widow had come in later that afternoon. Then perhaps Lola could have given the woman the peace she so desperately needed. "If you bring me his suit, you can see him this evening."

"Mom, no. Don't." Mascara smudged the teen's big brown eyes. "You'll be talking to a corpse, not Dad."

"Aubrey." Mrs. Eastlake's voice strengthened as she gently chastised her daughter. "Every part of your father is dear to me."

Aubrey sobbed.

A door opened and closed behind Lola.

"Everyone grieves differently." Lola spoke directly to Scotty's daughter. "If it makes your mother feel better to talk to your father in person, when he's ready, she should." Lola tapped a spot over her heart. "And if she talks to him through things he gave her, like that necklace, that's okay too."

Tears smudged more of Aubrey's makeup.

"I promise I'll let you know when Scotty's ready to hear your apology." At the sound of approaching footsteps, Lola looked up, expecting to see Augie ready to usher Scotty's family out.

It was Drew.

"Sheriff." Mrs. Eastlake held out a hand to him.

He took that hand, drew Mrs. Eastlake to her feet, and hugged her. He hugged her tight, as if he was grieving too.

Drew hadn't given Lola a hug when Randy had died. His dispatcher had called Lola and told her to get to the hospital in Greeley. When she'd arrived, she'd wanted to rush into Randy's room. Instead, the sheriff had blocked her path.

"His head injuries are severe," Drew had said, trying to prepare Lola.

She'd wondered later whether the sheriff had been trying to tell her Randy was brain-dead or whether he'd been trying to prepare her for the stained sheet they'd put over half of Randy's face. A hug that day would've been nice.

The Widows Club board entered with Edith and surrounded the Eastlake women.

Lola drifted across the room, giving the Sunshine natives space.

Drew followed her. "Do you know when Norma can see Scotty? I want to be here for her."

Lola didn't like putting a time on her preparations. It wasn't like Scotty was getting an updo for a wedding. She didn't know how long it was going to take. Those scars…

Mrs. Eastlake was waiting for Lola's answer. Lola took a breath and stitched together a smile for Scotty's wife. "Mrs. Eastlake, do you remember when you and Scotty were first dating?"

"What does that have to do with anything?" Edith's voice echoed off the green marble floors and the wall display of urns and headstones.

Mims shushed her.

"Who can remember first dates?" Mrs. Eastlake brought her daughter close with one hand and held her pendant with the other. "That was two decades and three children ago."

Lola remembered her first dates with Randy. That spark of anticipation that wouldn't let her sit still. That bubble of joy that had kept a smile on her face all day long. It'd taken her forever to get dressed. "I bet you both spent a little extra time getting ready. Pressed clothes. Fresh makeup."

"He'd always shave." Mrs. Eastlake kissed her daughter's forehead. "He grew a thick five-o'clock shadow."

Lola nodded encouragingly. "And you probably spent extra time preparing to get married."

"I was in the salon for hours with all my bridesmaids." The newest widow in the room blew out a breath. "I think I understand what you're trying to say."

Lola nodded again. "While I get Scotty ready, you should clean up too." Mrs. Eastlake's jeans and mint-green blouse looked slept in. "Call Barbara Hadley. She'll come in on a Sunday for you and do your hair. And if she's busy, you can call me. I'll do your hair and makeup."

Lola prepping the living to see the dead? That was a first.

Mrs. Eastlake caught Lola's reflection in the window as she fought tears. "The last time I saw him, I was in my bathrobe."

"A woman should always look her best," Edith said confidently, as if she hadn't looked like roadkill just last night.

Mims elbowed Edith aside and led Mrs. Eastlake toward the door. "Why don't we follow you home and pick up Scotty's suit?"

"I'll drive," Clarice offered cheerfully.

The Eastlakes exited with two of the Widows Club board members and Edith, leaving Bitsy behind with Drew and Lola. Sunlight cast Drew in a golden glow, softening the bump on his nose and that little scar cresting his cheek.

"That was nice," Drew said in his detached cop voice with a not-so-detached look in his eyes as he stared at Lola.

Bitsy joined them, her short blond hair as smooth as her voice. "You know, when spouses die..." Bitsy nodded to Lola. "Or become dead to us because of a bitter divorce..." She nodded to Drew. "Well, there's just so much emotion, it needs an outlet."

Uh-oh. Lola crossed her arms over her chest. "Is this an intervention for my window display?"

"It should be," Drew muttered.

"Now, now," Bitsy said before Lola could retort. "I understand needing a vent for wounded emotions, and so does Drew. After my first husband died, I didn't say a kind word to anyone for weeks. I felt wretched, and I acted wretched. People in town had to put up with me until I found a proper outlet for my grief."

"You were out of line?" Lola was dumbfounded.

"Yes." Bitsy gave Drew an expectant look.

He cleared his throat and reluctantly admitted, "After Jane left, I drank myself under the table at Shaw's every Saturday night for a month. People in town put up with me too until I realized what a blessing Becky was."

Lola narrowed her eyes. "So this means you'll lay off my window display?"

Drew shook his head.

"We're saying you need a different outlet, Lola," Bitsy said kindly, but the cat was out of the bag. This was an intervention. "And I have just the thing. The intersection at the interstate. No one else should lose their lives there. You and Norma Eastlake can channel your grief and be the voices for change."

"Great idea," Drew said.

Lola stared out the big plate-glass windows, feeling pressure to conform. "I'm not going to lie—I wish someone would take up that cause." Crimson tulips waved in the breeze, reminding Lola of the ruby earring and her betrayed and broken heart. "But I don't think anyone's going to fix that intersection because I ask for it."

Drew and Bitsy exchanged glances, perhaps telegraphing their thoughts for another round of arguments.

Lola didn't have time to argue, not if Mrs. Eastlake was going to see her husband later that day. "Excuse me. There's a gentleman waiting for me downstairs."

* * *

"You should model in our fashion show," Clarice said to Edith on the drive from the mortuary to the Eastlake house.

Mims couldn't believe it. "Isn't there a rule against that?" she muttered from the passenger seat.

"Nope." Clarice banked around a corner too hard. The tail end of the minivan slid. Clarice seemed unconcerned. She gave Mims an uncharacteristically sly glance. "We get a lot of men in the audience at the fashion show."

Suddenly, Mims felt less alone in her quest to match Edith. After that uncomfortable breakfast at the Saddle Horn, it seemed she had Clarice's full commitment.

"I could rock a bathing suit." Edith's voice plucked at Mims's nerves like a defective duck call on the first day of hunting season.

"Our models wear dresses." Mims ground her teeth. She was beginning to sound as uppity as Barbara Hadley. "We have a connection at a department store in Greeley. They loan us dresses." All models and attendees received coupons to shop there.

"We broke from tradition this year." Clarice raced toward a stop sign, bringing them to a jerking halt just in time. "Some women are wearing pantsuits."

"We could bend the rules for bathing suits," Edith persisted.

"It's hard not to admire your determination, Edith." Clarice slowed as they neared their destination.

The paint on the Eastlake house was a fresh blue. The yard was overgrown and needed mowing. Mims made a mental note to find volunteers to help them care for their home over the next few weeks.

"Charlie loved my curves." Edith's tone dared anyone to argue.

Why wasn't Clarice speeding up to the curb? They crawled toward the house.

"To honor Charlie, I should share my body with the world." Edith wasn't giving up. "Besides, I've got the best assets on the Widows Club board."

"You're not on the board," Mims snapped.

Edith raised her voice. "Bitsy's too skinny. Clarice sags from years without a bra. And Mims has no waistline."

There was the pot calling the kettle black. Edith and Mims had the same body type.

The minivan jerked to a halt.

"Edith, you can model," Mims said through stiff lips, racking her brain for available men to invite to the fashion show. "But only if you wear a *dress*."

The back seat reverberated with bikini protests.

"On the one hand, I admire her courage." Clarice rammed the minivan into park and stared at Mims. "On the other, she disregards the rules. What a dilemma."

"There is no dilemma," Mims said firmly over Edith harping about assets, rights, and honor.

"She's like a teenager, isn't she?" Clarice took out her hearing aids. "I knew I should have left these at home today."

Chapter Eleven

♥

After Lola was done with Scotty, she had an extra few hours before Mrs. Eastlake was due to return. Knowing Avery would be swamped, she rushed into the Grand movie theater without buying a ticket.

The noise from excited kids was nearly deafening. But that was balanced by the enticing scent of fresh popcorn.

Avery was behind the snack counter, ringing up customers faster than any of the teenage employees—none of whom were on duty. The line was twelve deep and growing.

"I can help." Lola moved behind the counter and washed her hands, knowing the routine. "Who's going to order a bucket?" Lola counted orders. "How many with butter?" She began filling popcorn and setting the buckets on the counter. When she finished, she looked up again. "How many child trays?"

The cardboard boxes were already made. All Lola had to do was fill half with popcorn and place a piece of candy on top. Avery would add the small drink.

Lola lowered her voice. "Randy's love nest was in

the garage apartment at the farmhouse. And..." She dropped her words to a whisper. "I found his lover's jewelry."

Avery did a double take. The soda she was filling overflowed. "Are you kidding me?"

Lola shook her head. "Anyone want a small bag of popcorn?" Lola looked up to find Drew, Becky, and Wendy at the head of the line. They looked like a family. Her heart panged with envy. "Hey, guys." She directed her greeting to Becky, who wore a green T-shirt, jean shorts, and a pair of white sneakers, not a trace of dripped whip in sight.

Drew motioned Lola to step aside. "You haven't taken down Randy and his—"

"*Lover?*" Lola said provocatively.

Although she hadn't raised her voice, heads turned, including Wendy's.

Drew moved farther away from the snack-bar line and motioned for Lola to move with him.

"I just got done with Scotty." Lola followed, crossing her arms over her chest. "I haven't been home yet. Besides, I told you—"

"Ramona Everly will continue to call until—"

"Ramona Everly doesn't know how to keep her nose in her own business," Avery snapped without taking her eyes off the soda cups she was filling. "And she's ungrateful. Lola mows that lawn of hers every weekend."

Drew's eyes widened but to his credit, he stayed on point. "Regardless, you should think about what Bitsy said and take your display down."

"No." Lola was angry. At Drew. At Randy. At the world.

"Whatever you do with those dolls should be a private thing." His authoritative gaze added a silent *Or else*.

Danger slid its cold fingers down Lola's spine. This was a man who wouldn't make idle threats. But Lola wasn't breaking any laws. "Careful, Sheriff. The more you try to convince me to let it all go, the more I think you know who this woman is." And that he wanted to protect her.

That earned her a dark look from the lawman.

"Drew." Wendy called him back to pay. She smiled at Lola without a hint of jealousy or annoyance. Nothing unsettled that woman.

After Drew paid, he picked up the bucket of popcorn and took Becky's hand. "I'll let you have your fun for a day or two, Lola, but then they need to come down."

Becky dragged him toward the theater.

"Hey, um..." Wendy lingered, smiling self-consciously, as if she were posing for a mug shot. "I'm producing the lower grades' school play this year, and I need a hair and makeup artist."

"Are you..." Lola blinked, trying to downshift from battle mode. "Are you asking me to help?"

No one ever asked Lola to help with anything. And now in the space of a few hours, she'd been asked to join in a bake sale and a school play.

"Yes, I'm asking." Wendy's head bobbed. She had a round face that would have benefited from a layered, fuller hairstyle. "Are you free during the evenings over the next two weeks?"

Holding Becky back with one hand, Drew paused at the theater door, waiting for his date.

"She's free," Avery blurted before Lola could make up her mind. "And she has free time."

"I'll get you a schedule." Wendy beamed and went to join Drew.

After the kiddie rush was over, Lola leaned her hip on the snack-bar counter and got right to the heart-stopping point. "I think Randy gave his lover my grandmother's pearl ring." She could let go of many things but not that ring.

"I'm sorry but you'll never see that again." Avery refilled the popcorn machine with kernels. "What's up with you and Drew?"

"Nothing." The words didn't ring true, mostly because she found his steady glance and sly humor appealing. But she hadn't come to the theater to talk about men. "I want to show you the box of jewelry. You grew up here. You see everyone in town. You might recognize something."

"Did you not see how chaotic that rush was?" Not one to waste time, Avery bent to restock candy in the display case. "I could tell you who came by, but I couldn't tell you what they were wearing, much less what kind of jewelry they had on."

"But..." Lola floundered.

Avery covered her ears. "Describe my earrings."

Lola couldn't remember what kind of earrings Avery was wearing, and said so.

Her friend's hands came down, revealing a dangly silver pair. "My point exactly. Don't waste another year on Randy."

"But...Sunshine isn't that big." Lola was as reluctant to let go of her quest as she was to shelve blow-up Randy and Candy.

"What if Randy's mistress is from Greeley?"

Lola's mouth went dry. Randy's spin class...His basketball games...All in Greeley.

Avery shooed Lola from behind the snack bar. "I've got to clean the other movie theater in the next thirty minutes. Go home. Get some sleep. Forget about this woman. Think about the future, not the past."

Lola couldn't, not without Nana's ring on her finger. "But..."

"Thanks for your help. I'll call you tomorrow." Avery tossed her ponytail over her shoulder. It fell neatly in place. That was the thing about Avery. She bounced back from adversity smoothly.

Lola wished she could say the same.

* * *

"Daddy, unlock the car." Becky skipped to the police cruiser after the movie, as energetic as the green leaves rustling in the trees lining Main Street.

Drew did as asked, using the remote, and then slowed his steps for some time alone with Wendy. He didn't think this counted as a date, and he needed to set one up. He'd been so consumed with the problem of convincing Wendy to marry him quickly that he'd hardly followed the movie at all. "Did you enjoy the show?"

"It was good." Wendy seemed lost in thought. The breeze blew a lock of her hair from behind her ear. She tucked it back in place before he thought about doing so. She was nice to look at, quiet and good-natured. She'd offered to guide Lola through the bake sale fund-raiser and asked her to volunteer for the school play. And she'd encouraged his daughter to dress conservatively and to try out for the lead in the elementary school production. She'd be an asset in his battle against Jane.

"Dad, Daddy, Papa, Padre." Becky climbed into the back seat. "Let's go!"

Drew planned on dropping Becky off at his mother's house while he joined Norma Eastlake at her private viewing. He needed to get going but he also needed a wife. So he put on the smile his mother said was handsome, stood up straight, and tried to forget what was at stake. "Who was your favorite character in the movie?"

"The heroine, of course." Wendy smiled. It was a gentle smile, a smile that said she had the patience to deal with a precocious little girl. And why not? As school secretary, she dealt with about a hundred kids every day.

"Dad, Daddy, Papa, Padre." Becky put more urgency in her request.

Despite Wendy being as sweet as sweet tea, it was becoming increasingly obvious that she was painfully shy. Was she wondering whether he liked her? He could put her mind at ease by asking her out. "Would you like to go to dinner on Wednesday? We could go into Greeley."

Her gaze moved down the sidewalk, away from him. "No."

She was rejecting him? He experienced an unusual sensation—the cold-skin prickle of panic.

"Have you forgotten?" Wendy's gaze returned to him, still a degree or two off-center. "There's a PTA meeting that night."

He hadn't forgotten. He just didn't normally attend. It was great that Wendy was so dedicated to her job. And fantastic that she wasn't turning him down flat.

Heartened, Drew pressed on. "How about Thursday?"

"No." Her attention drifted down the sidewalk again, and her brows lowered as if she was having a serious inner discussion.

Perhaps about the unwanted advances of the town sheriff?

Drew considered patience one of his virtues. So he waited for Wendy to say more, silently listing her attributes. She was committed to Sunshine, kind, and responsible. Becky seemed to like her, and it wasn't a hardship to look at her. Wendy's silences and deep inner thoughts could be a plus. They'd probably never argue, not like he did with Lola or had done with Jane.

Now Lola...Lola was a looker, and conversation with her kept Drew on his toes. She may have been going through a difficult time, but she was a reliable employee. After all, she'd insisted upon locking up the cemetery after he'd found her the other night, and she'd gone into work at the mortuary on a Sunday.

Drew frowned. He shouldn't be thinking of Lola when his future wife was standing in front of him. Wendy needed a softer approach than most women in his life. "I'd like to get to know you better. No pressure."

Just a whirlwind romance, a short engagement, and a small wedding.

"Thursday is our first evening rehearsal." Emotion rang in Wendy's normally stoic voice. She was proud of her special project. "Remember, Becky will be trying out for a role on Tuesday."

And knowing what a ham his daughter was, Drew had no doubt she'd be selected for a part. "How about Sunday?" He was working Friday and Saturday night.

"Okay." Wendy stared down the sidewalk with the intensity of Einstein caught in the middle of noodling the theory of relativity.

Now what? If Mims were here, she'd probably tell Drew to kiss her.

Great idea. Drew dutifully leaned in and pressed a kiss to Wendy's cheek. "I'll pick you up at six."

Wendy nodded and drifted in the direction of the thrift store.

"Did you just ask Wendy Adams out?" Pris stood just outside the pharmacy door, wearing a funky black print skirt that was hemmed too high and a plain black tank top that was cut too low. Fake black eyelashes. Fake black nails. She was a billboard advertising for the wrong man.

Drew beelined toward the cruiser. "Don't start." His sisters always thought they knew exactly what Drew needed.

"I don't know where to start." Pris jogged to his side with ragged steps. She wore impractical high-heeled sandals like the ones Lola had worn at the auction, but she hadn't mastered them. "I mean, Mom told me about Jane wanting custody and about the advice to get married, but you don't date. Ever. So I thought marriage wasn't an option. And then you bought Lola at the auction. And now…" She turned, walking backward, presumably staring at Wendy. "Wendy Adams? She's nice, but she's like the milk toast Mom used to make us eat when we had a fever. Zero personality."

Pris tripped on an uneven seam in the sidewalk. Drew caught her as her shoe fell off. Forget his legal needs. Now was the time to broach the topic of Randy. Slim though the chances of Pris having dated him might be, Drew had to close the loop. "Hey, do you remember when Ben gave you a bottle of perfume at Christmas one year?"

"Yeah." Pris held on to his shoulder while she slipped back into her high heel. "It was his apology for gambling away our vacation money."

"Do you still have that bottle?"

Pris straightened, flapping her false eyelashes. "Why? Did you want to regift it to Wendy?"

"No."

"Then why do you want to know?"

"Just answer the question." Why couldn't his sister be like a nervous criminal and come clean?

Pris gave him her you-are-an-impossible-brother look. "I don't know. It's probably in a box in Mom's garage."

Drew washed a hand over his face. There was no alternative but to ask a direct question. "Did you date Randy Williams after he got married?"

"What? No." Pris scowled and pushed Drew's shoulder. "What's wrong with you?"

Honestly, Drew didn't know, but he was relieved by her answer.

"Dad, Daddy, Papa, Padre!" Becky called from the cruiser.

"In a minute, Sunshine." Drew faced Pris and decided the partial truth was his best defense. "Jane. It's Jane." And Lola. God help him, it was Lola and her legs. But mostly, it was Jane. "Jane wants joint custody of Becky, and she's coming home to stay." The words burst from him in a panicked rush, as if they'd been waiting for hours to be shared, which they had. Drew hadn't told his mother the latest. "Jane sent me a text this morning."

"What?" Pris clutched his arm, digging in her false nails. "When is she moving back?"

"I don't know." Oxygen was a problem. Drew forced himself to fill his lungs with air.

"Let's not get all maudlin." Pris released his arm. "This is Jane we're talking about. She never does anything without an agenda that benefits Jane. How will gaining custody of Becky help her?" One set of Priscilla's fake eyelashes stuck together. She squinted and carefully pried her eyelids apart. "Wendy isn't the answer. Oh, I know, no one ever has a bad word to say about her. She lives at home with her parents and helps care for her mother. She donates her time to the community." Pris blinked the sticky-lash eye. "But she's boring. She came to Shaw's one Sunday, and I swear she never said a word."

"She's not like you or Eileen or the twins or Jane." Or Lola. Wendy was low maintenance, even-keeled, safe. "Maybe shy is what I need."

"Not hardly," Pris allowed, peeling off one black

eyelash and looking at it in disgust. "What do you like about Wendy other than she doesn't talk back to you?"

Drew couldn't think of a single thing.

"Do you know anything about her other than what you could fill in on a rap sheet—age, residence, employment history?"

"Um."

"*Drew.*" Pris loaded his name with sisterly disgust. "We live in Sunshine. I can tell you what kind of ice cream Pearl buys every week. I can tell you where Bitsy shops on Saturday. I can tell you who Iggy kissed on Saturday night." Her cheeks colored slightly. "But I can't, for the life of me, tell you one personal thing about Wendy, and you can't either."

Drew opened his mouth to say something, but he couldn't. He'd stood in line with Wendy for movie tickets and then for popcorn. Wendy had smiled and occasionally nodded in agreement to whatever he and Becky were talking about. He didn't know whether Wendy liked her job or enjoyed working with children or loved baking something other than Bundt cake.

"Don't jump in a well without a flashlight, Drew." Pris scrunched her nose, trying to find the right words, when she should have been peeling the other caterpillar off from her eye. "For all you know, Wendy could be a serial killer."

Drew had had enough. He turned away. "Someday, that imagination of yours is going to get you in trouble."

"In the meantime, go see Rupert Harper," Pris called after him. "Get a good lawyer, not a good wife."

Chapter Twelve

♥

"Good morning." Beatrice, the receptionist at the Sunshine Retirement Home, greeted Lola on Tuesday.

It'd been two days since Lola had featured Randy and Candy in her window. Two days since she'd breathed the same air as Drew and thought about kissing him.

That was a lie. She'd thought about kissing Drew every time she'd looked at Randy's mementos. So far, she'd learned nothing new by asking the grocer and the pharmacist if anyone had asked about a lost bracelet, necklace, or earring. But today would be different. Today would be spent with the most talkative and sometimes longest-memoried residents in Sunshine.

"You have a full schedule until three." Beatrice handed Lola a sheet of paper with her appointments on it. She was a slender woman in her fifties with gray-brown hair that could use a strong relaxer or, at the very least, stronger mousse.

Lola pretended to scan the sheet while she reached into her vest-jacket pocket for the clip-on ruby earring from Randy's box. Despite Drew and Avery's advice to the contrary, she couldn't let her search for the truth go. The best place to find the owner of a clip-on earring was the retirement home. And who saw everyone coming and going? Beatrice.

"Good morning, Ms. Stephens." Beatrice straightened in her chair before Lola got the earring out of her pocket.

Marcia Stephens entered. She was a well-preserved woman approaching fifty with precisely applied makeup and a thick white-blond bob she tucked behind her ears. A few kinked stragglers floated above her crown, like alert antennae. Marcia volunteered at the retirement home where her mother resided, reading romances to those who could no longer read for themselves. Like her daughter Barbara Hadley, she was always well turned out. Today she wore platform sandals, formfitting white capris, and a turquoise blouse that Lola wouldn't have minded wearing.

Marcia carried a brown jacket over her hands and greeted Beatrice warmly, acknowledging Lola with barely a nod because... Well, Lola never quite knew why Marcia gave her the cold shoulder, except that she was Barbara's mother.

"Don't mind her," Beatrice whispered as Marcia headed down the hall. "She's been low since Barbara refused to put blue streaks in her hair anymore. Barbara told her she had to grow up. No more fast cars. No more pool parties. No more anything."

Barbara may have been the mayor's wife, but she tried to rule everything in town, from the acceptance of outsiders, like Lola, to her own mother's hair. Barbara owned Prestige Salon and had refused to rent a station to Lola when she'd arrived in town. She had residents cowed when it came to hair. No one wanted to risk Barbara's wrath by going to Lola, not even Avery.

"Marcia hasn't had blue streaks for a long time," Lola said. Not since last year. It was Lola's business to notice hair, even if someone didn't notice her. She checked the time and realized she had none to spare to ask Beatrice about the earring.

Lola hurried down the hall toward the small room that housed the one-person beauty parlor, wheeling her supply kit behind her as if it were carry-on luggage. She worked Monday through Friday from midmorning to whenever she couldn't drum up any more work, revising her schedule to accommodate mortuary clients as needed.

When Lola had arrived in Sunshine, she'd been disappointed that doing hair at the retirement home and the mortuary was the only work she could get. After all, she'd been on an award-winning makeup team on Broadway. But she'd come to appreciate the spunk and gossip of the elderly and the emotionally satisfying mortuary work. However, the more she thought about it, the more she was looking forward to the faster work being involved with a play entailed, even if it was only a play for kids.

"My appointment is in two minutes." Harriet Bloom was waiting for Lola outside the salon door. She was perched on the seat of her walker, wearing a flowered blouse over a long jean skirt. Her tennis shoes were blue, her orthopedic hose bright white, and her hair a frizzy gray storm cloud around her head.

"I'll be ready," Lola sing-songed, because that was how she dealt with Harriet—with forced cheer.

Lola unlocked the door and began turning things on for the day—lights, fan, radio. Somewhere along the line, someone had painted the wall opposite the hair station a dull dusty rose. The color didn't flatter the pale complexions of the residents. Lola had tacked up a large black feathered headdress Nana had bought in the seventies from a Vegas showgirl. It was the only lively thing in the room.

"I should reschedule." Harriet bumped her walker against the doorframe a few times before getting through. She needed glasses and claimed she couldn't afford them. "You've got big hair today. You always have big hair when you're upset."

"I'm not upset." Lola caught her reflection in the mirror. Sure enough, she'd swept her hair up and twisted it for height above her forehead, letting the rest of her hair fall to her shoulders.

"If you say so." Harriet wheeled her way closer to the chair. "I'm sure I won't like the way you do my hair today—"

Harriet didn't like anything Lola did. It was a wonder she came back every week.

"—but you can do your best."

Since this complaint was as regular as Harriet's attendance, Lola replied with a mild dig of her own. "The shuttle can take you over to Prestige Salon."

Harriet harrumphed. "There's no privacy there." Meaning she didn't get the VIP treatment, like she did with Lola.

Lola snapped a pink polka-dot drape over Harriet and then helped her into the chair at the shampoo bowl. The old woman's shoulders were permanently slumped, hindering her ability to recline. Lola set the walker in the hall and then closed the lower half of the Dutch door. "We could try something really different. We could dye your hair silver, cut it short everywhere but on top, and spike it up. Spiky hair is in." And fit Harriet's prickly attitude.

"No big-city fluff for me. I live in Sunshine." Harriet lifted a bony hand to touch her frizzy mop. "I hope you can master the art of the pin curl today."

"You can talk me through it." Lola had mastered the art of the pin curl. And the perm. And the comb-out. That was practically all she'd done for two years.

"I heard you joined the Widows Club auction." Harriet chuckled. "They finally got you in their clutches."

It was Lola's turn to harrumph.

"I also heard the sheriff bought you." Harriet was merciless in her pursuit of information. "However did you manage that? The sheriff doesn't play Widows Club games."

"Harriet…" Lola knew she shouldn't let the woman get to her, but she couldn't keep the barb from her tone. "I clean up nice, you know."

Harriet cackled. "The sheriff was probably worried you'd start a *fire* at Shaw's."

Though Lola had to admit that might have been the case, it didn't take the sting out of Harriet's ribbing. Lola worked shampoo into Harriet's thin, kinked hair with more than her usual vigor. "I bet you started some fires in your day."

Most people didn't see the faded red rose tattoo on Harriet's shoulder. The petals peeked out from beneath her wide white bra strap, stretching toward her shoulder blade.

"I rode a Harley," Harriet said proudly. "I've been to Sturgis. Wish I could go for one last ride."

That was highly unlikely given how shaky Harriet was with her walker.

"Is that where you met your husband? Sturgis?"

The old woman chuckled. "I met my husband at a Widows Club fund-raiser. That club has been around for more than fifty years. You get better odds of landing a man than online dating. Or so I've been told. Do you have your eye on the sheriff?"

"Only because he's a shifty character." Lola toweled the excess moisture from Harriet's sparse hair. It really would look better spiked. Someday, when Harriet really annoyed her, Lola was going to do it anyway.

"Shifty? Not Sheriff Taylor. Now, my husband...he was a devious devil." Harriet continued to reminisce with stars in her faded blue eyes. "A ladies' man. But I made sure every woman in town knew if they messed with him, they'd have to mess with me."

Lola bit into her cheek to keep from smiling. Harriet was a ninety-pound weakling. "*Ow.*" That weakling had just pinched the underside of Lola's arm. "What was that for?"

"To show you I've still got it." Harriet's smile revealed silver-capped yellow teeth. "If you'd have given women in town a run for their money, like me, maybe your man wouldn't have strayed."

"How did you..." Lola could barely manage a whisper. "Do you know who Randy slept with?"

"No, but I recognized that look in his eyes, even as a boy." Harriet tsk-tsked. "He had a thing for damsels in distress."

"Where were you on my wedding day?" She could've used that bit of insight.

"I was here," Harriet said dejectedly. "Been here way too long. And I can tell you, I won't be here much longer."

"Promises, promises." Lola pulled her arm out of pinching distance. "And that'll cost you a nickel." She had a whining jar on a shelf in the corner. Last year, she'd donated a whopping five dollars to the home's Christmas fund.

"I brought a dime. Means I've got one more complaint in me."

She'd likely have more than one complaint, but Lola chose to change the subject, bringing Harriet to a sitting position. "I found some of the other woman's jewelry." She produced the ruby earring from her vest-jacket pocket and showed it to Harriet. "Have you ever seen it before?"

Harriet plucked the earring from Lola's hand and held it an inch from her face. "Ooh. Antique and real."

"How do you—"

"Hello." Bitsy appeared in the Dutch doorway, looking eighties chic in a pink tunic with shoulder pads. Two black plastic clips held her blond hair away from her face.

Before Lola could snatch her evidence back, Harriet clutched the earring in her fist.

Bitsy didn't seem to notice. "Lola, I wanted to give you more details about the bake sale tomorrow."

"Could you tell I've been having second thoughts?" Lola had been dreading the bake sale since the moment she'd agreed to participate. She helped Harriet from the shampoo bowl to the main chair. "I can make cupcakes from a box. It won't be anything special."

"Is it time for the bake sale?" Harriet gasped. "Someone promise me you'll bring me a slice of Wendy's Bundt cake."

Lola resisted pinching her disloyal customer on the arm while Bitsy promised to bring her a slice Wednesday morning.

"I'll loan you a cupcake recipe of mine." Bitsy was nothing if not persistent. "If you can mix hair color, you can bake from scratch."

"Scratch?" Lola shook her head. "I know my limits."

"The bake sale isn't for Betty Crocker," Harriet snapped. "It's why it's so popular." She drew herself up. "I used to make praline brownies. Let's see Betty make those from a box."

"Uh…" Lola had never been competent in the kitchen.

"Don't be afraid," Bitsy said in a voice that somehow settled Lola's nerves. "I'll bring everything you need to the viewing this afternoon. You'll have plenty of time to pull it off."

When Bitsy left, Harriet brought the earring from beneath her drape. "Never was one to wear baubles like this. Can't say I've seen it before." She handed it back to Lola. "You'd do better asking at the thrift store or one of those pawn shops in Greeley."

"I need to go to the thrift store anyway." After agreeing to pick up Randy's stuff from her driveway, they'd called Monday morning and canceled because his things were "unsuitable."

There was nothing wrong with Randy's things. No doubt Mrs. Everly was blackballing her. In retaliation, Lola had changed her window display. But a change of doll position wasn't enough. This was war.

"Do you still have that blond wig, Harriet?"

Harriet had defeated cancer the first year Lola was in Sunshine.

"I do."

"I'd like to borrow it." Lola thought it'd look better on Candy than her painted-on plastic curls did.

* * *

"Remind me again what we're here for," Drew said to Becky, having picked her up from school for some father-daughter time.

Later she was having an early dinner with his mother while he went to Scotty's viewing.

It'd been another long day filled with spring-thaw madness. There'd been a fender bender in the elementary school drop-off line, ten minutes before the bell, that had made thirty kids in five grades tardy. Joy Kendall's Labrador had escaped, which would have been nothing new, except she was in heat and other dogs had literally chewed through fences and gates to get to her. (Flo had called Eileen to help.) Then one of the town's two stoplights had gone on the fritz. It wasn't scheduled to be fixed until later tonight. That light happened to be in front of the mortuary, which meant Drew would be on traffic duty as people began to leave.

"*Da-addy.*" Using the superior tone of a sixteen-year-old, six-year-old Becky walked slowly down the aisle of Sunshine's thrift store. Thankfully, Becky still dressed like a little girl. She wore pink striped leggings and a neon-green shirt with a frilly hem. "I'm Etna in the school play. I tried out at lunchtime. Ms. Adams said I could have a sword."

The thrift store offered an eclectic mix of castoffs for sale but Drew was convinced they weren't likely to find a sword in Sunshine, much less at the thrift store, which smelled as dank as the farmhouse basement. "Isn't this something Granny Susie could help you order online?"

"Granny Susie always says we should look here first." Becky stopped and peered at a colorful display of rabbit-feet and then moved past a weight rack toward a display of gardening tools.

"I'm not going to argue about you not picking up my stuff." Lola's voice carried over aisles from the direction of the jewelry counter. Her tone drifted between diplomacy and disrespect. "If you don't want my garage sale treasures for free, it's your loss." There was a sound like a heel pounding on linoleum. "Can you just tell me if you have a pearl ring?"

There goes diplomacy.

"Nada," Ricky Parker, the store manager, wheezed. Ricky had emphysema from chain-smoking when he was younger and always seemed to be gasping for breath. It made him a man of few words.

Although he couldn't see Lola, Drew's pulse kicked up a notch. She hadn't taken down her plastic display nor was she giving up on the jewelry scavenger hunt.

At the next junction of aisles, Drew left Becky to wander, and cut toward the jewelry section.

Ricky sat on a stool. His bulk overflowed onto the counter.

Lola stood opposite him, dressed in black tights, black pumps, and a curve-clinging zebra-striped short dress. Half her brown hair was twisted and clipped high on top of her head. The rest fell in large loops over one shoulder. Her eyes were lined for business—the investigative business. And her lips? They were red and would have been attractive if they hadn't been moving.

"I don't suppose you recognize any of these." Lola laid out the pieces they'd found in the apartment—the turquoise pendant, silver bracelet with copper bells, and ruby earring. "The turquoise has a silver backing and is engraved. See?" She turned it over. "*Dream Big.*"

"Pass." Ricky slid the necklace toward Lola and sucked in air. "I've got ten like it in back."

"But this one's engraved."

"They all were. Generically." He picked up the ruby earring and squinted at it from behind small reading glasses. "These are real." He slurped in air. "I'll give you two hundred for the pair."

"I don't have the set." A thin layer of patience coated Lola's words. "I have nothing for sale. I just want to know if you've ever seen these before. What about the bracelet?"

"Don't answer that question, Ricky." Drew leaned

on the counter near Lola, near enough to smell her flowery scent. A smarter man would've backed away and dragged his gaze from those lips.

Unlike Wendy, Lola wasn't shy. She had a direct gaze and always got right to the point. "This is none of your business, Sheriff."

Ricky held up his hands. "Never seen it."

"You wouldn't lie just because *he's* here, would you?" Lola angled her thumb at Drew.

The store manager shook his head. "It wouldn't be good for business."

"Neither is rejecting donated goods." Slender brows pulled low, Lola picked up the bracelet, jingling the small copper bells.

Lola rearranged the jewelry on the counter and then stared at the pieces, as if contemplating different chess moves.

Drew knew the move she should be contemplating. "Have you thought about closing those drapes?" Ramona Everly was annoying Flo with the frequency of her complaints.

"Nope. I like the light." And she liked creating provocative window displays. Today's version had Randy's head buried in his love interest's neck mid-hickey.

"Daddy-O!" Becky ran around the corner, waving a plastic sword. It jangled with every slice through the air. *Clang-clang-clang!* It was just the kind of toy Drew would've loved as a boy and the kind he'd never allow in his house as a parent. That toy would give him no rest. "Look at me!" Becky stopped and raised the sword toward the ceiling. "*Booyah!*"

"That has got to be the coolest sword ever." Lola spared Becky an indulgent smile as she dropped the jewelry into her large black leather purse.

Lola could afford to be indulgent. That sword wasn't coming home with her.

"I need this." Becky displayed more attack poses, as if she'd been taking fencing all her life. The reality was that she'd watched too many Bruce Lee movies with Drew. The sword jangled and swept dangerously close to Drew's knees. "I'm going to be in the school play, and I'm going to kill people."

Drew's shoulders tensed. Bloodthirsty girls weren't good examples of proper parenting. "I thought you were an owl." Drew reached for the sword before his daughter could do damage to something like the display of vases nearby or his privates.

Becky spun away. "I am the goddess of war!" She thrust her sword at a large stuffed lion propped next to the counter that was almost as big as she was.

Jane would love to video Becky like this and show it to the court. Exhibit A.

Drew reached for the sword again. "You said you were Etna."

Becky shuffled two steps back and made a high-pitched strength-gathering sound Bruce would've been proud of.

"I think you mean you're Athena." Lola grinned, revealing a dimple in her right cheek. "Goddess of wisdom and war."

He'd never seen that dimple before. He couldn't remember her being that amused or happy in his presence.

“Sheriff?” Ricky lowered his voice. “You buyin’ the lion too?”

“No.” Drew scowled at Ricky and then at Lola’s dimple. “Becky, stop that.”

“All I need now is armor.” Becky jabbed her stuffed enemy with her sword until the beast fell over.

“Oh, honey.” Lola shook her head. “Athena wears a toga, not armor.”

A toga? Drew attempted to give Lola the high sign.

Becky stopped attacking long enough to ask, “What’s a yoga?”

“A *toga*…,” Lola said before Drew could stop her, “is a dress.”

Becky made a strangled noise. “I’m not wearing a dress. I never wear dresses.” And then she raised her face to the ceiling and howled. “Nobody told me there’d be dresses!”

“What’s wrong with dresses?” Lola held out her skirt and curtsied, displaying less cleavage than Pris on a conservative day. “Dresses are fun. Dresses are cool.”

“Dresses are stupid.” Becky crossed her arms over her chest—no small feat, given she still held the clanging sword.

“I feel pretty in a dress.” Lola glanced down. “And look. I’m wearing tights. That’s like wearing pants and a dress at the same time.” She gave Becky two thumbs up. “Double bonus.”

Both Taylors stared at Lola in silence. Becky appeared to be fascinated with Lola, struck as dumb as Drew was.

Lola leaned over until her face was even with Becky’s. The rising hem of her skirt raised the heat in

Drew's blood. She tweaked Becky's nose. "When you get old enough to go to Shaw's—"

"Which will be never," Drew choked out.

"—you can wear a dress with cowboy boots."

Drew had the strangest feeling, as if he were stuck in a snowdrift up to his neck. He could move his eyes to track Lola, but everything else? Everything else was frozen in place.

He was certain he'd seen legs as long as Lola's somewhere on someone. He just couldn't remember where or whom.

All he knew was that when she was teasing as she was now, and that dimple appeared in her right cheek, it made him stare at her more intently, just to see whether a left dimple would appear.

And Lola's eyes…They were as deep blue and unpredictable as the South Platte River in early spring. One moment calm and reasonable; the next snapping with energy—energy that could make him laugh or bind him in place.

"I am *not* wearing a dress," Becky reiterated, glaring at Lola. Her cheeks were a blotchy red.

Lola straightened, and her skirt fell back to appropriate levels, which made Drew's breath come easier. "Don't you have sisters, Sheriff?" Lola asked, without dimpling.

Drew's mouth was dry. He managed a nod.

"Don't your sisters wear dresses?" Lola's gaze demanded answers.

"Yes." Drew managed to push the word past his dry throat.

"My twin aunties always try and dress me up." Becky waved her sword again. "I am *not* their doll."

Lola's gaze bounced from one Taylor to the other, settling on Drew. "Good thing the no-dress rule isn't the end of the world."

"It is...if she wants to play Athena." Drew grinned at Lola recklessly, forgetting for a moment that she was unpredictable, eccentric, and out of control. "Sometimes kids back themselves into corners."

Becky made a huffing noise. The sword clanged softly.

"Kids?" Lola grinned back at Drew, flashing that dimple. "Sometimes *people* back themselves into corners."

The reckless grin was still on his face—he could feel it—but his next question was serious. That window dressing and this search would lead her nowhere. "Have you backed yourself into a corner?"

"Nope." Lola stopped smiling.

"You two"—Ricky came around the counter to pick up the defeated lion—"need a chaperone."

Lola's heels clicked on the linoleum as she backed up a few steps.

Drew blinked. When Lola was near, he felt like a compass near a magnet. She made him lose his bearings.

What just happened?

Besides the grinning and the recklessness.

"Worse than high schoolers." Ricky carried the lion toward the back of the store, breathing heavier than Darth Vader.

"This is awkward," Lola said, shifting on her heels.

Becky stared back and forth between the two adults. "I'm confused."

"That's a common occurrence when Lola is around." Drew swung his daughter into his arms, clinging to the familiar.

"Thou hath wounded me with your verbal sword." Lola swept her arm into the air as if she were a bad actor on a stage. "Excuse me. I have a viewing and then cupcakes to make." She pivoted on her heels with more grace than Pris had ever managed.

"I like that lady. She's funny." Becky wrapped her arms around Drew's neck and laid her head on his shoulder. The sword clanged against his back. "But I'm not wearing a dress."

Chapter Thirteen

♥

Scotty Eastlake looked good.

Nice blue suit. Yellow Jerry Garcia tie. Clean-shaven chin. Clean-cut hair.

His casket had a brown finish and a burgundy lining, warm complements to the color Lola had applied to his face. The darkly paneled viewing room was full.

Lola blended into the black-clad mourners, still shaken by the thrift-store episode with Drew.

Ricky was right. Their banter had felt like flirting. And the way Drew had grinned at her…Well, if he was dating Wendy, he shouldn't be grinning at Lola like that. Because that grin sent messages no taken man should be sending.

What was wrong with her? She wasn't looking for a man. She was looking for Randy's mistress and the truth.

Augie set another bouquet of flowers in the corner. This one was in front of Lola's emergency makeup supply case, kept there in case last-minute touch-ups were needed. Augie straightened his suit jacket, caught

Lola's eye, and smiled. It felt nice to be appreciated by her boss. Lola smiled back.

Mrs. Eastlake stood alone at Scotty's side. When she saw Lola, she held out a hand and drew her close. "My girls don't want to see him." Her nose was red, and her eyes glazed. The brown hair color Barbara had applied on Sunday was bright but her hair hung limply over her ears, as if she hadn't washed it in two days. "The girls are in the back. And people feel weird around me and Scotty." She tilted her head and touched Lola's forehead with her own. "But not you."

The unexpected gesture warmed Lola inside. "I'll be here as long as you need me."

After two years working at the funeral home, Lola was used to being one of the rocks people clung to during the emotional upheaval of death. Scotty's widow might feel close to Lola today but a month or two from now she'd associate Lola with this awful time and look the other way when she saw her.

Mims appeared at Mrs. Eastlake's side, followed by Clarice, Bitsy, and Edith.

Edith walked up to the coffin and peered at Scotty. "He looks so lifelike. Lola is the best, isn't she? When we laid my Charlie to rest, he looked as if he could jump up and grab his fishing pole."

Mrs. Eastlake tried to contain a shuddering sob. Like bookends, Mims and Lola each wrapped an arm around her.

"Edith." Clarice used her walking stick to put distance between the offending widow and the coffin. "There are rules to a viewing. Show some class."

"I am." Edith lifted her chin and sniffed. She wore the same black pantsuit she'd worn for her husband's funeral, this time pairing it with scuffed black sneakers. "No one complimented my Charlie. He was a handsome man, both in life and in death."

Mrs. Eastlake released a sound like a wounded animal and lunged for Edith, but not to take her down. She wrapped her arms around the outspoken widow and gave her a bear hug. "Thank you. Scotty *is* handsome."

Lola took some pride in that, surprising as it was to hear.

Bitsy tapped Lola's shoulder and handed her a green cloth grocery bag filled to the handles. She'd exchanged her cheerful pink tunic for a plain black dress. "These are your cupcake supplies and my recipe. The trick is to refrigerate all the ingredients in step two until you mix them together."

"Thank you." Lola dutifully looked inside the bag. She'd have to tote it around for a bit. She didn't have a key to the office, and her bosses were nowhere in sight.

"You'll have no problem," Bitsy reassured her, moving to pay her respects to Scotty.

Carrying the bag, Lola went to the rear of the room to check on Scotty's daughters. They sat huddled together with their little Yorkie, which Mrs. Eastlake had insisted was her therapy dog. "We set up punch and cookies in the reception area. You don't have to sit here the entire time."

The two younger girls scampered away.

Aubrey frowned at her clasped hands. She wore a

black sundress beneath a short, tight-fitting jean jacket. Her brown hair had had the life straightened out of it. The ends were broken and flyaway, in need of a good conditioner. "Mom wants us to stay here."

Lola sat next to the teen, setting Bitsy's cupcake groceries between her black pumps. "Your mom wants your emotional support but she also wants to be there for you if you break down."

The Yorkie tried to rummage through Lola's supplies. Lola shooed him away. Augie and Rowena were still absent from the viewing room.

"She's cried every night since Dad..." Aubrey pursed her chapped lips.

Lola wanted to rub the teen's shoulder or give her a hug but was afraid Aubrey would reject physical comfort from a relative stranger. "That won't change anytime soon, I'm afraid. Especially if you don't give your mom something to keep her mind occupied." Guilt began to pound at Lola's temples. If she did as Bitsy suggested and took up the crusade for a safer intersection, she might help Mrs. Eastlake through her grief. It was the right thing to do, but it didn't feel like the right time for Lola. "Anyway... voice of experience. I spent too much time mourning my husband alone."

"Did you love him?" Aubrey stared at her mother. "Sometimes I wasn't sure if my parents loved each other. They fought a lot."

"I loved him." Lola was surprised to find it was true, despite her anger at Randy's infidelity. "You can love somebody and not like them sometimes."

They sat silently for a few moments. The Yorkie

sniffed Lola's bag again, earning a nudge from Lola's foot.

"How do you do it?" Aubrey's features scrunched in a fight against tears. "How do you touch…"

Lola had been asked that question many times. She'd given many answers but none seemed as important as the answer the teen was seeking. "I talk to them. As if they're still alive." Risking rejection, Lola put her arm around the girl. "Because they are still alive. To their loved ones."

Drew appeared at the end of the pew, making Lola's heart burst into an inappropriate tap dance. He gestured for Lola to follow him. In his brown-and-tan uniform, he should have looked out of place amid the black-clad mourners. Unlike Lola, he fit in anywhere in Sunshine, no matter what he wore.

"It'll get better, Aubrey," Lola promised, unable to resist Drew's summons. "Maybe not every day, but it will get easier in time." She picked up Bitsy's bag of groceries and joined Drew.

Drew took Lola's arm. She went willingly, her steps light as air. The sheriff was escorting her, and he wasn't escorting her to jail. It was hard not to smile.

"I thought now might be an appropriate time to meet the mayor and mention you want a traffic light or overpass by the interstate." Drew nodded toward Mrs. Eastlake, who was still surrounded by the Widows Club and was speaking with the mayor and his wife.

Lola stopped smiling. "This is a viewing. It's not the right time for crusades."

"It's the perfect time." He led her toward a cluster

of floor vases with big colorful floral arrangements. "Emotions are high. And hard to say no to."

Mayor Kevin Hadley turned and led his wife, Barbara, their way.

Drew's grip on Lola's arm tightened, holding her in place. "Kevin, you remember Lola Williams, Randy's wife."

The mayor was young and handsome, a fitting match for Barbara, who was blond and beautiful. Lola would bet they'd gone to high school together and been crowned at the Homecoming Ball. Theirs was the kind of love Lola had dreamed of. A perfect partnership.

"Lola?" Drew prompted.

The mayor was waiting for her to speak. Possibly more importantly, Barbara was waiting for Lola to speak, wearing the kind of expression that said she was expecting Lola to fall on her face.

Lola's shoulders sagged. Her marriage had been a sham. No one in Sunshine who wasn't nearing a grave wanted her to do their hair, not even her best friend. Why would anyone listen to her?

"Lola," Drew repeated with a little less sensitivity.

Kevin smiled at her patiently, perhaps used to awestruck constituents. He was really, really good-looking. Barbara smirked, perhaps reveling in her power to cow the town peasants.

If Lola said nothing, Barbara would most likely say something, most likely something unpleasant. And Lola would stand stupidly and take it, because no one talked back to the queen of Sunshine. The woman had no flaws. Not an ounce of cellulite. Not a blemish on her face.

Lola stared at Barbara, feeling like a mouse about to be squished by a lion's paw.

And that was when she saw it—Barbara's flaw. It took her a second to recognize it for what it was. Barbara wasn't perfect. Her dark roots were showing through the blond hair at her temple.

"Right." Lola set the cupcake supplies at her feet and cleared her throat, because Barbara might still jump down it, flaw and all. "I don't want to take too much of your time." She glanced at Drew, who nodded encouragingly. "I just…My husband died at the same intersection as Mr. Eastlake. I don't want anyone else to lose someone they love. I feel so empty inside without him. It's…" Her throat nearly closed with an unexpected wave of grief.

She'd thought she was past the word-stealing, gut-wrenching phase of loss, especially now.

Drew's grip on her arm loosened. His hand moved across her shoulders, leaving a trail of heat in its wake. It was all she could do not to lean on him.

The mayor gave Lola a compassionate smile. He wore an expensive suit and an expert haircut. Barbara might have been cruel but she had good taste in clothes, and she was a good hairstylist. "This is an issue I can take to the planning commission at the city and county level." Kevin seemed pleased Lola had brought her concern to him. He could have blown her off. She wouldn't have blamed him. "Why don't you tell me your thoughts?"

A group of women approached, having paid their respects. Kevin and Barbara closed ranks to allow them to pass.

A scent drifted in the air. Expensive. Familiar. *The*

scent. The one from the perfume bottle she'd found in Randy's keepsake box. Lola hadn't realized she should be searching for Randy's mistress here.

It was too late.

The women moved on. Kevin and Barbara backed away. The trail of perfume went cold. And so did Lola's ability to speak. She stared after the retreating women—Tiffany Winslow, Mary Margaret Sneed, and Darcy Jones. All she had to do was follow them out and get close enough for a whiff, and she'd find Randy's lover.

Drew's radio chirped. "Go on, Lola. I've got to take this." He walked out to the reception area.

The three women kept walking, right out the front door. There was no way she'd catch up to them now.

"Lola?" Kevin prompted. "Your thoughts?"

Barbara made a noise that sounded suspiciously like a stifled laugh.

"I…um…" Lola had no thoughts. "Other than wanting the intersection to be safer, I don't know what to say except…perhaps…we can include Mrs. Eastlake somehow?"

"Fair enough." Kevin's teeth were blindingly white. "How about I keep you informed as things progress?" It was no surprise why Kevin was mayor. He was polished and gracious.

Barbara, on the other hand…

She had a way of smiling and turning up her nose at the same time. "That dog is eating your groceries."

Mrs. Eastlake's therapy dog was chewing the cream cheese. And from the ravaged state of the package, he'd been snacking on it for some time.

* * *

Drew's pulse was racing faster than the cruiser's engine when he pulled in front of his sister Eileen's small house in an older neighborhood.

Flo had alerted Drew while he was at Scotty Eastlake's viewing that she couldn't reach Gary on his radio after he'd been sent on a call to Eileen's place. Procedure demanded backup be sent. Drew just hadn't ever expected a call like that to be at a family member's home.

Drew parked next to the department's second vehicle, the SUV. His rookie deputy, who happened to be his younger cousin Gary, stood on the walk, gun drawn.

On Eileen!

For a moment, Drew played out a scenario where he winged his cousin. Drew was a good shot, and Gary wasn't far away. But the paperwork and potential lectures from his mother deterred him from taking that course of action.

His sister stood on the porch like a human *X*, as if Gary had tried to get past her and might try to get by again. Her faded blue jeans were stained, and her T-shirt torn. Was she harboring that deadbeat boyfriend?

Drew got out of the car. "Gary, you need to stand down, or my mom is never going to invite you to Sunday dinner again."

"Boss, someone is screaming inside." Gary didn't take his eyes off Eileen. A bead of sweat trickled down the side of his face. He was only two years out of high school, too young to fill out his uniform, too green to stay calm in a crisis. "If this was one of those hypothetical situations you quiz me on, you'd want me to have gun in hand."

In a way, Gary was right. Until you added in the fact that this situation involved Eileen.

This could go to hell in a handbasket quicker than you could say *my sister rescues loud strays*.

"Stand down," Drew commanded, coming around the cruiser, hand on his own weapon.

Forget Sunday dinner; Aunt Cindy wasn't going to invite Drew to Thanksgiving if he shot her son. And she made the best gravy this side of Denver. And the town...Jeez...Gary had broken the state record for the hundred-yard dash in high school. He was the first Sunshine native to make it to the state record books. He was a local folk hero.

"Someone's screaming inside." The panic in Gary's voice made him sound prepubescent. "Eileen won't let me in."

"Gary always did have an overactive imagination." Eileen had never been one to deliver a properly timed punch line. She was hiding something all right. But a human victim? Not likely.

There was a crash inside, followed by the sound of a woman's garbled scream.

"See? See?" Gary lowered his head to take aim. "I told you."

Drew continued to work his way to his deputy's side but his sister needed to work with him. "Eileen, you need to stand down too."

"I've got this covered." Eileen blushed the way she did when she lied, all the way from her throat to her ears. At the sound of glass breaking, she cringed but held her ground. "I'm...I'm...wonderful."

Wonderful? He wasn't buying that.

"Nice try, Eileen. No one here is wonderful." He reached Gary's side and channeled the voice of his former drill sergeant, the one that sounded like a cross between a bark and a bellow. "Holster your weapon, Deputy." He never should have listened to his mother and hired family.

"But..." Gary reluctantly turned his gaze Drew's way. "What about the woman inside?"

"Gary." Drew placed a hand on his cousin's slender shoulder. "Eileen rescues animals. She's not the kind of woman to lock up humans. Shooting a constituent you're supposed to protect will get you fired." And possibly put in jail.

"Oh, man." Gary wiped sweat from his brow. "Eileen, you better not have robbed a bank or something."

"She didn't," Drew reassured him, except Gary wasn't reassured or backing off. "Gary, do you really want me to tell your mother you drew a bead on your cousin?"

"You wouldn't." Gary swallowed and then nodded. "You would." He lowered his weapon. "Okay, I'll be your backup."

Drew shook his head. "Busy day in town. Emily's off, and there's no working stoplight at the mortuary. Go direct traffic coming out of Scotty Eastlake's viewing. It should be ending now, but commuters from Greeley will be hitting town at the same time." Sunshine didn't need another traffic tragedy.

Gary's face puckered. "You're demoting me?"

"No." Drew sighed. "I'm allocating resources where they're needed." He ignored Gary's grumbling and waited until his cousin drove off before climbing the steps to Eileen's door. "I'm not Gary. Tell me what's going on."

"You're not coming inside." Eileen held her ground, chin jutting.

Another crash. Another cry of anguish, too high-pitched to be her last boyfriend, Tyrell the car thief.

Drew indulged in a sigh and a wistful thought about quiet, trouble-free Wendy. "Whatever's in there should *not* be in there."

"I can handle it," Eileen insisted.

There was a loud bang. The house shuddered, along with Eileen.

Drew took advantage of her shock to push past her. As soon as he opened the door, something the size of a minibike and as white as snow crashed into his legs, knocking him against the doorframe. He sucked in air and breathed in barnyard.

Squealing like the cruiser's siren, a large pig lurched sideways, pinning Drew's legs to the wall. The swine wore a pink rhinestone-studded collar that was large enough to fit two Saint Bernards.

"Rosie!" Eileen lunged for the beast.

"Stay back!" Feeling his feet go numb, Drew blocked Eileen's entry with one arm.

Rosie found her footing on top of Drew's boot and charged away, banging into upended furniture and puffing like a runaway steam engine.

"Eileen…" Drew chased the perp. "When I catch that pig, I'm taking it to the Bodine Meat Company."

"You can't eat Rosie," Eileen whined and followed him inside, closing the door behind her.

"I like bacon." And he hated chaos, especially spring-thaw madness that upset his sister.

Rosie banked into the kitchen, stumbling over one of two upended kitchen chairs. Squealing, she circled back to the living room, veering toward Drew.

He jumped onto the sofa, hauling Eileen with him. "Why is this pig hell-bent on knocking us over?"

"She's overweight. The fat in her cheeks means she can't open her eyes." Eileen was the kind of athlete to sit in right field picking dandelions. She lost her balance on the cushion and stumbled against the wall. "It helps to cover her in a jacket or a blanket."

He was supposed to swaddle three hundred pounds of panic? "I need something to throw over her. Give me that." Drew held out his hand, keeping an eye on the pig, who was completing a second lap, crashing into the stove.

"No." Eileen snatched up the gold-colored afghan and held it to her chest. "Grandma Lucille made this for me."

"I'll have to tase her." Drew reached for his Taser.

Eileen swatted his hand away. "You'll do no such thing."

He recognized that voice. His sister had made her decision. If he didn't abide by it, she'd do something foolish. Something worse than bringing a blind, high-strung pig into her home. Rosie would need to be calmed down in a humanitarian way without damage to Grandma Lucille's afghan. "Tell me you have no emotional attachment to the tablecloth over there."

He didn't wait for her answer. He made a run for it because the pig was playing bumper cars with the couch. At least Rosie was consistent. She kept running her circuit. Drew was able to grab the tablecloth and cover her with it as she ran out of the kitchen. The tablecloth hooked on her snout and trailed behind her like a rose-colored cape.

"Eileen, she's not stopping."

"Um..." Eileen's cheeks flamed. "You have to give her a hug too."

"A hug?" Drew stood in the center of the house, turning with the circling pig as if she were a horse and he had her on a lunge line. "I think I'd rather tase her."

"Drew..."

"Fine. I'll hug her." He shook his finger at his sister. "But you owe me. You owe me big."

When Rosie circled her way out of the kitchen, Drew tackled her, dragging her down to the hardwood floor and his lap. It was like being on the bottom of a dog pile. And yet the beast's legs kept moving as if she was still running.

"You're too rough." Eileen was at Rosie's side instantly, cooing and stroking the pig beneath the blanket.

Drew grunted. "Is this what you had in your SUV Sunday morning? Is this why you swerved on the road?"

"Don't play detective."

"Answer the question, or I'll tell your landlord." Tom Bodine, the largest landowner in Sunshine, the owner of Bodine Meat Company.

The pig didn't like either of their tones. She squealed and did the sideways running man. Drew held on tight, ruing the fact that his mother hadn't given birth to more than one sensible child.

"Yes," Eileen cooed, practically singing her words. "Rosie rammed my seat back, and I swerved. Are you happy now?"

"No." But thank heavens she hadn't been at the intersection near the interstate when it happened, the one where Scotty and Randy had died. The pig's legs didn't slow, and Drew's legs were growing numb. "How long do we have to stay like this?"

"Lower your voice." Eileen cooed at the large ham sandwich as if it were a beautiful baby. "Just a few more minutes."

Rosie didn't want to settle. She'd worked herself up into a royal state the way Becky used to do when she was overly tired and stuck on scream mode. Back then, he'd buckled her in her car seat and played the soundtrack from *Beauty and the Beast* on full volume.

"You need to sing," he whispered.

"What?"

Rosie squealed.

"Sing a lullaby. Or a Christmas carol or something." If being a parent had taught Drew anything, it was that pride was less important than a happy child. When Eileen didn't start singing, Drew did. He sang "Hush, Little Baby" and "Baby Mine." He sang "Silent Night" and "Rudolph the Red-Nosed Reindeer." He was about to start "It Came Upon a Midnight Clear" when Eileen stopped him.

"She's all better. Aren't you, Rosie?" Eileen stood,

removed the tablecloth, and helped the pig stand. She led it into the kitchen, where she stroked its face and told it to sit.

Drew stayed where he was, letting his numb legs tingle back to life.

The pig rested on its haunches, as well-behaved as any dog. Except most dogs didn't do this much damage. Overturned furniture, spilled litter box, broken picture frames.

"Mom is not going to be happy." She'd convinced Tom Bodine to rent the house to Eileen without a security deposit.

"You wouldn't tell her." Eileen's eyes were huge.

"I don't need to tell her. She always stops by unannounced." Drew got to his feet and picked up a family photo from when Becky was born. The glass was cracked over Drew's grinning face. "This pig isn't a house pet. Tell me you're not keeping it permanently."

Eileen set a plastic child gate between the kitchen cabinets and a wall, a configuration that would be about as effective at stopping a runaway hog as a bedsheet hung on a clothesline. His sister was always making houses out of straw.

"You run an animal shelter." He reinforced the child gate with a kitchen chair. "I can drive Rosie there."

"You can't." Eileen sniffed. "I have some dogs I'm working with who won't stop barking at her. They gave Rosie a nervous breakdown."

"So you're keeping her here?" Drew gestured to the remains of Eileen's home. "Now I'm having a nervous breakdown."

Eileen lifted her chin. "She'll be fine once she loses weight."

"*If* she loses weight." And it wasn't as if she was going on a cleanse. There was an extra-large dog bowl on the kitchen counter.

"Why can't you ever support what I do?" Eileen's big brown eyes filled with tears.

Rosie snuffled.

Eileen knelt and hugged her, promising her everything would be all right.

Drew took in the destruction in Eileen's small house. And then he looked at Eileen's paper-thin T-shirt and her tennis shoes with slick soles. She needed to get a real job, a real life, and a real plan for the future. But first, she needed to rescue this overweight, overly sensitive pig.

"She can't see the threats around her," Eileen said softly, petting Rosie like she would a dog. "And that upsets her. She needs to be confident in her surroundings. I can adopt her out if she loses some weight."

Eileen had always been the sensitive one in the bunch. The peacemaker. The sister who went without if there was too little to go around. The one most deserving of Wonderful status year-round.

Drew knew Eileen wanted to save the world. And he supposed it wouldn't kill him to help her save this corner of it.

One pig at a time.

Chapter Fourteen

♥

"I never should have agreed to the bake sale," Lola mumbled to herself as she ran inside the school gymnasium with a box of baked goods. The gym served as the town's multipurpose center, home of basketball games, town hall meetings, and Widows Club fund-raisers.

It was less than two hours after the viewing ended. Bitsy's recipe had been complicated, more fitting for a team of veteran bakers than an inexperienced one. Lola had struggled with the frosting's consistency. It probably hadn't helped that she'd had to apply frosting while the cupcakes were still warm.

Before she'd left home, she'd impulsively decided to wear the turquoise necklace from Randy's stash over her zebra-print dress in case Mary Margaret, Tiffany, or Darcy came to the bake sale. She didn't immediately see the trio but the gym was crowded; tables snaked their way back and forth across the basketball court. Mims was selling water on the stage at the far end.

"I'm here." Lola slid on her heels behind the table between Wendy's and Bitsy's.

"Good. Let me be the first to buy one of those red-velvet chocolate snowballs." Bitsy wrinkled her brow at the boot box Lola had used to transport her goods. It didn't stop her from putting a five-dollar bill on Lola's table. She took one of the smooshed cupcakes from the corner.

"Shoot." Lola took in the fancy tablecloths on Bitsy's and Wendy's tables, their elaborate decorations, and their coordinated napkins and paper plates. "I didn't realize we were decorating too." She was new to the charity biz, and it showed.

"People are only here for the food." Wendy should talk. She had a line at least ten deep. She might have been a whiz at baking but her hair could use some help. It was nearly as limp as Mrs. Eastlake's had been.

Lola's fingers itched to repay Wendy's kindness with a complimentary haircut and style.

"I suspected you might not know about table dressing." Bitsy had Lola covered. She'd brought two of everything and had Lola's table decorated in no time.

Lola couldn't thank her enough. Now if only her cupcakes tasted better than they looked, everything would be fine.

"Cupcakes!" Becky skipped toward Lola, having added a child's belt to her outfit. The sword she'd found at the thrift store swung from it.

Drew and his mother trailed behind her. They seemed to be having a strained conversation. It was hard to hear when the crowd was thick enough to bump elbows.

Drew stopped where Wendy's and Lola's tables met. His uniform was streaked with dirt, and one pocket was torn. He eyed Lola's cupcakes suspiciously. "Why do your cupcakes look so...gloopy?"

"Like you've never eaten my gloop before." His mother checked out Lola's cupcakes from where she stood at the back of Wendy's line. "And you liked it."

"You'll like Lola's cupcakes," Bitsy said to Drew.

"I think I heard somewhere that coconut is supposed to gloop." Lola wished that were true. She'd had a lot of trouble mixing the coconut and what was left of the cream cheese. There weren't any drips or globs on Wendy's frosting. Her Bundt cakes looked professionally made. "Besides, I've heard if it looks too pretty to eat, it probably doesn't taste good." As soon as the words left her mouth, Lola wanted to snatch them back. "No offense, Wendy."

"None taken," Wendy said cheerfully.

Wendy had no reason for the grumps. She had a lengthy line and was busy slicing. A couple of people had brought Tupperware and bought two slices.

Lola had only one person in her line. "Go ahead." She handed Becky a cupcake. "Take one. On me."

"There is no gifting," Bitsy said primly between selling bags of fudge. Her line was half that of Wendy's but doing a brisk business nonetheless. "All proceeds go to help build a new fence around the Little League outfield."

"Becky only needs one dessert." Drew took a half step toward the Bundt-cake line.

"Cupcakes are messy." Wendy had a rhythm—collect money, slice, serve, collect money, slice, serve. "No offense, Lola."

"None taken." Because it was only what Lola deserved after what she'd said.

Becky licked the cupcake's frosting. "Mmmm. Yummy."

Lola grinned. Drew's daughter was officially her favorite person in Sunshine.

"Rebecca Maureen Taylor." Drew's voice rose above the crowd. "Did I give you permission to eat that?"

Traffic around their tables slowed. Wendy froze midslice.

Becky took one look at her father's face and set the cupcake down, wiping trails of white frosting on her pink-flowered blouse. "Sorry."

And Drew called Lola wound too tight? She rubbed the turquoise pendant. Maybe it was time someone told the sheriff what to do.

"Now, normally," Lola said in a voice sweetened by justice, "I'd say it's okay to put it back, but if you taste it, your dad kind of needs to buy it." Lola nudged the cupcake toward the girl and smiled. "Which means you get to finish it. Pay up, Sheriff."

"Let's have Becky taste Wendy's Bundt cake and decide which one we buy." Drew guided Becky toward the end of the Bundt-cake line. "What?" he said when his mom gave him a disapproving look.

Susie Taylor shook her head. Drew's mother was probably a customer of Barbara Hadley. There was no gray showing in her shoulder-length warm-brown hair. "We'll talk about this when we get home."

"Are you going to ground me?" Drew chuckled, a sound nearly swallowed by the crowd.

Susie crossed her arms over her chest and turned away. She was ahead of him in line.

"Looks like you're in trouble, Sheriff," Lola taunted.

Becky giggled, which made Lola feel great until she realized no one was stopping at her table. She'd need some master salesmanship to get things started.

"These cupcakes are awesome," Lola said at megaphone volume. "Right, Bitsy?" Lola gestured toward the cupcake the older widow had taken. And then she gestured again, because she had a sinking feeling she wasn't going to sell any cupcakes and she'd have to stand here for an hour, watch Wendy's Bundt cakes disappear, and smile as if it didn't matter.

Bitsy looked at Lola the way you did when your boss asked you how good his crappy work was. But she had game. She nibbled on the cupcake. "It's good."

"That hardly seems enough to make a judgment." Drew grinned. He was about eight back in Wendy's line.

"Can I finish mine?" Becky had slipped back to Lola's table and her cupcake.

Drew reluctantly waved his approval. Becky didn't need to be told twice.

"You need to pay for that cupcake." Drew's mom studied Lola with unabashed curiosity. "And buy yourself one too."

"No." Drew's smile disappeared. "I'm saving room for Wendy's Bundt cake."

Disappointment tried to shrink Lola's shoulders inward. Pride kept them thrust upward.

"I'm all sold out." Wendy shouted and threw her

hands in the air as if someone had called *Time!* in a baking competition.

Sold out? Lola's jaw dropped. How had that happened?

Lola took advantage of the situation and held a cupcake toward the rest of Wendy's line. It was one of the prettier ones with a near-perfect swirl of coconut and cream cheese. "Get your red-velvet chocolate snowballs before they're gone."

Most people in Wendy's line moved away.

With a sigh of defeat and a regretful glance toward Wendy's empty cake plate, Drew reached for his wallet. "We'll take three." He handed over some bills and picked out two cupcakes, handing one to his mother.

"Mmmm." Becky's smile revealed teeth covered in chocolate.

Behind her table, Bitsy was sucking down water. Her cupcake was half eaten.

"It's gloopy," Drew said, sounding like he'd eaten too much peanut butter. He turned to his mother, who didn't seem able to pry her lips open.

Lola had a gut-dropping suspicion that her cupcakes hadn't cooked all the way.

Bitsy sidled closer, running her tongue around her teeth and looking a tad judgmental. "Did you follow my directions?"

"I tried to." And based on the reactions of her customers, Lola hadn't been successful. She lowered her voice. "Should I give them their money back?"

Bitsy shook her head, still working her tongue around her mouth. "No refunds."

"We'b gotta glow," Drew said, mouth full of gloop. He looked surprised by Lola's cupcakes, and not in a good way. "It's a stool knife." Drew led his family toward the door, presumably because it was a school night. He stopped to buy water from Mims.

People walked past Lola's table without slowing or looking her in the eye. The dull burn of being a misfit flared to life in Lola's chest, more unsettling than the heartburn she'd gotten after that cheap Cabernet she'd drunk with Avery's five-alarm chili last week.

"I should go," she told Bitsy. The widow would probably never ask her to do a fund-raiser again.

The older woman grabbed onto Lola's shoulders and gave her a gentle shake. "Nothing was ever solved by running away." She smiled, trying to reassure Lola, but one of her top teeth was covered with chocolate.

"Oh, I'm sorry." Feeling her cheeks heat, Lola waved a hand over her mouth. "You have—"

"What did I miss? I was passing out flyers about Frank trying to buy the block downtown. He's determined to ruin my life. And I'm determined to stop him." Avery ran to Lola's side, taking in her sad-looking inventory. "What did I miss other than why your cupcakes look like a two-year-old frosted them."

"No one wants my gloopy cupcakes," Lola whispered, fighting the sting of rejection. She wanted to go home.

"It's their loss." Avery set a small stack of flyers in front of Lola's display, plunked a five-dollar bill on the table, and grabbed a cupcake. "I bet they taste good."

Lola felt obliged to say, "You don't have to try one."

"I want to." Avery peeled back the wrapper.

"Thank you for being such a good friend." With five cupcakes gone, Lola's display looked like she'd sold some, so it wasn't a total embarrassment. If she didn't count the peanut butter texture of her product or the cake stuck in Bitsy's teeth.

Which she would have told Bitsy about if her fudge business hadn't been booming now that Wendy was sold out. Lola felt guilty every time Bitsy smiled.

Out of desperation, Lola turned to Wendy, prepared to help her pack up her decorations. But Wendy wasn't near ready to go. Despite having nothing to sell, she still had a line, this time with people expressing regret that they hadn't gotten to her before she'd sold out.

"You should have made more Bundts," Lola said, wondering how hard it was to make one. She'd bet it was easier than red-velvet chocolate snowballs.

"Two is enough." Wendy spared Lola that mellow, no-worries smile. "Thank you for helping with my play."

"My pleasure." And it was. She needed to spend more time with kids like Becky, who didn't care where she was from or what she did for a living. Lola tried to catch the eye of one of the last of Wendy's disappointed customers but the man's glance flicked to her cupcakes, and he spun away.

Wendy accepted someone else's regrets. Rather than feeling sorry, she actually seemed to be happy about it.

Lola was beginning to wonder whether Wendy planned to run out so she could receive accolades.

"Dat's a letty neckface," Avery said around a mouthful of cupcake. "I used to hap one dust mike it."

Lola took a moment to translate frosting-mouth into English, and even then she couldn't quite believe it. "*You* used to have a necklace like this one?"

Avery nodded.

The room turned cold. So cold Lola's lips froze shut, her neck hardened in place, and the cogs in her brain ground to a halt.

Avery was Randy's mistress?

No. But it was a weak *no.*

"Waler?" Avery asked.

With effort, Lola pried her lips apart. "Water? Mims is selling it on the stage." Lola glanced down at the pendant, trying to think clearly as Avery hurried off.

Avery. It's Avery.

No.

Just because Avery had once owned a necklace like this one didn't mean she was Randy's mistress. Avery didn't wear delicate floral perfume. And she'd dated at least six men in town or in Greeley in the two years since Lola had moved here. Avery didn't need Randy.

Needing is different than wanting.

Plus she'd encouraged Lola to drop her search for Randy's mistress.

Avery. Avery. Avery.

Lola didn't want Randy's lover to be her best friend. She shivered, still cold as ice.

The attractive man who'd bought Avery at the Widows Club auction approached her in the water line and said something.

Brows drawing down, Avery held her hand over her mouth and said something back.

"Did you chill the coconut milk?" Bitsy was too classy to declare her disappointment in Lola but it was there in her repeated questioning of Lola's methods.

"I didn't have time to chill anything. I had to stay through the entire viewing." Lola tried to discreetly see whether the chocolate still covered Bitsy's teeth, but Bitsy's lips were closed.

Across the gym, the man with Avery gave her a strained smile. He didn't look like he was dead set on trashing Avery's life. He looked like an ex-boyfriend trying to get back in his woman's good graces. And Avery didn't look like a home-wrecker. She looked like an annoyed, thirsty woman.

But Lola had been deceived by looks before. Most notably, Randy's.

A man in a brown-and-tan uniform entered the gym and was immediately swallowed up by the crowd.

Drew.

He was back. He'd know what to do. He'd tell Lola to stick to the facts, which leaned toward Avery's innocence. He'd ask whether Avery had been with Lola on those nights when Randy attended spin class or played basketball in Greeley. (She often had been.) He'd get her through this just by standing near.

But the man in tan wasn't the sheriff. It was his deputy Gary, a man so young he wasn't old enough to drink beer at Shaw's. In his first week on the job, he'd set up a speed trap just outside city limits and ticketed the mayor. A few weeks ago, he'd tried to arrest one of the Bodine twins for texting during a movie. His was not a stabilizing presence, but it was a popular one.

People slapped him on the back as if he was a hometown hero.

"You didn't refrigerate the cream cheese or the butter for hours?" Bitsy's gaze had sharpened. "Not even when you got home?"

Hadn't she tried to tell Bitsy she wasn't good in the kitchen? Not that it mattered. Her continued questioning had thawed Lola out from top to bottom. It wasn't Avery. It couldn't be.

"Lola?" Bitsy asked.

"No fridge. Sorry." Every time Lola had thought about getting the keys to the office, where the refrigerator was located, something at the viewing had required her attention. "By the time I got home, I had to start baking." And then what good was refrigeration? There was a point of diminishing returns in the kitchen, wasn't there? A place where the damage was done. Like now with Bitsy's food-covered tooth. If Lola didn't say anything, Bitsy would know she *could have* said something but didn't. The time to point out this embarrassment was now. "Really, I'm sorry, but you have—"

"We should leave." Avery stomped back with two bottles of water, handing one to Lola. "Frank is trying to talk me out of passing out flyers. Can you believe he thinks tearing down town history and destroying jobs, even temporarily, is a good thing?"

Avery stared at Lola. At the necklace.

Avery. Avery. Avery.

Lola teetered on her heels. She shouldn't have skipped dinner. She shouldn't have ventured out of the realm of the retirement home and the mortuary. She shouldn't have agreed to bake. She didn't fit in. And if Avery was Randy's mistress, she'd have no friends in Sunshine. Not now. Not ever.

Not Avery.

But the truth hung in the air like too much hair spray. Lola teetered on her heels once more. Where was her fight? Where was her anger? Her gaze swept the floor, looking for a soft spot to land if she passed out.

Avery drew a slow breath. "Where did you get that necklace? My grandmother gave me one just like it." Avery glared at Frank, her auction date, who was approaching. "It was engraved on the back, but I lost it in high school."

The hair stood up on the back of Lola's neck. "What did it say?"

"Dream big."

Avery. It was Avery.

The air rushed out of Lola's lungs. She leaned on the table, trying to tell herself it didn't mean anything. There were other necklaces out there. Ricky had said as much at the thrift store.

"Dream big. That's what my grandmother always told me." Avery speared her fingers through her hair. "My dad wants to sell the theater to Frank instead of me. Can you believe it? It's hard to keep dreaming when reality keeps body-slamming me."

Lola could relate. "This is yours. I found it in Randy's love shack." She fumbled with the pendant and turned it around to show Avery the engraving. "Dream big. It was you. Randy's lover. All this time."

Color flared high in Avery's cheeks. "Lola…"

Lola couldn't look at Avery. She couldn't not look at Avery. Her gaze bounced on her and away. "I thought you were my friend. I thought... but you..."

"Don't say it," Avery warned, not even trying to deny it. She was staring at her auction date.

Betrayal wasn't cold. It was as hot as a tighty-whitie blaze. "You were sleeping with my husband!" Lola shouted as loud as any cheerleader ever had in this gymnasium. And she'd been so certain Randy's lover had been a blond. "You knew about blow-up dolls."

A crowd began to form.

"I'm not having this conversation here." Avery thrust out her hand. "Give me my necklace back."

"No." Swaying, Lola held her ground. She'd picked the wrong occasion to wear super-high heels. "First, tell me. Did he love—"

"Give it to me." Lola's soon-to-be former best friend lunged for the necklace.

Lola stumbled back. Her slender heel gave way, and she reached for the table for balance. Her hand squashed several cupcakes and tipped over the tiered tray but she stayed upright. "You can have it when I have my grandmother's ring back."

"I don't have your ring." Avery latched on to the pendant. She yanked on the chain, sawing it into the back of Lola's neck.

Gasping, Lola clasped her hands around Avery's. She'd been unable to hold on to her husband. She wasn't going to lose her hold on the necklace.

Her hand was coated in melting coconut icing. It dripped to the floor between them. They slipped and slid and lost their footing. The clasp gave way, and the necklace flew into the air. The momentum carried them in the other direction—on top of the red-velvet chocolate snowballs. The folding table collapsed beneath them, and they crashed to the floor.

For a moment, Lola heard nothing but the rasp of her own breathing. And then people started to laugh.

Coconut gloop was everywhere. In their hair. Up the back of Lola's dress. There was a stripe of frosting war paint on Avery's face.

"Back it up! Back it up!" Deputy Gary swaggered onto the scene, smiling at the gathered crowd as if they were going to be happy with the upcoming show. His gaze lit on Lola and Avery. "Put your hands in the air."

Lola complied. Avery did not.

Unflustered by the melee, Bitsy was using her tablecloth like a mop, trying to clear a safe path to Lola and Avery. She glanced up at Gary. "Is that necessary?"

"I'm sure this is all a misunderstanding." Wendy handed Lola a small flowery napkin when what she really needed was a large towel. Maybe two.

The young deputy snorted. "Both of you put your hands up and come with me."

"Gary," Mims said in a commanding voice that made the deputy waver, "we've never had anyone arrested at one of our functions, and we aren't going to start now."

Avery got to her feet, slipping by increments but staying upright. She glared at Gary. "If you arrest me, I'm going to tell your mother what you and Sheree did at the midnight showing of *Dirty Harry* last summer."

It must have been bad, because the young deputy faced Lola. "Ms. Williams, I'm taking you in."

"No thanks." Lola got to her knees and picked up the necklace. There was cupcake mush on her tights, on her dress, and in her pumps.

Bitsy had barely wiped the floor clean when Edith appeared. She held her pantsuit hems high and waded to Lola's side to help her stand. "So, Avery's your Jezebel."

Lola couldn't bring herself to say yes. Through the lingering audience, she spotted Avery's cake-stained, retreating back. Her betrayal hurt almost as much as the day she'd found the box of condoms. But there was nothing to purge, nothing to burn.

"That's the way it always is." Edith led her to dry ground near Gary. "Best friends have the sharpest knife and the deadliest aim."

"Oh, please." Mims gestured for Lola to come toward her, away from the deputy.

"Not so fast." Gary grabbed onto Lola's arm. "I said, you're coming with me."

Chapter Fifteen

♥

"Gary, we need to talk." Drew was so close to firing his cousin that he could already hear the lecture his mother would give him when he picked up Becky later.

"Before you start on me, you need to know that Lola was disturbing the peace." Gary rocked back in his desk chair. "And she might have thought about resisting arrest."

"Gary, you're family." And his mother had encouraged Drew to hire him despite Gary's low rank in the academy and the fact that he still had acne. "But this isn't the big city. When you arrest people in Sunshine, it's like dropping a boulder in a fishing pond. People get upset. And not just the people you arrest. I've already had a call from the mayor, Mims, and your mother." Not to mention Flo had given him an earful about how power was corrupting Gary.

"I know one way to keep the peace, Drew. One way." Gary laced his fingers over his chest and continued rocking as if it were Sunday and he were sitting on his front porch. "Uphold the law and show no favoritism."

"So it wasn't favoritism when you let Avery walk?" Drew had the strongest urge to strip Gary of his badge, his weapon, and his duty belt. Instead, he planted his hands on Gary's desk and leaned forward. "You better find another way to keep the peace, or you're going to have to find another job." Family or not. "Your mother gave me her blessing to fire you. I guess she still holds a grudge from the safety citation you gave her last month." The one for a burned-out taillight.

Gary had paled at the mention of Avery's name but he went white when he heard about his mother's blessing.

"Lucky you, I believe in second chances." Or maybe fifth chances. Drew had lost count.

Gary gave a small, almost imperceptible nod.

Still fuming, Drew grabbed the jail-cell key ring off its hook and made his way back to Lola. From what he'd heard, Lola didn't deserve to be locked up. If he'd been there, he would've given both parties a chance to tell their sides and then given both women a warning.

Drew stopped when he reached her jail cell. Lola's legs were propped against the back wall. She still wore black tights and the zebra dress. Her black pumps were on the floor next to the bench. She had frosting in her brown hair and chocolate smudges on her cheek, and she wouldn't meet his gaze. She was deep in Woe-Is-Me mode. A little levity was called for, but Drew needed another minute to swallow back his anger at Gary.

Like last time, Lola's feet moved over the wall in intricate dance steps to a rhythm only she could hear. If it'd been Wendy in the cell, she'd have been sitting primly, staring at the wall in quiet contemplation. Not that Wendy would ever find herself in his jail cell. And that was what he liked about her.

"Congratulations." He blew out a breath. "There aren't many people who've been in my jail two times in the span of a week."

"There's an honor I didn't aspire to." Lola's feet kept moving.

Drew opened the cell door, thinking her feet might stop when he did so.

She kept dancing. That was the thing about Lola. She was never predictable. The only thing you could count on her doing was the unexpected, which was why she was on his Watch-Over list. Who knew she'd need watching over at a bake sale?

For two years, he'd thought he knew Lola. He'd thought she was a polite, too-proud woman who didn't care if she never fit in in Sunshine. He hadn't realized until this week—until this moment—that she was more than polite. She was caring. He'd seen it at the mortuary and the Saddle Horn. Pearl liked her, and Pearl didn't like anyone.

Lola didn't keep her head up because she thought she was above people here. She kept her head up because of the way people in Sunshine treated her. She deserved better from Sunshine. She deserved better from him.

Drew moved to stand next to Lola, which made it impossible to look at her long legs without getting caught. "You can go home now."

"I'm not cooled down." She sniffed and swiped a hand at her nose, which was possibly the cleanest feature on her face. "My best friend…"

"It can't be Avery."

"It was her necklace in Randy's box." Her words spilled out too quickly. But those feet...those feet kept moving slowly. "She tried to take it back."

"If Avery was the other woman, at least now you know who all those things belonged to. You can move on."

"No husband. No best friend. No pearl ring." Her feet stilled. "I'm at a dead end."

He'd been staring at her legs again. Drew took a step back. "Time to end this sad song. You've got a lot going for you. You're employed. You own property." He moved toward the door, keeping his gaze on the keys in his hand. "You should go home, shower, order a pizza, and count your blessings." Drew silently cursed Gary because, from this point on, every time he looked at the jail cell, he'd see Lola's dancing feet. Once, he could forget. Twice, and it was imprinted on his memory. "Besides, you could still be wrong. I've never seen Avery with a married man." He looked at her.

"That must be Avery's secret talent." Lola's feet slowed even more, and she glanced up at him with watery blue eyes. "Everyone has a secret talent. At least that's what my grandmother used to say."

"And Avery's talent would be..."

"Invisibility. You didn't see her with Randy, and I didn't see this coming." Lola pressed the backs of her hands over her eyes.

Drew wanted to ask Lola what her secret talent was and what she thought his might be, but therein lay danger. Of what sort, he wasn't sure. "Come on. I'll get you a towel and a ride home."

"You mean..." Lola sat up. "Avery didn't...?"

"She didn't press charges." And Gary didn't have enough to book Lola on. "Ms. Everly will be happy tomorrow when you deflate those dolls." Ramona Everly's secret talent was disapproval. Although that wasn't so secret.

"I guess." Lola sighed, still not making her way to the door. "What happened to Marvin?"

"Who?" He'd been pondering secret powers again.

"Marvin." She gestured toward the end of the bench. "The rooster."

"Oh, Marvin. He made bail and relocated outside city limits." Tom Bodine had taken him to his ranch.

If Lola relocated, she could put whatever she wanted in her front window, and Drew wouldn't worry about her. What with Jane coming and spring thaw in full swing, he could use a break.

Lola stood, shedding a fine layer of cake crumbs. "I don't suppose you have a hose."

"Not even ones for riots." Drew fought a smile. Lola was more resilient than his sisters. Or maybe more accustomed to adversity. "No shower either."

"If I'm free to go, I'll just walk home."

"I could call for pizza," Drew said, thinking she shouldn't be alone, belatedly realizing she shouldn't be alone with him. "I mean, it'd be there when you get home."

She bent to pick up her heels without so much as a wide-eyed blink of surprise, as if Drew offered to feed her every day. "I think I'll just raid my chocolate stash." Her first few steps were stiffer than a professional football player on Monday morning.

Drew could almost hear her joints creaking. "Heard you and Avery took out a table, just like professional wrestlers."

"Not on purpose." Lola had her back to Drew but it sounded as if she was smiling.

Suddenly, Drew couldn't resist asking, "What's your secret talent?"

Her steps slowed. "Nana would say I love too deeply." There was a melancholy quality to her words that reached out to Drew and squeezed his heart. "My mom would say it's my naivete, which isn't really a talent."

Drew suspected both women were right. "I don't think either one of those is a bad thing."

Lola turned and sniffed, leaning closer to sniff again. "What's that smell?"

Uh-oh. He lifted his shirt front and sniffed. Yep, it was pig. "It's Rosie."

She straightened and then shook her head. "I'm too tired to make sense of that." Lola resumed her slow march toward the door.

In no time, she'd be gone.

He couldn't resist asking, "What do you think my secret talent is?" He didn't expect her to know but he'd been taught never to leave a question unanswered.

"Loyalty." She didn't hesitate. "You're loyal to a fault." She'd reached the outer door and leaned against the wall, waiting for him to unlock it.

Their eyes met.

She was close enough to touch. Close enough to draw into his arms and kiss. He'd bet she tasted like chocolate, coconut frosting, and hope because, no matter how low she got, Lola didn't seem to give up.

She'd called him loyal but his thoughts had him feeling disloyal to Wendy.

"Loyal?" he choked out, unable to look her in the eye anymore. "That's a good thing, right?"

"I suppose. It's hard for me to say. You aren't loyal to me."

He said nothing. But he was afraid she was wrong.

* * *

If not for Edith rushing forward, Lola might not have noticed the Widows Club waiting for her when she was released from the slammer a second time.

Her pulse was pounding, and her knees weren't steady. She could swear Drew had been staring at her legs when she was in the jail cell. And then he'd moved in close at the outer cell door, almost as if he was moving in for a kiss.

Which only proved she was delusional. Or lonely.

Or both.

Lola refused to be demoralized. Most women in town probably indulged in a fantasy or two about their handsome sheriff. Most single women might experience a moment or two of loneliness. No need to consult a therapist or call a hotline or FaceTime with your best friend.

"You poor thing." Edith opened her arms to give Lola a hug and then thought better of it when she saw the state of Lola's ruined dress. She picked a piece of frosting from Lola's hair and tsk-tsked. "Your best friend." Her gaze slanted toward Mims. "It's always the bestie."

Lola grimaced.

"It isn't always the best friend," Mims grumbled, tugging down her neon-yellow sweatshirt, which had a perfect pink cupcake on the front. She was frowning and swinging her purse as if warming up to swing it at someone's head.

Someone who'd ruined the bake sale fund-raiser?

Lola kept her distance.

"It's not always a friend," Bitsy said with a faraway look in her eye.

"Sometimes it's the town floozy." Clarice leaned on her cane, gray braids hanging down on either side.

Lola didn't know who the town floozy was, but it wasn't Avery. She was picky about whom she dated. "I'm sorry about ruining your cupcake recipe," Lola said to Bitsy, staring at the older woman's mouth to see whether her teeth were finally clean.

Her lips were sealed.

Darn. "And I apologize for causing a scene. I didn't mean for it to get so...so..."

"Physical? Dangerous? Deadly?" Gary returned Lola's purse. His chin jutted, as if he was unhappy Lola had been released without charges being filed.

"*Gary*," Drew warned from too close behind Lola.

Lola resisted the urge to turn around, resisted the craving to log Drew's expression and give it context, like *Interested* or *Just being kind.*

"These things happen sometimes." Bitsy smiled.

And there it was. The chocolate-covered tooth.

Lola gasped. Now was her time to make amends. "Bitsy—"

"We probably should have known." Clarice cut Lola off. "If it happened to anyone, it would happen to you."

"*Clarice*," Bitsy said. For whatever reason, she always stuck up for Lola. She deserved a save in return.

"Bitsy!" Lola practically shouted before anyone else interrupted. "You have . . . something in your teeth." She didn't say *cupcake*. After all, it could have been fudge.

Bitsy delicately covered her lips with her fingers.

"Let me see." Edith moved into Bitsy's grill, acting as a mirror and rubbing her own tooth. "Golly, yes. This one. I can't believe none of us saw that."

Lola wanted to disappear. There was no way that had been fudge.

Mims stood near the door, frowning Lola's way. Lola wouldn't be surprised if her invitation to join the Widows Club was rescinded. But she was surprised to realize she'd be disappointed if it was.

Despite everything, Lola was still golden in Edith's eyes, perhaps because the older woman was an outcast among the widows as well. She returned to Lola's side. "What are you going to do about Avery?"

"Nothing," Drew said at the same time as Mims.

"How are you going to make her pay?" Edith added, ignoring the pair.

"She's not," Drew and Mims said as a unit.

"I'm not," Lola agreed. She felt defeated, as unsteady on her feet as Randy and Candy would be when she pulled their plugs.

"Ladies." Drew took Lola by the arm and led her to the door, smelling of Rosie, whatever that meant. "Lola wants to walk home. She needs time to herself."

"Walk home?" Edith hurried around them to the door. "Nonsense. She's one of us. We'll drive her."

"I've got a plastic drop cloth in the back of my van." Despite Clarice's dig about the inevitability of Lola wreaking havoc, she hurried forward, thunking her walking stick on the floor with authority. "She can sit on it as long as she sits still."

Lola didn't want to be crowded into the back seat of a minivan. She wanted space and the freedom outside a jail cell. But mostly, she wanted to have friends she trusted and somebody to love.

Frosting smooshed inside her pumps.

And yes, she wanted to be clean.

"I can walk," Lola said, not wanting to be a bother.

"You shouldn't be alone just yet," Mims said in a much gentler voice than Lola had expected given the events of the evening.

Edith put her small hands on Lola's back and guided her out the door. "That's our cue to leave."

Lola climbed into the middle seat of Clarice's van, sitting on the thin plastic drop cloth. She brushed her black pumps free of white frosting and palmed a quarter from the floor, planning to hand it to Clarice when she got out, assuming it was hers.

Clarice took off with a squeal of tires and an illegal U-turn. Off-road, she may have been an environmentalist and a lover of her fellow man. But on the road, the old woman was a menace.

"About this thing with Avery." Mims patted Lola's thigh. "You are not a victim."

Lola hadn't been thinking she was, but if the necklace fit…

"Someone told me you used to do hair and makeup on Broadway." Edith ignored Mims. "What shows did you work on?"

"The most well-known show I did was *Chicago*." Those days seemed a lifetime ago. "But one of my favorite jobs was working for a magic show off Broadway." Far, far off Broadway. Between shows, Magic Merle had taught Lola the basics of sleight of hand, escape, and distraction. She snapped her fingers in front of Edith and magically produced the quarter she'd picked up.

Edith squealed. "What else can you do? I love it when magicians saw people in half." She leaned forward to eye Mims's midsection and then leaned back to eye Lola's. "Do you know how to do that?"

"Blast." Mims tugged at her ear, saving Lola from answering. "I've lost an earring."

For one stomach-dropping moment, Lola imagined Mims had lost the ruby earring on her dresser. Mims and Randy? A ridiculous thought.

"What does your earring look like?" Lola peered at the floor mats.

"It's a clip-on with a purple doodad." Mims shook out her sweatshirt but all that flew free was cupcake dust. "Darn. You can hardly find clip-ons in stores nowadays. We clip-on wearers are a dying breed."

A clip-on earring.

Avery had pierced ears. Avery wouldn't be caught dead wearing a clip-on earring like the one in Randy's keepsake box. The ruby earring couldn't have been Avery's. But the necklace was and had been lost when she was in high school, which meant…

Clarice took the corner onto Skyview Drive with too much speed.

Lola's stomach plunged and was left at the corner as the truth pressed in on her.

Avery might not have slept with Randy recently.

And Randy had more than one lover.

Clip-on earrings.

At least one of Randy's lovers might have been an older woman.

Chapter Sixteen

♥

The light was on in the apartment over the farmhouse garage on Saturday night.

Drew saw it from his kitchen window. He'd finished a shift thirty minutes ago and sent his mother, who'd been babysitting, home. Becky was asleep upstairs.

He'd just swallowed a shot of whiskey to take the edge off, because earlier Gigi had called 911—not because she'd seen a rabid rodent in her backyard but to report chest pains. An ambulance had taken her to the hospital in Greeley for tests. Drew still wore his uniform and duty belt. He should tuck himself into the corner of the couch and close his eyes. He should catch up on the sporting news on television. He should think about topics of conversation for his date tomorrow with Wendy. What he shouldn't have done was look out the window toward the garage apartment.

He could swear that light hadn't been on when he'd pulled in ten minutes ago.

That light…

Drew had two guesses as to who was up there—

Avery, because she was presumably Randy's lover and had a key, or Lola.

His money was on Lola.

It was dark outside. Sultry music drifted from the garage apartment. Drew climbed the stairs slowly. He shouldn't be out here at all but he'd always been too curious for his own good. When had curiosity not bitten him in the ass?

Drew opened the door at the top of the stairs. The room was dark, lit only by a candle on the bureau. But the occupant wasn't Avery or Lola.

A blonde wore a cop uniform. *The* cop uniform from the bottom bureau drawer. It wasn't like any uniform he'd ever seen. Gray halter top, blue pants, black high heels, and a duty belt, complete with handcuffs and a small nightstick. Back to him, the blonde danced slowly, moving pale limbs with languid grace.

He didn't recognize her, and that bothered him. He knew everyone in town. It was his duty to.

He still wore his uniform. He should tell her to freeze and demand to know what she was doing here. The last thing he needed was a stranger hanging around the property.

The blonde began a slow set of steps with an intricate pattern that had her doing a gradual turn. By increments, her face came into view. A straight nose. A delicate chin.

"Holy Mary, Mother of God." The blond siren was Lola.

There was a bottle of red wine on the bureau and a half-empty glass next to it. Drew almost reached for it.

With a wife like that, why would Randy cheat?

Lola had frozen at his outburst. Their gazes collided, locked. And then, instead of blushing, instead of covering herself up and kicking him out, instead of laughing as she'd predicted when they'd discovered the costumes, Lola picked up her footwork where she'd left off. Only this time, she danced toward him.

There's no way this is Lola.

But it was. Those blue eyes. Those lips that were moving, lip-syncing.

He had it coming.

And those feet. He recognized the slow pattern from the other night in jail.

Drew couldn't move. He felt like Blow-Up Drew, left wherever Lola propped him, patiently awaiting her return.

Lola danced closer. Her arms wove in a pattern as mesmerizing as her feet. She had a pair of handcuffs dangling from the fingers of one hand.

Step away.

Those arms undulated near his chest.

Move.

He couldn't. He was that blow-up doll. *Her* blow-up doll.

He waited obediently.

Her lips swam closer, brushed the corner of his mouth. He could feel her smile.

She's enjoying this.

Drew's blood pounded in his veins.

He claimed her arms, drawing them around his neck.

He claimed her shoulders and held her immobile so he could look at her—at blond hair, at blue eyes, at red lips—searching for the Lola he knew and could resist. He didn't find her.

He claimed the wig, tossing it aside.

And then he claimed her mouth.

* * *

Lola had missed kissing.

She'd missed the warmth of a strong body filling her arms, the tug of a man who wanted her.

Her eyes drifted closed, and her hands slid from his neck, down his solid chest, around his waist, and toward his back and…

Lola jerked back an inch. She'd been in a lovely wine-induced haze, dancing to the soundtrack from *Chicago*, imagining she was dancing for Randy in a way she'd never been brave enough to when he was alive. And then Randy was there in the shadow of the door, wearing his tool belt.

Except it wasn't Randy in the doorway. It was Drew!

Lola froze like a kid caught playing with her mother's makeup. Her right hand clenched the trick handcuffs from Randy's drawer.

Drew stared down at her, not saying a word.

"What are you doing here?" Lola whispered, afraid to back up, because she was wearing next to nothing, just a thin layer of stretchy polyester and her panties.

She should put some distance between them. Instead, her fingers wandered around the back of his belt.

"I'm wondering what I can arrest you for." His deep voice rumbled with unmistakable longing.

Lola licked her lips. "Last I heard, lip-locking wasn't a crime." Her fingers encountered another set of handcuffs. His.

Drew was staring at her mouth, not speaking.

Lola was staring at his mouth, wishing…

Things she had no right to be wishing.

She had to say something. She had to break the spell between them. "Avery doesn't wear clip-on earrings."

"What?" Drew seemed dazed.

"Each one of those items in the box came from a different woman. The clip-on earring? It can't be Avery's. She has pierced ears."

His gaze drifted to the ceiling. "You've got to be kidding me."

"No." She traced the handcuffs at the back of Drew's belt. She liked them better than Randy's. "I'm going to go to Shaw's at midnight. That's when all the late-night action happens."

Metal clinked softly.

Lola added quickly, "I'm going to find a woman who wears clip-on earrings and—"

"And do what?" Drew's dark eyes flashed a warning.

Lola lifted her chin. "I'm going to ask her if she's lost an earring." Why did Drew always talk to her as if she were one step away from a violent break in behavior? "I made a decision today. I'm leaving Sunshine just as soon as I talk to all of Randy's lovers." It wasn't as much a decision as a thought. But it felt right. "I need to find a place where I belong, where I can settle down and have a family and a future."

Drew grabbed Lola's shoulders and backed her toward

the bed. "You aren't going to Shaw's tonight." He pushed her onto the blue bedspread and stared down at her.

For a moment, Lola thought he might cover her body with his and kiss her again. She licked her lips, wondering why he wasn't. Really, the man overthought everything. Why wasn't he making a move?

Ah, yes. There'd been a command in his statement somewhere. About Shaw's. He was waiting for her to confirm she'd obey.

Obey?

That opened the floodgates of anger and had her scrambling to sit. "You can't stop me."

"I can." Drew reached behind his back and produced a pair of handcuffs. He snapped one on her wrist and then attached the other to the brass headboard. "You'll thank me in the morning."

His gaze burned so hot she just knew he was going to kiss her.

Instead, Drew walked away.

"Hey!" Tethered, Lola pulled against the bed frame.

Drew stopped at the door and glanced at her over his shoulder. "If I've learned anything about you, Lola, it's that you need time to cool down. I'll be back in an hour."

He was putting her in time-out?

Lola vowed to make him pay.

* * *

Something landed on Drew and nestled in the crook of his legs. Something bigger than a cat.

The TV came on. A familiar cartoon theme song filled the air.

Drew cracked open one eye. Sun glinted through the blinds and picked up the highlights in Becky's brown hair.

His daughter yawned. "You slept on the couch again, Daddy."

His back confirmed her detective work. It was kinked worse than an old hose. He extended his legs and arched his back.

"You aren't a good pillow." Becky shifted to lean on the opposite arm of the couch.

Speaking of pillows, Drew missed his. He was still in his uniform. His duty belt was on the coffee table. At least he'd locked his weapon in the gun safe after he'd—

"Lola." He bolted off the couch. He was supposed to have let her go after an hour. And now…he'd kidnapped a woman. If she pressed charges, he'd go to jail and Jane would get Becky, no questions asked.

"What about Ms. Williams?" Becky yawned. "Does she always wear pretty dresses? Is she a hooker?"

"No. No no no no." Drew tugged on his boots without bothering to lace them. "Stay here. I'll be right back." He raced out the back door and took the stairs to the garage apartment two at a time.

"Lola?" Drew opened the door. And then opened it wider. His gut clenched.

The apartment was empty.

She'd escaped? Drew spun around. Not possible. She would've had to call someone with a handcuff key, and that someone would've arrested Drew.

Just to be sure she was gone, Drew checked the shower and under the bed.

His pulse was racing, pounding at his temples. He needed coffee. He needed his cop sense to kick in. He needed a miracle to avoid prison.

Drew took slow, deep breaths and surveyed the room one more time.

The headboard hadn't been hacksawed. The bed was still neatly made. The cop uniform was strewed on the floor but the blond wig was nowhere to be seen.

If she'd been rescued, she wouldn't have stopped to change. Which meant...she'd escaped?

Drew ran a hand over his hair and back again. "She picked the lock?" It hardly seemed possible. But she had. And she also had a new theory about Randy and multiple lovers.

He slammed the door and ran down the stairs. In no time, he was in the farmhouse. "Becky, we need to leave early for Sunday breakfast."

Becky sat up. She had a bad case of bedhead. "Can you braid my hair?"

Drew bit back a groan. Braids. He hated braids. "Not today, honey."

She huffed. "That's what you always say."

She was right. He avoided braiding her hair like his mother avoided going to the dentist. Drew went to get a brush and some hair bands. If he was going to be arrested for kidnapping, he wanted to make his baby happy one last time.

Nearly forty minutes and what seemed like forty failed attempts at a decent braid later, Drew parked the cruiser in front of Lola's house. "Stay in the car."

Becky undid her booster buckle, hopped over the seat, and reached for the radio. "Can I talk to Flo while I wait?"

"No."

Becky pouted, turning to stare out the window at Lola's house. "Who's that in the window?"

"It's just a doll." The male blow-up doll rode a mounted deer head like a horse. His plastic mistress was nowhere to be seen, but the blond wig Lola had worn last night sat on the deer's head.

"Can I play with her doll? It looks like fun."

"No." Drew hurried up the drive, past the crisply cut grass, past Lola's impractical Fiat, past boxes and bags of Randy's stuff. He pounded on Lola's door.

"Are you finally going to do something about that hideous display?" Ramona Everly called from across the street, standing on a well-kept lawn with mower tracks on it. "Someone should be arrested!"

"But then who would mow your lawn?" That was it. Drew had fallen victim to spring-thaw madness.

Scowling, the older woman retreated, leaving Drew to stab Lola's doorbell. When she didn't answer, Drew pounded on the door again. "Lola, open up!"

"Do you think she's dead?" Bloodthirsty Becky called from the cruiser.

"No." He drew on previously uncalled-upon reserves of patience. "Lola, I know you're in there."

The door swung open. Lola had bedhead to rival Becky's, big loops of brown hair in need of a brush. Her eyes were mere slits, as if alcohol made the light hard to bear. But her lips…her lips were still full and kissable.

Not that Drew had any right to kiss her again.

"Sheriff, if my house isn't on fire, I hope your pants are." She shoved a pair of handcuffs into his chest.

"We need to talk. Can I come in?"

"Why? So you can handcuff me to my banister? No thanks." She tried to close the door.

Drew was quicker, stopping her with the flat of his palm. "I'm sorry. I fell asleep. I never meant to leave you locked up for long."

"You never should have locked me up in the first place." She pushed harder on the door.

Drew didn't let it budge. "If you make a scene, Ramona will call Flo for backup." That shocked Lola enough that he was able to hustle her inside. He rattled his handcuffs at her. "How did you get free? Did you go to Shaw's? Did you accuse another woman of sleeping with Randy?"

The questions continued in his head. Had she tugged the ears of every woman in the bar? Had there been a catfight to rival the cupcake smackdown? Had she been hurt?

He gave Lola's body what should have been a quick and clinical once-over. Mistake. She wore a pair of men's boxers and a clingy tank top. His mouth went dry.

He slapped his forehead to put his rampant thoughts on pause. "Forget all that. How did you get free?"

"I switched your handcuffs with Randy's when we were…" Her cheeks turned a deep shade of pink.

"You knew I was going to cuff you?"

"No." She scowled and ran her fingers through her

hair, only slightly taming the unruly brown locks. "I wanted you to arrest someone with fake cuffs." Her cheeks went from pink to red, and her gaze fell to the floor. "I didn't think you'd use them on me."

He hadn't either. "So you didn't go to Shaw's last night?"

Those blue eyes came firing back up at him. "Why do you always think I'm on the brink of creating an incident?"

"Maybe because you're unlike anyone I've ever known before." Drew swallowed, trying to take it down a notch so her feelings wouldn't be hurt. "I have no idea what you're capable of."

She crossed her arms.

"I need to apologize for last night," he said quickly. "I never should have handcuffed you or left you afterward." What a mess. "Are you going to press charges? I won't talk you out of it." But he prayed she didn't want to. For Becky's sake and his own.

Lola waved her hand as if waving a wand to make the entire episode disappear from their memories. "If I pressed charges, everyone would know what happened. What I wore. That I kissed you." A deeper color emerged on her cheeks. She stared at her bare toes. Her toenails were painted a sparkly, happy purple. "What you did was over the line."

"Yes." He was quick to agree, perhaps quicker to realize his mistake had created a shift in power between them. He being the powerless one, a position he was by no means familiar with and didn't like in the least.

Lola sensed the gain in power too. Her mouth

quirked, and she dropped her hands to her hips. "I think we should make a pact."

"Go on," he said cautiously.

Her blue eyes narrowed. "You stop locking me up and demanding I take Randy down…"

"In exchange for your silence," Drew guessed, relieved.

She nodded. "Shake on it."

"Deal." He didn't have to think twice on the terms. Bullet dodged. Drew clasped Lola's much smaller hand in his. Hers was warm and soft, a contrast to the determined look in her eyes.

"And I want my gun back."

Drew dropped her hand as if it burned. "Too late. That wasn't part of the agreement." He headed for the door. "Apply for a permit if you want it that badly."

She scurried after him. "You were scared, weren't you? When you woke up this morning?"

Her words stopped him at the door, his hand on the knob.

Lola looked a mess, from the crooked part in her hair to her bloodshot eyes to the faded blue boxers she wore. She didn't seem to care how she looked. She was bringing it, challenging Drew as if she were in her man-eater armor.

"Yeah, I was scared." He was man enough to admit it. "But not for the reason you might think. My ex, who doesn't know the meaning of the word *mother*, wants joint custody of Becky."

"You thought your actions last night meant you'd lost Becky." Her gaze softened. "Over something you did in the heat of passion."

He glossed over the mention of passion. "I lost my focus. I made a bad choice." Her kiss may have been the stimulus, but he'd chosen the improper response. "In law enforcement, a bad choice could be catastrophic."

"Deadly." Lola's gaze drifted to the plastic doll posed at the window.

"I prefer the word *catastrophic*."

Lola's gaze was distant but not as spacey as Wendy's. "Randy made a series of bad choices."

"Randy probably didn't see it that way." When her eyes snapped to him, Drew held up his hands. "He didn't strike me as a tortured man." Not by any stretch. Randy had been happy-go-lucky with the disposition of a well-fed Labrador.

"Randy wasn't as content as he appeared. He was searching for something, or he wouldn't have strayed."

"We're all searching," Drew said, more because philosophical ground seemed safer with Lola than re-hashing his mistake last night.

"I'm searching for names." Her slender brows bent together. "But what are you searching for?"

"The perfect sole-custody defense." He smoothed a loop of hair over her ear, as if he touched her hair every day. "And you want answers, not names."

"What I want is peace." Her features scrunched as if she was fighting tears. "Right here." She tapped her chest, letting her gaze fall away and her voice weaken. "Why wasn't I enough for him?"

Drew wanted to know that too. Her kiss would keep any man at home.

They stood without speaking, her looking pained,

him feeling her anguish and wanting to do something about it.

Becky honked the cruiser's horn.

"I need to go." He didn't move, which was stupid. Lola wasn't the woman he needed. It was Wendy. Wendy was the plan. After a week of waiting, they had a date scheduled for tonight.

Lola opened her eyes and stared at the floor. "You should go. Hot chocolate with mile-high whip is only served until eleven."

How did she know that? He'd never seen her in the Saddle Horn on a Sunday until last week. Had she been waiting to go until she had kids of her own? The sadness of it struck Drew like a blow to the gut.

"Why don't you come with us?" As soon as the invitation left his mouth, he regretted it.

Predictably, Lola regretted nothing.

She smiled and accepted.

Chapter Seventeen

♥

Lola had never eaten at the Saddle Horn on a Sunday. Both Randy and Avery had outgrown the whipped cream tradition and pooh-poohed it when she'd asked about it.

To Lola, making whipped cream whiskers was theater she viewed in limited doses when she purchased coffee to go. She wanted an excuse to be able to sit in the audience. Just once. Her acceptance of Drew's offer had nothing to do with the thrilling taste of his kiss and everything to do with the longing to experience Sunshine as one of them.

The Saddle Horn didn't disappoint.

There was Clarice in the corner booth, building layers of white facial hair.

A group of young Holly Scouts sat in the small private room, dunking, dipping, and plunging their faces without any finesse. Their joy more than made up for their amateur efforts.

And then there was Becky, the master of the goatee, sitting next to Lola at the counter with one of the crookedest braids Lola had ever seen. According to Drew's daughter, she had a repertoire of whipped facial hair, but mostly they looked like the same puffy beard and mustache combination.

"Dad said when he was a kid, he could make a pointy mustache. But I think he might be 'xaggerating." Becky babbled, which was great since it meant Drew and Lola didn't have to speak to each other.

What did you say to a man who'd locked you up after a hot kiss? A man you'd bested? A man who was fighting for his daughter?

Becky's hot-pink rainboots clashed with the burnt-orange tank top she wore over pea-green leggings. "But Dad's never shown me, so I don't know if it's true." She flashed her father an impish smile.

Drew drank black coffee and looked straight ahead. Although he wore a tan polo instead of his tan sheriff's shirt, he still sat with rigid authority, as if ready to spring into action when duty called. He didn't rise to Becky's challenge though. "Beard-making is for kids."

"Da-ad."

Lola leaned back on her stool so she could see the Widows Club in the corner booth. "Clarice seems to be having fun." Lola envied the old woman's indifference to what people thought of her.

"Dad misses out on all the fun." Becky waved to Pearl for more whip. "Were you good at Saddle Horn beards when you were little, Ms. Williams?"

"We didn't have a Saddle Horn in New York."

Becky made a horrified sound. "So you've never..."

"Nope."

"Ooh. You have to do it." Becky clapped her hands. "It's fun. You'll see."

Drew's mouth might have twitched up, and his glance meandered Lola's way but Lola knew it wasn't her reaction he was enjoying. He was a dedicated father, unlike her own, and he'd do anything to protect and keep his daughter. He was the father every man should be. The dad she'd wished for as a child. When he'd told her about the challenge to his custody of Becky, she'd known she was right not to tell anyone he'd handcuffed her to a bed.

Drew turned to Becky and Lola. His eyes gleamed with that rare humor that made Lola's heart beat faster. "Lola's fully grown." Meaning she was too old for mile-high whips.

Something wild and thrilling took hold of Lola, an energetic, freeing sense that she could be herself. With Drew and Becky. All she needed to make the moment complete was Avery. Her necklace was in Lola's purse. Her apology on the tip of Lola's tongue.

"Lola won't do it," Drew teased.

Lola raised her hand to catch Pearl's attention. "One adult-size hot chocolate. Right here. For the woman who's brave enough to *get 'er done.*"

"Really?" Becky grinned.

"Oh yeah, I'm doing it." She wasn't brave enough to grin at Drew so she beamed at Becky instead.

Pearl set a mug in front of Lola that seemed to be a foot tall, a guaranteed messy-faced sugar high with a certain crash later.

"It's not for the faint of heart," Drew murmured with that teasing glint in his eyes, egging her on.

Had she ever thought Drew wasn't as handsome as Randy? That he was stiff and stuffy? She'd been wrong on both counts.

"Like this?" Lola asked Becky, and without waiting for an answer, she plunged face-first into the mountain of whipped cream. She lifted her head and swiveled in her stool to show Becky. "What does it look like?" Lola asked without moving her lips. "Why aren't there mirrors in here?"

And then Lola remembered she had her cell phone. She swiveled her back to Becky and took a selfie of the two of them and their bearded faces. Drew sat in the background, drinking his coffee but smiling at his daughter this time.

"You can make a bad-guy beard." Becky pinched the whipped cream near her little chin. "But if you try too hard, it melts." Half of Becky's beard plopped into her lap.

Lola laughed.

Drew handed Becky a napkin faster than you could say, *Melted snowman.*

Becky did a good job of smearing whip across her leggings. And then she wiped her mouth clean with one big circular motion. She crumpled her napkin and tossed it on the counter. "Try again, Ms. Williams."

While Lola cleaned her face, Wendy Adams entered the coffee shop, holding the door for Marcia (she of the no longer blue hair), who took one look at Lola and scurried to a back booth where her daughter, Barbara, sat with a toddler. Wendy walked right to the stool on the other side of Drew and sat down.

It seemed as though Drew went from relaxed to high alert, like an unprepared understudy who suddenly found himself on stage. He gathered his shoulders (probably to make him seem larger), put on a smile (seemingly forced but pleasant), and barely contained a sigh (possibly resigned).

Okay, the latter assessment might have been wishful thinking on Lola's part.

Wendy wasn't a discerning theater critic. She smiled at Drew as if his performance were Oscar-worthy. And then she critiqued Lola's participation in the Saddle Horn's tradition with the barest of frowns.

Deep inside Lola, jealousy rumbled awake, urging her to harden her stare, to lean forward and catch Drew's eye, to mark her territory. That's what Avery would do. But Avery had more confidence than Lola when it came to men.

Lola placed her palms together and slid them between her legs. She had no more right to claim Drew than Avery did to claim Randy. That didn't stop her from staring at the pair and wondering why Drew was dating Wendy and kissing Lola.

Or maybe he wasn't dating Wendy. They exchanged a greeting that was practically a handshake.

Bitsy appeared at Lola's shoulder and asked her to accompany the Widows Club board on Monday to pick up the clothing for their fashion show. Lola was so shocked by the Drew-Wendy thing that she agreed, although it meant she had to reschedule her retirement home appointments.

"Hey, Ms. Williams." Becky dipped her face in the

whip and scooped it with her chin. The motion created an almost pointy beard. She thrust her chin toward Lola. "Do yours."

Instead of dunking her face in the whip, Lola raised her mug and drew it around her face as if it were lipstick.

"You made whiskers like my Aunt Eileen's pig." Becky giggled, causing a drip, creating a chain reaction in Drew, who cleaned her face with a supply of napkins. When he was done, Becky leaned over and whispered, "Ms. Adams wants to marry my dad."

Lola snorted whipped cream up her nose.

Drew's spine stiffened, and he turned to stare at his daughter with his stern cop face. "*Becky*..."

Becky shrugged. "Granny Susie says it's true."

* * *

On paper, Wendy was perfect for Drew.

She lived at home to help care for her mother, who had multiple sclerosis. She had a solid employment record working with kids. She'd never been arrested. (Yeah, Drew had checked.) And she looked good in a pink calico dress and cowboy boots.

But she was as boring as a glass of water on a table filled with imported beer. And in a loud, colorful Mexican restaurant, Drew could drink a lot of imported beer.

He sat across the table from Wendy, demolishing a basket of chips and salsa and washing it down with a Corona. Stress was building in his chest like plaque in an old man's artery.

After only fifteen minutes of their date, he was tired of holding one-sided conversations. Wendy sat across from him, stirring guacamole with a chip and nodding at everything he said.

Drew should be willing to put up with one-sided conversations. Wendy was his best defense against losing primary custody of Becky. He'd keep to the plan unless he met with Rupert Harper on Wednesday and heard differently. Rupert's secretary had promised he'd come by the sheriff's office first thing the day he returned from vacation.

Still…Wendy's lips didn't entice him like Lola's. Her conversation didn't keep him on his toes like Lola's. And her presence didn't make him want to smile like Lola's.

Drew crumbled a chip in one hand. He needed to stop thinking about Lola.

The door to Los Consuelos opened, and Pris walked in with Eileen. They stopped at the hostess stand and spotted him.

Saved!

Drew waved his sisters over.

"You don't mind if my sisters join us, do you?" Drew didn't wait for Wendy's agreement. He scooted toward the wall and indicated to his siblings that they should fill the booth.

Pris hesitated at the table, holding Eileen back with a nearly imperceptibly placed elbow. Pris wore black boots, jeans, and a plunging blouse that she tugged higher when a teenage busboy stopped wiping a table to stare at her. She might have been looking for male attention but obviously she drew the line at jailbait.

"Hey, guys," Pris said casually, as if she ran into her brother with a woman every day. "Are you having dinner together?"

"We are but we just ordered." Drew bared his teeth in what he hoped wasn't the smile of a man backed into a corner. "You can join us. My treat."

If Pris noted the desperate look in his eyes, she made no note of it. Her elbow came down and she sat next to Wendy, most likely so she could smirk at Drew, because that's what she did immediately, as if to say, *I was right about Wendy, wasn't I? Milk toast?*

Drew signaled their waitress and latched on to a topic of conversation before Pris did. "Eileen, how is Rosie?"

Eileen was fiddling with a set of plastic bandages on her knuckles. She put her hands under the table and out of sight. She was dressed to work at the rescue shelter in black rubber boots, stained gray sweats, and a dingy green Sunshine High School T-shirt that was so old the buffalo's horns had worn off. "Rosie is good. She's a gem. She's absolutely no trouble."

In addition to damaging Eileen's fingers, Rosie had probably trashed Eileen's house down to the studs. And what would happen when Rosie lost enough weight to see again and was ready to go to a new home? Eileen would call Drew to repair the damage, just as she had that time she'd rescued a llama and it'd pawed through her backyard fence.

"Rosie could use a dog walker." Apparently, Pris

had more than witnessing Drew's embarrassment on her mind.

Drew half expected her to ask him to change the oil in her car too, which, come to think of it, was probably due.

"I think the Bodine boys could use some extra work." Drew sat back in the booth, pushing the basket of chips toward Eileen. "They're in shape, and they'll have time since high school baseball is coming to a close."

Pris tsk-tsked. "Eileen doesn't have the money to pay anyone."

Eileen nodded, confiscating Drew's salsa bowl and digging in as if it was her first meal of the day. "I need a volunteer. Someone strong enough to hold her. Someone who can sing a good lullaby."

"I'm busy," Drew grumbled.

Wendy was watching them and smiling wanly as if happy to be sitting with them. "Is Rosalie okay?" she asked.

"She needs to lose weight," Eileen said, having missed the subtext of the question while cleaning out the chip basket. "It's affecting her eyesight."

"Rosalie's going blind?" Wendy's forehead scrunched. "That's horrible."

"Eileen rescued a pig called *Rosie*," Drew explained patiently. "We're not talking about Rosalie Bollinger." He raised his beer bottle, intending to take a drink.

"Rosie and Rosalie. I was mixed up," Wendy said with a flash of a smile that was more than milk toast. "Have you seen Lola Williams's window? A man riding a deer. It made me laugh."

The salsa Pris had loaded on her chip fell to the table. Drew set his beer down untouched.

Shy, withdrawn Wendy had a sense of humor. Maybe things weren't as grim as he'd thought. Maybe there was a personality to Wendy after all, buried deep down where only the most desperate of men could find it.

"I thought her window was funny too." Eileen signaled the waitress for more chips. "I drive by it every day. Why is she doing it?"

"Who knows?" Drew's sister was getting them off track. "Do you have any pets, Wendy?" Drew motioned to the waitress to bring him another beer.

"I have a tortoise. He lives in my basement." Wendy slid a glance Drew's way. "He's not as exciting as a pig. He doesn't need walking."

Pris raised her brows, and Drew could almost tell what his sister was thinking: *She has a pet she keeps in her basement… along with her personality.*

Drew shook his head, brushing his sister off. Wendy had just given a big speech. He continued to be heartened and waited for Wendy to say more.

And waited…

"What's your turtle's name?" Drew couldn't stand it any longer. This was almost a conversation.

"Archie. And he's a tortoise," Wendy said tolerantly.

Pris leaned back and studied Wendy. "How old is Archie?"

Wendy shrugged.

"How did you find a turtle…" Even Eileen was caught up in it now. "Er… a tortoise in Colorado?"

"I visited an animal rescue."

Eileen frowned. "You haven't visited *my* animal rescue."

"I already have a pet." Wendy took a bite of a chip.

"There's logic to that, I suppose," Eileen said, oddly supportive.

Pris's eyebrows went higher, as if to say, *Whose side is she on?*

Drew gave Pris a very brief, very dark look.

"Have you heard anything from Jane?" Eileen asked, further proving she wasn't with the program. She should've known the topic of Jane was taboo in front of Wendy.

Wendy blinked and then stared at Drew.

"I haven't heard a word from her." Drew brought the near-empty basket of chips closer and took one. "How am I going to walk a pig who can't see?"

"Oh, she's very docile." Eileen took the bait. "She heels better than any dog I've rescued."

"She has a leash," Pris said with a superior expression, possibly imagining Drew walking her.

"Oh, you've taken Rosie out, Pris?" Drew bared his teeth.

"Nope." Pris returned his smile in kind. "I just saw her leash."

"Tomorrow," Wendy said.

As one, the Taylors looked at her.

"You should walk Rosie tomorrow, Drew." Wendy brushed the few chip crumbs she'd made to the side of the table. "Since she needs to lose weight."

The woman he intended to marry wanted him to walk a pig? How could Drew refuse?

Chapter Eighteen

♥

"What are you doing here so early?" Eileen opened the door a crack on Monday morning and stared at Drew as if she hadn't had her first cup of coffee.

Behind Drew, the last efforts of a weak spring storm spit at the cruiser's windshield.

Behind Eileen, Rosie grunted in the same unwelcome tone as his sister's greeting.

"I'm here to walk the pig." He usually spent the hour after dropping Becky off at school making rounds, but if walking an overweight piece of bacon helped make Eileen's life safer, it was worth rearranging his schedule. Besides, it kept him from driving past Lola's house.

His sister didn't open the door, smile, or say, *Thanks for coming*. Something clanked behind her. It sounded like a fork settling on china.

A breakfasting guest realizing the law was at the door?

Drew shifted his weight to the balls of his feet, ready to charge inside. "Is there someone in there?" Someone besides an overweight pig?

"No." Eileen's cheeks flushed. She was lying.

His sisters lied to him all the time. Little white lies about why they were short on cash. Bold-faced lies about where they'd been the night before. Brave lies told around sniffles after a breakup, reassuring him they'd be fine.

What kind of lie was Eileen trying to get past him?

Drew inched closer to the door and saw that the white paint on its frame was peeling. "Is it Tyrell? I told you to call me if he came back. I told you I'd take care of him." Drew's hands fisted.

"*No.*" Eileen stuffed that one word with more sibling disgust than Pris and the twins combined. She gave the doorknob a quick turn and release, as if she were revving a motorcycle engine at a red light, preparing to leave the car in the lane beside her behind. "I changed my mind." Her brown eyes didn't often flare with rebellion. They were on fire now. "I don't need your help."

Drew stopped listening to his sister and took stock of the situation. Eileen's SUV and his cruiser were the only vehicles in her driveway. Her dark hair hung about her shoulders, thick and frizzing from the humidity. She wore a man's red T-shirt that bunched over her hips (he couldn't remember whether he'd seen it before), a pair of black sweats Drew could swear had belonged to him once, and fuzzy pink slippers with a hole revealing her big toe. Her fingers were still bandaged but there were circles under her eyes that hadn't been there last night. If Eileen was in trouble, it came with four hooves and several hundred pounds of bacon.

"Eileen..."

She pursed her lips.

It had stopped raining altogether. Inside, something cracked, something as fragile as china. The pig made an anxious sound.

"What was that?" Drew did more than inch forward. He filled the doorway, breathing in a barnyard scent that was anything but reassuring.

Eileen cast a worried glance behind her. "Keep your voice down."

Drew was done talking. He rested his hands on his duty belt and fixed Eileen with the look he gave speeders near the interstate, the look that said he had a fresh ticket book and a quota to fill. That look caused lawbreakers to confess every time.

Eileen was caving. "If I let you in, you can't lecture."

If? He was already through the door. "Me? Lecture?" And then the state of her house registered. Drew didn't dare move, didn't dare take his hands off his belt for fear he'd reach for his weapon and shoot Rosie.

Every stick of furniture was smashed, except for the couch where Rosie lay. The lower kitchen-cabinet doors were cracked. The humongous litter box had been overturned and trampled. A square shovel had been used to scoop up excrement from the wood floor.

Drew swallowed back his disgust and took shallow breaths.

"I can explain." Eileen stepped in front of him and whispered, "It wasn't Rosie's fault."

"*You* did this?" Not likely.

"It was my fault." Eileen kept up that desperate secret-pouring whisper. "I was asleep, and I felt a body get into bed with me. I screamed. Rosie panicked. And..." Her eyes teared up. "Before I could calm her down, she'd done all this. By the time I got her relaxed, she was in my bed, and I couldn't sleep." Her eyes swept the room. Her expression crumpled. "What am I going to do? It's all ruined. Go ahead. You can say it. I'm a failure."

"You're not a failure," Drew said wearily. "You're in trouble, that's all."

The pig rolled off the couch, ambled over to Eileen, and sat on her foot the way any loyal, loving, paws-too-big-for-his-brain puppy would when he knew he'd done wrong.

There were two ways Drew could proceed. The first was the most obvious. Read Eileen the riot act, bully her into turning over custody of the pig, and invite the family over next week for barbecued spareribs. It was so logical that he almost didn't consider the second option at all.

But he'd been picking up after his sisters for too long to let logic rule where they were concerned. Drew pulled his sister into his arms and gave her a hearty hug. "It's going to be all right."

Her shoulders tensed and then shook as she began to cry. "*How how how how ho-ow?*"

"Shhh." Drew patted her on the back and stared down at the pig, whose eyes he could almost see. "We'll figure something out."

Rosie turned her face his way and snorted, but it was an appreciative kind of snort, not a derogatory one.

"Why don't you open up the windows and then shower?" Drew would've released Eileen from the hug but she held on, still sobbing. He needed more solutions to this mess. "I'll take Rosie to the station and put her in jail. It's quiet in there, and she should get some rest." Not to mention he could return to Eileen's and clean the place out while she was at work.

"Behave," Drew said to Rosie a few minutes later as he walked her down the sidewalk. "We're going to kill two birds with one stone and go on my rounds."

He'd walked rescue dogs for Eileen with worse manners than Rosie. The pig ambled along at his heel, most likely so she could follow him blindly.

The streets were nearly empty. Those who drove by gave him shocked stares. Drew walked through the old residential district, passing the Victorian he'd grown up in. Thankfully, his mom wasn't an early riser. Pris lived in a small Craftsman converted into a duplex around the corner, which was down the street from Lola's house.

It was trash day. Most residents had their cans on the curb already. Not Pris. Her curb was neat and her car gone, which was odd considering she didn't have to be at work at the bank for another forty-five minutes. Drew made a mental note to swing by to take her cans out after he got Rosie settled in jail, and walked on.

At the intersection he'd just crossed, a car took a corner too fast. Rosie stopped, dead weight behind him.

Drew turned, half expecting to see Clarice barreling down the street in her faded blue minivan.

Pris scraped her front end as she sailed up her driveway. She hopped out of her car and froze when she saw Drew. Her dark hair was mussed, and she wore the same clothes she'd had on last night at dinner with Wendy.

"Really?" Drew turned around and paced the length

of the leash, unable to go any farther with Rosie in anchor mode. “The walk of shame?”

Rosie snuffled nervously.

“Don’t judge.” Pris shook her finger at him. “And don’t lecture.”

This time, Drew had no choice but to lecture. “Can’t you date like a normal person without…” His hand wound in circles in the air.

“You’re just jealous because Wendy would never present the opportunity to get shameful.” Pris backed up to the porch steps, raising her voice for the neighbors to hear. “And you wouldn’t do anything if Wendy was easy, because you’re a pious…” She stomped on a step. “Boring…” She stomped on another. “Eunich!” She leaped onto the porch, landing with both feet. And then she opened the front door and slammed it behind her.

“You were gone all night, and you didn’t lock your door?” he shouted after her.

His sister’s reply was muffled, but Rosie squealed as if in agony.

“Don’t you have a meltdown too.” Drew returned to her side and gave her a pat.

Snorting nonstop, Rosie bumped her head against his knee in a love tap strong enough to bruise.

A loud engine roared down another street, heading their way.

Rosie’s ears twitched. She squealed again, louder this time.

“No no, piggy.” Drew stroked her ears closed, speaking in baby talk. “It’s just a truck. A big loud truck. It’ll drive past. You’ll see.”

A few houses down, someone dragged their trash can to the curb with a loud rumble.

Rosie was trembling now, releasing off-key squeals like an opera singer struggling to hit the right high note.

A large white truck with a lift kit and a holey muffler rounded the corner. Iggy King leaned out the open window. "Nice dog, Sheriff!" He hit his horn. *A-ooo-gah! A-ooo-gah!*

Rosie bolted faster than a defensive end blitzing the quarterback, dragging Drew into a sprint behind her. Her panicked wails twined with Iggy's hearty guffaws.

In an effort to stop, Drew dug in his heels and leaned against the leash. He had to lean back, or he'd fall forward and be dragged, because he wasn't letting go. Dragging was most likely how Eileen's knuckles had gotten scraped.

Rosie plowed on, past Joni Russell's house, past the Bastions' place, and toward Lola's. Lola was dumping black towels into her trash can, which was on the sidewalk.

Despite the pace, despite the shock of hard pavement beneath his boots, Drew didn't panic. He shouted commands. "Lola, throw a towel on her and get out of the way."

Iggy gunned his truck forward and parked in Lola's driveway, blocking the sidewalk with one oversized rear wheel in case Rosie got past Lola's trash can.

This is not going to end well.

Lola shook out a towel and held it in front of her body like a reckless bullfighter. Before Drew could say anything, Iggy pushed Lola out of the way and grabbed the towel. Lola stumbled in her heels and landed on her butt on her lawn.

Rosie crashed into Lola's trash can. Iggy tossed the towel over her head. Together, the men tackled the pig on Lola's grass. Not surprisingly, Rosie's hooves kept galloping.

"Just... like... old... times," Iggy rasped from beneath the hog pile. They'd played defense together on the high school football team.

"That a girl." Drew rubbed the massive pig's belly. "She can't see and gets stressed out by loud noises."

"My... bad," Iggy rasped.

Lola came to stand in Drew's line of vision. All he could see were her legs. She wore tight jeans that had red bows fastened at each ankle and black half boots with a tall heel. "You have a pet pig?"

Drew explained Rosie's situation to his landlady and then sang an urgent rendition of "Rock-A-Bye Baby."

Lola added her voice and knelt in front of Rosie. She had her brown hair in a French braid and wore a blue checked button-down that accentuated her curves without showing an inch of cleavage.

Why couldn't Pris dress more like Lola?

"Not... singing." Iggy's face was turning red.

"Easy now." Drew got to his feet when Rosie had calmed, and helped the pig to hers.

Still draped in a black towel, Rosie pressed her snout against Lola's thigh and snuffled.

"Yes. That must have been very scary," Lola said sympathetically, scratching Rosie behind her ears.

"Pigs." Iggy stood, stretched from side to side,

cracking his back, and then returned to his truck. "I'll stick with bulls."

"Are you okay?" Drew asked Lola softly.

"Maybe you should be asking Rosie that." She smiled but not big enough to show her dimple.

Drew wanted to kiss her good morning. Why couldn't he want to kiss Wendy?

A surge of annoyance made him say, "Next time a pig charges you, hold the towel to the side. If Iggy wasn't around, you would've been trampled."

Smirking, Iggy was backing out of the driveway. "Way to thank a woman, Taylor."

Using the leash, Drew led Rosie back to his side. "Lola knows I'm grateful and thinking about her safety."

"I suppose," Lola said grudgingly. "Sometimes it's hard to tell when you're being the sheriff and not Drew. What's next? A lecture about my window?"

"No." The drapes were closed, which was a relief until Drew noticed a plastic arm holding a lacy bra extending between the curtains. "And I don't always lecture people." But Lola was the third woman to chastise him about lecturing this morning. And it wasn't even nine.

He led Rosie toward the sidewalk. "It's a sheriff's job to be honest." Criminy. If he were being honest, he'd admit he wanted to see her dimpled smile again.

"There's a difference between supportive honesty and being a pessimistic pain in the neck."

Drew rubbed the back of his neck before he realized what he was doing, and dropped his hand. He should find out whom Pris was getting busy with and tell them to back off, because they were rebound bait. He should give up on Rosie, load her into the back of the cruiser, and take her to the Bodine ranch. He should call his mother and ask her to meet him at Eileen's to help clean out the place.

Instead of attending to the hard duties of older brother and sheriff, he turned at the sidewalk and leaned down to pet Rosie so he could spend a few more minutes with Lola. "Does it hurt your feelings? When I tell you the hard truth?" He kept his gaze on the pig. It was safer than looking at the attractive woman on the lawn.

"Sometimes the truth hurts no matter who points it out to you." Lola meandered to the end of the driveway.

His eyes started at the pointed toe of her boots, up those legs, across those gentle curves, and landed on her face. "You're beautiful."

"And you…" Lola stepped closer, bringing a light flowery scent that was worlds different than Rosie smell. She smoothed his uniform over his shoulders, letting her palms rest there, letting her gaze rest on his.

His hand found its way to her hip. His mind encouraged his mouth to find its way to hers.

Rosie sighed and sat on his foot, as if he needed a reminder that he'd chosen a different path, an uninspired, humdrum path. One that would ensure Becky stayed true to her Taylor genes.

Lola sighed too, letting her hands drift to her sides, easing his hand free. "You're dating Wendy."

He opened his mouth to deny it but nothing came out.

She glanced across the street to Ramona Everly's house and lowered her voice. "Someone went through

Randy's stuff. I put a tarp over it last night. It's been moved, and some things are missing."

"Things you wanted to donate to the thrift store?" The items Ricky had turned down.

Her eyes narrowed. "Yes. Can you dust for prints? In case it was one of Randy's mistresses?"

"No."

"Why not?"

"Because I'm tired of hearing about Randy and his lovers." Rosie bumped into his leg, and he softened his tone. "You want the truth from someone who's flawed? Take it from me. The past will trip you up if you don't move on."

He should have seen Jane coming. He should have gotten remarried long ago. He'd just never come across anyone who made him want to share his life, his bed, his closet…

His gaze fell to the high heels of Lola's boots. "Those shoes aren't practical for the high country."

Lola sniffed and whirled away, tossing over her shoulder, "Who said I was practical?"

And that was the trouble.

Lola wasn't practical.

She was Jane all over again.

* * *

"I should have driven," Lola said in a stress-punctured voice.

Mims patted Lola's knee while Clarice parked her minivan at the mall in Greeley. She was used to her friend's radical driving style. Much as she liked Lola, despite all her drama, she was a distraction from Mims's goal of matching Edith. Bitsy had never gotten with the program as it pertained to Edith. It was the poker game all over again. The matchmaking board remained divided.

"But if you drove"—Clarice glanced over her shoulder at Lola—"we wouldn't all fit in your little car."

They could have squeezed into Mims's Subaru or Bitsy's compact sedan. Mims drew the line at Edith's small truck. It was bad enough the woman had wormed her way into the trip. Three months ago, before Charlie died, Mims wouldn't have allowed it. She'd have been firm in her refusal. She'd have known what to say to help Lola settle down. She'd have known how to get herself out of this funk.

"The dresses wouldn't fit in Lola's car either," Bitsy added from the front seat.

"I meant, I should have driven for you." Lola released her seat belt. "I can drive us home."

"Why?" Clarice shook her head. "The seat and mirrors are adjusted for me."

"She doesn't like your driving," Edith said in a loud voice, most likely in case Clarice wasn't wearing her hearing aids.

"You don't have to shout." Clarice tapped her ears, pointing out her hearing aids were in. She opened her door. "There's no problem with my driving. I've never gotten a ticket or been in an accident."

"*Yet*," Lola added under her breath.

Mims patted her knee again. "It's best if you remember

her clean accident record." Whereas Mims had backed into someone at the supermarket last month. "And better if you don't dwell on her technique." She dug in her purse for gum, finding it beneath her handgun.

Everyone got out and walked toward the largest department store at the mall. Lola brought up the rear, her heels keeping a slow cadence behind them.

"We're meeting with the nicest man." Mims sidled closer to Edith. "Sonny Baker. He's the store manager. He's always supportive of our causes. And he's single."

Edith glanced back at Lola, who was falling behind with Bitsy.

"Lola, dear," Bitsy said in her pleasing customer service voice, "I was wondering if you felt up to doing the fashion show."

"I'm fine. My hips are a little stiff from my cupcake fall but..." Lola cleared her throat. "But that's not what you're asking. You're wondering if I'll behave."

Lola may have been going through a rough patch but she was one sharp cookie.

"It's not that we don't want you there," Bitsy said before Mims could say Lola passing on the show was for the best. "It's just that we don't want any...disruptions."

"I understand," Lola said woodenly, immediately eliciting Mims's sympathy and causing the Widows Club president some guilt.

"Everyone's welcome to model," Mims said gruffly.

"I remember the first time I was widowed." Bitsy held on to her black hair bow against a stiff gust of wind. "It took me a long time to get over Jim's death."

"Longer than a year?" That note in Lola's voice… Was it loneliness?

Mims glanced back. Lola's eyes were wide and a bit teary.

Bitsy was nodding. "And do you know what finally made the pain ease?"

Mims's toe caught on the pavement. She turned back around before she could fall and break a hip.

"No," Lola said. "What?"

"I met my second husband, Terry."

Mims was reminded why the Matchmakers Club existed—to help women find true love. If only Edith would fall for a man's charms, then Mims could help Lola find a new purpose in life.

"I don't think a new man can answer the questions left by my old one." Lola's voice was firm.

"Sometimes a new man makes the old questions less important," Bitsy soothed as they reached the department store's doors.

Only then did Mims realize Edith had been unusually silent. She hoped she got the message Bitsy was sending: *Love heals*.

A distinguished-looking gentleman wearing a crisp shirt the same color as his white hair and a plain burgundy tie unlocked the glass door for them and held it open. Sonny Baker always made a good first impression. He wore glossy black loafers, a big shiny watch, and a lady-killer smile. If he couldn't charm Edith out of the Widows Club, no man could.

"My girls!" He hugged the board, complimenting each woman. Bitsy on her ruffled silk blouse. Clarice on her comfortable shoes. Mims on the pink purse she'd bought used online. "And who are these two lovely ladies?"

"Two of our models." Mims introduced Edith and Lola.

"Edith." Sonny kissed the back of her hand. "Welcome to the team." He surveyed Edith as if she were a line of shoes he was considering buying. And then he took Edith's arm and whisked her inside. "I chose all the ensembles and accessories. This year, I added pantsuits."

"I requested a bikini," Edith said testily, head swiveling back and forth as if she'd never been in a department store before.

"No bathing suits," Mims hissed.

"That's against the rules," Clarice added.

Sonny chuckled. "As I recall, I chose an evening gown for you, Edith." He led them to a back room with a rack of clothing on wheels and a box filled with accessories and handbags. He handed Mims a clipboard. "Here's your list of what we chose, along with the names and sizes of the models you gave us. I added product descriptions your emcee can read for each model." Flashing his well-rehearsed smile, Sonny produced a business card from his wallet and handed it to Edith. "If you need anything, call me. Or walk down the hall until you find the biggest office." He winked. "And we can talk."

He'd laid it on too thick. Mims shook her head.

Sonny was a ladies' man, and he enjoyed the finer things in life. He might not whisk Edith away from

Sunshine forever but he might be the distraction she needed to realize she could love more than one man in her lifetime.

Edith watched Sonny walk away, a frown wrinkling her already wrinkled brow. And then she handed the business card to Lola. "I think this is for you."

Mims nearly choked on her gum.

Lola dropped back a step and waved Edith off. "He didn't kiss my hand or ask me to his office."

Edith stared at the card again. "Whatever would he want with an old biddy like me?"

"A dinner date," Clarice suggested, taking a seat in a chair in the corner.

"A cruise companion," Bitsy said somewhat wistfully, stroking a purple feather on an evening gown.

Trying to keep her tone casual, Mims didn't look up from the clipboard. "Someone to take moonlit walks with."

"He was clearly smitten," Lola said with a straight face.

Mims nearly hugged Lola for joining their cause.

"He's after the wrong gal." Edith picked up the gown with the purple feathers and pulled a face. "And the wrong dress."

"I don't know." Mims angled the clipboard so Edith could see the list Sonny had made. "It says right here, 'Purple-Passion Plumes for Edith.' The ideal choice for a romantic dinner at the Bar None." Which was the most expensive steakhouse in Greeley.

Edith studied Sonny's card and said nothing for a long time.

Chapter Nineteen

♥

The light was on in the garage apartment when Drew got home near midnight.

He sent his teenage babysitter home and changed out of his uniform, locking his gun in the safe. Becky was sprawled on her stomach in bed, her arm dangling over the edge of the mattress. Drew rolled her over and tucked her in. And then he went to the garage apartment to check on Lola.

There was no music. No candlelight. No woman dancing.

Drew was almost disappointed.

Lola sat on the floor in the corner, her back against the wall, staring at the bed. Her hair was looped high on her head. She wore a pair of plain black leggings, a plain gray jacket, and a plain old frown.

When she didn't acknowledge Drew, he sat on the floor nearby, back to the wall, legs stretched out in front of him. "Looking for clues?"

"Looking for perspective." She leaned her head against the wall and gazed at the ceiling. "My dad left my mom for the pregnant woman he was having an affair with. Would he have stayed if they had better birth control?"

It was easy to see where she was going with this line of thought. "Randy didn't leave you."

"But he might have. Eventually. If the condoms failed." She turned her head to look at him.

There was pain in her blue eyes, and something else. Something he couldn't quite place. Something that reached into his chest and took hold.

"I was in a race without knowing I was in the running." Lola's eyes drifted toward the blue bedspread. "Remember, Randy married me even though technically he didn't ask. He had some measure of honor. If one of his mistresses had gotten pregnant, he'd have left me."

"Then it would have been his loss." Drew knew it was true.

Judging by the worried slant to her eyes, he could tell she didn't believe him. "After Dad left, every little thing was a big deal to my mom. She couldn't let things go, especially if she felt lied to." She slipped Drew a sideways smile, so fleeting he might have missed it if he hadn't been staring at her. "I know I can overreact a little sometimes."

"Cue sarcasm."

"And when Mom finally got her head on straight where Dad was concerned, she clung to me." She hugged her knees. "Well, not exactly me. But the idea of me. Of family. Of something that was hers that couldn't be taken away like a husband could. A daughter she wanted to make sure had her eyes wide open so she'd never make her mother's mistakes." Lola sniffed but it wasn't a juicy, I'm-about-to-cry sniff. It was more of a draw-a-breath-for-courage sniff. "You'd think I'd be the wiser, what with all her clinging and prophesizing."

He nodded, thinking about being broadsided by Jane.

"I was lucky. I had my grandmother, who was the most positive woman on the planet. She wanted me to follow my dreams…" Her voice trailed off, and then she added in a soft voice, "Just like Avery's grandmother did. I miss Avery so much. She won't answer my calls or texts."

"You'll patch things up with her." Drew reached across the space dividing them and took her cold hand.

Lola stared at his fingers wrapped around hers. "When my half sister was born, my grandmother took me to visit. My dad barely acknowledged my presence. He held his new daughter and told her and his new wife how much he loved them."

"But not you." He laced his fingers with hers. "What an idiot."

She shrugged. "When Randy came along, I told myself my mother wasn't right about love being shallow. Randy loved me deeply. But I was wrong, and Mom was right." Lola squeezed Drew's hand, just a gentle pulse, more of a reflex than a need to strengthen their connection. "One way or the other, people leave. Dad left Mom. I left Mom to come here. Jane left you." Lola raised those blue eyes to his. "If Randy hadn't died, he'd have left me eventually, right?"

Drew wanted to say no. But he was a man of the law.

Right and wrong. Facts versus circumstantial evidence. He had no proof. "It might help if you asked me questions I could answer."

"I save the hard ones for you." She tried to laugh, leaning back against the wall. "This is where you tell me I shouldn't let things like this keep me up at night." She spoke so calmly, without drama or self-pity, without any of the myriad emotional demands his sisters tossed at him.

She wasn't in a place that was Wonderful. She wasn't in Woe-Is-Me or Watch-Out-World mode. Wherever she was, Drew hadn't mapped it before.

Lola was waiting for him to say something. He'd prefer she talk so he could puzzle out her mood, find something in his past he could compare it to, and put it in context. But talk, he did.

"It's no secret my father left my family and didn't look back. I guess when I returned to Sunshine and saw Jane after all those years..." Drew, who prided himself on his interrogation skills, couldn't remember how to keep his mouth shut. He felt his way through the past, shoulders tense. "Jane with all her dreams of leaving Sunshine...In a way...I thought..."

"That you could stop her," Lola finished for him.

The accuracy of her words relaxed his shoulders, relaxed the stopper he kept on his past. "I'd been overseas. I'd been a big-city cop in New York. Jane didn't know how good she had it here." Explosions. Gunshots. Turf wars. Angry commuters. Angry protestors. Angry tourists. "We got married, and I told her we could move someday."

She squeezed his hand again. "But you didn't really mean it. You love it here."

How did Lola know that when Jane hadn't? "I thought she'd settle down and embrace the idea of staying." Of singing on Saturday nights at Shaw's or Sunday in church.

"She had to experience the world beyond Sunshine for herself." Lola's eyes were luminous.

She understood. The feeling he couldn't identify in his chest ratcheted tighter. "I don't regret it. I have Becky."

"I sense a *but* coming."

The tension returned to his shoulder blades, this time as a knot he had no idea how to unravel. Lola was the type of woman he didn't want. Impulsive. Controversial. Unpopular. And she'd said she was going to leave town once she had her answers. It made no sense that he wanted to pull her into his lap, wrap his arms around her, and kiss her senseless.

Well, it would have made perfect sense if Becky were quiet and grounded, like her best friend, Mia, and Jane weren't coming back to town.

Lola continued to stare into his eyes. Maybe she expected a kiss. Maybe she just had a way of looking at a man, any man, with an intensity that could be mistaken for interest. Whatever she felt, whatever the reason she looked at him that way, he had no right to mirror that longing back at her.

It was time he admitted it to himself. He was attracted to Lola. Her wit. Her humor. Her legs. Her kindness.

She deserves to know why I can't kiss her.

The knot in his shoulder blades doubled. Drew didn't

want to tell her. He eased his shoulders back against the wall and stared at the bed.

Hadn't he just been thinking that Lola deserved to be treated with more respect? If he didn't tell her now, she'd know in a few days when Jane returned.

"I need a wife." Drew tried to shrug. It felt more like a shudder.

Lola released his hand. Hers fluttered in the air before she figured out what to do with it. A knee pat (his). A hair pat (hers).

If only Lola were Wendy, this was where Drew would happily pull her into his lap and kiss her. He'd propose marriage—people were marrying strangers all the time on television. Not that he and Lola were strangers. Because they knew each other, they had a better shot than most. But…

Not only was Lola not holding his hand, she was scooting back from him.

Which was good. Excellent, really. He might as well tell her the rest. "I need a wife who's stable, above reproach, and respected in the community. I don't know if you're familiar with Judge Harper but when it comes to family law, give an uncaring ex-wife an inch, and he'll give her a mile."

Lola stared at him as if he'd grown a snout and straggly whiskers. "I didn't come here tonight to start something with you."

"I didn't say you did." His voice was barely above a whisper. "I wanted you to know why I can't kiss you again, why even holding your hand is a one-and-done experience."

He knew the moment she understood what he was saying—that she wasn't in the running for the position of wife—by the way her jaw firmed and her eyes took on a chill.

"Lola—"

"You need to stop talking. You... You need to stop talking *to me*."

"I'm clearing the air." Trying to keep himself honest and his hands off her.

She shook her head. "You're making yourself feel better, because I'm not good enough to be a pawn you use in some game against your ex-wife. That would be Wendy." She scrambled to her feet, one hand over her abdomen, halfway between her stomach and her heart. "Wendy, who you treat like a secretary, while you... you kissed me." She pulled in a deep breath and met his gaze. "Let me make this harder on you. I liked kissing you. I've thought about kissing you again."

Drew couldn't help it. He stared at her lips as male pride swelled in his chest.

"But I can't change who I am or who people in Sunshine think I am." She gave him a wide berth as she walked to the door. "And I won't give in to kissing a man who doesn't even like me."

"I like you," he said as she walked out the door.

I like you just the way you are.

But being a father meant he couldn't always have what he wanted. Not that second beer at Shaw's, not dinner without vegetables, and not a caring, vulnerable woman who pushed small-town boundaries in a way that wasn't the best example for an impressionable little girl.

Chapter Twenty

♥

"What's up, Flo?" Drew was making his early morning rounds while Gary walked Rosie.

"Victor Yates wouldn't tell me." On the radio, Flo sounded more than miffed. Drew's ex-father-in-law rubbed most people the wrong way. "Since it's not an emergency, take your time."

The luxury of time. How Drew wished he had more of it where his personal life was concerned. Time would tell if the town would ever accept Lola as one of their own. And if they did…

He'd be married to Wendy.

A few minutes later, Drew climbed the steps to the feedstore. It was a mild sixty degrees, and the double doors were propped open.

Victor's sourpuss expression awaited him just inside. "'Bout time you got here." His ex-father-in-law was a tall, rangy man who didn't fill out his blue coveralls.

"Can't justify the siren if it's not an emergency." Drew hooked his thumbs in his duty belt.

"My wife got word. Jane's coming." Victor's features

were screwed up so tight he could have passed for one of those apple dolls Drew's grandmother used to make for the fair every year. He wasn't a warm, cuddly grandfather to Becky, but he showed up on birthdays and holidays, which was what mattered most, Drew supposed.

"And..."

"I want to know the details." Victor's cheeks flushed. He was a proud man. Having to ask Drew anything must have cost him.

"Ask Jane." Drew turned to leave. He had a busy day and had volunteered to help out at Becky's play rehearsal this evening.

Lincoln Lee backed his truck up to the loading dock.

"Wait." Victor gripped Drew's shoulder. "Jane doesn't talk to us. Her message was a surprise. Molly wants to know if she's staying with you."

"No." Drew nearly recoiled. "She's not staying with me."

Lincoln got out of his truck and ambled over to the stairs.

Victor's frown deepened, most likely because they no longer had any privacy. "You let me know when you hear anything." His voice was low and unyielding. "We've got Becky to protect."

Victor wanted to put Becky's well-being above Jane's?

The unexpected sentiment nearly sent Drew stumbling.

* * *

Lola hadn't known there were this many young children in all of Sunshine Valley. She'd certainly never seen them all in one place.

Kindergartners and first graders ran around the high school gymnasium like ants on the remains of a spilled ice cream.

It was the first dress rehearsal for the lower grades' play, and the first time Lola had been in the high school gym since she and Avery had done battle at the bake sale.

Lola missed Avery. She'd called and texted without response.

When Wendy saw Lola, she waved and headed right over. As usual, she was understated in dress—a plain red blouse, a whitewashed blue jean skirt that hit below the knee, and white Keds. "I'm going to send you the actors who need help with hair and makeup." Wendy had to shout above the din. Despite the chaos, she was calmer than a cat in a sunny window seat. "You can set up at the table in the corner." She paused. "Strike that. Bitsy is moving your table next to Drew's. He's doing photos for the program."

Lola followed the direction of Wendy's gaze.

Drew was trying to make a little boy stand still while he took his picture against a painted backdrop of the Parthenon. Bitsy finished dragging Lola's table next to his and tried to help Drew get the boy to hold still.

Lola swallowed. After his rejection the other night, this was going to be uncomfortable.

"Your kids all need to be done and ready for dress rehearsal in an hour." Wendy flapped a hand in front of Lola. "Did you hear me?"

"Yes." Lola stopped watching Drew. "How many kids do you need me to do?"

"Ten."

Ten was a lot in an hour. She'd be so busy that she'd have no time to talk to Drew. "What about all the other ones?" The thirty or so running around like they'd consumed multiple cups of mile-high hot chocolate.

"They don't need it." Wendy gazed upon the bedlam fondly, pushing her flat blond hair behind one ear. "The ones with blue capes are the Greek army. The ones with white capes are the Greek chorus and…Hey!" shouted Wendy. "Nathan! Take your cape off June's head." She hurried off to save the poor girl from a member of the Greek chorus.

Power made Wendy seem like an entirely different person. And she spoke with volume and authority. Now this woman…Lola could see Drew dating her.

Gathering her pride, Lola went to her table. At least she wouldn't be alone with Drew. Bitsy stood next to him, encouraging his subject to strike a pose.

"Grandma!" A little girl with short brown pigtails and a blue cape ran up, doing the potty dance. "I need a bathroom."

The pair rushed off, leaving Lola chaperonless.

The little boy Drew was trying to photograph ran off to join the rest of the chorus, white cape fluttering behind him. From the look on Drew's face, he hadn't gotten his photograph.

"Wendy's in her element." Lola feigned nonchalance, shedding her blue-fringed suede jacket. She set out bobby pins and a case of bright eye shadow in many colors. "Did Wendy ask you to volunteer too?"

"Becky wanted me to help." Drew grinned, glancing toward the stage, where Becky waved her sword. "I've got to make the most of it now. Another eight to ten years and she won't want to have anything to do with me."

"That won't happen." He cared too much to let go of people, especially his daughter. The man was a great father.

"After my dad left, I practically raised my sisters. They drove me nuts." Drew lifted a hand to catch Becky's eye. His daughter's sword swung dangerously close to Wendy's bare knees. "When my sisters were younger, they wouldn't leave me alone. And when they were older, they pretended I didn't exist."

Becky lowered her weapon, and then Drew turned toward Lola. "When Becky was born, there was a moment when I was disappointed. Another girl? How could life be so cruel?" He chuckled. "And then I held her in my arms, and I knew all the drama my sisters put me through was just practice so I'd be a good father to Becky."

For a moment, Lola forgot all about Drew's rejection. All she could see was what an amazing husband and father Drew could be.

Mary Margaret Sneed stopped by Lola's table. She was a kindergarten teacher, and one of the women who'd passed her at Scotty's viewing. One of the women who might have left a trace of that expensive perfume she'd found in Randy's keepsake box. She had a mane of long red hair and was tall with enviable curves. She knew how to dress too. She wore a plain pink sheath accessorized with a looped and knotted teal-flowered scarf. "The kids are super excited about the play, and I'm super excited that Wendy's doing it this year. That means I'm backup for the first time in years."

"Lucky you," Drew said.

Mary Margaret smiled at Lola, a tenuous expression that said, *Yeah, I can't believe I'm a widow either*. They were about the same age. Mary Margaret's husband had passed last December but she and Lola hadn't crossed paths, because she'd chosen cremation.

"*Mary Margaret Sneed*," Lola breathed her name as if she were a rock star, and then launched herself at the woman, wrapping her arms around the kindergarten teacher and sucking air through her nose like a new Hoover.

"*Lola...*" Drew's voice permeated Lola's brain just as she realized Mary Margaret didn't smell like Joy perfume.

"I'm sorry." Lola released her suspect and backed away, noting her pierced ears. She'd just made a fool of herself. And now she had to say something. Anything. She scrambled for words. "I used to work on Broadway and...and...I'm just so-o-o excited to be here tonight." Lola clapped her hands in mock glee, feeling her cheeks heat. Mary Margaret must think she was an idiot.

Yep. The tall redhead made a hasty retreat. And who could blame her?

"You were sniffing Mary Margaret like a trained police dog on an escaped convict's jumpsuit." Drew crossed his arms over his chest and aimed his starchy cop expression her way. “Did you come here to smell every woman in town?”

“Oh yeah, that’s why I volunteered,” Lola deadpanned. Drew thought she was that desperate? He could be such a…such a…cop. She unpacked the rest of her supplies on the table and then stopped, needing to defend herself. “I miss helping with plays, okay? I miss the energy of the cast, and the bustle of performances.” Lola turned away, nearly dropping her basket of lipsticks. Why was she bothering to explain? He didn’t care.

“There’s no reason this should be hard.” His tone sounded conciliatory.

She turned back around. “Are you giving me the friend speech?”

“Why not?” He shrugged. “We know a lot about each other.”

Yep. Like the taste of your kiss.

Smirking, Lola rummaged through her supplies without knowing what she was looking for.

“For example, you like being behind the scenes but a part of things.” Drew touched her shoulder, pulling her gaze back to him. “Like when you work at the mortuary.”

“I like minding my own business,” Lola said firmly, planting a can of mousse on the table with a thud.

“Sheriff.” Drew tapped his chest, smiling like he’d just solved a crime. “The job gives me license to be a busybody.”

She wanted to return his smile. She wanted to accept his friendship. But the sting of rejection was too fresh.

“Ms. Adams says I get a fake nose.” A little boy laid his torso across Lola’s table, turning so he could see her. He wore a flesh-colored shirt with muscles drawn on it and a pair of brown faux-fur pants. "A pointy nose. Right here." He tapped his little nose and grinned.

"No, Caden," Wendy called, having heard him from the stage with her bionic hearing. "You need ears. Pointy ears. You're a satyr."

"Come sit here." Lola directed Caden to a chair. There was a headband around his neck with pointy pink ears glued to either side. She put the ears on his overgrown dark-brown locks. "Let's see how this looks."

"I wanted a nose." Caden crossed his arms and kicked out his feet. "Hair stuff is for girls."

"It's too bad you feel that way, Caden." Lola considered her plan of attack. "I was going to spike your hair into satyr horns."

Caden stopped kicking and angled his cherubic face toward hers. "Horns? For reals?"

"Yep." Lola kept a straight face. "With your permission, of course." She had some spray-on colors in her case—red, pink, green, blue, plus the traditional hair colors for those last-minute touch-ups. Red horns would be awesome on Caden.

The little boy pursed his lips and then frowned, giving her proposition careful consideration. "I guess you could do horns in my hair."

"Well, only if you *really* want them." There was something about the boy that made her want to tease him a little. Maybe it was the mischief built into his smile or the sparkle in his eyes that said he wasn't going to be one of those kids who sat quietly at his desk during story time.

Caden popped up in his seat. "I *really* want horns."

While she worked product into Caden's hair, several kids gathered round. Drew took advantage and pulled some over to have their pictures taken.

After the horns were made of Caden's dark hair and his ears were put back on, Lola opened her makeup kit.

"That's for girls." Caden began sliding out of the chair like melted butter.

Lola gasped and clutched the makeup kit to her chest. "I was going to make you look truly evil, but if you want to look like Caden with horns, suit yourself."

Caden halted, flipped around, and climbed back into the chair as if that had been his plan all along. "Evil, evil, evil." He made claws out of his fingers and snarled.

The children around them let out shrieks of joy.

Drew captured another child in a photograph. "Lola, are you sure you aren't a child whisperer?"

"Sheriff, I'm a beautician." Lola lifted her nose in the air and sniffed. "We have superpowers."

"Superpowers and horns all in the same day." Caden squirmed in his chair. "*Suh-weet!*"

Lola went to work with her makeup brush, intent upon giving the boy the fairy treatment, which involved creating overly dramatic eyes. She shaded red streaks on either side of his nose that climbed beneath his eyebrows. And then she lined his eyes thickly with black and filled in his eyelids with sparkly gold.

"Not that," Caden said, horrified when Lola knelt in front of him with lipstick. "My mom does that."

"This is *not* your mama's lipstick." Lola needed to hurry. She had principal players in line waiting for makeup. She'd gone a little overboard with Caden. "This is the black I reserve for evil characters. I've never used this on a mom. Not ever." At least no one who played a mom on stage.

"I want some." Becky popped up at the table, wearing a disheveled toga over a pair of blue jeans and red cowboy boots. She carried the clanking sword. "I want to look like Caden."

There was a chorus of "Me too."

"Girls can't have this." Caden scowled, looking like the evil satyr he was going to be playing. "This is for bad guys only." He jutted his chin toward Lola and commanded, "Do it."

When Lola finished with his lips, Caden snarled at his friends and ran to Drew for a picture.

Several moms had drifted Lola's way. Not close enough to engage Lola in conversation but close enough to see what she was doing.

Amid a cacophony of "Me nexts," Becky claimed Lola's client chair. "It's me. I'm Athena." She'd pulled the bottom half of the toga through a corded belt. It hung in double folds around her waist. She dropped her sword. It clattered and clanked and stopped several conversations before it quieted.

Lola made quick work of Becky's hair, threading it with plastic pearls. And then she lined her eyes with gold eye shadow.

After the ten main players had their makeup on, Lola couldn't turn down the requests from the chorus and the army, at least not when Wendy gave her approval.

Moms drifted closer. They smiled at their children

and Lola, who felt something she hadn't in a long time—that she belonged somewhere besides the retirement home and the mortuary. She could have a place here, if only she twisted hair and applied makeup fast enough.

Eventually, she ran out of time. Wendy called the cast for a run-through of their lines. Parents and children moved to the stage but not without thank-yous for Lola and a couple of exuberant hugs from the acting troupe.

Lola collapsed onto her chair, feeling as drained as if she'd been called in at the last minute to work a wedding party with twelve bridesmaids.

"That was cool." Drew handed her a bottle of water. "Not at all what I expected when Wendy said you'd be doing makeup."

"I don't like to be limited to tradition."

"Clearly." His gaze drifted to the blue suede jacket hanging behind her and then toward Wendy standing on the side of the stage with her boring hair and her forgettable wardrobe.

Lola sighed, stopped staring at Drew, and turned her attention to the stage to enjoy rehearsal.

The kids in the chorus and the army were adorable. They sang, twirled their capes, and as time dragged on, yawned. Not surprisingly, Becky was a ham. She and Caden stole the show. Good casting on Wendy's part.

Lola could have left at any time but didn't. This was her troupe, her tribe. She knew the texture of Soldier Number Four's hair and who had dimples in the chorus. She knew that Laura, who played an owl, had recently battled chicken pox, and that Eric, Soldier Number Nine, had a new puppy.

When rehearsal was over, Lola packed up her supplies. "Becky is a pistol. Her high school years are going to be fun for you."

Drew bristled like a commuter who'd been told the train was too full. "Becky's not like you."

"Like me?" Lola did a double take. "I was shy in school. I sat at the back of the class and never said anything without a teacher prying it out of me. I never would've tried out for a school play." She'd rejected the offer to be a tree one year in favor of working backstage. "Becky is nothing like me, and I think she's wonderful."

"Wonderful..." Drew's protests died out, and his guard slipped. There was longing in his dark-brown eyes, a yearning that called to Lola. "She's just... She's not a pistol, okay?" His guard came back up.

"No," Lola agreed, because he seemed to need her to. "Becky's not a pistol." And he thought Lola was. Heart heavy, she turned away.

Wendy hurried down the stage stairs, Pied Piper to a string of children. She gushed her thanks to Lola. "You injected the production with a level of excitement the kids needed."

The unadorned, pink-cheeked faces of children who hadn't received makeup clustered around Wendy and Lola.

A little redheaded girl twirled her hair around her finger. "I want an evil face."

"You're in for it now." Drew had somehow managed

to stand between Lola and Wendy, despite the crush of children. He pointed to a little boy with big brown eyes and a shock of black hair. "Try saying no to that."

Wendy added a pleading look of her own. "It would make them so happy."

Lola felt sucker punched. But she was a realist. "I can't do makeup for forty kids." It would take hours.

"Then we'll recruit assistants for you." Wendy beamed and then looked at Drew, as if recruiting him.

"I can't braid hair." He held up his hands. "Or do makeup."

"I can help." Mary Margaret stood a few rows of children away. "And I can recruit some of the room mothers, if Lola can come up with a makeup design they can follow. It'll be like coloring."

It would *not* be like coloring but before Lola could protest, several moms volunteered.

They volunteered knowing they'd be working with Lola. A warm, fuzzy feeling enveloped her, silencing her protests.

Wendy plowed through the crowd and hugged Mary Margaret.

"That's how you hug someone." Drew grinned the way Becky had when she'd found her sword in the thrift store.

That grin made Lola forget he'd said he needed a wife who wasn't like her.

It wasn't fair. He could only ever be the staid, standoffish sheriff to her.

Her heart ka-thumped anyway.

Needing to gain emotional space, Lola angled her

face toward Drew's ear. "That's how you hug friends. I was hugging a suspect."

Drew frowned, the austere sheriff once more.

A few reminders of rehearsal schedules later, the auditorium was nearly empty. Wendy disappeared backstage. Lola finished packing up and reached for her jacket. The air in the gym was chilly from everyone opening the door as they left. She needed an extra layer to keep warm.

"Daddy-O, I'm tired." Becky rubbed the side of her face on Drew's pants, creating a gold streak next to the brown stripe on his sheriff's uniform.

"We can leave as soon as Ms. Adams is ready to go." With an almost reverent touch, Drew stroked the updo Lola had made with Becky's hair. "We don't want her walking out to the parking lot alone."

Wendy poked her head out from behind a stage curtain. "Drew, I'm going to stay here another hour. I need to rearrange the lights with Edgar and make adjustments to the scenery." She beamed at Lola. "But you can walk Lola out."

Lola's arm got stuck in her jacket sleeve. "No need."

Despite her protests, Drew and Becky walked her out anyway. The parking lot was nearly empty, and the High Plains wind had picked up, ruffling Lola's hair and the suede fringe on her jacket. She wheeled her kit behind her. The case made more noise on the asphalt than a red wagon with squeaky wheels.

"I'm looking forward to the play next week," Lola said loudly, feeling the need to make conversation.

"Me too." Becky was a limp noodle in her father's

arms. Her toga billowed from beneath her purple windbreaker.

"Where's your car?" Drew reached his cruiser.

"I walked here." Lola stopped to say her goodbyes and noted his questioning look at her high heels. "Remember, I'm a city girl. I grew up walking everywhere." It was only six blocks or so. Nothing by New York City standards. Not even in heels.

"We don't walk at night in Colorado." Of course Drew overrode her. "I'm giving you a ride." Of course Drew commanded her. "Get in front." He opened the cruiser's back door and deposited Becky in a child seat. And when Lola continued to protest, he stopped her. "Get in the front seat and quit arguing." Drew opened the front passenger door and quirked an eyebrow.

Attraction shimmied down Lola's spine, flooding her veins with adrenaline. Her heart should have been keeping its cool, not pounding in her chest.

"You've been on your feet all day." Drew swept his hand toward the passenger seat. "And it's getting chilly."

If he'd smirked…If he'd frowned like giving her a ride was an obligation…If he'd only been annoying, Lola would have refused. But he was being nice, which meant he might make a joke and she might see a hint of that smile, which she liked.

And then I'll be in colossal trouble, heart at risk of falling.

Too late.

She got in the car.

"Why do I feel like I'm about to give you a root canal?" Drew telescoped the handle of her case and stowed it in the trunk, presumably with his big guns, bulletproof vest, and fire extinguisher. He slid behind the wheel. "You really don't want to be friends, do you?"

"A little less talk, please." Lola looked out her window.

Drew brought the car roaring to life.

"Everybody gets to ride up front but me," Becky mumbled sleepily from the back seat.

Lola turned to smile at little Athena but her eyes were closed. "I think she was talking in her sleep."

Drew didn't say anything.

"Did you hear me?" she asked.

"I thought I wasn't allowed to talk," he whispered.

Lola made a frustrated noise. Five blocks to go.

Drew glanced in the rearview mirror. "She's dozing. Kids that age burn out quick."

Kids. She ran her fingers through her jacket fringe and watched Sunshine through the window, seeing it the way she had when she'd first come to town. Quaint older homes. White picket fences. The promise of Norman Rockwell and the small-town American dream. Babies with walnut-brown hair, serious brown eyes, and hard-won smiles.

That isn't right.

Babies with blond hair, blue eyes, and charismatic smiles.

Lola sighed. "Did you always want to have kids?"

His hand drifted up the steering wheel and back without turning it. "Maybe not in the way women envision having a family, but I love my kid."

The streetlights in Sunshine were few and far between,

which made it seem as if they were sitting in the dark, sharing secrets the way lovers did late at night.

It means nothing. I *mean nothing like that to him.*

"I always wanted to have kids." She was fishing for more from him. "I hated being an only child with a stepsister I rarely saw and didn't know."

"Are you trying to prove your dad once loved your mother by proving Randy loved you?"

"You think that's what my search is about?" Lola did a quick gut check. "I don't think so, Dr. Freud."

He'd gone silent again and been waiting too long at a deserted four-way stop.

"Anyway," she continued, because when she got home, she'd have no one to talk to but Randy and Candy, and they weren't much for conversation. "I thought when people got married, part of the attraction included having the same goals about life and family."

He slowed as he approached her street. "My marriage…Turns out we had nothing in common. She was looking for a helping hand to get away from Sunshine, and I was looking to build a family." He took the corner at a safe speed, a welcome change from Clarice's driving.

"I thought Jane wanted to be a country-music star."

"That too." Drew came to a smooth stop in front of Lola's house.

"Would you take it wrong if I told you this conversation made me feel less depressed about my marriage?" Because it had. Hanging around with widows who worshipped their departed spouses had made her feel she'd bombed at marriage, big time.

He tapped his fingers on the steering wheel and made a noncommittal noise.

"Good night, Drew." Lola reached for the door handle.

"Wait." He touched her arm, so lightly she almost missed it.

And just like that, her heart was rattling its cage.

He gave her a wry smile. "Your case is in my trunk."

Be still, you stupid heart.

"Don't forget a good-night kiss, Daddy," Becky mumbled.

Lola's hand froze on the door handle. Her eyes flew to Drew's.

"Kids," Drew said but he was looking at Lola's mouth. "Can't control what they say."

Lola's body parts began to tremble. It took her two tries to work the door handle. And once out of the car, she had to make a few adjustments to her stance to handle the heave and roll of the concrete beneath her feet.

Meanwhile, Drew got out of the car, retrieved Lola's case from the trunk, and headed toward her door. His longer legs had him waiting on her porch when she finally caught up to him.

"I'll take that." She reached for the case.

He didn't release the handle. "Open the door first."

And what would come second? A good-night kiss? A friendly handshake? Extreme disappointment?

That will happen regardless.

Despite fingers that shook, Lola managed to open the door. She stepped inside and stared at Drew. At his warm brown eyes and ruffled brown hair. At that starched uniform with a streak of gold makeup on the pant leg. At broad shoulders and a broader moral code.

Wendy would make him a good wife. She'd probably never burn his skivvies in anger or engage in a cupcake war. Wendy would give Drew beautiful, boring babies, who'd look up to wonderful, colorful Becky in awe without ever truly understanding her.

Drew set Lola's case down just inside the door with barely a glance toward her window display. "Good night, Lola." He leaned in, perhaps propelled by the wind.

Lola couldn't move. Not. One. Inch. She held her breath, knowing that whatever happened, she wouldn't sleep easy tonight.

And then Drew pressed a kiss to her cheek, so soft, so tender, so gut-wrenchingly disappointing.

As quick as her sigh, he was gone.

Lola closed the door.

She looked at Randy and Candy. The couple stood on their heads in a moving box, their world as upside down as Lola's life had been since she'd discovered Randy's secret life.

Wanting to uncover those secrets had nothing to do with her parents and everything to do with last straws. So what if Sunshine had had enough of Lola? Lola had had enough of Sunshine. She'd ask only one more thing of the town before she left—the who and the why. And then she'd be able to sleep at night.

Her knees locked. Her shoulders lifted.

Wendy would have Drew.

Lola would have the truth.

Chapter Twenty-One

♥

The drive to the farmhouse seemed longer than usual that night.

The open High Plains seemed to stretch forever beneath the full moon.

Drew had kissed Lola's cheek.

He'd been about to press his lips to hers when he came to his senses and veered toward safer ground.

If only he'd discovered Lola's big heart sooner, before she'd found out about Randy and before he'd heard from Jane. He might have been a calming influence on her. And she might have been an asset in his fight against his ex-wife.

Drew turned down the long gravel driveway to his place. There was a beat-up small red sedan parked in front of the farmhouse.

A slight, familiar figure with short, choppy blond hair got out of the car.

Jane.

Drew wanted to back out of the driveway and pull away but retreat implied weakness. And he couldn't afford to be weak with his ex-wife. He got out of the car and leaned on the doorframe, facing her.

"Hello, Drew." Under the exterior lights, she looked like country royalty in her rose-colored boots, black jeans, and shearling coat. She'd always been good at presentation, just not at being present. "Is that her in the car?"

Her. As if Jane couldn't remember their daughter's name.

Anger burned in Drew's veins, making it hard to move slow, hard to close the door quietly to shield Becky from the argument that was about to ensue. "You're trespassing, Jane."

"I have visitation rights," Jane reminded him, although she'd never used them before. She wore heavy makeup. But whatever she'd slathered on her face to smooth over the lies she told herself didn't fool him.

"She's asleep. Come back…" He bit back the word *later*. Rethought about the word *tomorrow*. And settled on "another time." No way was she—a stranger to Becky—going to wake her up and start playing at being Mommy.

Jane moved close, possibly to catch a glimpse of Becky, more likely to rattle him. Up close, she looked thinner, exhausted, tense.

She was tense?

Drew gritted his teeth, refusing to be rattled yet unable to shake the tension.

Jane set her boots down in front of him and nodded toward the farmhouse. "I thought I could stay here."

"You thought wrong." Was that Drew's voice? He hardly recognized the sharp edges. "Stay with your parents."

"It's late." Her gaze fell. "And I'm worried I don't have enough gas to make it into town."

Drew wanted to tell her to write that worry into one of her songs. Instead, he glanced toward her car. He couldn't see through the rear windshield to the front. There were boxy shadows filling the empty spaces. She'd said she was coming back, but he'd hoped that was an idle threat or a ploy for money. "Why?"

Why here? Why now? Why the sudden desire to be a mother?

"It wasn't my time." Jane's husky voice hitched. Her gaze slid to the skirting around the house. "Is that what you wanted to hear?"

Hell to the no!

"You aren't moving back in with me." He couldn't get the words out fast enough.

"But Drew." She sidled closer, reaching for his shoulders, smiling at him the way she used to when he'd first returned to Sunshine, like he was all she needed to keep her happy. "You haven't gotten married again. That must mean—"

"That I'm a devoted father. One who doesn't have time to date." He brushed her hands away. "At least, not until recently. I found someone." Lola's bright face and brighter-colored clothing came to mind.

His jaw ticked as he tried to pull forth an image of Wendy and failed.

Dang it. He'd never had trouble making the responsible choice before. Never.

"We could work it out." Jane's words were laden with promises. "And then in a year or so, we could move to Nashville, just like we planned. Maybe the timing will be better industry-wise."

And there it was. Her real reason for returning.

"I'm not your fallback plan." Drew knew how Jane's mind worked. She took risks, sure. But she also covered her bases. Her weakness had always been her lack of patience. "I haven't been pining for you. I can barely stand the sight of you."

Jane dropped back a step. "But—"

"Becky deserves better than you." There. He'd said it. The harsh words that he'd kept inside all this time.

"But—"

"Becky deserves someone who loves her and understands her and…" Lola's face came to mind again, grinning at Becky in the thrift store. "She deserves better than you!" He shouted it this time and had to swallow twice before he could go on with any control. "Leave. Leave before I arrest you for trespassing." And before his shouts woke up their daughter.

Jane's face paled. Not even Lola's magic with the dead could have brought her color back. She backtracked with stumbling steps.

Drew knew he wouldn't sleep that night.

Jane was back. And the things she wanted…

No. Absolutely not.

* * *

"You wanted to see me, Sheriff?" Rupert Harper was a third-generation lawyer with aspirations to be a second-generation judge.

Those aspirations meant Rupert lived a conservative life, one that wasn't too austere or too flashy. Still, he had to be at least fifty, and there wasn't a gray hair on his head. He wore a dark suit, wool so fine it had to have cost a month of Drew's salary. A vacation to the Bahamas had left Rupert looking tan and rested.

Anyone would look more rested than Drew the morning after Jane's return to town.

Rupert had arrived at the sheriff's office just as Drew finished walking Rosie.

Drew ushered Rupert into a seat and closed the door, explaining the situation with Jane. "All she wants is a sugar daddy to take her back to Nashville. She doesn't want to be a mother." Drew might have repeated that sentiment more than once.

Rupert nodded, tapping something into his cell phone. "Does Jane have a record?"

"Of course she does," Drew said, realizing he'd worked himself up into a near panic. He took a slow breath. "Marijuana and indecent exposure."

"I hear you're dating Wendy Adams. Good choice, considering." Rupert handed Drew a sheet of paper. "Marriage will definitely help you out. Sign this agreement, and I'll take your case."

Drew looked it over without reaching for a pen. "Just so you know, I called your brother, Oliver, when I heard you were out of town, but he was unavailable."

"No surprise there. Oliver and I agree to be out of town at the same time every year to level the playing field." Rupert's smile was wide and sharklike. He and his brother being the only two attorneys in town, it was a coin toss as to which one would be chosen when the need for legal representation arose. "What might surprise you is that Oliver took Jane's case."

"*What?*" Drew felt as if Rosie were sitting on his chest. He'd assumed Jane couldn't afford legal representation. He scanned Rupert's agreement. "There's nothing on here about fees."

"If you have to ask, you consider money more important than your daughter." Rupert's cell phone buzzed. He checked the display. "You're in luck. My father is willing to see you now."

"Why would that be lucky?"

"Because apparently, he's with Jane."

Chapter Twenty-Two

♥

As much as Jane had looked like a polished country star last night, this morning she looked like a young woman who'd never left Sunshine.

Big green eyes, artfully tousled hair, blue jeans, and a white T-shirt. She sat demurely in a chair in Judge Harper's chambers, trying to look innocent.

Lucky for Drew, Judge Harper wasn't the kind of man to fall for an innocent appearance.

A century or so before, the old man would've been labeled a hanging judge. The silver-tipped cowboy boots and black bolo tie with a turquoise clip enhanced the impression that Judge Harper was from another era.

Part of the reason crime was so low in the area was that Judge Harper believed in alternative sentencing. When you came into court, he gave you a choice—jail time or a punishment of his own making.

Steal someone's bicycle? You might find yourself walking around the high school track for twenty miles. Drunk and disorderly? If you were an annoyance, you might find yourself locked in a jail cell for twelve hours with one song playing loudly on repeat. Steal from your boss? You might find yourself standing next to the road out of town on a Saturday with a sign that said you were a thief.

With sentencing like that, no one wanted to go back in front of him.

Tension sat at the base of Drew's throat, loaded with arguments he could spring on Jane.

Rupert sat to Drew's right in the judge's chambers, which were darkly paneled and somber.

Rupert's brother, Oliver, sat to Jane's left. Oliver seemed to be wearing the same high-quality suit as his younger brother but he didn't look as sophisticated. His tie was too wide and a dirty gray color. He'd also gotten sun on vacation but his skin wasn't the smooth tan Rupert had achieved. He had the shiny red skin of a man who'd forgotten sunscreen.

Judge Harper cleared his throat, sounding like Bob Lumley's '57 Chevy. He looked like he hadn't been eating well or sleeping much, unlike his vacationing sons. He scowled at the assembled. "Well?" The judge stared at Jane. "Six years ago, you said I was done with you."

"A lot can happen in six years," Jane said quietly, staring at her clasped hands as if she folded those hands together every Sunday at church.

Drew struggled to sit still.

"A lot has happened." The judge flipped through a folder. "Rebecca Maureen Taylor won a sack race at the county fair in the Under Five division. She fell attempting to climb a tree in the town square and sprained her wrist. She's about to star in the lower grades' annual school play." He stared at Jane over the top of his round reading glasses. "Did you know any of this?"

"No," Jane said, hands clenching.

Drew derived some level of satisfaction from Jane being outed as an absentee mother. But it was a small measure and did nothing to ease the tension gripping the base of his neck.

The judge rocked back in his big leather chair, steepling his hands in front of his chest. "Is that because you didn't ask?"

"Yes." Her voice seemed very small now.

Beside Drew, Rupert relaxed and smiled at his brother.

"Now, before you resort to tears..." Judge Harper held up a gnarled and spotted hand. "And before my son decides he's won a case that has yet to be filed..." He shot Rupert a stern look. "I respect a parent's right to be involved in their child's life."

Now it was Jane who relaxed. Jane who smiled.

Drew felt his gut wind into a tight little ball.

Judge Harper rested his elbows on the desk. "But first, the court needs to determine if the parent who signed away rights to Becky will be a good influence."

"Dad." Oliver wasn't as distinguished as his younger brother, Rupert, but he had the Harper killer instinct, as evidenced by his take-no-prisoners tone. "Not another one of your tests."

The judge slapped the top of his desk with the flat of his hand. "I'm Judge Harper while I'm in the courthouse."

Had Drew thought Judge Harper looked worn out? Anger sparked in the old man's gray eyes.

Rupert smirked at his brother. Oliver smirked back.

The fire in Judge Harper's eyes turned on Jane. "Young lady, you left your child and never looked back for six long years. Do you know what it's like to be abandoned like that? To be left?"

Jane gave a little half shrug.

"Well, you're going to know now. For the next week, you'll be spending your days looking for work, and you'll be spending your nights camping out on the land the cemetery annexed last year, checked on every night by the sheriff's department."

"What?" Jane's hands moved to the arms of her chair, as if she was going to push herself out of it and do something impulsive.

Oliver's hand came down on her arm.

"You'll find out what it means to be on your own—"

"I know what it feels like to be on my own," Jane said hotly, jerking her arm free from Oliver's grip.

"*And*"—the judge raised his voice to a near shout—"you'll know what it's like to be alone and forgotten."

"Becky wasn't forgotten." Jane was digging her own grave. "She had Drew and his family. And my parents. I was the one who was forgotten." She tapped her chest. "Me."

Oliver shushed her but most likely the only reason Jane stopped speaking was because she'd run out of things to say.

Rupert wore a grin the size of China.

"I don't think anyone in Sunshine ever forgot you,"

Judge Harper said gruffly. "My assistant has what you need to camp. You'll return the supplies in the condition you borrowed them in, or there will be further consequences."

Oliver cleared his throat. "Judge Harper—"

"If you do this"—the judge coughed and then worked hard to clear his throat—"I'm granting supervised visits while in Sunshine."

"What?" Drew couldn't believe it. He gave Jane a contemptuous look. "After everything she's said and done?"

"*Daily* visits," the judge said firmly. "Of up to one hour in length. We'll reconvene next week, and each of you will submit to further review."

Now Drew knew how a driver caught speeding felt—trapped. "I'll need time to prepare Becky."

"One day," Judge Harper allowed. "Two max."

Drew thanked the judge and left the office.

"This is a good thing." Rupert followed him out, a bounce to his step. "As is your dating Wendy."

"Is it?" Drew barely kept himself from slamming the outer office door against the wall.

"Yes. If Jane's not good for your daughter, you'll know it. And if by some twist of fate she is, you'll know it. I know you, Sheriff. You're a good judge of people. And you're fair." Rupert walked down the hall toward the courtroom and a waiting defendant, Ellery Finkle, who'd been charged with drunk and disorderly conduct.

"Fair?" Drew didn't want to be fair. He wanted to play dirty.

It was time to get serious about Wendy.

* * *

"My kids are in love with you." Mary Margaret hung her dress next to Lola's fashion-show outfit in the room beneath the stage at the high school. "The boys all want horns like you did for Caden, and the girls are dreaming of fairy makeup."

"Your class is adorable." Lola meant it. She couldn't wait for the next rehearsal with those five- and six-year-olds. It helped that Mary Margaret seemed to have forgotten the hug Lola had given her. "And your dress is lovely."

"It is, isn't it?" The kindergarten teacher held it up to admire it. Mary Margaret had been given a midcalf midnight-blue sleeveless sheath. It would show off her cover-model figure and provide a rich contrast to that mane of red hair. "I wish I could afford it." Her expression wavered between wistfulness and melancholy. Word was just now spreading about the debt her husband had left her with. "Three hundred dollars. Yeesh. How much is yours?"

"Three seventy-five." Lola wouldn't be buying her outfit either. She'd been given a robin's-egg-blue formfitting pantsuit with a sleeveless tunic and a cream-colored scarf. The ruby earring she'd found in Randy's keepsake box was going to stand out on that scarf and look like an antique brooch. Only Randy's lover would recognize it for what it was.

And this time, if anyone asked Lola for it, she was giving it to them. She still had a bruise on her backside from falling on the table at the bake sale.

"I drove by your house the other day." Mary Margaret looked around to see who might overhear and lowered her voice. "Loved the couple in the window."

Her praise went a long way to settling Lola's nerves. "My husband bought them. It's kind of my revenge for him being a jerk, you know? They've been up for more than a week, and I'm starting to talk to them." Starting? That was a stretch. "Do you think that's weird?"

"No." Mary Margaret took Lola's arm and leaned in close as if they were best friends sharing secrets. "People talk to plants. My mother-in-law talks to her dog." She had a sweet smile but it turned mischievous. "If you want to talk to somebody who'll talk back, come to Shaw's on Sunday afternoons. You'll fit right in with the girls."

Lola nodded. Sunday afternoons at Shaw's. Avery might be there. Lola had been too busy to track her down to apologize in person.

"Question." Drew's sister Priscilla had been given a black cocktail dress with a plunging neckline. She had curves and filled out every inch of the dress. "Should I hitch the dress up?" Priscilla tugged the shoulders and turned her torso from side to side. "Or pull it down?" She tugged the dress at her hips.

"It rides more naturally up," Lola said diplomatically.

"Up, definitely," Mary Margaret agreed. "Otherwise it bunches over your hips and makes your butt look big."

"It does not." Priscilla swatted playfully at Mary Margaret's arm and then tugged the dress down. "Does it?"

Mary Margaret assured her she'd been teasing.

"When you're done with those dolls in your window," Pris said, nudging Lola's shoulder, "I'd like to borrow them. They'd drive my brother crazy."

No matter what happened in her search for Randy's mistresses, Lola would always remember this day. She belonged to a club that included her in fund-raisers. She'd been invited to hang out at a bar. And she had friends again.

While Lola changed, her gaze strayed to the corner where Avery sat alone, as far away from Lola as she could get. She wore a vintage-style white dress with lace cap sleeves and an A-line skirt. She looked like a 1950s bride. Her hair should have been styled in wrap-around braids with a few wisps of hair framing her face and softening that scowl.

Holding a wedding bouquet, Mims walked over to Avery. "How did you end up with this dress?" She frowned and searched the room until her gaze found Wendy in the opposite corner with her back to them all as she put on makeup. She wore a floor-length black satin gown. It was a look Avery would have rocked. Obviously, there'd been a mix-up somewhere.

"It's too late to change now," Bitsy said brightly as she zipped Darcy Jones into a denim jumpsuit.

"I suppose..." Mims didn't sound convinced.

Avery's shoulders rounded. She snatched the bouquet from Mims's hands.

"Where's Edith?" Mims marched over to where the purple evening gown with feathers still hung from a rack, leaving Avery alone once more.

Lola's heart went out to her. Avery needed some

TLC. This was a fashion show but that didn't mean Avery's hair couldn't look fabulous. She walked over to Avery's corner, intending to apologize. "Hey."

Avery's back was to Lola. She stiffened beneath all that lace but didn't turn.

"That dress is beautiful." Lola took a few steps closer. "How about I pin up your hair?"

"Nobody touches Avery's hair but me." Barbara's blond hair was slicked back into a severe ponytail, and her makeup was flawless. The mayor's wife stared down her nose at Lola, intimidating the curl right out of Lola's hair.

Not today. That was what Lola should have said. *Not today, Barbara. Avery needs me.*

Instead, Lola shuffled her feet. "I . . . uh . . ."

Avery still hadn't turned around.

"I think Avery would look lovely with an updo," Lola said meekly.

Barbara blew out a puff of air in apparent disgust. "There's no time for that. Her hair is fine as is. And if there were time, she'd need a style more sophisticated than you could achieve with pin curls."

Lola felt her cheeks burn with embarrassment.

When Barbara sauntered off and Avery still said nothing, Lola turned away and clipped the antique ruby earring onto her scarf.

* * *

"Smile at Wendy when she comes out," Drew's mother said from her seat next to her son at the fashion show. "You should have gotten her flowers. Women love flowers."

"Mom, I don't need your dating advice." Drew intended to smile at Wendy. There was no way she wouldn't see him smiling in his front-row seat. And with Becky at his side, his mother was going to see Wendy smiling too.

Seats were filling rapidly in the high school gymnasium, and the volume of the crowd's conversations was rising. The fashion show was starting soon.

"It's been a long time since you dated." His mom waved at Augie and Rowena Bruce, who'd sat down on the other side of the runway.

"It's been longer for you, Mom."

"Sheriff." Tom Bodine tapped his shoulder and leaned close. "Jane applied for a job at my butcher business." He gave Drew's shoulder a squeeze and Drew's mother a thumbs-up. "I told her we weren't hiring." Tom moved on without waiting for Drew's response.

The protective father in Drew wanted to cheer. No job meant Jane couldn't stay. But the sheriff in him, the man who played fair and did the right thing, knew what Tom had done was wrong.

"Friends have been calling all day to tell me Jane's back," his mom said, trying to be heard without shouting. "And, like Tom, no one will hire her, out of loyalty to you." She sighed. "I almost feel sorry for her."

"Let's not go that far." Drew jerked back in his seat because his mother wasn't above contacting Tom and asking him to reconsider Jane's request for work. "She wants to return to Nashville. Do you want Becky to go with her?"

"Go with who?" Becky piped up. She was becoming a class-A eavesdropper.

Drew didn't say. He hadn't told Becky yet that Jane was back in town, and now wasn't the time.

"Sweet, sweet child." Edith appeared before them. She wore a pink terry bathrobe and black flip-flops. She grabbed Becky's hand. "Can I borrow you?" Without waiting for Drew's approval, Edith led his daughter away.

"What do you suppose that's all about?" his mom asked.

"I'm afraid to ask," Drew said.

Mims stepped up to the podium and called for quiet. She wore a bright-green dress, a black silk jacket, and her usual broad-faced grin. "Ladies and gentlemen, thank you for coming to the Twelfth Annual Widows Club Fashion Show to benefit our college scholarship fund. If you've been chomping at the bit for the snow to melt and your social life to resume, have we got ideas for you! But first, let's give a warm welcome to our emcee, Mayor Kevin Hadley."

As the applause died down and the music began to play, Drew's mother said, "I'd date a man like Kevin. But there are no single men like him on the market."

"You mean no men your age," Drew corrected.

"No." She volleyed the word back at him sharply. "If Kevin were single, I'd make a move on him."

Drew nearly fell out of his folding chair. "He's my age."

"Who cares?" Drew's mom steadied him. "Honestly, you're lucky he's taken. Less competition for you. You can be such a stick in the mud, which is why Wendy is perfect for you."

Drew choked while trying to spit out a protest, struggling to come to terms with what his mother thought of him. No wonder she was the only one in the family to approve of him going out with Wendy.

Kevin read from index cards. "You never hear bridesmaids complain about a dress they can wear more than one time. Kindergarten teacher Mary Margaret Sneed is wearing a dress that could go from Sunday service to brunch in Greeley to dinner at the Bar None."

Mary Margaret was as sweet as Wendy and smiled just the way a kindergarten teacher should. But she strutted down the runway like she'd been born in high heels.

"Wow," Kevin said into the microphone as Mary Margaret made her way back. "Look at the way she owns the runway. Let's give her a round of applause."

Mary Margaret disappeared behind the stage curtain, and the next model appeared.

"Here's a familiar face. My wife, Barbara." Kevin doted on his wife. And why wouldn't he? His ambition and her drive had propelled him into office. It didn't matter to him that Barbara thought of herself as the mayor too. "Barb's wearing thigh-high rain boots and a polka-dot fire-engine-red raincoat." Kevin's voice turned playful. "Honey, if you've got nothing on underneath that, proceed directly to our house. Do not pass Go."

The crowd laughed.

"Of course I have something under here." Barbara undid the belt at her waist. "Read the cue card, honey."

"Right. Read." Kevin chuckled. "And here it is. Barb's got clothes on. Those are moisture-wicking alligator leggings and a white tank top, a perfect ensemble for unpredictable High Plains weather."

Barbara worked the runway, greeting constituents by name.

"I always thought you dodged a bullet by not marrying Barbara." His mother was on a roll tonight.

"She never looked twice at me." Drew glanced around to see whether Becky was somewhere near the stage passing out programs or bottles of water. A twinge of concern had him looking for his daughter elsewhere. "Besides, she probably doesn't like sticks in the mud."

"Thank heavens."

"That's right, ladies." Kevin's voice filled the gym. "You can mix polka dot and alligator. Multiple patterns are in. Let's hear it for my wife, the mother of my child, the love of my life." Kevin called for a round of applause for his wife. "Next up is Lola Williams. Lola's wearing a blue pantsuit that flatters any body type. She can wear this outfit to work and on a dinner date."

Lola stepped out from behind the curtain, looking tame compared to her regular appearance and that of the models who'd gone before her. Her brown hair was held away from her face with a rhinestone clip. Her shoes were flat. Normal. Boring.

Why hadn't she worn something more like what Mary Margaret or Barbara had? Where were the heels? The big hair? The wide, I-got-you-Sheriff smile?

Lola walked the aisle, blushing the entire time and staring above everyone's heads, just as she'd done at the bachelorette auction. There was no smile. No dimple.

The only thing she did differently than on auction night was wave a hand at the scarf tied around her neck. The flutter of her hand was continuous, hovering over…

A ruby earring.

She just couldn't let this thing with Randy's infidelity go. Drew fought the impulse to leap onto the runway as she passed and snatch the earring away.

"And double thanks that you aren't interested in that one," his mother whispered. "She's the kind of woman who'd go after a man with a gun."

"No. She'd go after a blow-up doll," Drew muttered.

"Next up is Priscilla Taylor-Barnes," Kevin announced.

"Priscilla Taylor," Pris corrected, striking a pose next to the mayor.

"Jeez, Mom." Drew covered his eyes while Kevin described what his sister was wearing. "Where did you go wrong with her?"

"I think she looks charming." Drew's mom blew a kiss at Pris as she walked by. "I think I'd look good in that dress too."

Drew groaned.

His mother elbowed him. "Do you know how hard it is to find a man in Sunshine? The Taylor females have curves. You better learn how to deal with it before Becky gets hers."

Drew groaned again. "I think I'm gonna be sick."

"And now here's Wendy Adams."

"Smile, smile, smile," his mom said, turning to look.

Surprise rippled through the crowd like a strong breeze through a wheat field.

Drew glanced up, and his jaw dropped.

Even Kevin, who was never at a loss for words, hesitated.

"That is *not* Wendy Adams." Drew's mom put a hand to her throat.

Quiet, demure Wendy had a tortoise for a pet, could barely speak in Drew's presence when they were alone, and was perfect as the last layer of defense against Jane.

That wasn't the Wendy on stage.

"What happened to her?" Drew's stomach turned, for real this time.

This Wendy...She wore a long black dress, which would have been fine if the halter top hadn't tied two inches above her navel and there hadn't been a slit worthy of Angelina Jolie on her right side. She'd clipped her hair away from her face and applied the same kind of fairy makeup Lola had used on the kids at dress rehearsal.

Kevin shuffled through his index cards. "I'm sorry. I was expecting Wendy to wear a different dress."

"Weren't we all," Drew's mom murmured.

"Ah, here it is." Kevin sounded relieved. "Wendy is wearing the ideal dress to take on a cruise for a formal night." Kevin glanced up at Wendy again, waving her toward the runway. "Or you could wear it anytime you want to make your ex jealous."

It was too warm. It was too loud. Drew's head pounded.

Wendy began her walk. It was obvious she wasn't comfortable in high heels. It was equally clear she wasn't comfortable with the height of the slit in her dress. She kept tugging it together.

She was a hometown girl though. The crowd began applauding before she made it to the end of the runway.

"Smile," Drew's mom said past a clenched jaw. "And don't look for any wardrobe malfunctions."

How could he not? Every man and woman in the gym was looking to see whether she wore panties. Iggy stood at the top of the bleachers, clapping. Wendy had overtaken Lola as the talk of the town.

After she passed, his mother sat back and glared at Drew. "You didn't smile."

"She didn't look at me." Which was a blessing since he didn't think he could've mustered a smile.

"Maybe she didn't look at you because you frowned like a stick in the mud."

Drew sat back, ready for the fashion show to end.

"Our next model is Edith Archer." Kevin turned toward the part in the curtains. "Edith is wearing a purple-passion plumed evening gown..."

Becky stepped through the curtain. She wore a sparkly purple dress that fell onto her red cowboy boots. Feathers fluttered in her wake as she strutted forward.

Someone shrieked behind the scenes.

Edith stumbled on stage. She wore a black bikini and should have waxed.

The audience went silent. Even the mayor was struck mute.

"I dedicate this to my Charlie." And then Edith began to dance down the runway, giving Becky a high five as she passed the other way.

Instead of laughing, the crowd began to clap to the beat of the music.

Chapter Twenty-Three

♥

Did someone give you that to wear?" Mary Margaret pointed to the ruby earring on Lola's scarf.

"No. I brought it from home." Lola had dillydallied backstage, postponing a costume change as she circled the room like a guppy taunting a lurking shark.

No one paid attention to her, what with Wendy and Edith being showstoppers. Sadly, no one smelled of Joy.

But what could Lola do? Change and go mingle with the crowd?

"Is that…" Mary Margaret leaned closer. She was tall. Earrings swung from her pierced ears. "Is that an earring?"

"It is." Lola removed the earring and held it in her palm. Why not? It couldn't belong to Mary Margaret.

"May I?" Mary Margaret's fingers hovered over Lola's palm.

Lola raised her hand higher.

The kindergarten teacher took the earring and stared at it for several silent seconds. "I think this was my great-aunt Bunny's. She gave me a pair just like it, and I lost one. Where did you find it?"

Lola's body jolted as if she'd downed a large energy drink. "You..." She took a step back in case Mary Margaret turned out to be the possessive-aggressive type, like Avery. "You slept with Randy."

"Please." Mary Margaret blanched. "Keep your voice down. That was a long time ago. Before you were married. My husband and I... We went through a rough patch and were separated."

Before you were married.

Mary Margaret wouldn't know whether Randy had loved Lola or not.

"What's all the hubbub?" Edith was still bikini-clad.

"Grandma Edith, look." Mary Margaret showed her the earring. "Isn't this Great-Aunt Bunny's earring?"

Edith nodded, plucking the piece from Mary Margaret's hand and snapping it onto her ear. "I told you it'd turn up someday."

"I used to wear those earrings because my father refused to let me pierce my ears." Mary Margaret was calm, regal even; only the deepening color in her cheeks gave away she was upset. "Randy and I... It was one night and long before Randy met you. I... I needed someone to hold me, and Randy seemed to really care."

"He seemed to have cared about a lot of women," Lola murmured.

Mary Margaret winced.

Mims hurried over, Bitsy and Clarice in her wake.

"I just want to know if he loved me." Lola couldn't

help but notice that her voice had the hoarse, hurt quality of her mother's.

Mary Margaret blinked. "I…I'm sorry. I can't answer that."

"Of course not. And you did nothing wrong, Mary Margaret." Mims took off her black silky jacket and put it around Edith's shoulders.

Several women, including Avery, slipped out the door. Only widows remained.

"Where did you get this?" Mary Margaret asked softly. "It's been missing since—"

"He stole things from the women he slept with," Lola blurted, still in that hoarse, hurt voice. "Are you missing a bracelet too?" That would be neat and tidy, and one less woman to wonder about.

"No." Mary Margaret turned on her heel and left, leaving Lola alone in the dressing room with the Widows Club board.

"There are others, you say?" Edith stomped her foot. "Your husband was worse than—"

"Shush." Mims put her arm around Lola. "People are human and make mistakes."

Avery had lost her necklace in high school. Mary Margaret had lost her earring before Lola and Randy married. Lola might have hypothesized that all Randy's liaisons had occurred before her marriage, if not for the nearly empty box of condoms.

"Mistakes hurt." Edith raised her face to the floor joists above them and cried, "Mims slept with my husband. I can't keep it in any longer." And then she began to cry in big, heaping sobs with a rain shower of tears.

Mims stood as still as a tree trunk, not denying anything.

Bitsy and Clarice cast disappointed glances at Mims and then gathered Edith between them and led her away.

The sudden silence rang in Lola's ears. All Edith's talk about best friends and betrayals made sense. She had to ask Mims, "Did you sleep with my husband?"

"No," Mims snapped.

"Hmm." Lola began changing her clothes. "Did you sleep with Edith's husband?"

It took Mims longer to answer, and when she did, it was without snap. "No."

Lola wasn't buying it. "Then why didn't you tell Edith that?"

"Because she wouldn't believe me, just like you don't believe me." Mims sank onto a wooden folding chair. Her head was tucked tight to her shoulders, like a turtle hunkering down in its shell. "I'm too old and too tired to have an affair."

"But..." Lola sensed there was more coming.

"But after Hamm died, Charlie would come over and hold me." Mims wiped her nose with the back of her hand. "And when hunting season rolled around, we went hunting together, just like we did when Hamm was alive. And then came fishing. And..." She raised tear-filled eyes to Lola. "We did everything we used to."

Lola slipped into her boots, pausing to catch Mims's eye. "There was no hanky-panky?"

"What we had was platonic." Mims struggled to sit tall, to regain some of her confidence. "We did nothing wrong."

"You don't have to be physical for it to be cheating," Lola said softly. "Charlie betrayed his wife emotionally. And you betrayed your friendship."

Mims shook her head. "Charlie gave me what I needed—the strength to keep going." Her gaze turned pleading. "My children couldn't give me that. They've all moved away. The Widows Club couldn't give me that. No one but Charlie understood."

"I understand." Lola tugged on her jacket. "I'm going through the same thing. The loneliness seems unbearable. It's a deep hole in my chest that I can't seem to fix." The void had lessened after Drew kissed her but now she was hollow once more. "My chest aches so bad it keeps me awake at night. And I've been floundering, looking for the truth in the hopes it'll make me feel better."

Lola shouldered her purse, clinging to the strap the way she clung to the hope that she'd find peace when she discovered the names of the women who'd seen her husband naked.

* * *

On Thursday after his shift, Drew's mother met him at her front door. She had flour on her cheek and something on her mind. "Drew, you need to help your sister."

"Which one?" He'd had a long day at work and been out of the loop family-wise.

In addition to his regular rounds and continued reports that Jane was in town, there'd been an illegal burn at the Handelman Ranch and a drunk riding his horse through town, and Gary had pulled Iggy over for speeding. Iggy had called Drew, complaining he'd been going five miles over the legal limit and urging Drew to fire Gary.

Surprisingly, there'd been no calls or complaints on the Lola front.

"Which sister?" Drew repeated.

"Eileen. I'm talking about Eileen." His mom cast a glance over her shoulder to make sure Becky wasn't listening and then lowered her voice. "Why didn't you tell me that pig has made a ruin of her house?"

"Eileen's place was a wreck before Rosie got there." Drew had meant to check on Eileen's home after his initial cleaning but each day seemed to get away from him. Spring-thaw madness seemed like it'd never end. "Have you seen it lately?"

His mom nodded. "You know Tom Bodine owns that house. He gave Eileen a steep discount because I said she was such a good tenant. I said she'd be no trouble at all."

Drew was too tired to cover common ground. He shifted his feet on the Victorian's porch. "If you let me in, I can work on repairing everything."

His mom was a tough negotiator. She made the gimme gesture with her hand.

Drew sighed. "And I can find someone to take Rosie if you're worried Eileen wants to keep her."

His mother gave a full-body shake, like a dog coming in from a rainstorm. "If you're suggesting the pig goes to Tom Bodine and his butcher shop, I'm going to slam this door in your face."

Drew reached for his most patient voice, the one that calmed hyperventilating moms when they parked in the fire lane when they were late for the Christmas pageant. "Tom has the largest working ranch in the valley. He'd have no problem—"

"Eating Rosie," his mom finished for him firmly. "No way. That pig is a sweetheart."

He agreed but the topic of conversation was Eileen and the condition of her rental. Drew closed his eyes. He and his mother approached problems from different angles. He always wanted to divest people of trouble. She and Eileen always wanted to redeem trouble. Heaven help him if they decided they wanted to redeem Lola.

He opened his eyes and tried for clarity. "Are you asking me to help Eileen fix her house or to help the pig?"

"Yes." His mom frowned, meaning both. "Why do you have to ask?"

The weight of the town and his family and Jane suddenly seemed too much. Drew didn't have time to date Wendy, much less get close enough to her to ask her to marry him. He sagged against the doorframe. "All right. I'll work on Eileen's house. I'll try and find someone to adopt Rosie. And I'll talk to Eileen about...whatever is bothering her. Can I see my daughter now? I was going to take her to the park." To meet Jane. God help him.

His mother wasn't done. She held to her blockade. "Becky said you wouldn't let her wear her rain boots and tutu to school today."

"I need Becky to look more like her friend Mia." Drew couldn't keep the desperation from his voice.

"But she's not Mia. She's Becky." His mom was whispering now. "Don't try to make her be like everyone else."

"At the expense of custody?" His throat threatened to close. "To Jane?"

"Love and parenting is about finding the right balance." His mother opened the door wider. "Think about it. You'll do the right thing. You always do."

Rupert had said much the same to him at the courthouse. It didn't make Drew feel any better about wanting things that didn't align with the "right thing," like being with Lola or letting his daughter express herself through unique clothing choices.

"Becky," Drew called out, "grab your things. We're going to the park before dinner."

"Dad, Daddy, Papa, Padre." His daughter lumbered out of the kitchen like a sleepy elephant. Her mouth was ringed with chocolate. "We made cookies. I think I ate too many." She groaned.

"And you ate them *before* dinner." Drew gave his mother a significant look. He expected the rules to be bent by the teenage babysitters he hired sometimes, not his mother. Why had she let Becky go overboard today? He needed his daughter to be rested and in a good mood. Meeting Jane wasn't going to be easy.

"What good is being a grandmother if you can't break a few rules?" His mother shrugged. "Besides, you're going to the park. She'll run off that sugar."

"You can have a cookie." Becky held up a burned one. "I saved this for you."

"No thanks, Sunshine."

It took a few minutes to gather Becky's things and a few more to get her buckled into the back seat of the cruiser. The park was nestled between the elementary and junior high schools. There were swings and a merry-go-round on the elementary school side of the park; trees, picnic tables, and barbecues in the middle; and a wide expanse of grass and benches near the junior high.

Jane sat on a swing, elbows hooked around the chains as if she needed the tenuous grounding.

He'd pushed her on that same swing when they were in high school. She'd always sat in it and gazed up at him, silently begging for a kiss before the ride began. He'd loved her then. He'd loved the way she hadn't cared what other people thought of her. The motorcycle boots. The leather vest. The lace skirt. The heavy eye makeup one day, the bare face the next. She'd had talent, and she'd known it. Her talent had always been her shield. But now it looked as if her shield was gone.

Drew parked near the merry-go-round, which was Becky's favorite, and took his time unbuckling her. Becky was nothing like her mother. She was kind and thoughtful. She put others first. She called everyone in her class *friend*.

"My stomach hurts," Becky moaned.

"You ate too many cookies."

"I ate too many cookies," she agreed with a sigh. "I don't wanna go to the park. I wanna go home."

Drew paused. Here was his out. An excuse, so tempting to use.

But it would only postpone the inevitable and get him into trouble with Judge Harper.

"There's someone here." Drew tried to make his voice light.

"Is it Mia?" Her best friend in the whole wide world.

Drew cringed, ashamed that he'd wanted Becky to conform. "No."

"Is it Ms. Williams?"

"No." Why would she want to see Lola? Had she noticed the interest Drew tried so hard to hide?

Becky dropped her head back. "Then I wanna go home."

He couldn't leave without letting Jane meet her. Gary had checked up on Jane last night. She'd held up her end of the judge's bargain and camped on the undug grounds of the cemetery. If Drew didn't make an effort to comply, Jane would use it against him. "Come on. Let's walk out and see this lady. The fresh air will make you feel better, and then we can go home."

Becky scooted to the edge of the car seat before holding out her arms. Drew picked her up and kept her close.

Jane stopped swinging and stood. She looked like a good wind could blow her over and out of town. But she stood her ground, short blond hair blowing in the breeze. "Becky?"

Becky turned her head, keeping it resting on Drew's shoulder. "Hi."

Drew's heart swelled with pride. He'd taught his daughter good manners. He'd raised her right. Judge Harper would have to see that unemployed, drifting Jane wasn't fit for custody.

"Becky, honey." Jane came closer. "I'm so happy to meet you. I'm your—"

"Biggest fan." Drew cut Jane off. She was just going to blurt out who she was without any warning? "She heard you were going to star in a play."

"I'm Athena," Becky said in a shy voice that was totally unlike her normal boisterous tone. "Goddess of war."

"And wisdom," Drew added, thinking of Lola, who would never walk away from her child.

There was a crease between Jane's blond brows.

"I wanna go home." Becky buried her face in Drew's neck.

"She needs to know," Jane said with the same steel in her voice she'd used the day she'd left him. "Judge Harper said I could visit."

"He said no more than an hour, and Becky isn't feeling well." Drew turned. "I'm taking her home."

"No." Jane trotted around to block his way. "Tell her, or I will."

"I don't feel good." Becky's cheek felt hot against his neck.

Drew's gaze collided with Jane's. The news of who Jane was wasn't going to go over well, not when Becky wasn't feeling good. But he shrugged and set Becky down. "If you insist."

Becky wailed and clung to Drew's legs. Her face was red and sweaty, the portent of bad things to come.

Jane knelt to Becky's level and spread her arms in welcome. "Becky, I'm your mama."

Becky raised her green eyes to Drew's. There

was no disbelief. No longing. No shock. Just upset stomach.

"It's true. This is your mother." The words stuck to the roof of Drew's mouth like one of Lola's cupcakes.

Becky stared at Jane and her open arms. Burped. And vomited.

Chapter Twenty-Four

♥

Augie and Rowena were taking a rare long weekend off.

To cover for them at the mortuary, Lola had rescheduled all her hair appointments at the retirement home's beauty parlor. There was just one she couldn't reschedule—Harriet Bloom's. The woman had requested a special Friday appointment to coincide with a visit from her great-grandkids.

Lola was just ushering Harriet out the door when Drew appeared. His gaze connected with Lola's and sent a familiar howdy-do that went straight to her heart and made her blood pump faster.

Harriet paused in the doorway and looked at Lola over her shoulder. "I almost forgot. Come watch *Phantom of the Opera* tomorrow morning. It's at the movie theater. They beam these things in live from Broadway now."

Broadway.

Lola felt homesick.

"And..." Harriet laughed, banging her handles on the doorframe as she wheeled her walker into the hallway. "Rumor has it Avery Blackstone is going to protest the sale of the downtown buildings tomorrow morning with signs, chanting, and everything. Should be quite the spectacle."

Avery would hate being a spectacle.

Harriet left.

Drew handed Lola a small stack of photographs. "Wendy wanted me to drop off some pictures I took of the kids you made up for rehearsal."

Lola flipped through the photos: Caden with his hair horns, Becky with her updo, soldiers and kids in the chorus. That night she'd felt like she had a future in Sunshine, like she was a part of the community.

"You're not saying anything." Drew's gaze softened. "Are you okay?"

"I'm not sure what to say to you anymore, Sheriff."

His eyes narrowed at the word *sheriff* but it took him a moment to speak. "You know, we had a pretty brutal winter with lots of snow late in the year."

He's trying to make small talk?

Lola should be packing up to get to the mortuary. The Larsons were supposed to come in and proof their grandfather's headstone at nine thirty. It was nine now. But Drew's retrospective weather report, or maybe just the sound of his deep voice, kept Lola's high heels in place.

"A hard winter gives people cabin fever," Drew went on. "The sun comes out, and suddenly you can do things you couldn't before. For a couple of weeks during spring thaw, it's like spring break for the entire town." Drew paused and looked at Lola the way he had the night he'd found her dancing.

And then he kissed me.

She shivered.

"I call it spring-thaw madness. We're in it now." He blew out a small breath and shook his head. "My dad left my mom during spring thaw. Pris met a cowboy during spring thaw and eloped with him. And then there was me and Jane."

"Quite a track record." Or a series of coincidences. Although Drew's cop sense wouldn't lead him to believe in coincidences. He'd collect the evidence and...

Decide her hunt for Randy's mistresses was a product of the spring thaw.

Decide their attraction was a product of the spring thaw.

Decide he never wanted to see her again come June.

Anger made her pulse pound this time. Lola shut off the fan and the low-playing radio. She loaded the photos, hair spray, and shampoo into her supply case and snapped it shut. She wheeled it toward the door and turned off the light.

Drew didn't leave, standing in her way without taking his eyes off her.

"I suppose if you think about it hard enough," Lola said, back straight enough to make a ballerina proud, "you'll find a way to blame kissing me on spring thaw."

"The need to kiss you does seem like madness," he murmured, staring at her lips.

She'd never wanted to kiss someone as much as she wanted to kiss Drew right now, if only to prove it had everything to do with chemistry and nothing to do with the season.

But he wasn't done with his hypotheses. "As does your need to have proof that your husband strayed because he didn't love you. I'm sure he did in his own way."

She tried to push past him.

Drew caught her arm. "What is love, Lola, but an acceptance of someone for who they are and what they can give you emotionally? Let the rest go, Lola. The perfume, the bracelet."

"Would I be good enough for you then?" Lola wanted the words back as soon as she uttered them.

His eyes widened. "You've always been good enough for me."

"But not for Sunshine or your custody battle." Lola was aware of people moving up and down the hall, of their voices and their laughter. "And my grandmother's ring? The one that was *stolen* from me?"

His gaze was filled with regret. "Don't hold on too tight to things you've lost. Or you might find yourself stuck in a place where no one can find you." Drew walked away.

Lola stood in the midst of the hall for a good minute more, gripping the case handle so tight her bones ached.

A lot of people in town thought she was a disgrace for bringing up her husband's indiscretions. She tried hard not to care, tried hard not to take it personally or let it keep her up at night. But what Drew thought of her did matter, did hurt, did leave her sleepless. He wanted her to move on, to be the bigger person.

Could she let questions about Randy go unanswered?

Could she pretend knowing the truth about her marriage wasn't important to her?

* * *

"Why does this mama want to see me?" Becky placed her cowboy boots on the back of the cruiser's front seat and pushed. "She didn't come to my last birthday. Or Christmas."

Drew's boundaries were being pushed as hard as his seatback. "Jane wants you to like her."

Drew had been sure Jane would give up her quest for motherhood after Becky got sick on her yesterday but she'd texted last night asking for a time to meet again. He'd picked Becky up after school and taken her home to clean up and get a light snack. He'd talked about Jane in a distant way, and for some reason, Becky started referring to her as "this mama," as if she had more than one.

Could that be the result of all the talk and jokes about marriage to Wendy?

"Do you like this mama?" Becky pumped the seatbacks as if they were failed brakes. "I like people you like. Ms. Adams. Ms. Williams. Granny Susie."

"I used to like Jane." Was that what he'd say about Lola one day? His chest ached. He admired Lola's honesty but that didn't change his obligation to protect Becky.

"I like everybody I know." Becky pumped the seats again. "I s'pose I'll hate somebody someday."

"I s'pose." Uncomfortable with Jane's visitation,

he'd called Rupert last night, needing the advice of his lawyer.

"Stick out the week, Sheriff," Rupert had said. "Haven't you ever done anything hard in your life?"

Drew had, but nothing this hard, nothing that had felt as if half his heart were going to be ripped out of his chest if he wasn't careful.

In the back seat, Becky flexed her leg muscles again. "Mia hates Caden because he tried to kiss her at recess."

"She'll get over that." But could Drew get over Jane wanting to be back in their lives?

The schools and the park came into view, along with Jane sitting on the swing. Maddie Robertson pushed a stroller along the sidewalk. Over by the junior high, the Bodine boys sat on a bench, bookending a girl Drew didn't immediately recognize.

"Can I like this mama once?"

"You can like her more than once." It killed Drew to say it. He parked and turned to face his daughter. "I love you, Sunshine. Nothing will ever change that. You're always going to live with me no matter what this mama says."

Becky stared out the window with a worried expression on her face. "I promise not to throw up on her."

"I know, sweetheart." Drew patted her boot. "Let's take a ride on the merry-go-round and see what this mama has to say."

As soon as he opened the car door, he heard Jane sing.

"*Blue jean baby...*" Jane's sultry voice carried across the grass, hitting the opening notes to "Tiny Dancer" with power and full-on country soul. She walked toward the cruiser, continuing to sing.

Drew's stomach clenched into a tight ball. Nashville had been blind to Jane's talent. Did she want to use Becky or Drew to get their attention? Contestants on those singing shows always had some kind of sappy life story.

Maddie's steps slowed as she brought the stroller to a halt. The Bodine twins stopped flirting with the girl Drew now recognized as Jami Iverson.

"Who's that singing?" Becky asked, twisting in her car seat. Jane was approaching from behind her.

Drew unbuckled Becky's seat. "That's her."

"This mama?" His daughter scrambled out and stood in front of Drew, awestruck by that throaty voice. She reached for his hand.

Jane looked like she'd been roughing it. Her clothes were wrinkled. Her hair was a limp and rumpled mess. But that voice... She sounded as if she'd slept in a five-star hotel. She came to a stop in front of Becky and sang another verse.

And then the chorus.

And then another verse.

And...

Maddie had moved on. The Bodine boys were back to double-teaming Jami.

Drew raised his hand in a cutting motion across his throat.

With a slight frown, Jane took the hint and stopped singing. She smiled at Becky broadly as if Jane were a judge on one of those singing competition shows. "Hi, baby girl."

"Hi," Becky whispered, spellbound. "Did you just make that song up?"

"No." Stopping a few feet away on the grass, Jane stuck her hands in her back pockets. "That's a classic song about life on the road. I think, anyway."

"Life on the road," Becky echoed, fairly trembling with excitement. She let go of Drew's hand and stepped toward the grass.

Becky was worshipping Jane. His temples throbbed, and reflexively, he reached for Becky's shoulders, keeping her on the sidewalk. "We're going to ride on the merry-go-round."

Jane hadn't looked at him since he'd cut her song short. "Does your stomach feel well enough for a spin, baby girl?"

With a nod, Becky marched forward, and Drew's hands fell to his sides.

For a moment, he couldn't move. His baby was walking away, chattering with Jane as if she'd known her all her life.

He forced his feet to move. He forced air in and out of his lungs. He forced himself to listen in case Jane revealed the real reason she wanted custody.

Chapter Twenty-Five

♥

Lola was in Rowena's office at the mortuary when the call came in.

"My mother-in-law died last night," Kevin said on the other end of the line. "Can I talk to Augie or Rowena?"

Holy gone too soon.

Lola had just seen Marcia toting a stack of romances at the retirement home yesterday. Lola grabbed a pencil and the pickup paperwork. "They're in Denver at their daughter's college graduation. They won't be back until Sunday night."

The mayor relayed the message to Barbara.

"I don't care," Lola heard his wife say. "We need to have a plan."

"It's settled," Kevin said in an even voice. "We're coming in."

Inwardly Lola cringed. Kevin and Barbara were Sunshine royalty. Serving them was above her pay grade. Not to mention Barbara didn't like her. "I know this is a difficult time but I have to ask. What is Marcia's location and has she been declared dead by a doctor?"

On the other end of the line, Lola heard a door open and close.

Kevin lowered his voice. "Obviously, this is unexpected. Barbara's demanding an autopsy, so there's no immediate need for a hearse."

"Then you can wait for Augie and Rowena. I can schedule an appointment for Monday." Lola tried not to sound relieved.

She heard a door open again.

"*Kevin*," Barbara wailed. "You left me alone."

"We'll be there within the hour." Kevin hung up.

Needless to say, Lola quaked in her heels.

The Barbara Hadley who strutted around town and intimidated people into submission wasn't the Barbara Hadley who showed up at the mortuary. Her blond hair was frizzed, and her clothes were rumpled, as if she'd pulled on what she'd worn the day before. Her eyes were red-rimmed and puffy, completely devoid of makeup. There was moisture on her upper lip, and her green silk blouse had sweat stains beneath her arms.

"I found her." Barbara clutched Lola's hand, only to immediately release it. "I call her every morning, and this morning she didn't answer." Her voice was high-pitched, very un-Barbara-like. "She lives in a little house on our property, and when I went over to check, she was..."

"It's okay." Kevin had his arm around his wife's shoulders but rather than lean into him, Barbara held herself stiffly.

"I want the best." Barbara crumpled a tissue in one hand. She held a blue velvet drawstring bag in the other. "That's why I'm here. The best doesn't come quickly."

She was right about that.

If Barbara was in the mood to buy, Lola could be in the mood to sell, especially with a commission involved. She led them to the showroom, which was lined with more caskets, urns, and headstones than Happy Motors had cars in its used-car lot. "I don't want to overwhelm you with options." They'd start with the easy stuff. "Are you thinking burial or cremation?"

"Burial. Top-of-the-line casket. Top-of-the-line interior. Top-of-the-line headstone." Barbara rattled off her demands like a general directing his troops through an important drill. "Visitation beginning during business hours and extending into the evening. I want real food, none of those store-bought cookies."

So much for the easy stuff.

The mayor tried to inject some sanity into the equation. "Barb—"

"Slideshow. A printed color program on quality paper stock." Barbara jerked from beneath Kevin's arm. "There needs to be a string quartet. Hymns. Eulogies. Prayer."

Kevin lifted a hand to draw Barbara back but thought better of it. His arm fell to his side. "Your mother didn't believe in God, honey."

"It's the right thing to do," Barbara snapped, moving to stand apart from them. "When you run for governor, do you want people to look back and say you're a devoted family man? Or do you want them to look at Mom's passing and wonder if you considered her a nuisance, because we skimped on everything?"

Lola wanted to disappear into the paneling so they could fight without an audience.

"Marcia wrote her wishes in a will." Kevin's tone was as gentle as a morning breeze. His expression as compassionate as a minister's. If he ever retired from public service, he had all the skills to work in the bereavement industry. "We should get it out of her safe-deposit box and read it."

"No." Barbara slashed her hand through the air. "I know exactly how to produce this."

"We don't have to do this today," Lola said. If this was how the session was going to go, she'd prefer her bosses handle all the drama.

"Oh, we'll do this today." The edge returned to Barbara's voice, sharp enough to cut. Her eyes roved the showroom, seemingly without seeing anything. "I can't do it tomorrow. I'm working. I have seven clients coming in. It's bad enough I had to let Sheree cover for me today. Give clients one reason to leave, and they go elsewhere."

"Baby, your mother just died. You need to take time off." Kevin came to Barbara's side and pressed a kiss to her forehead.

Barbara's shoulders sagged, and her face tilted heavenward but she said nothing.

Meanwhile, Lola thanked heaven for Kevin's presence. Without him, this would be a raging fiasco.

Kevin's phone rang. He checked the display and then lowered the phone but didn't put it away, clearly torn.

Barbara sighed. "If it's Frank, you need to answer it. I don't care if you were friends when you were seventeen or how much money he has—you can't let him buy and demolish downtown." When he hesitated, she shooed him away. "Go, please."

Kevin took the call, drifting back to the lobby and speaking quietly.

"Men." Barbara gave Lola a watery smile. "I'm barely holding it together, and when Kevin tries to be supportive, it just makes me want to shatter. I can't be weak. I've got a business to run and the wife of the mayor's office to uphold."

Lola wasn't aware the wife of the mayor had an office.

"I mean, if I broke down, I'd end up doing something rash, like you and those window displays." Barbara wiped her nose with a tissue. "People expect more from me. My mother expected more from me. Someday, I'm going to be First Lady." She said it with complete confidence.

The scary part was Lola believed her.

"Let's look at caskets." Lola walked deeper into the showroom. The farther she went, the higher the price, and the more lucrative her time with Barbara would be. "I didn't know your mother personally but this seems like something you'd want to consider." She opened the casket. "This is our ultra-premium unit. Eighteen-gauge steel, beveled edges, hand-waxed teal powder finish, diamond-tuck rose interior in satin, eternal-rest reclining couch base and matching pillow, triple-rose embroidery above the head position." It had everything but a TV remote.

Barbara clung to the side of the casket as if it were the edge of the deep end of a pool and she couldn't swim. "She was so young. She hadn't even gone through menopause yet. She had me in high school, you know."

Lola hadn't known.

"Daddy was twenty years older than she was." Barbara shook the casket. "Why did this happen? We were supposed to go to dinner in Greeley tonight." She bowed her head. "She's had a rough year. The doctor said she was depressed. What did she have to be blue about?"

"I couldn't say." A strange feeling was taking hold of Lola—the impulse to comfort Barbara with a touch or a hug.

"Not that it was suicide." Barbara lifted her head to stare at Lola, perhaps to see whether Lola thought it might have been.

"No one said it was." Had it been? Marcia's body would tell the tale even if Barbara didn't.

There was an uncomfortable silence but since Barbara was so upset, it didn't last long.

"What am I going to do?" wailed Barbara. "We were so close. She was my room mother all through elementary school. She was my cheerleading coach. She judged the debate team. My friends all loved her. She gave up everything for me." Barbara turned tear-filled red eyes to Lola. Her lips trembled, and she looked like she might crumple.

Lola gave in to impulse and hugged her. It was one of the most uncomfortable hugs ever. Quick. Awkward. With a hint of unwashed body odor—Barbara's.

"This casket is perfect," Barbara said into the ensuing void. "The lining will match her skin tone." She drew herself up and held her head high as a tear rolled down her cheek. "You'll do her hair and makeup because... because..."

"It's my job." And from the horrified look on Barbara's face, she loathed the idea of doing it herself.

"I want to get her something nice to wear. A power suit or a nice sheath dress and matching jacket." Barbara wiped at her eyes with the remains of her tissue. "Is it all right if I bring that in tomorrow?"

"We have a few days, depending upon when they can do her"—Lola almost said *autopsy* but thought better of it—"*final procedure*. You can also bring in any personal items you want her buried with. And a picture would help me with her final preparations."

"I have pictures in here." Barbara handed Lola the small blue velvet bag. "She had blue streaks in her hair up until last year. She said it was because she liked to set herself apart from the crowd but I think she was having a midlife crisis." Barbara stared at her hands. "I stopped letting my colorist put blue in her hair a year ago. I thought a change would do her good. Was I wrong?"

"I couldn't say." But Lola was thinking yes.

"I don't want her to look like the pictures," Barbara continued as if Lola hadn't spoken. "No bright makeup. No funky hair colors. I want her to look like the mother of a First Lady."

No way! "No problem." What Barbara was asking was wrong. Marcia hadn't been the staid and stuffy type.

But disappointing this client? That was a scary thought.

"Her wedding ring is in there too. She didn't wear it

anymore, and she'd probably kill me for burying her with it on but Daddy died years and years ago so technically it's the right thing to do." Barbara heaved a sigh and kept babbling. "She and Daddy fought like wolves but they loved each other, and he did leave her a life insurance policy big enough that she could retire early."

Marcia had been lucky her husband hadn't left that insurance money to his mother, like Randy had.

"And there's a pearl ring in there she was fond of," Barbara was saying. She glanced over her shoulder toward the door and then leaned in to whisper, "She had a special someone for years. He gave it to her two Christmases ago. She never told me who she was seeing. I always imagined he was someone incredibly romantic. He made her so happy."

A pearl ring. A secret man.

The hair on the back of Lola's neck went up, along with her suspicions.

She was wrong, of course. There was the age difference. Since Barbara and Randy had been in the same class in high school, Marcia had literally been old enough to be his mother. When Lola had suspected Randy of having an affair with an older woman because of the clip-on earring, she hadn't thought she'd be that much older. She'd pictured someone pushing forty who'd never pierced her ears. An eight-year age difference, max.

But still... a pearl ring.

"Honey." Kevin entered the room and put his arm around his wife again. "I think that's enough for one day."

Rigid in his arms, Barbara stared at the casket.

Lola murmured her agreement and then reassured Barbara that she'd get the paperwork started and call about casket availability. They rarely sold stock off the showroom floor, and Barbara probably wouldn't accept it if they did.

With fits and starts and soft reassurances, Kevin managed to escort Barbara out.

Lola shut the front door behind them and then sat on the green burlap couch in the lobby, staring at the blue velvet bag.

When he was younger, Randy had slept with two knockouts—Avery and Mary Margaret. And Lola wasn't exactly chopped liver in the looks department either. By comparison, Marcia was...not bland, but a different cup of tea. And older.

Randy and Marcia?

There was no way that was true.

Yet there was only one way to find out.

She opened the drawstring bag and dumped the contents onto the couch cushion. Simple clip-on pearl earrings. A simple diamond band. And a simple ring with a fleur-de-lis to either side of the pearl. A pretty ring. A familiar ring.

Nana's ring.

Lola fell forward onto her knees, trying to breathe, trying to pretend she was wrong.

Randy and Marcia had been lovers.

She'd prefer to believe he'd had a deep friendship with Marcia, like Mims claimed to have had with Charlie. But Randy hadn't had female friends.

Things Barbara had said about her mother swam through the muck in Lola's head. "*She was depressed... She had a special someone for years. He gave it to her two Christmases ago... He made her so happy.*" And the depression had started about a year ago, around the time Randy had died. Randy, whose favorite color was blue, the color Marcia liked to put in her hair. When combined with the pearl ring, the pieces fit.

"Oh, Randy."

Now Lola knew why Marcia had avoided talking to her, why Marcia turned the other way when she saw Lola. It had nothing to do with Barbara and everything to do with Lola being married to Randy.

Lola felt so inadequate. Her husband had been having an affair with an older woman.

Her insides twisted. She could understand Randy falling for a beautiful woman. She could understand him falling for a woman who stocked the contents of the garage-apartment bureau. But the age difference...

How could this have happened? They'd been newly-weds. He'd seemed so happy.

Unless Drew was right and Randy's affair with Marcia pre-dated her marriage. In which case Lola had been the other woman, and Marcia had been wronged.

Chest on her thighs, Lola stared at a small dust bunny behind her heels. Maybe it was Randy who'd had the midlife crisis and wanted to settle down, have a few kids, be more traditional.

What if, after she and Randy arrived in Sunshine married, Marcia had wanted to take their clandestine relationship public? Would Randy have divorced Lola if Marcia had said the word? Or had he married Lola to spite Marcia because she wouldn't marry a younger man? That kind of thing would put a kink in Barbara's White House plans.

Lola had too many unanswered questions, more now than before.

She was falling apart inside. Chunk by chunk, her heart was breaking away. If she discovered one more of Randy's illusions, one more piece of his past, she'd shatter.

She sat with her head between her legs for several minutes, feeling nauseated and breathless and more than a bit used. Finally, she recovered enough to look at Marcia's pictures.

The first photograph was professionally done, a picture of Barbara sitting and Marcia standing behind her. Marcia's hands were on Barbara's shoulders. The neck of Marcia's baby-blue sweater was decorated with shiny blue beads. Her white-blond hair had a bright-blue streak. She wore the small pearl ear studs and was smiling broadly without a bevy of wrinkles. She could afford Botox when Lola could barely afford new brakes for her car.

The others were candid shots. Marcia wearing a leather jacket and sitting behind the wheel of an impractical convertible with the top down and zebra glasses on. Marcia in a yoga pose on a ledge beneath the Saddle Horn mountaintop. Marcia wearing an evening gown with cleavage Pris would envy.

Marcia didn't just dress like she was in her thirties. She'd lived like she was in her thirties. Emotionally, she and Randy must have been the same age.

Lola put her head between her legs again.

When she didn't feel so light-headed, she shoved everything but Nana's ring into the blue velvet bag.

So what if Marcia was hip for her age? That didn't mean Randy had the right to give her Lola's ring.

But why had he given it to Marcia?

And how was Lola going to keep it from being buried with her?

Chapter Twenty-Six

♥

By Saturday, Mims had been avoiding the Widows Club board for days.

First, she'd gone fishing. Hadn't caught anything.

Then she'd gone shopping in Greeley. Hadn't bought anything.

Finally, she'd gone for a drive but all roads eventually led back to Sunshine. Nothing she tried erased what she'd done.

The other woman.

There was a title Mims had never aspired to.

It played on a loop in her head. Along with thoughts like *If only Hamm's death hadn't hit me so hard* and *If only I'd told Charlie that I was fine*. Because deep down, Mims had always been strong. It had just felt better to have Charlie's arms around her and had been so much easier to lean on him when her children and grandchildren were hundreds of miles away.

But after days of self-loathing, Mims discovered something: clarity. All her grief, all her guilt, it'd bogged down her brain. She watched *Jeopardy!* and shouted out the questions before the contestants. She felt as if she could play poker and win.

"I'm back," she said to herself on Saturday morning, which meant there was work to be done.

Mims found Wendy at the town library, where she volunteered for a shift one day a week.

If Mims hadn't seen it, she would never have guessed that Wendy was the same woman who'd sashayed down the runway a few days ago in a sexy dress with sparkly makeup on her face. Today she wore almost no makeup and a T-shirt with what looked like a finger-painted rainbow across her chest.

Mims stood at the checkout desk and surveyed the patrons. Unlike other libraries across the country, the Sunshine Valley Library still thrived, most likely because the town was thirty miles from the nearest bookstore.

Susie Taylor was reading a Curious George book to a circle of children in the cozy corner, her granddaughter, Becky, among them. George Brewer was helping some high school kids with math at a table nearby. Pearl was in the paperback-romance section, wearing her name tag from the Saddle Horn. And Beatrice was carrying a stack of thrillers, most likely to bring back to the retirement home.

"How are things going with Drew?" Mims asked Wendy in hushed tones.

"Oh, I don't know." Wendy placed a stack of books on a cart, looking uncomfortable. "He and I..."

"You haven't found common ground," Mims guessed.

Wendy nodded, looking relieved. "He talks a lot. Or at least, a lot more than I do."

Mims processed her remark in the context of the shy Wendy she'd seen at the Saddle Horn and the glowing Wendy she'd seen at the bake sale and fashion show, and combined it with the confident Wendy she'd encountered at the elementary school. "You need someone a bit more sensitive, don't you?"

Wendy, being Wendy, shrugged.

Mims was more decisive. Wendy needed someone bookish and comfortable with silences. And yet someone who could enjoy the limelight a little and support Wendy when she occasionally stepped into it herself. In hindsight, Drew was totally wrong for Wendy. He was under pressure with Jane's return, and she'd never seen him spark to Wendy. In fact, there'd been more sparks between him and Lola.

Mims chuckled.

Darned if Bitsy hadn't been right all along. At least when it came to chemistry. With Drew's worries about child custody and Lola's obsession with her husband's paramours, neither one of them was ready for romance. But they could be. With a little help from the Matchmakers Club.

* * *

Folks in Sunshine usually greeted Mims with a smile.

But Lola sat, not smiling, in the same webbed folding chair she'd sat in when she'd been burning her husband's underwear. Only this time, she was surrounded by opened boxes of clothing, the mounted head of a four-point buck, beer mirrors, a coffee table, and a flimsy sign that read, MOVING SALE.

"Are you moving?" Mims wandered through the maze of castoffs to reach the young widow.

"Someday." Lola watched a car pass slowly by. "For now, Randy is moving out." She waved a hand toward the house behind her.

In her front window, a pair of blow-up dolls were involved in a steamy clench. The man wore a black leather jacket, and the woman wore a black nightgown.

Mims would bet Ramona was having a conniption fit across the street. Her mauve curtains twitched. "Have you had much traffic?" There seemed to be a lot going by, although it was still early.

"I've had no traffic." Lola had her legs crossed at the knee. She kicked out her foot in rapid succession, like a cat that was annoyed and about to take a swipe at something, claws drawn. "Should you be seen talking to me? Some of my stink might rub off on you."

"I might say the same to you." Mims reached Lola and shoved her hands in her hunting-vest pockets, taking stock of Lola in a different light. She and Lola had something in common—the emptiness of heartache. Mims tried to fill her well with good works. Lola with her window displays, which snubbed the husband who'd hurt her. Mims studied the items for sale closely. "What's really going on here?"

"The thrift store canceled picking up Randy's things." Lola's gaze swept her husband's possessions littering the drive and front lawn. "Marcia Stephens died." She cast a glance over her shoulder toward the couple in her front window. "And I received a warning from town hall that my front yard is a fire hazard and violating some city code."

One of the three things Lola had mentioned threw Mims off—Marcia's death. What did that sad event have to do with Lola?

"Let's do a dump run." Mims sat down on a footlocker. "I've got a truck at home."

"Since I'm not selling anything..." Lola frowned at a passing car. "I hope it's a big truck."

"It is." Mims picked up a stained pink fabric scrapbook at Lola's feet. "What's this?"

"Nothing."

Mims opened it, noting Lola's name in flowery script on the inside cover. She flipped past autographed playbills and magazine photos of wedding dresses and baby nurseries. There was a picture of Lola with a grandmotherly figure. Mims kept flipping, not knowing what she was looking for, until she turned to the last page. "There's a love letter here from Randy."

Lola grunted again. Her leg swung faster.

"He admits he's loved more than his share of women," Mims said, feeling uncomfortable for reading but compelled to do so nonetheless. "He says you'll be the last woman he loves."

"There was a tie," Lola said gruffly, staring at the street. "Or maybe he wasn't discerning when he decided to marry me. He had a long-term affair with Marcia Stephens."

"No." Mims nearly tumbled backward off the footlocker.

"I suspect it pre-dated me." Lola swept her brown hair into her hands, twisted it, and piled it on top of her head, only to let it fall back down on her shoulders.

"I don't think Randy ever stopped loving Marcia. Or seeing her after we were married. He gave her a pearl ring that was my grandmother's." She showed Mims the ring she wore. "Barbara told me Marcia had a man on the side, a man she'd been seeing for years. I've been looking for his mistresses but I think he only had one. I think he only loved one."

Mims stared at Randy's note. "Did he write this before you were married?"

Lola nodded.

"He wanted to be faithful to you, I think." Mims returned to a passage he'd written. "*Our love is innocent, and I intend to do right by you.*"

"But he didn't. He didn't love me."

"He loved you." Mims held the scrapbook out to Lola. "He loved you the same way Charlie loved me while still loving Edith."

Lola blinked back tears, her hands in her lap. "I didn't sign up to share my husband's heart with anyone."

"But the fact is, you did share him. You shared him with a good woman. Marcia was kind. She was reliable. She was my friend." Mims continued to extend the book to Lola. "And so are you."

Lola hesitated before accepting it. "I have very few friends nowadays."

"Jealousy and misperception make us lonely beings."

Lola crossed her arms over her chest and her scrapbook. "Avery's protesting today."

Lola's former best friend had been leading a picket line when Mims drove down Main Street.

"Avery will be all right without you." Mims's thoughts

turned to her former friend Edith. She'd been more determined than a tick in a border collie's ear to serve on the board. But maybe that was only because Edith had been working up the courage to confront Mims.

"But I won't be all right without Avery." Lola sat up, looking less teary. "No excuses anymore. I'm going to apologize for the Cupcake War and the necklace. I'm going to ask her to forgive me. And you're going to convince Edith to do the same."

Mims nearly fell off the storage locker again. "Edith and I weren't as close as Charlie and I, or you and Avery." Not since grade school.

"That's a cop-out." Lola pressed the pages of her scrapbook tighter together. "Sunshine is a small town. You can't avoid Edith, which means no matter what your friendship status was before Charlie died, you need to make this right between you."

Lola might be impulsive but she knew in her heart what was right.

And even if Mims was unhappy about it, she knew it too.

Chapter Twenty-Seven

♥

Gary shot to his feet the moment Drew came through the door. "Boss, I need to tell you something and ask you about procedure."

"Are you going to tell me about arresting Avery for protesting outside her family's movie theater?" Drew had Becky in tow and expected Jane any minute for a supervised visit but he'd already fielded two phone calls about Gary's latest arrest. "I hope you had good reason."

"Avery didn't have a demonstration permit." Gary hitched up his pants. "And that Frank fella held me back when I tried to take her sign, and then Avery disrespected the uniform and pushed me when I tried to cuff him."

Drew sighed. Those actions were against the law but Gary was always bringing a sledgehammer to a fence-building party.

"Uncle Gary." Becky had been jumping up and down near his desk, where she'd been waiting for a break in the conversation. "Wanna see me sing?"

"Of course." Gary sat down and dutifully put a smile on his face but his gaze kept darting to Drew.

Becky burst into song, an off-key rendition of "Yankee Doodle." She may have inherited her mother's love of the limelight but she'd received Granny Susie's set of pipes. She sang completely off-key and had been doing so often since she'd met Jane.

One day. It'd taken only one day for Becky to idolize her mother. And how would she feel when Jane disappeared again? Devastated, that's how.

Becky finished and struck a pose as if she'd been freeze-framed while marching. "That's a little song about life on the road!"

Rosie's shrill, frightened squeals filled the air, as sharp as fingernails scraping on a chalkboard.

As Gary applauded, Drew turned toward the door leading to the jail cells. "Quiet down. I think we've set off Rosie." He grabbed the keys and opened the door.

The pig continued to squeal.

The three of them ran down the hallway to her cell, past Avery and Frank, calling out to the pig. All that noise didn't help. Rosie squealed louder. By the time they reached her cell door, she was making a circuit. She crashed into the bars in front of Drew and swayed as if she'd just given herself a concussion.

"Becky, go get the blanket from the storage closet. It's by the med kit." Drew put the key in the lock and exchanged a glance with Gary. "You always sucked as a tackler. Don't suck today."

"You know," Gary said smugly, "I was going to ask you what to do, seeing as how we're in violation of Ordinance 102—no livestock in town."

"You have crap timing, Gary." Drew turned the key,

opened the door, and leaped forward, arms spread wide, catching Rosie's neck as if he were a steer wrangler.

His arms alone weren't strong enough to wrestle Rosie to the ground. But she did slow.

"Gary!" Drew glared at his deputy, who stood blocking the doorway with a stunned look on his face.

Rosie slammed Drew into a wall.

Gary set his feet as if he were going to start running a competitive mile. His hands moved in circles, tracking the pig's path.

Drew was losing his grip. "Go, you idiot!" When Gary still hesitated, he commanded, "Tackle us!"

Apparently, Gary held some resentment toward his cousin, because he didn't hesitate to body-slam Drew. Rosie slowed beneath them but she was still squealing and digging in her hooves.

"I got the blanket, Daddy." Becky stood in the doorway.

Drew held out a hand.

Rosie lurched forward.

"Don't hurt her." Becky tossed the blanket.

"Get back." Boots searching for purchase, Drew shook out the wool blanket with one hand and tried to cover Rosie's head with it. "We need to sing."

"I demand to see a lawyer," Frank shouted.

Gary grunted. "My arms are tired."

"Don't you dare let go." Drew struggled to cover Rosie, imagining he was wrapping the blanket around Gary's neck.

"*Rock-a-bye, baby.*" Becky burst into song, too loud, too off-key.

Rosie let out a pig scream and lunged toward her just as Gary let go.

Becky screamed. Rosie squealed. Drew shouted. The bars jangled from the impact of the three of them. Rosie dragged Drew along the side wall. He dug in his heels and tried to hold on to all that girth. A couple more turns and she'd ram Gary, who was trying to comfort Becky, who was sobbing but still standing in the way.

"*Rock-a-bye, baby, on the tree tops.*" The deep sultry voice sounded like that of an angel as it echoed through the jail.

And for the first time in years, Drew didn't want to stuff his ears with cotton when Jane sang.

Without missing a note, Jane picked up Becky and carried her to safety.

Gary shut the jail-cell door and prepared to take another crack at pig tackling.

Fifteen minutes later, Drew was on the phone with Tom Bodine, making arrangements for Rosie to be picked up.

"But, Daddy," Becky said from her seat on top of his desk. She was going to have some bruises on her backside from the bars (like her daddy), and some tall tales to tell her classmates on Monday, but otherwise, she was going to be fine. "Mr. Bodine is going to eat Rosie."

"That's what people do." Jane sat in a chair in the corner. "People eat pigs and cows and lambs and chickens. You've eaten plenty of Rosies in your lifetime."

"Becky, can you go check on Gary? He looks scared." Drew lifted Becky to the floor as carefully as if she were fine china, and closed the door behind her. "You can't talk to Becky like that."

"It's true." Jane's mouth set in a mutinous expression. Her hair looked better today, and her clothing less wrinkled, as if she'd found a place to shower.

Mental note: ask Emily if she checked up on Jane last night.

"I don't care if it's true." Drew leaned against his desk and crossed his arms over his chest. "You don't tell children their pet pig is going to be bacon. She's still of an age to believe in Santa and fairy tales."

Jane's chin jutted out. "The sooner she learns the harsh realities of life, the better off she'll be."

"Why? Because life was tough on you and your dreams?" He held up a hand when it looked as though she was about to argue. "Look, you did a good thing in there. Thank you, but leave the parenting to me."

Jane stood, her green eyes cold. "I'm not leaving anything to you. I'm calling my lawyer and telling him you've been reckless with our child." She opened the door.

"Jane." Drew had several things he'd like to toss into the verbal sparring match they were having but none of them would help his cause in the courtroom. And none of them were appropriate for Becky's prying ears. So he let Jane walk out with the last word.

"Here." Gary handed Drew a ticket when he emerged from his office.

Becky stood on the porch, waving as Jane drove away.

"What's this?" Drew looked down at the ticket Gary had given him.

"It's my hypothetical question about procedure." Gary fidgeted, standing with his thumbs in his duty belt. "A citation for violation of Ordinance 102."

Anger rumbled through Drew's veins. "You're citing me for having Rosie in jail?" He crumpled the ticket.

"Boss, I wrote myself up too." Gary rocked from side to side. "It seemed only fair. We both broke the law."

What could Drew say to that?

* * *

Drawing a deep breath, Lola walked into the sheriff's office of her own free will.

That, in itself, was unusual. Unusual enough that Drew stopped reprimanding Gary to stare at her.

"I'm here to see Avery." Who'd been arrested for protesting and called Lola. She met Drew's gaze squarely.

"*See?*" Gary demanded. "Or bail out?"

"*Gary*..." Drew traipsed over to open the door to the cells for Lola. "Clear up the paperwork. We're not pressing charges."

Lola walked slowly to Avery's cell, listening to the sound of Gary's complaints and then paper being shredded.

Avery hung on to the bars, looking miserable. The man who'd bought her at the date auction sat on the bench, looking oddly happy. Rosie was stretched out on the floor in the next cell.

"Hey." Lola came to a stop across from Avery.

"I didn't think you'd come." Avery didn't quite meet

Lola's gaze. Her normally perfect hair was in disarray. "Thanks for bailing me out."

"And me." The man stood. He was tall and ruggedly handsome. "I'm Frank."

"She's not here for you," Avery snapped.

Rosie snorted and sat up.

"Be very quiet," Lola said softly. "And use your chipper voice."

"I don't have a chipper voice." Avery crossed her arms over her chest.

"Lola, technically, you were my phone call." Frank had the friendliest smile but it lacked Drew's howdy-do. "Avery's mother hung up on her so I let her have my phone call, which means you're going to bail us both out. I'm good for it, whatever it is. And I'll cover Avery's too."

"You won't." Avery wrapped her arms tighter around her chest.

"Avery, I'm not offering to marry you and give you my AmEx. I'm offering to help straighten out the fallout from your protest." Frank didn't raise his voice or sound impatient. For Lola's benefit, he added, "I'm buying the block downtown if the town council approves the deal."

Avery shook the bars and ground out a frustrating sound that made Rosie's ears twitch. "I suppose you want to know the details of my big *romance* with Randy."

"No," Lola said quickly. "Things got out of hand at the bake sale and—"

"Is that what your tussle was all about?" Frank began to laugh.

Avery whirled on him. "Don't you say a word, Frank Dell Quincy, or I'll—"

"Stop," Frank said, reaching for her, but Avery moved away. "There was no romance with Randy. And it was my fault. I made Avery cry at prom, and Randy took advantage of her."

"Do you ever shut up?" Avery glared at him.

"Randy liked to rescue the ladies," Frank explained.

Lola wrapped her arms around her waist because Randy had pretty much rescued her too when they'd met on the streets of New York.

"I'm sorry." Avery's chin jutted out. "I suppose you hate me."

"No." Lola moved closer to the bars, closer to her friend. "Why didn't you tell me all this at the bake sale?" Or anytime in the past two years?

"Because—"

"We're all set." Drew entered the hallway. Then he opened the jail-cell door. "You're free to go."

Avery darted out of the cell and ran down the hall.

"I'm sorry," Lola said but she wasn't sure Avery heard her.

Drew looked Lola up and down, and then his gaze drifted to Frank. "You still have it bad for Avery?"

"Not bad." Frank looked demoralized for the first time since Lola had entered the jail. "Worse."

Chapter Twenty-Eight

♥

From the window of the sheriff's office, Drew watched Lola walk away, a little piece of himself walking away with her. He felt a lot like Frank. Whatever he felt for Lola… It wasn't bad; it was worse.

His head hurt. He wasn't fond of whom he was becoming—a man without patience for his green deputy, a brother unwilling to go the extra mile for his sister's rescue, a father so scared of losing his daughter that he was considering marrying a woman he barely knew. The week Judge Harper had given him was halfway gone. He had to wrap up his defense and get engaged to Wendy. Maybe then things would go back to normal.

"You have a lot to learn, Gary." Drew wasn't proud of the contempt in his voice.

"They broke the law." Gary was nothing if not predictable. His chin went up, and his hands went to his duty belt. If Gary weren't a cop, he'd be the kind of driver who argued about the accuracy of a radar gun when receiving a speeding ticket. "And we swore to uphold the law."

"What if you were arresting Avery and Frank and a heart attack call came in?" Like the one Drew had received recently about Gigi. "Or a report of arson? Or heaven forbid, a suicide attempt?" He captured Gary's gaze. "Would you still insist upon arresting them when you had a life-threatening call?"

"That didn't happen." Gary's expression turned mulish.

"But it could." Drew continued to press, despite the blood pounding in his temples. "What would you do?"

"I'd order them to turn themselves in, and then I'd take the call."

"Gary, you know the law." Drew shook his head. He really didn't want to do this. There was going to be hell to pay. "But you don't know how to be a lawman."

Tom Bodine pulled up outside with a truck outfitted to carry small livestock.

"They say you can turn lemons into lemonade. I really hope you can, Gary." Drew heaved a sigh. "You're fired."

* * *

Mims stood outside Edith's door as the sun came up on Sunday morning.

She'd knocked several times. Edith wasn't answering.

"I'm going to stay out here until you open this door," Mims called out. "We need to talk."

Edith opened the door in her pink terry-cloth bathrobe. "Slut! Whore! Floozy!"

Mims had been prepared for an attack but Edith's

words still stung. She tugged down her fishing vest and squared her shoulders. "You said you wanted to know the details. If that's true, come along." She turned and walked to her car.

"I'm not dressed." Edith slammed the door.

Mims took that to mean she was to wait for her. Good thing she'd brought coffee. To pass the time, she watched the birds flit through Edith's apple tree searching for bugs, appreciated the colorful sunrise, and braced herself for another round of insults.

Fifteen minutes later, Edith dropped into the front seat, wearing blue jeans, a neatly pressed neon-yellow T-shirt, and a scowl that knotted her entire face. "Did you have a love nest, like Lola's man? Is that where we're going?"

"No. Don't talk until we get there." Or Mims might just change her mind, pull over, and leave her alongside the road.

"Whore." The slur popped out of Edith's mouth like burnt toast from a new toaster. "You were my friend once. I feel so betrayed."

"Don't talk," Mims warned again.

"Jezebel." Edith was incapable of being silent. "Do you remember our freshman year of high school?"

Mims rolled her eyes and shook her head, slowing for a turn.

"That's when I knew Charlie was mine, you floozy." Edith grabbed onto the handle above the door, as if Mims drove like Clarice. "You'd dated him all summer but come September, he was mine."

Mims held her tongue.

"Slut, slut, slut." Edith couldn't hold hers. "We used to do things together. We used to go to the movies and make cookies for the football team."

"You forget what happened after you professed your love to Charlie." Mims's vow of silence didn't just break. It shattered. "You didn't want to hang out with me. You only wanted to do things with Charlie. You went to the movies together. You went shopping together. You had a baby together." There. She'd said it. She'd said what she'd kept inside for more than fifty years. And then she said more. "You weren't married. You didn't finish high school, and neither did he." Edith had trapped Charlie more completely than Mims ever could, because Mims had wanted to wait to have sex until after marriage. "You won Charlie but it wasn't fair and square."

"He loved me," Edith said mutinously.

"He did," Mims agreed, accelerating onto the highway heading out of town. "He loved you despite your insecurities." He'd probably loved her because of them. Charlie liked being needed. He hadn't been Mims's emotional rock out of kindness alone. He'd treated Mims as if she needed a man to survive. She didn't. But in her extended grief over Hamm, she'd forgotten.

"I am not insecure," Edith shouted, tugging at the handle.

"You have got to be the least confident person I know." Mims was shouting now too. "It's why you barge in and pretend not to notice you hurt other people's feelings. You don't let anyone else get a word in. I can't have a conversation with you—I have to yell at you. That's why we stopped being best friends fifty years ago. It had nothing to do with Charlie and everything to do with you being insecure and annoying!"

"Stop the car. I want to get out."

Mims accelerated. "You wanted to know what we did."

"I lied." Edith was pale. Tears streamed down her red cheeks. She wiped them away. "I don't want to know. I only said that because of Lola."

"Lola is a brave woman." Impetuous but brave. "I wouldn't be doing this if not for her." Mims turned down a side road toward the river. She parked by a shallow bend. "Get out."

"I don't understand." Edith backed up against the door. "Are you going to shoot me? Is this a hit?"

"You watch too much TV." Mims got out and opened the back hatch of the Subaru. "You want to know what we did? This is what we did." She took out her waders and put them on. "We fished. We sat in duck blinds. We hunted."

Edith opened the door and scowled at the river. "I hate the outdoors."

"Exactly." Mims got out her tackle box and began tying a fly to her line. "Charlie did everything you enjoyed with you. But you did nothing he enjoyed with him. Charlie and Hamm and I used to hunt and fish together. After Hamm died, Charlie and I hunted and fished together."

"So there's no love shack? You didn't sneak off to some sleazy motel in Greeley?" Edith looked disappointed.

"No."

"Okay." Edith blew out a breath. "You can take me home now. I still hate you but I'll see you at the board meeting later."

"I don't think you understand." Mims gritted her teeth. It really would be easier to shoot her. "You're going to fish *with* me today."

Edith crossed her arms. "Fat chance of that."

"As a way to honor your husband, you'll do it." Mims used her stern voice, the one that had kept many a hungry schoolchild in line. "And if this is the last time you fish, so be it." She held up a pair of waders. "You honored Charlie your way with that bikini. Now honor him his way."

Edith hesitated instead of firing back. She eyed the river. "If I fall in—"

"You'll get wet."

"If I drown—"

"You'll be with Charlie in heaven." She wouldn't let her friend drown.

Edith's eyes narrowed. "I hate you."

"I know." Mims sighed. "I'm sorry I leaned on Charlie after Hamm died. But now it's just you and me. Get your waders on."

* * *

Today was the day Drew would become bulletproof against Jane.

Of course, he was nervous. There were unknowns, and the Saddle Horn was busy, even for a Sunday.

Still, he and Becky had the same seats they always had, next to Iggy. Jason was out on the road, trying his best to win another belt buckle for bull riding. Crazy thing, bull riding. Drew would have gladly switched places with Jason. Not that he had much skill at handling two-thousand-pound bulls, given he couldn't handle a three-hundred-pound pig by himself.

Beside him, Becky was perfecting her beard-making skills with a tall mug of hot chocolate, same as she did every Sunday.

There should have been comfort in the usual but something was off.

Pearl had harrumphed when she poured his coffee. The entire Widows Club board had frowned at him when he walked in. Even Norma Eastlake had looked away when he smiled at her.

Drew spun his mug in a slow circle with sweaty palms. His bad Saturday was turning into a worse Sunday. He'd gotten a call from Rupert last night. Jane was trying to work the system to her advantage, calling Drew reckless in his care of Becky because of Rosie. Drew had fought back this morning, reporting to Rupert that Jane hadn't spent the night camping out in the cemetery. His part-time deputy, Emily, had checked every two hours, starting at midnight. No Jane. Rupert claimed that wasn't enough, not if Drew wasn't married.

The bell over the door rang. Drew jumped, expecting Wendy.

Eileen charged inside instead and slugged Drew's shoulder. "How could you? Rosie doesn't belong on a farm."

"She's on a *ranch.*" Drew tilted out of slugging range, ruing his childish need to teach his sisters how to take care of themselves. He'd taught Eileen to hit hard. "And a ranch is exactly where Rosie belongs."

"In a pigsty." Eileen choked on a sob. "I just saw her, Drew. How could you do that to her?"

"I heard she nearly killed Becky," Iggy said, nosy as always.

"Stay out of this," Drew growled.

"Daddy said Mr. Bodine wouldn't eat Rosie." Becky spun in her stool to face Eileen, wearing a heavy whip beard. "But that new mama said that's what people do. Eat animals." The bulk of the beard plopped into her lap.

Eileen gasped. A tear spilled down her cheek.

The bell over the door rang, and Wendy entered. She headed for the empty seat next to Drew without looking at anyone, not even Becky and her lap of whipped cream.

"Eileen, come on." Drew tried to reach for her arm. "Be reasonable. Tom said he could have Rosie down to fighting weight in a few weeks."

"And you believed him?" Eileen looked around the coffee shop, gathering support.

"That pig was so sweet," Norma said from a side booth. "Say you aren't going to eat her."

"Sweet?" Iggy scoffed. "It took the two of us to take her down one day."

"And you say that with pride." Eileen clenched her fists.

Becky hadn't wiped any of the whip off her lap. She

stared at Drew with wide eyes. "Rosie's going to be okay, isn't she?"

"She'll be fine." Drew grabbed a handful of napkins and wiped Becky clean. "She went to fat camp, that's all."

Eileen made a noise of disbelief and ran out the door.

Lola came in before the door could close again. She wore those sky-blue leggings again—the ones that would stop Drew in traffic if he were behind the wheel. She carried her thermos. No doubt, she was working on Marcia Stephens this morning. Augie and Rowena had returned from their vacation early. He'd seen their truck at the mortuary on his way to the coffee shop.

"What happened to your window display?" Wendy asked Lola, unusually chatty.

"I took it down." Lola glanced at Drew and then away.

All eyes seemed to turn to Drew.

"I didn't make her." What was wrong with people? Half his complaints the past week had been about Lola's window.

"Well, you asked me to do it." Lola handed Pearl her thermos. "Lots of times."

Drew heard a guttural sound and realized it'd come from his own throat. "Why now?"

Lola tilted her head toward one shrugging shoulder. "I decided you were right."

"Next thing you know," Pearl said, topping off his coffee, "you'll be telling me to be nice to people."

"Can you do that, Daddy?" Becky stopped messing with the whipped cream.

"No." Drew scowled.

"He sure can." Iggy laughed.

"What is wrong with you people today?" Drew said to no one in particular.

"You fired Gary, for one." Iggy settled his straw cowboy hat farther back on his head. "He's a town legend, the first person from Sunshine to make it on the state record books."

There was a synchronized wave of head nods.

Drew scowled. "You told me to fire Gary when he pulled you over a few days ago."

"Gary's an..." Iggy's gaze caught on Becky. "Gary's a little green around the edges but he means well."

The bell over the door rang, and Drew's mother entered. She never came to the Saddle Horn on a Sunday anymore. Never.

"This is how you treat family? You fire your cousin? You sentence a pet to death? You don't answer your phone when your mother calls?" She shook her finger at Drew, spun around, and left.

Okay, Drew got it. He'd made some hard decisions over the past twenty-four hours. But he didn't deserve to be treated like he'd sold the town downriver. Everything he'd done had been in Sunshine's best interests.

"No one gets it." Anger coiled around his lungs, and Drew struggled to fill them with air. "You can't have it both ways, people."

"It's okay, Daddy." Becky patted his shoulder. "Do you want to go for a walk? You've got your angry face on."

"Count to ten," Pearl said.

"Deep cleansing breaths," Iggy said.

"Are you okay?"

Although his back was to her, Drew recognized Lola's voice.

"I'm fine," he said wearily, because nothing was going to play out the way he wanted it to but he'd never been a quitter. "Or I'll be fine when this thing with Jane is under control." He'd come here today not just to spoil Becky but to close the deal with Wendy. He turned to her and got down to business. "How'd you like to get married?"

There was a collective gasp in the coffee shop, and then everyone went silent.

Wendy sat very still, so still he almost thought she'd stopped breathing.

Pearl had been pouring coffee in Lola's thermos. It overflowed. At the Widows Club booth, forks clattered. Even Iggy had nothing to say.

Wendy blew out a breath. "Um, wow. I wasn't sure we were dating, and..." She lifted her sweet gaze to Drew's. "I was going to tell you this morning that we shouldn't see each other anymore."

"You're...breaking up with me?" Drew's vision tunneled, and he swayed on the stool.

Wendy nodded and got to her feet. "And I'm turning down your proposal of marriage."

A few minutes later, Drew pushed out the door, tugging Becky behind him.

"But I wasn't finished," Becky whined.

"You've had enough whipped cream for one day." He needed a backup plan. He should have had one to begin with.

The bell rang behind them. It was Lola.

"Don't say a word." Drew yanked open the cruiser's back door for Becky to climb in.

Lola followed, giving him a wide berth. "You shouldn't drive like this."

"Like what?" He leaned in to buckle Becky's seat belt and then straightened to face Lola.

"You shouldn't drive when the spring-thaw madness is at its peak. Walk Becky over to the park. Stroll down the block to the movies." Lola moved closer, close enough to touch, close enough that he couldn't see her long legs without looking down. And then she laid a palm across his cheek. "It will get better."

Drew wanted to snarl and shout and thrust her hand away. He wanted to speed and take corners too fast. He wanted to rant about injustices. He wanted to rail about employees who didn't wield the rules wisely. He wanted to howl about ex-wives who tried to bend the rules to their advantage.

Instead, he stared into Lola's blue eyes and was calmed by her gentle touch.

"It's a beautiful day, Sheriff." Lola's gaze and touch fell away. "A wonderful day to be alive."

Chapter Twenty-Nine

♥

"Get dressed," Lola said to Avery when she opened the door to her small apartment. "We're going to Shaw's."

Avery tugged up the sweats she'd cut off at the knee and stared at Lola's black Keds. "You don't like Shaw's."

"I know, but you do, and it's Sunday and I need a drink." Lola wasn't proud of those words.

It was Sunday afternoon. Augie had come back yesterday to prep Marcia's body because Barbara had decided against an autopsy.

Lola had finished working on Marcia, and she couldn't stand to go home alone. It had nothing to do with Drew (almost) proposing to Wendy and everything to do with prepping the body of her husband's lover. Oh, at first it'd been hard not to make Marcia look like a Kardashian. And then, as they'd listened to eighties classics, something odd had happened. Lola had read Marcia's file and begun to get a feel for the woman's personality.

Marcia had had a baby in high school and married

a much older man. She'd been a devoted mother and most likely a good wife. Widowed early, she'd taken the insurance money, to spend not on a midlife crisis but on the youth she'd cheated herself of. And then along came Randy (that part wasn't in the file). He might have thought she was grieving (a damsel in distress), or he might have thought she was ready for a rebound. And then because Marcia was ready to settle down and was a great person, they'd stuck. And then because her daughter had aspirations of the White House in her future, Marcia couldn't go public with a much younger man. And then because Lola had an overactive imagination, she'd forgiven her husband's mistress.

That was a lot of *and thens*.

"I'm sorry we had a food fight over a man. I really need a drink." The Marcia-Randy epiphany had been profound but having to watch Drew propose to Wendy had hurt. Because while he set a record for making the most awkward proposal ever for the best of reasons, Lola had realized something.

She loved Drew.

It wasn't the insta-love she'd felt for Randy, a love that had grown over time. It was the unhurried kind of love, built on the solid foundation of finally knowing him inside out.

Until a day ago, Drew had always taken care of everyone in the right way at the right time. Siblings, mother, deputies, townspeople. Even a slightly overreactive young widow who'd lost her way. He took his job seriously and let only a few people in on a secret—he had a sly sense of humor to go with that big heart.

Love. Lotta good it did Lola.

"I'm sorry I didn't explain about my one night with Randy," Avery said. "You know I don't like everyone in my personal business, but I should have told you. I should have told you a long time ago." Avery wasn't being as hard of a sell on reconciliation as Lola had thought she'd be. "Let's go to Shaw's. It's Ladies' Day, you know." The afternoon was reserved for female customers.

"I know." Lola shrugged. "I figure a lot of my critics will be there." Mary Margaret, for sure.

Interest sparked in Avery's eyes. "And you want to face them because..."

"I deflated Randy and Candy."

Avery pulled Lola inside and shut the door. "Don't tell me you found all the women Randy slept with?"

"I found enough. I'm not looking anymore." It was too painful, as was applying Marcia's makeup. That woman had flawless skin.

"So why do you want to go to Shaw's?" Avery studied her, suddenly skeptical.

"Because you like it." Lola tugged Avery's necklace out of her purse. "Isn't that what friends do? They do the things the other likes." And there it was. The question that would confirm whether they were still friends. Lola held her breath.

"Yes." Avery didn't hesitate. She hugged Lola fiercely, not even taking the necklace. "Would you think I'm a wuss if I admitted I missed you?"

"I would but it's okay since I'm a wuss too." Lola hugged her back, just as fiercely. "I'm sorry I let you demonstrate alone. If we were twenty years younger, we'd make a pact never to fight again."

"We'd pinkie swear." Avery pulled away, grinning, and it was just as if the last two weeks hadn't happened.

"Hey." Lola peered at Avery's hairline. "Is that a gray hair?" She didn't wait for confirmation. She plucked it out of Avery's head.

"OMG!" Avery accepted the gray strand. "I need an appointment with Barbara."

Lola sighed. There were some things about Sunshine even the bonds of friendship couldn't change.

* * *

Shaw's on a Sunday was different than Shaw's on a Saturday night. The lights were brighter. The décor appeared dingier. And the clientele more judgmental.

Mary Margaret, Tiffany, Darcy. The three women Lola had smelled at Scotty's wake, one of whom was one of Randy's one-night stands. They stood around the pool table and stared Lola down.

Lola balked at the door.

"Oh no you don't." Avery pushed her forward. "Ladies, we come in peace. Noah, two glasses of what they're drinking."

Tiffany and Mary Margaret went for their purses. Darcy gathered a pile of what looked like law books.

Lola swallowed her pride. "Ladies, I'm not on a witch hunt for anyone Randy slept with." It was enough that she'd come to terms with the woman he'd loved, creating a story for their relationship that was romantic. And if it wasn't true, for once, she didn't want to know.

"I'm kind of…" Lola wasn't kind of anything. "I'm moving on and letting Randy go." The declaration gave her a sense of peace.

"And to prove she's over Randy…" Avery collected Tiffany's and Mary Margaret's purses and tossed them in a booth. She took Darcy's books next and dropped them on a nearby table. "She's buying the next round."

It took another round after the one Lola bought to break down their defenses.

"I'm sorry your husband died," Lola said to Mary Margaret.

The redhead put a hand to her throat, as if it had suddenly closed.

"Yeah, widowhood sucks. But it gets better." Lola squeezed her arm. "Let me know if there's anything I can do." She dug in her purse. "Tiff, I think this is yours." She held up the silver and copper bracelet.

Tiffany drew back. "That's not mine."

"Let me see." Mary Margaret shook the bracelet when Lola handed it over, making the tiny bells ring. "I got one of these from one of my room mothers a few years back. *And…* I still have it." She grinned. "I saw it in my jewelry box when I tucked my great-aunt's earring away." She handed it back to Lola.

Lola stared at it and then at Tiffany. "If it isn't yours, then you must wear Joy."

"Hardly." Tiffany held out her wrist. "I get cologne at the pharmacy for cost. Smell me."

They all did.

Lola didn't recognize the scent. "So...you didn't sleep with Randy?"

"No."

"Then why did you look guilty when I came in with Avery earlier?"

Tiffany's cheeks began to redden. "Because Randy never invoiced me for retiling my shower and then I spent the money on new tires. I kept thinking you were going to bill me."

"Debt forgiven." Lola waved it away with one hand. "I've already squared Randy's books with the accountant. It'll cost me too much to go back." Despite her vow to let the rest of Randy's secrets rest, she looked at Darcy. "And your excuse for avoiding me is..."

"I didn't want you to accuse me too. I've been studying for the bar. If I got in a brawl with you, Judge Harper would skin me alive. In fact, he still might. I'm supposed to be studying now." She gestured to the books on the table.

"Darcy's supposed to be studying every Sunday." Mary Margaret tugged a lock of Darcy's hair gently. "But if we aren't corrupting her, Jason is."

"Speaking of which"—Avery pointed at the television—"Jason's about to ride."

Lola knew next to nothing about bull riding but when Jason stayed on the beast to the buzzer, she clapped and cheered with the rest of the women. And when he climbed the fence into the stands and kissed a beautiful brunette, she got silent like the rest of the women.

Darcy's cheeks paled. "I'm okay." She tried to smile, clearly not okay.

Two cell phones rang.

"It's the judge." Darcy moved away to take the call from her boss.

"It's Frank." Avery stared at the display with a frown.

"Take the call," Lola urged Avery. "Frank seems like a nice guy." And from what she'd heard Barbara say to Kevin in the mortuary, the town council wouldn't approve his purchase.

"That's just it. Nice guys never like me." But Avery answered. She spoke in low monosyllables, ending with "Thank you."

"Did he ask you out?" Lola hoped so.

"No. He's decided to pull out of the downtown development project." Avery looked perplexed. "I won." She looked at Lola. "I convinced him it was wrong."

Avery had no idea Frank was in love with her. Lola congratulated her anyway.

"I need to go." Darcy gathered her books. "The judge wants me to come over and study for the bar."

"I swear," Mary Margaret said after Darcy left, "if I didn't know better, I'd say old Judge Harper had a thing for Darcy."

"That'll never happen," Avery said absently. "He's like fifty years older than she is."

"May-December romance?" Lola shook her head, thinking of Marcia and Randy. "Never say never."

* * *

"We've got to stop meeting like this." Drew entered the garage apartment.

His landlady sat on the floor, propped against the bed. Lola wore blue jeans, the kind of high-heeled black boots women in New York City wore, and a pensive expression beneath the hair piled high on her head. "I should lock the door, I suppose." She stared at something in her hand.

He moved closer, curious as to what had her attention. "If it was locked, I'd just knock." He couldn't tell what she held. "If you've come to gloat over my botched marriage proposal, don't. The entire town has been rubbing it in my face all day."

"As proposals go, it was pretty terrible." Lola curled her fingers and tilted her head to look at him. "I understood why you did it. You want to protect Becky."

"The sign of a desperate man." He sat next to her.

"You've got no need to feel desperation. You're a good dad." Lola shook her hand and something jingled.

It was the clue Drew needed. She held the bracelet she'd found in this room.

They sat in silence for a few moments, staring at the bureau.

She sighed. "I never had anyone pine for me the way Frank pines after Avery."

"Give it time." Drew might have pined for her, in between the madness caused by spring thaw. "You're young."

"And foolish." She held out her hand to show him the pearl ring she wore. "It's Nana's."

Unbelievable. She'd found it? Lola didn't think like him at all but he was beginning to suspect she'd make a good police detective. Or...a good backup plan. "Are you going to tell me who had it?"

"I don't think so." Her eyes held a secret, and her cheeks glowed a soft pink. "How did you break your nose?"

"My nose?" He fingered the bridge.

"Never mind." Lola waved a hand. "I need to keep to the facts, not..." She sneaked a glance at him. "The facts are that Mary Margaret and Avery both said they spent the night with Randy when they were at a low point in their lives, and I met him right after my grandmother died."

"Which means..." He was still wondering why she wanted to know about his nose.

"I don't think Randy was the town man-whore." Lola smiled. Not a dimpled smile but a smile nonetheless. "I think he sensed when women were lonely and vulnerable."

"You think he seduced them with the best of intentions." It was hard to keep the sarcasm out of his voice.

Based on her elbowing him, he hadn't succeeded. "Randy was a romantic, not a seducer. He kept a memento from every woman. I think he cared for each of them." She shook the bracelet. "I don't know who this belonged to. Or the perfume."

But she'd found who had her ring, and no one had called 911.

"Randy had your ring in that box too," Drew realized. "You have your answer. He loved you."

"I'd like to think so." And then Lola did something

so unexpected that Drew almost fell over. She laid her head on his shoulder.

A surge of…something passed through him, crowding his lungs.

It wasn't the breath-freeing feeling of relief. It wasn't the pulse-pounding feeling of annoyance. It spread from his chest like a sip of smooth whiskey, warming him from head to toe, melting away the stress of the choices behind and the choices ahead.

She'd deflated the blow-up dolls. She'd found the answers she was looking for regarding Randy. She was no longer a woman he had to monitor with caution.

He captured Lola's hand and pressed a kiss to her knuckles.

She didn't move. "What was that for?"

He didn't know. He couldn't say.

There was only the languid feeling of the two of them together. Lola understanding him. He understanding her. And this peaceful, contented feeling that he was meant to be nowhere else but at her side.

Images drifted through his mind. Lola's feet dancing on the jail-cell wall. Lola giving Becky two thumbs up in the thrift store. Lola covering her face in whipped cream at the Saddle Horn. Lola coaxing little Caden into letting her style his hair and apply makeup. Lola dancing in the cop uniform and blond wig. Lola winding her arms around him and kissing him as if his touch were more important than air.

There was a reason he couldn't shake the need to kiss her again.

He turned her face to his. "I love you."

She drew back a smidge, not screaming that she loved him too. “You sound surprised.”

“It’s just so...unexpected.” On paper, Lola was everything he didn’t want in a woman. Spontaneous. Unpredictable. Year-round spring-thaw madness.

She had yet to smile. “Didn’t you just propose to Wendy this morning?”

He nodded, cupping her cheek with his hand, stroking the corner of her mouth with his thumb.

“Do you still need a wife in your custody case?”

“It would help.” He traced the shape of her ear with his fingers. Maybe that blond wig was back in the bureau, next to the cop uniform.

“You’re such a jerk.” Lola scrambled to her feet.

Drew stared up at her, still drifting in the ambiance of love. “What are you talking about?”

“You still need a wife.” She leaned over him, hands on hips. “Your proposal technique sucked today with Wendy so you decided to try something different.” She sounded just like his sisters, ramping up into Watch-Out-World mode. “You dropped the L-bomb hoping I wouldn’t turn you down the way Wendy did.”

Drew refused to be drawn into an argument. He remained cool, hoping calm would prevail, hoping they’d find common ground. “Maybe you noticed I didn’t ask you to marry me.” He’d take it slow this time.

Her mouth dropped open. And then she was moving, gathering her car keys and her indignation on the way out.

“You’re such a jerk,” she said one more time before slamming the door behind her.

Chapter Thirty

♥

Drew loves me?

Lola couldn't believe it.

Literally. She couldn't believe he felt love for her. No man who proposed to one woman in the morning would tell another woman that night that he loved her.

Even Randy would agree I deserve to be treated better.

Lola couldn't sleep. She tossed and turned and got out of bed. She ate half a bag of cookies and opened the box Randy and Candy came in, debating whether to inflate them again, if only to have someone to talk to. She rummaged through her lingerie drawer—one black bra, one white thong, one red teddy. Pathetic. She shopped Victoria's Secret online without buying anything, because she got distracted by a sidebar of cute kitten videos.

Four hours of sleep, six hours of doing hair at the retirement home, and a shared plate of loaded nachos with Avery later, Lola walked to the last dress rehearsal, feeling like someone had stuffed her head with cotton. She hoped no one wanted to have a scintillating conversation.

Drew pulled into the high school gym's parking lot just as she arrived.

She fought the impulse to run back home. Instead, she put on her brightest smile and waited for Drew to get out of the police cruiser, jingling the bells on the bracelet she wore. This first meeting after his declaration had to be handled deftly, or she'd never be able to face him again.

Lola planted her heels on the blue paint of the empty handicapped parking space. "How are you, Sheriff?"

"I'm fine," he grumbled, walking quickly toward the gym. "Didn't arrest anybody, didn't walk any runaway pigs, didn't fire any relatives, didn't lose custody of my daughter." His steps faltered on that last statement.

What judge would look at Drew and revoke custody? He's ninety-nine percent perfect.

Drew grabbed hold of Lola's arm and stopped her. "What did you say?"

Lola blinked. "Did I say that out loud?" She hesitated at his jerky nod. "Which part?"

He rolled his eyes and released her.

"All of it?" she squeaked. When he nodded, she added, "I need more sleep."

Drew sighed and moved on with the purposeful steps of an irritated man. He couldn't be irritated with her slip of the tongue. Come to think of it, he'd slammed the car door with too much gusto before she'd ever spoken.

"Still getting the business from everybody, Sheriff?" For firing Gary, dooming Rosie, and asking Wendy to marry him at the Saddle Horn.

"Yep."

Good thing no one knows you told me you loved me. The town would have a field day.

"You're sleep-talking again." Drew opened the gym door for her, releasing the sound of hundreds of children chattering at the same time. Both the upper and the lower grades were rehearsing tonight, and it was nearly deafening inside.

But only one child mattered to Drew. And she sat right by the door.

"Daddy." Becky had tears in her eyes. Her wrist was wrapped in an elastic bandage.

"Hey." Drew knelt before her. "What happened?"

Lola lingered, feeling a little awkward, but she was early and cared too much about Becky not to eavesdrop.

Becky wiped at her cheeks. "I was practicing the sword fight with Caden, and he hit me. Ha-ard." She gave a shaky sob and flung herself into Drew's arms.

"She's fine." Wendy appeared next to him. She was wearing white overalls and a white T-shirt today. Her short blond hair was pinned back over her ears with black bobby pins. "That's what rehearsals are for—shaking out the kinks."

Lola glanced at Drew, wondering whether he was thinking what she was thinking: *Wendy's not exactly the soft, cuddly type, is she?*

"No, she's not," Drew said. "You are."

She'd spoken out loud again? Lola pressed her lips together.

"Caden didn't shake anything. He hit me." Becky

turned in Drew's arms and gave Wendy a mutinous scowl. "Fire Caden, Daddy. You're good at firing people."

"Why don't you quit, Becky?" A spitfire blonde Lola didn't recognize had come through the gym doors. She had choppy hair, as if she'd cut it herself, and wore more makeup than most women in Sunshine.

Drew's arms tightened around Becky. It didn't take a detective to figure out this was his ex-wife, Jane.

Becky's expression crumpled into tears. She buried her face in Drew's shoulder.

"Quit?" For once, Wendy's calm exterior was ruffled. She frowned at Jane. "Caden apologized and promised not to swing his sword too hard."

"He shouldn't have to be soft on her." Jane wasn't being soft on anyone. She glared at Wendy. She glared at Drew. She glared at Lola, and Lola hadn't even said anything.

"Maybe you should use cardboard swords." Drew stood, still holding Becky. "Those plastic ones can be dangerous."

"If you say you could poke someone's eye out..." Wendy toned down the heat and tried to smile but it was a strained lifting of lips. "I want the kids to have fun."

"I'm not having fun," Becky said in a muffled voice.

Jane put her hands on her hips. "Then you should quit and stay here for the rest of your life. Life is too hard outside of Sunshine."

Lola disagreed. She'd found life to be pretty hard in Sunshine.

Everyone stared at Lola, even Wendy.

Lola realized she'd spoken her thoughts aloud again. "Sorry. Lack of sleep."

Jane narrowed her eyes in the direction of Drew and Becky. "I don't want my daughter's heart to be broken. She shouldn't think she can make it big just because she does well here."

"Every child should dream," Lola said.

Wendy nodded. "So true."

"Drew, why didn't you tell me you were dating?" Jane demanded, glaring at Lola.

"We broke up," Wendy said matter-of-factly. She touched Lola's shoulder. "I need you to take Becky to hair and makeup below the stage. Curtain goes up in ninety minutes."

"Wendy, I wouldn't call what you were doing with Drew dating." Jane dismissed Wendy with a wave of her hand. "I'm talking about her." She pointed at Lola.

"Oh. No. Um." Lola edged toward the stage. "Drew and I are just friends."

Drew's gaze was sharp, and his words sharper, aimed at his ex. "How do you know what kind of dates Wendy and I had?"

"Wendy told me." Jane planted her boots in line with her hips and sliced right back at Drew. "I'm staying with her."

Drew frowned.

"Busy night." Now Wendy was backing toward the stage. "Talk later." She lifted Becky from Drew's arms and set her on the floor, taking hold of her hand. She grabbed on to Lola's wrist with her other hand and dragged them both toward the stairs leading backstage.

"That mama is staying with you?" Becky asked, as curious as Lola about Wendy and Jane.

"We were kind of friends in high school." Wendy slowed as they approached the stairs. "We bonded in drama class when I was too shy to take on an acting role and became the script coordinator." She released Lola's wrist. "What is that?" She peered at the silver and copper bracelet. "How cute. I used to have one just like it but I..." Her eyes flew to Lola's, and the color drained from her face.

The color might have drained from Lola's too. She certainly felt as if someone had knocked her to the floor. Wendy had slept with Randy? He was beginning to make Tony Stark look like a Boy Scout.

The fact that she'd found another one of her husband's paramours wasn't all that shocking. The fact that it was Wendy was. Put Wendy in a lineup with Mary Margaret, Avery, even Marçia, and people would assume they were playing a game of Which One of These Objects Doesn't Belong?

Which wasn't fair. When it came to Randy, Lola was increasingly convinced that her husband didn't have a type.

"Becky, honey," Lola said, "go downstairs and tell everyone to line up for makeup. You can go first."

"Yes, Ms. Williams." Becky gathered the ends of her toga and scampered off.

Wendy stood frozen, her shoulders hunched and her eyes cast down, as if someone had warned her a *T. rex* was in the building and it would find her if she moved.

Lola held up her hands. "I'm not mad."

"Please don't tell Drew." Wendy swallowed and rephrased. "Please don't tell anyone. It was after Jane left and long before you came to town. I felt so alone."

"Your secret is safe with me." And Lola meant it. Besides, no one would believe her anyway. "Hold up. Why wouldn't you want Drew to know?"

"Because he might start asking other questions." Wendy glanced around, making sure they were alone. "He's so curious about my life, and I..." Here her voice dropped to a whisper. "I don't make those Bundt cakes."

Lola wobbled in her heels and latched on to Wendy's shoulders for balance. "Get out."

"I'm a terrible person." Wendy looked like she might crumple. "I wasn't supposed to wear that evening gown at the fashion show. I switched it." She glanced around again, making sure they still wouldn't be overheard. "And I stole that fairy makeup idea from you. The town saw it on me first so I'll get the credit when they see it on the kids in the play. I just...I've always taken care of my mom, and sometimes I feel like I have to take shortcuts to catch up."

"Your secrets are safe with me." Lola righted herself. "I think...I think I'm honored that you shared them with me."

"Really?" Wendy's eyes teared up. "And I'm not a terrible person?"

"You're a fantastic person, deserving of the limelight." Lola would gladly give it up to her. She handed the bracelet to Wendy. "You don't wear perfume, do you?"

Wendy shook her head.

"That's a shame." Because somewhere, when Lola least expected it, the scent of Joy would ambush her.

* * *

"You're late," Rupert said in a low voice on Wednesday morning when Drew made it into Judge Harper's office at 8:01.

Jane and Oliver were just passing through the open door to the judge's chambers.

"I'm almost late," Drew said in an equally low voice. He'd gotten caught in school drop-off traffic. He hurried inside, taking the same seat he'd occupied last week.

Judge Harper sat behind his desk, drumming his fingers together as he studied Drew with beady eyes.

"You feeling okay, Judge?" Drew asked, because if anything, the old man looked worse than he had last week. Cheeks more hollow. Eyes more sunken. Lips paler than…

"I'll most likely outlive you, the way you're going," the judge snapped.

Drew wasn't sure what that was supposed to mean. A quick glance at Rupert didn't shed any light on the old man's comments either.

"I'll start with you, young lady." Judge Harper scowled. "I told you what I wanted you to do. I've got a report here from the sheriff that says you only did as I asked for two nights."

"With all due respect…" Oliver leaned forward. "It was cold out there, Dad."

"It's Judge Harper in the courthouse!" The old man slapped the flat of his hand on his desk. "I may have forgotten more things than you'll ever know about the law but I would never forget to give a judge about to hear your case the respect his office deserves."

Rupert didn't bother smirking at his brother. He smirked at the dark-green velvet curtains behind the judge instead.

"Sorry, Judge Harper." Oliver cleared his throat. "My client was cold and sought shelter."

"Your client was weak and continues to be unemployed." Judge Harper tossed his hands. "What could you possibly have learned, young lady, when you couldn't stomach a week alone?"

Jane sat straight, her hands clasped as they'd been last week. "I learned who my friends are in town."

The judge's shaggy gray brows wagged up and down. "Go on."

"I learned who I can rely on." Her eyes were wide and innocent, and she had a rueful slant to her lips. "And I know who'd rather see me disappear in the cemetery for good."

Drew waited for the judge to see right through her epiphany ruse.

"That wasn't what I wanted you to learn," the judge said gruffly.

Jane shrugged. "Sometimes what you want to learn and what you need to learn are two different things."

The judge made a contemplative noise. He wrote something in a file on his desk that looked like seismic scribbles.

Oliver gave Rupert a half smile.

"And you..." Judge Harper's sharp gaze swiveled around to Drew. "You screwed up, Sheriff."

"Me?" Drew pointed at Jane. "*She cheated!*"

"And you fell apart under the stress," the old man said.

Drew could swear Oliver tsk-tsked.

Judge Harper leaned forward. His big leather chair creaked. "Mishandled a termination. Sent a pet to certain death. And botched a marriage proposal."

"Everybody has a bad day occasionally." Drew strove to keep his voice casual.

"Or two," Oliver murmured.

Drew fought the frown trying to form on his face. He hadn't expected his behavior to be under scrutiny. He'd abided by the visitation rules, hadn't he?

"You run the sheriff's department alone." The old man tilted his head and stared at Drew as if he were a bug in a science experiment. "You've been raising your daughter alone. You lost your composure under pressure."

Drew kept his mouth shut, certain this was a trap.

"Judge Harper," Rupert said, "with all due respect, my client didn't leave town. He made tough decisions when he had to, and he's stood by them." He smoothed his very expensive-looking tie. "I'm sure you'll agree that consistency is a sign of a good parent."

Judge Harper's eyes narrowed. "It always comes back to that, I suppose." He closed the file on his desk. "I don't want to make a decision today. I want to wait a week. Continue visitation." He nodded at Drew. "And get a job." He nodded at Jane.

Drew waited until he and Rupert were outside the courthouse alone to ask, "What does he want from me?"

"Whatever it is, don't worry." Despite Rupert's words, he looked worried. "The longer he gives us, the more likely Jane is to make a mistake."

Chapter Thirty-One

♥

Kevin told me she looks beautiful." Barbara stood in the doorway to the viewing room, hesitating. She'd been unable to bring herself to see her mother.

Lola took pity on her. "I'll be right by your side." And by Marcia's.

There were fifteen minutes left for visitation before the service began. Everything was ready. Everyone was ready. Everyone had moved into the chapel. Except Barbara.

Barbara took a few mincing steps into the room. She looked lovely in a black dress and conservative heels. And those dark roots? Gone. Barbara slid a half glance toward the casket but there wasn't much to see from this angle thirty feet away.

Lola had done an excellent job giving Barbara what she wanted. Marcia looked like a middle-aged mom. She had soft pink lipstick instead of bold red, and mascara on her lashes instead of extensions. Her white-blond bob softly framed her face. And if Lola felt she was betraying her husband's mistress here at the end, she wasn't going to say a word in front of Barbara. What good would it do? Marcia couldn't argue.

Not that Marcia seemed to have argued while she was alive.

And Marcia wore Nana's pearl ring. Lola was still torn about that. Barbara expected to see it on her mother...if she ever worked up the nerve to look at her. Lola would have an opportunity to retrieve it before the burial but she'd never be able to wear it in Sunshine. What if Barbara noticed?

"I don't need anybody," Barbara said half under her breath. She took a step forward and then another. "I don't need anybody." She froze in the middle of the room, still too far away to see much more than her mother's white-blond part.

"You don't have to do this." Lola gave her the out she must have wanted. "You can turn around. No one's going to fault you for wanting to remember your mother the way you saw her last."

"I found her," Barbara whispered, mistaking Lola's meaning. "She was sitting on the couch. She'd taken out the cushions for some reason. She was sitting on the springs in her underwear with the television on. Her hair looked as if she'd been electrocuted and left out to dry on a humid afternoon."

Well, at least she looks better than that now.

Lola laid her palm on Barbara's shoulder, intending to rub her hand across her back.

Without warning, Barbara wrapped her arms around Lola and held on tight. And then she made a keening noise so sharp it hurt Lola's ears. "What am I going to do? She was my rock."

"You'll have to be the rock now." Lola drew in a

deep breath, realizing she had to heed her own advice. Maybe she'd rent a station at a salon in Greeley and give up her mortuary and retirement home clientele.

Barbara's perfume filled her nostrils. It took Lola a moment to process the scent.

Is it…? Could it be…?

Lola buried her face in Barbara's neck and drew a deeper breath. "Is that Joy?"

"Yes. Mother always gave me a bottle at Christmas." Barbara pushed free and eyed Lola like a woman who'd just been unexpectedly groped.

Lola wasn't making any apologies for sniffing Randy's lover out.

"I'm…" Barbara hesitated at the sound of voices in the lobby. She was in uncharted territory—her mother in a casket on one side of the room and Lola, a person she needed to get through the services and burial of her mother, on the other. A hint of First Lady Barbara returned to her expression but it was only a hint, and it collapsed when her glance found her mother's casket. "I only wear Joy on special occasions." Barbara was off her game. Babbling. "The campaign trail, weddings, funerals, meetings, date night."

In other words, she wore it almost daily.

Lola tried to look the part of the downtrodden, helpful mortuary employee but the anger that had made her burn Randy's underpants had ignited in her chest and begun flowing in her veins. "It's very expensive."

"They don't sell it in Sunshine." Barbara continued to try to regain queen of Sunshine footing. Her eyes darted about the room. Her feet shifted. "They don't even sell it in Greeley. That's why I like it. I don't like to smell like anyone else."

No. But she did smell like the other woman.

There was no mistaking the meaning of Joy. Barbara Hadley was married and one of Randy's lovers. It was her near empty vial of perfume in Randy's keepsake box. It was hard to imagine Barbara had ever been at rock bottom and fueled Randy's rescue instincts.

And at around one hundred dollars an ounce, Lola didn't think Barbara had been buying Joy when she was in high school. If Marcia and Randy had been a thing for years, as Barbara claimed, that meant...*ew*. It was hard to think about mother and daughter having affairs with Randy at the same time.

But that might explain the number of condoms missing from the box.

Poor Marcia.

Lola had talked herself into understanding Marcia's motivation for keeping her thing with Randy quiet. They'd loved each other. But Barbara had the perfect husband and, by all accounts, an adorable little boy. She wanted to see Kevin elected to the White House.

Okay, reality check. Barbara wanted the White House gig for herself.

Whatever Barbara had had with Randy, he'd felt something for her, or he wouldn't have kept the perfume bottle. But Lola couldn't imagine any scenario where Barbara felt anything in her heart for Randy.

Lola's pulse was pounding, demanding action, demanding retribution. For herself. For Marcia. And maybe for Randy.

Outside in the lobby, the last of the mourners were drifting toward the chapel at Augie's urging. Barbara glanced toward the casket but didn't move her feet.

"If it'd help..." Lola's mouth was on autopilot while her brain was a muddled mess. "You could just wait for the broadcast during the service." They'd be moving the coffin into the chapel soon. Barbara had requested they open the casket one last time at the end of the service. A camera above would project Marcia onto the big screen.

It was one of the grandest services Lola had ever been a part of. And Barbara had been involved in every step of its planning. When did Barbara find time to cheat? She cut hair. She ran a business. She attended all those events with her husband.

"I could wait to see her," Barbara was saying. "And no one would have to know that I couldn't do her hair."

Oh, dear heavens above. Lola's blood nearly boiled over. Barbara must have been telling people she'd done her mother's hair and makeup. She was taking credit for Lola's work. And it wasn't even Lola's best work, what with all of Barbara's restrictions.

Lola nodded, unable to speak.

Barbara left the viewing room.

That woman had everyone from Lola to Avery to her own mother—when Marcia had been alive—running scared, afraid to open their own salon, afraid to let anyone but Barbara touch their hair, afraid to buy some blue hair color at the pharmacy. It wasn't right.

Marcia was being presented to town the way Barbara wanted her to be remembered.

Lola came to stand next to the casket. Marcia's lips were starting to fade into her chin. It was all that pale color Barbara had requested. She looked as if she were seventy, what with her paleness emphasized by a yellow crew-neck dress embroidered with rosettes.

"Girl, I wish I could do something for you." Lola patted her hand, her fingers brushing over Nana's ring.

And there was still a decision to be made about that.

Augie stuck his head in. "Are we ready to close her up for the move? Should I ask the pallbearers to come in?"

Lola nearly nodded, nearly said yes. This was her job. Augie was relying on her.

Her mouth opened, and words began to form. "She needs a touch-up. Can you give us a little privacy?"

What am I doing?

Augie closed the door.

Lola was having an out-of-body experience. She went to the back of the room, where her supply case was half-hidden behind vases of flowers. She wheeled it over to the casket and opened it up.

No one will forgive me for this. Not the town, not Barbara, not Drew.

She'd never belong.

It didn't matter. It had to be done.

"You'll thank me for this when I see you in heaven," Lola said to Marcia, certain it was true.

* * *

Drew sat in an aisle seat in a pew next to Pris, who was the only family member besides Becky who was talking to him at the moment. Thankfully, Pris wore a blouse that covered her Taylor assets.

Gary was a few rows behind them, wearing a suit. Aunt Cindy, Gary's mother, sat beside his former deputy. Her death-ray glare was burning a hole in Drew's head. A few rows up, Judge Harper sat next to Victor Yates, Jane's father. And in the front row, Kevin sat with his arm around Barbara, who kept wiping her eyes and nodding to whatever anyone said about her mother during the open-mic eulogy portion of the program.

Drew had attended many funerals in the mortuary chapel. Not everyone in town belonged to the church so it saw its share of business. But he'd never seen Lola stand to the side during a service. She usually sat in the back with Augie. But today...

Lola stood against the wall near the stage stairs. She didn't fidget. She didn't slouch. She stood at the ready.

Ready for what?

The hair on the back of Drew's neck prickled. He tried to concentrate on what the speaker was saying about Marcia.

"She knew how to drive," Darnell Tucker, a local mechanic, said. He glanced up at the assembled and added, "Not all of you do."

Truer words had never been spoken. About Marcia, who'd loved fast cars and been left enough money to indulge in that passion. And about most of the people in Sunshine, who slid off the road in ice storms, tumbled into ditches during rainstorms, and rear-ended their fellow man at Emory's Grocery.

"One spring, long after we had a thaw, Marcia was

driving her convertible." Darnell was surprisingly at ease with public speaking, even if the suit he wore wasn't at ease with him. The sleeves looked like he might never get them off his big biceps. "It snowed. One of those fast, freaky storms that blow in and blow out without so much as a how-ya-doin'."

Heads nodded in the audience...in agreement, not sleep.

"Marcia pulled up in the midst of it all, honked her horn, and told me to get my ass—*sorry*, my butt in the car." Darnell wasn't sorry. He was grinning. "We drove around—within the speed limit, Sheriff—listening to the Eagles and ABBA, and pretty soon the car had three inches of snow on the interior and on us. And do you know what Marcia said to me?"

Drew and Pris and the rest of the audience shook their heads.

"She said, 'We lived today, didn't we?' " Darnell left the podium and patted the teal coffin. "And we did."

On the side of the room, Lola wiped her eyes.

Drew didn't understand it. Had Lola known Marcia? Or was she in Woe-Is-Me mode? He'd been encouraging Lola to let things rest. And she was. The plastic dolls were gone from her window. She hadn't gotten into a fight with anyone in days. But she was crying.

Drew almost got out of his seat to put his arm around her.

Pris clutched Drew's arm. "What's Jane doing up there?"

Sure enough, while Drew had been mooning over Lola, his ex-wife had been climbing the stage steps on the other side of the chapel. Drew shifted in his seat, prepared to move, prepared to stop whatever trouble Jane was about to cause.

Jane took her place at the podium. She was wearing a crocheted black sweater and a long black skirt. Her hair was spiked up, and her makeup toned down.

"I didn't know Marcia Stephens very well," Jane said in that deep voice of hers. "She hosted a party for everyone after high school graduation. She pulled me aside and told me I had talent. She told me that meant I had to make difficult trade-offs." Jane hauled in a deep breath. "Like having a family or pursuing my art. She told me whatever choice I made, she'd always support me. And when I left town..."

Drew was several rows back in the chapel but he could tell Jane's eyes were filling with tears.

"When I left town, she sent me care packages. Cookies. A gift card to Walmart. Notes of encouragement." Jane looked at Barbara and tried to smile. "That meant a lot to me. As did her hug when I came back to town." Jane's gaze dropped down, and then her head lifted and her voice filled the chapel.

She sang "Amazing Grace."

Over to the side, Lola cried some more. Next to him, Pris sniffed.

And Drew? He was deep in thought.

If Jane had taken the stage and simply began to sing, he would have sworn she'd done it for all the wrong reasons. But her story about Marcia...It seemed heartfelt. And as much as he hated to admit it, her efforts with Becky seemed genuine too.

He wasn't in church but he was having a revelation.

Lola had forgiven Avery. And Mary Margaret. And whoever had given her the pearl ring Randy had stolen. She might even have forgiven Randy. If Lola could do all that, Drew was going to have to forgive Jane for leaving and support her right to visitation. He was also going to have to forgive Gary and one overweight pig. It wasn't Rosie's fault she'd banged up Becky. He'd do his best to find her a good home somewhere else or convince Eileen that Tom's intentions were good.

Spring-thaw madness is over.

Jane finished. She came down the steps and was met by Victor. He hugged his daughter and accompanied her to a pew. Forgiveness. It was in the air.

Pastor Mike stood behind the podium once more and spoke in a soft, whispery voice. "Marcia's casket is going to be open one last time for friends and family to pay their final respects. Her image will also be broadcast on the screen above me. If you've already said your goodbyes, please move outside. Augie will be leading the procession to the cemetery with the white hearse."

It was an announcement warning those uncomfortable with the face of death to head for the hills.

Most people got up and began to leave.

A string quartet played classical music. Overall, it was just the kind of service Barbara would have wanted had she died. If it'd been up to Marcia, a band might have been playing the Eagles or ABBA.

Mourners were still clogging the aisles when the image on the screen above the pulpit changed from the words of the last song the choir had performed to an image of Marcia, who looked more like Marcia than she had an hour before in the visitation room. Her makeup was more lifelike, and her hair had a streak of blue.

Whispers and murmurs rolled through the assembled mourners. People on their way out paused and turned.

Barbara made a keening noise. She rose to her feet and faced Lola. "What have you done? Did she look like this the entire time?"

Lola's chin was up, her shoulders back, her eyes flashing in Watch-Out-World mode.

Drew choked on air.

Spring-thaw madness is never going to end!

"I honored Marcia," Lola said, loud enough for everyone to hear. "This is who she is. You tried to make her into someone she wasn't when she was alive. I won't let you do that to her in death."

"I'm going to hug that girl," Darnell said.

Augie was trying to push his way down the aisle, followed by Mims and the Widows Club board. It was too congested. They weren't getting very far, not as people turned to see what all the fuss was about.

"Barbara?" Kevin stood, looking perplexed. "I thought you did your mother's hair and makeup."

Too late, Barbara became aware she still had an audience. "I didn't. I couldn't. I..." She tried to put the mask of grief back on but she was scowling too hard.

"She lied." Lola walked up the stairs, hanging on to the railing as if she needed support. "She lied about a lot of things."

Drew was moving before he realized it, trying to work his way through the twenty people packed in the aisle to reach Lola's side.

"Stop lying, Barbara, and tell everyone how much your mother loved my husband." Lola's words silenced everyone in the chapel.

Movement stopped. Commentary stopped. There was more drama here than the town would see at Becky's play that night.

Drew's gut tensed as if readying for a blow. "*Lola...*"

Lola was beyond warnings, beyond the protection of Watch-Over status, which had never worked when it came to her anyway.

She stood strong and righteous before the town, beneath the projection of Marcia on the screen. "Or maybe you should tell your husband how much my husband liked your perfume. Randy kept a little bottle of Joy for you, didn't he?"

The assembled might have been shocked into limbo but Drew wasn't. He kept inching his way toward Lola.

"Don't you dare," Barbara warned Lola in a voice that didn't crack.

Lola choked out something that sounded like a laugh. "Don't dare what? Face the truth? Death is the end, Barbara. And at the end, you have nothing left but the truth. I loved Randy. And I love that my husband made your mother feel young again. But when he died, a part of her died with him." She sniffed and pulled herself together. "But what did Randy give you, Barbara? Did he accept you, dark roots and all? Did he let you be imperfect?"

"Shut up!" Barbara's entire body went rigid. Her face was beet red.

Whereas Kevin's was pale. "Barb?"

Barbara turned to him as if in slow motion. She laid her hands on Kevin's lapels. "She's lying, honey."

"You know I'm not." Lola scanned the crowd. "Since I found out Randy was unfaithful, I've never lied about anything. And trust me, it would have been easier on me to live with a lie but I didn't." Lola's expression turned grim. "I admitted my husband cheated at the bachelorette auction. I confronted Avery at the bake sale. I confronted Mary Margaret at the fashion show. But I never lied." Her gaze found Drew's. "All I've ever wanted is the truth."

"And peace," Drew said softly, thinking Lola should never be anyone's backup plan.

"And peace," Lola repeated with a rueful smile.

"You've ruined everything." Barbara refused to give up. "This was supposed to be a special day to honor an angel." Barbara pounded Kevin's chest. "Do something. Tell Drew to arrest her." And then she spotted Drew. "Arrest her!"

Judge Harper turned, squinting until his gaze found Drew.

Drew didn't care what the judge thought. Nevertheless, he stopped trying to reach Lola, afraid to give the impression he was going to cuff her.

As if in solidarity, Kevin sat down.

High school students could have taken their college entrance exams in the chapel. It was that quiet. But there was a tension to the silence. Drew didn't know which way the remaining members of the crowd would turn when they awoke from their stupor. Would they rally around Lola? Or would they back Barbara, the local favorite?

Barbara spun every which way, trying to find

someone, anyone who might be sympathetic. Finding no one, she turned back to Lola. "You suffocated Randy." Barbara was panicking, trying to save herself. "You wanted to be with him every minute of every day. And he couldn't take it. He needed an outlet."

"Barb?" Kevin's voice was weak.

"Of course Randy would look elsewhere." Barbara was like a runaway train headed off a cliff. Everyone could see the hopelessness but Barbara couldn't seem to work the brake. "Anyone who can't breathe in a marriage looks elsewhere."

"Did you need an outlet?" Kevin looked up at his wife, the truth clear in his eyes.

Barbara's features contorted. She couldn't pull all that rage back to the façade of tranquility. "Kev?" And her voice... It was raw from desperation. "Why would you ask me that?"

Someone laughed. It wasn't an amused laugh. It was the shocked laughter after a really bad storm. But laughter was what the room needed. More joined in. By laughing, they didn't have to choose sides—to gravitate to truth or continue to support a lie.

Kevin walked out.

"Why are you wearing my mother's pearl ring?" Barbara's voice bounced off the rafters. "If you won't arrest her for ruining everything, arrest her for stealing my mother's ring."

The pearl ring. That was how Lola had figured all this out. She was smart. She was kind. And justice was important to her. More important than the status quo. In that moment, Drew couldn't have loved her more.

If only she would let him love her.

Lola didn't argue with Barbara. She extended her hands toward Drew and waited for him to cuff her.

"We need to talk," Drew said, taking her by the arm. He wasn't in uniform and didn't have any cuffs with him.

Lola allowed herself to be led out, and above the noise, he thought he heard her say, "I'm afraid I'm all talked out."

Chapter Thirty-Two

♥

Lola sat in a jail cell, huddled on the bench.

It would have been better if she'd had a cellmate—Avery, Marvin the rooster, or Rosie the pig. At least then she'd have someone in her corner.

On the other side of the bars, Drew was refereeing an argument between Augie and Barbara. Judge Harper leaned against the far wall, watching it all and making Lola very nervous.

"My mother will be buried today, and she will be buried with that pearl ring!" Barbara glared at Lola.

"Lola says the ring is hers." Augie kept trying to argue. "I have no records at the mortuary of Marcia's personal effects including a pearl ring."

Lola felt guilty about that. She hadn't logged in the ring with the rest of the items in that blue velvet bag Barbara had given her.

"Lola, do you have proof the ring is yours?" Drew's gaze was sympathetic but he'd been the one to throw her in the pokey.

"I have the original ring box it came in."

Barbara huffed. "That's not proof."

About the time Drew reached her at the service, the anger that had driven Lola to change Marcia's appearance and confront Barbara had left her. She had no fight remaining. For all she knew, Barbara could have had an affair with Randy before Lola's marriage.

"My grandmother's wedding date is inscribed inside," Lola said wearily.

"Anyone can memorize a date." Barbara looked to Judge Harper for agreement but he wasn't saying anything.

Was he deliberating her punishment? Lola tried to make herself smaller.

There was a scuffle down the hall.

"Wait!" Mims traipsed to the cell, trailed by Avery. She held Lola's scrapbook. "Lola is innocent. It's her ring, and I have proof." She flipped through the book. "Here's a picture of Lola and her grandmother. And look." Mims tapped the page. "Her grandmother is wearing that pearl ring."

Barbara growled in frustration, refusing to look. "A coincidence. Nothing more."

"Looks like the ring to me." Augie smiled kindly at Lola.

"Me too." Drew handed the book to the judge, who nodded.

"Don't you dare let her go." Barbara struck a bar with the heel of her hand, making the bars shake. "There's still the matter of Lola disturbing my peace."

"That's why I'm here." Judge Harper pushed clear of the wall on legs that were visibly unsteady. "Ms. Williams, the charge against you is disturbing the peace. How do you plead?"

Lola stood, prepared to face the consequences. "I'm guilty, your honor."

Judge Harper nodded, looking less severe than a moment earlier. "You disrupted a beautiful tribute to a woman beloved by this community."

"I did." She hoped he wasn't going to ask whether she'd do it all again, because the answer would be yes.

"Don't forget," Barbara said snidely, "she defaced my mother's body."

"No, she didn't." Kevin joined the crowd on the other side of the bars. He held a stack of papers with blue paper backing. "This is Marcia's will. It says, *I wish to be buried the way I lived.* I think most of us would agree she wanted to look more like herself." He caught the judge's eye. "I'm not pressing charges."

He was handsome and had moral fiber? Lola was definitely voting for Kevin in the next election.

"But I'm pressing charges, and it's my opinion that counts." Barbara edged her way around Mims and Avery. "Kevin, we need to go somewhere and talk."

"No, we don't." Kevin wasn't smiling, and there was a quality to his voice Lola hadn't heard before—the harsh barb of reality. "I hired Rupert. We're getting a divorce." He walked out.

"But…Kev! Wait." Barbara scurried after him.

Drew's lips were moving upward. He put the key in the cell door lock.

"Not so fast." Judge Harper's stern voice struck fear into Lola's heart. "There is still the matter of disturbing the peace."

"Yes." Lola nodded.

"I can throw you in jail for thirty days—"

Mims gasped.

"—or you can serve a sentence of thirty hours of community service."

"Service," Lola blurted, incredibly grateful for leniency, since she'd heard the judge was hard on lawbreakers.

Judge Harper nodded. "You'll work with the mayor to cut through the red tape and get us a safe intersection at the highway." He clapped his hands once and walked out.

Drew unlocked Lola's cell door and hurried after him.

* * *

"Judge Harper." Drew followed the old man to the outer office. "I need to talk to you about Jane."

The old man turned with a wobble, reaching out to steady himself on what used to be Gary's desk. He gave Drew the same unwelcome glare he'd given his two sons in chambers.

"I mean..." Drew gathered himself and started again. "I've changed my mind. I'd like Jane to have visitation. Preferably supervised, at least at first."

"Hmm." Judge Harper tapped his fingers on Gary's desk. "And..."

"And you should know that I've decided to hire Gary Wycliff back." He'd have to shift some line items in the budget to send Gary to additional training, but it felt like the right thing to do.

"Good." The judge tilted his head. "And the pig..."

"The pig?" Drew blew out a breath. "Legally, Rosie can't live in Sunshine. She's better off on a ranch."

The judge leaned down and pounded his fist on the desk as if it were his gavel. "I didn't think you were the kind of man to allow an animal who was raised as a pet to be shot and butchered."

That wasn't a pretty visual. "I'm not. I keep telling people when she loses weight, she can go to a good home."

"A pig that size?" Judge Harper's gaze hardened. "You believe Tom Bodine will let her go?"

"I have no reason to believe otherwise." Tom had always been an upstanding citizen, if a hard businessman.

"Get that pig back." The judge straightened, more well-connected to the happenings in town than Drew. "I'm going to grant your wish for supervised visitation, Sheriff. We'll revisit the issue in six months." He glanced at the phone on the desk. "Call Gary. I'm tired of complaints from angry townsfolk who think I can influence our sheriff." With a wink, the judge tottered out the door.

Lola and her supporters filed out of the cell hallway.

Lola wasn't wearing the bracelet. That must mean...

"You found all five of Randy's lovers." Drew had thought he'd be relieved when this moment came.

She nodded.

Drew wasn't relieved. He felt as if he couldn't breathe.

Lola walked slowly toward the door in her New York clothes with her Sunshine friends. She'd never blend in. And he didn't want her to try. He loved all that color and impracticality. He loved her unpredictability.

But... "Does this mean you'll be leaving town?" he

asked. That's what she'd said, after all. That she'd leave when she found Randy's lovers.

Lola's eyes widened. Mims and Avery protested but Drew could see the truth of it in her blue eyes. Lola was returning to New York.

The pressure in his chest increased until he labored for each breath.

He loved Lola.

And she was leaving.

* * *

"You have balls, Lola." Avery poured Randy's whiskey into shot glasses. "I can't believe you outed Barbara when I couldn't even publicly admit at the bake sale that I'd slept with Randy more than a decade ago."

Lola sat on the couch, sandwiched between Edith and Mims, which was a good thing since she'd have fallen over without their support. At the service, Drew had said he wanted to talk, but the only thing he'd asked her was whether she was leaving town. Had her outing Barbara cured Drew of whatever love he'd claimed to have felt for her? Because he'd been right. The truth had brought no peace.

Mims downed her third shot of whiskey. "I can't believe Kevin and I got you out of jail." Mims patted her pink purse. "Although we had backup."

Lola mustered a smile, grateful it hadn't come to guns being drawn.

There were friends in her living room, people livelier than Randy and Candy. She'd been talking to blow-up dolls for weeks but she couldn't seem to form any words to talk to this group of caring women.

"You did a fabulous job on Marcia." Edith declined a third round of whiskey, as clear-eyed as ever. "She looked so lifelike I thought she might jump out of her casket at the end and tell Barbara what for."

"I'm going to cancel all my hair appointments with Barbara," Avery said from the bar. "How do you think I'd look with bangs, Lola?"

Tears pressed the back of Lola's throat. She couldn't speak. Not even to acknowledge her best friend's loyalty.

"Mims told me what Drew said earlier." Bitsy knelt in front of Lola. She wore a little black dress with a little black jacket and black kitten heels. Her trademark black bow sat at the base of her neck. "He didn't mean it."

Lola sniffed.

"Who?" Edith demanded, turning to face Lola.

"Drew wanted to know what your plans were." Bitsy ignored Edith. "He wasn't saying he wanted you to leave town."

Tears pressed at the backs of Lola's eyes.

"Are you talking about the sheriff?" Edith asked in a demanding voice.

Avery came to sit next to Bitsy and tossed down another shot. "Drew dumped you?"

Lola sucked in a breath that got stuck in her throat, and then she sobbed, "He said he loved me."

Arms encompassed her. Tissues and drinks and advice were offered. It was the first time Lola felt she truly belonged in Sunshine.

And yet she couldn't stay.

Chapter Thirty-Three

♥

Drew hadn't seen Lola for nearly two weeks.

He ached for her.

He'd tried to talk to her after the play but she'd slipped away in the crowd.

She hadn't come to the farmhouse.

She never answered the door at her home.

But Drew kept busy making things right in his life—rehiring Gary and signing a custody agreement with Jane, who'd taken a job with her father at the feedstore.

He'd been preparing for the day when he'd see Lola again. Sunshine was a small town. She couldn't avoid him forever.

"Daddy-O, I was the star of the play," Becky said from the back seat of the cruiser. She'd pulled out her Halloween costume this morning—black leggings, a black-and-yellow striped T-shirt, golden wings, and green antennae.

"You were, Sunshine." Drew caught sight of her wobbly antennae in the mirror. "You know, I love you no matter what you wear or what you sing."

"I know, Daddy-O."

He'd apologized to Becky for hindering her self-expression—not that she completely understood his apology, but she understood he loved her and always would.

There was a new sign in Lola's yard: FOR SALE. Her drapes were closed.

Drew's chest squeezed. He couldn't be too late. She hadn't even talked to him yet. He kept on driving toward the Saddle Horn, gripping and regripping the steering wheel.

When they entered the coffee shop, reactions were mixed.

"Still no word on Rosie?" Norma Eastlake asked. She sat with Drew's mother in the first booth.

Drew shook his head. The judge had been right. Tom Bodine was claiming possession of Rosie. Eileen was in for a fight, and Drew was backing her all the way, going so far as to pay Rupert's legal retainer.

He and Becky took their usual seats at the counter.

"Darcy won't see me," Jason was saying to Iggy.

Drew could relate.

"Dude, you kissed another woman on national television." Iggy elbowed his business partner. "Of course Darcy isn't going to talk to you. You're scum." Iggy turned to Drew, pushing his straw hat back. "Anything I can do to help you get that pig back?"

"As much as I appreciate the offer, I hear the Bodines don't just shoot cattle rustlers." Drew nodded his thanks to Pearl for a cup of coffee. "They also shoot pig poachers."

Pearl set a mug of hot chocolate with mile-high whip in front of Becky. "Let the judge handle this one."

"Words of wisdom, Pearl." Drew glanced over his shoulder to the street. It was empty of long-legged women. "Words of wisdom."

"Would you like to hear my words of wisdom?" With a soft touch to his shoulder and a softer voice, Bitsy sat next to Drew. "When you see Lola—"

"*If* I see Lola." She'd been avoiding him. She might go back to New York without saying goodbye. The thought had been keeping him up at night.

"—build up to the question." Bitsy cupped his chin, and then she shook it as if she were pulling on an imaginary beard. With a private smile, she returned to the corner booth and the Widows Club.

"Look, Daddy-O. Look." Becky lifted her face. She'd managed to get a thick layer of whip on both cheeks, which was more than her usual pointy beard.

"That's awesome." He'd had that skill once.

Color in the street caught Drew's eye. *Lola.* His heart started to pound.

Ninety-year-old Jorge De La Cruz had passed in his sleep at the retirement home on Friday. Augie had assured Drew that Lola would be working on him today, which meant she'd be stopping in for a carafe of coffee.

Lola wore the blue leggings he was so fond of and a black T-shirt and carried her thermos. Her hair was in a messy ponytail that looked no better than what Drew had done with Becky's hair that morning.

Drew had formulated a plan but he flagged Pearl

down, choosing to be spontaneous. "Another hot chocolate, please. And hurry."

Before Lola pushed open the door and rang the bell, Pearl had delivered a towering mug of hot chocolate to the empty seat next to Drew.

Everyone stopped talking and stared at Lola.

"Hey, everybody," Lola said, barely above a whisper. She headed for the cash register without looking at Drew. "Fill her up, Pearl."

Pearl frowned and glanced at the empty seat next to Drew.

Diners returned to their meals and conversations but kept their eyes on Lola.

Drew whispered some quick instructions to Becky. She nodded and grinned.

A moment later, Becky said, "Look, Ms. Williams. Look." Becky's face was clean. She pointed at Drew, who wore what felt like the most raggedy whipped cream beard ever made.

Apparently, beard-making wasn't like riding a bike.

Conversation dwindled and then stopped.

Lola's clear blue gaze landed on Drew. "I thought Saddle Horn beards were for kids."

"I think..." Drew jutted his chin to keep the whip on a little while longer, to keep Lola interested a little while longer. "Saddle Horn beards are for the young at heart."

Lola's gaze cut to Becky. "Has your father been drinking beer?"

"No, ma'am." His little bumblebee hopped off the stool, golden wings fluttering behind her. "But he did say a skirt would look good over my bee leggings." She curtsied the way Wendy had taught her for the play. "And he said he'd take me dress shopping later."

"Nice." Lola gave Becky a grin that created a dimple, plus she added two thumbs up.

Drew's heart swelled.

"Double bonus." Becky flashed two thumbs back at Lola.

Drew's beard plopped onto the counter, to the delight of the peanut gallery. He wiped his face clean, holding Lola's gaze. It didn't escape him that she'd moved two steps in their direction. "I was wrong."

A crease appeared in Lola's forehead. "About Saddle Horn beards?"

"No. About spring-thaw madness and women with attitude and what my daughter needs." Drew hadn't practiced what he'd say to Lola when she walked in. What he wanted to say was coming out in a rush. "I was wrong about everything. But I was especially wrong about you."

"Really?" Lola took another hip-swaying step closer, grinning at him the way she had in the thrift store, dimple and all.

That dimple gave him hope. "My mother was right," he said.

"I've waited years to hear this," his mom said from the booth she shared with Norma.

"Women in Sunshine have always been a bit exuberant, unpredictable, and expressive."

"The word I used was *intense*," his mom supplied, earning a dark look from Drew, which she shrugged off. "I just want you to be accurate."

He never should have told his mom what he had planned. He captured Lola's gaze once more. "I had a list of women I had to watch over, which was essentially my family and you."

Lola's dimple disappeared. "Should I be flattered?"

"Yes and no. I used to think my life would be easier without so many women to look after. But my life would be worse. Much, much worse without them." He hugged Becky. "I put you on my care-for list for all the wrong reasons but once I did, I couldn't stop thinking about you. And do you know what I learned?"

"What, Daddy-O?" Becky twirled at his feet, sending her golden wings flying through the air.

Drew grinned. "I learned that women who follow the rules and settle for the status quo bore me."

"Hmm." Lola had moved closer. She stood on the other side of Becky. So close. So very, very close.

"I want wild. I want unpredictable. I want fun." Drew hesitated, and then he said what he was really thinking. "I want you, Lola. I want to be with you whether you stay in Sunshine or we all pick up and go to New York."

Lola gasped.

Encouraged, he continued, "I've never met anyone as kind as you are. Who else could do hair and makeup for a retirement home and a mortuary? An angel, that's who."

Becky's eyes widened. "An angel?"

Drew nodded. "And I've never met anyone as courageous as you are. Who else could stand up to a bunch of yahoos at Shaw's or to the sheriff or the wife of the mayor?" He stood, because Lola was holding her ground. "Only a woman with wondrous, secret superpowers."

"*Wow*," Becky breathed.

Good thing someone was breathing. Drew wasn't sure he was. "And I've never met anyone as generous as you are. Who else could forgive the women who had affairs with her husband, or the man who told her she wasn't good enough to marry?" Drew got down on one knee and held out what he hoped would close the deal. "The woman I love, that's who."

"Drew?" Lola leaned forward, blinking at the small box he held. "What is this?"

He flipped the lid open. "I wanted to give you a new box of keepsakes. Go on. Look at what's inside."

She inched closer.

"Take notes," Iggy told Jason. "This is how it's done."

Lola picked out a slip of paper. It was a coupon for a box of Betty Crocker. She showed it to the crowd. "Really?"

"I promise to eat your cupcakes anytime you bake them, be they undercooked or overdone."

That had the crowd sighing.

Lola chose a silk rose petal next. It'd come from Randy's jar in the bureau.

"A reminder from a romantic to always be romantic." Drew knew Randy would always be important to her. He'd wanted to honor the man somehow.

It must have worked, because Lola's eyes filled with tears. She picked up a pair of pink trick handcuffs.

Drew's smile was gentle. "That's for when I need to cool down."

A tear tracked down her cheek.

Drew's heart pounded hard. All that was left in the box was an engagement ring.

He took it out and handed the box to Becky, who had rehearsed this part with him and was grinning. "And this is the most colorful, most beautiful ring I could find." A diamond solitaire framed by rubies and sapphires. "But it doesn't hold a candle to you. I love you, Lola. Will you marry me?" He wanted her to know exactly what he was asking and why.

"Drew, I..." Lola sniffed and wiped away a tear. "Who broke your nose?"

"Um..." Her question took him by surprise. He'd hoped she'd be falling into his arms by now. "I was trying to teach Eileen how to pitch. She hit me with a softball." And she'd told everyone she'd done it. It had taken years to live it down.

"I'm so glad." Lola fell to her knees with him. "I was hoping you got that bump from one of the wild, impetuous women in your life and not in some barroom brawl."

"Why?" he asked.

She sniffed. "Because that would mean you'd forgiven her, and you could forgive me too."

"Forgive you for what? Being honest and demanding honesty in return? I don't need to forgive you for that." He cradled her beautiful face in his palms. "Honesty is your secret talent, and I love you for it."

Tears flowed freely down her cheeks. "I love you, Drew. Home is where true love resides. And for me, home is right here with you and Becky and everyone in Sunshine."

"Is that a yes?" A wonderful yes?

She nodded.

Drew pulled Lola into his lap, gathered her in his arms, and kissed her until she was senseless.

Or at least until his mother and the Widows Club interrupted them.

About the Author

Melinda Curtis is the *USA Today* bestselling author of lighthearted contemporary romance. In addition to her Sunshine Valley series from Forever, she's published books independently and with Harlequin Heartwarming, including her novel *Dandelion Wishes*, which is currently being made into a TV movie. She lives in California's hot Central Valley with her hot husband—her basketball-playing college sweetheart. While raising three kids, the couple did the soccer thing, the karate thing, the dance thing, the Little League thing, and, of course, the basketball thing. Between books, Melinda spends time remodeling her home by swinging a hammer, grouting tile, and wielding a paintbrush with her husband and other family members.

Kiss Me in Sweetwater Springs

Annie Rains

If Lacy Shaw could have one wish, it'd be that the past would stay in the past. And with her high school reunion coming up, she has no intention of reliving the worst four years of her life. Ditching the event seems like the best option until a blistering-hot alternative roars into Lacy's life. Perhaps riding into the reunion on the back of Paris Montgomery's motorcycle will show her classmates how much she really has changed...

A bonus novella from *USA Today* best-selling author Annie Rains follows.

FOREVER

Chapter One

Lacy Shaw looked around the Sweetwater Springs Library for the culprit of the noise, a "shhh" waiting on the tip of her tongue. There were several people reading quietly at the tables along the wall. A few patrons were wandering the aisles of books.

The high-pitched giggle broke through the silence again.

Lacy stood and walked out from behind her counter, going in the direction of the sound. She wasn't a stickler for quiet, but the giggling had been going on for at least ten minutes now, and a few of the college students studying in the far corner kept getting distracted and looking up. They'd come here to focus, and Lacy wanted them to keep coming.

She stopped when she was standing at the end of one of the nonfiction aisles where two little girls were seated on the floor with a large book about animals in their lap. The *shhh* finally tumbled off her lips. The sound made her feel even more like the stuffy librarian she tried not to be.

The girls looked up, their little smiles wilting.

Lacy stepped closer to see what was so funny about animals and saw a large picture of a donkey with the heading "Asses" at the top of the page. A small giggle tumbled off Lacy's lips as well. She quickly regained control of herself and offered a stern expression. "Girls, we need to be quiet in the library. People come here to read and study."

"That's why we're here," Abigail Fields, the girl with long, white-blond curls, said. They came in often with their nanny, Mrs. Townsend, who usually fell asleep in the back corner of the room. The woman was somewhere in her eighties and probably wasn't the best choice to be taking care of two energetic little girls.

"I have to write a paper on my favorite animal," Abigail said.

Lacy made a show of looking at the page. "And it's a donkey?"

"That's not what that says," Willow, Abigail's younger sister, said. "It says..."

"Whoa!" Lacy held up a hand. "I can read, but let's not say that word out loud, okay? Why don't you two take that book to a table and look at it quietly," she suggested.

The little girls got up, the older one lugging the large book with both hands.

Lacy watched them for a moment and then turned and headed back to her counter. She walked more slowly as she stared at the back of a man waiting for her. He wore dark jeans and a fitted black T-shirt that hugged muscles she didn't even have a name for. There was probably an anatomy book here that did. She wouldn't mind locating it and taking her time labeling each muscle, one by one.

She'd seen the man before at the local café, she realized, but never in here. And every time he'd walked into the café, she'd noticed him. He, of course, had never noticed her. He was too gorgeous and cool. There was also the fact that Lacy usually sat in the back corner reading a book or people-watching from behind her coffee cup.

What is he doing here?

The man shifted as he leaned against her counter, his messenger bag swinging softly at his lower hip. Then he glanced over his shoulder and met her gaze. He had blue crystalline eyes, inky black hair, and a heart-stopping smile that made her look away shyly—a nervous remnant of her high school years when the cool kids like him had picked on her because of the heavy back brace she wore.

The brace was gone. No one was going to laugh at her anymore, and even if they did, she was confident enough not to find the closest closet to cry in these days.

"Hey," he said. "Are you Lacy Shaw, the librarian here?"

She forced her feet to keep walking forward. "I am. And you are?"

He turned and held out a hand. "Paris." He suspended his hand in midair, waiting for her to take it. When she hesitated, his gaze flicked from her face to her hand and then back again.

She blinked, collected herself, and took his hand. "Nice to meet you. I'm Lacy Shaw."

Paris's dark brows dipped farther.

"Right," she giggled nervously. "You didn't need me to introduce myself. You just asked if that's who I was. Do you, um, need help with something? Finding a book maybe?"

"I'm actually here for the class," he said.

"The computer skills class?" She walked around the counter to stand behind her computer. "The course instructor hasn't arrived yet." She looked at the Apple Watch on her wrist. "It's still a little early though. You're not late until you're less than five minutes early. That's what my mom always says."

Lacy had been wanting to offer a computer skills class here for months. There was a roomful of laptops in the back just begging for people to use them. She'd gotten the computer skills teacher's name from one of her regular patrons here, and she'd practically begged Mr. Montgomery over the phone to take the job.

"The class runs from today to next Thursday. It's aimed toward people sixty-five and over," she told the man standing across from her, briefly meeting his eyes and then looking away. "But you're welcome to attend, of course." Although she doubted he'd fit in. He appeared to be in his early thirties, wore dark clothes, and looked like his idea of fun might be adding a tattoo to the impressive collection on his arms.

Paris cleared his throat. "Unless I'm mistaken, I *am* the instructor," he said. "Paris Montgomery at your service."

"Oh." She gave him another assessing look. She'd been expecting someone...different. Alice Hampton had been the one to recommend Paris. She was a sweet old lady who had sung the praises of the man who'd rented the room above her garage last year. Lacy never would've envisioned the likes of this man staying with Mrs. Hampton. "Oh, I'm sorry. Thank you for agreeing to offer some of your time to our senior citizens. A lot of them have expressed excitement over the class."

Paris gave a cursory glance around the room. "It's no problem. I'm self-employed, and as I told you on the phone, I had time between projects."

"You're a graphic designer, right?" she asked, remembering what Alice had told her. "You created the designs for the Sweetwater Bed and Breakfast."

"Guilty. And for a few other businesses in Sweetwater Springs."

Lacy remembered how much she'd loved the designs when she'd seen them. "I've been thinking about getting something done for the library," she found herself saying.

"Yeah? I'd be happy to talk it over with you when you're ready. I'm sure we can come up with something simple yet classy. Modern. Inviting."

"Inviting. Yes!" she agreed in a spurt of enthusiasm before quickly feeling embarrassed. But that was her whole goal for the library this year. She wanted the community to love coming in as much as she did. As a child growing up, the library had been her haven, especially during those years of being bullied. The smell of books had come to mean freedom to her. The sound of pages turning was music to her ears.

"Well, I guess I better go set up for class." Paris

angled his body toward the computer room. "Five minutes early is bordering on late, right?" he asked, repeating her words and making her smile.

He was cool, gorgeous, *and* charming—a dangerous combination.

* * *

Paris still wasn't sure why he'd agreed to this proposition. It paid very little, and he doubted it would help with his graphic design business. The librarian had been so insistent on the phone that it'd been hard to say no to her. Was that the same woman who'd blushed and had a hard time making eye contact with him just now? She looked familiar, but he wasn't sure where or when they'd ever crossed paths.

He walked into the computer room in the back of the library and looked around at the laptops set up. How hard could it be to teach a group of older adults to turn on a computer, utilize the search engine, or set up an email account? It was only two weeks. He could handle that.

"You're the teacher?" a man's voice asked behind him.

Paris whirled to face him. The older man wore a ball cap and a plaid button-down shirt. In a way, he looked familiar. "Yes, sir. Are you here for the class?"

The man frowned. "Why else would I ask if you were the teacher?"

Paris ignored the attitude and gestured to the empty room. "You have your pick of seats right now, sir,"

Paris told him. Then he directed his attention to a few more seniors who strolled in behind the older man. Paris recognized a couple of them. Greta Merchant used a cane, but he knew she walked just fine. The cane was for show, and Paris had seen her beat it against someone's foot a couple of times. She waved and took a seat next to the frowning man.

"Paris!" Alice Hampton said, walking into the room.

He greeted her with a hug. After coming to town last winter and staying at the Sweetwater B&B for a week, he'd rented a room from Alice for a while. Now he had his own place, a little cabin that sat across the river.

All in all, he was happy these days, which is more than he could say when he lived in Florida. After his divorce, the Sunshine State had felt gloomy. He hadn't been able to shake the feeling, and then he'd remembered being a foster kid here in Sweetwater Springs, North Carolina. A charity event for bikers had given him an excuse to come back for a visit, and he'd never left. Not yet, at least.

"I told all my friends about this class," Alice said. "You're going to have a full and captive audience with us."

Nerves buzzed to life in his stomach. He didn't mind public speaking, but he hoped most were happy to be here, unlike the frowner in the corner.

More students piled in and took their seats, and then the timid librarian came to the door. She nibbled on her lower lip, her gaze skittering everywhere but to meet his directly. "Do you need anything?"

Paris shook his head. "No, we have plenty of

computers. We'll just get acquainted with them and go from there."

She looked up at him now, a blush rising over her high cheekbones. She had light brown hair spilling out of a messy bun and curling softly around her jawline. She had a pretty face, made more beautiful by her rich brown eyes and rose-colored mouth. "Well, you know where I am if you do need something." She looked at the group. "Enjoy!"

"You hired a looker!" Greta Merchant hollered at Lacy. "And for that, there'll be cookies in your future, Ms. Lacy! I'll bring a plate next class!"

The blush on Lacy's cheeks deepened as her gaze jumped to meet his momentarily. "Well, I won't turn down your cookies, Ms. Greta," she said.

Paris watched her for a moment as she waved and headed back to her post.

"The ink in those tattoos going to your brain?" the frowner called to him. "It's time to get started. I don't have all day, you know."

Paris pulled his gaze from the librarian and faced the man. "Neither do I. Let's learn something new, shall we?"

An hour later, Paris had taught the class of eleven to turn on and turn off the laptops. It'd taken an excruciating amount of time to teach everyone to open a browser and use a search engine. Overall, it'd gone well, and the hour had flown by.

"Great job," Alice said to him approvingly. She patted a motherly hand on his back that made him feel warm and appreciated. That feeling quickly dissipated as the frowner headed out the door.

"I already knew most of what you taught," he said.

Who was this person, and why was he so grouchy?

"Well, then you probably didn't need this class," Paris pointed out politely. "Actually, you probably could've taught it yourself."

The frowner harrumphed. "Next time *teach* something."

Paris nodded. "Yes, sir. I'll do my best."

"Your best is the only acceptable thing," the man said before walking out.

Paris froze for a moment, reaching for the memory that the frowner had just stirred. *Your best is the only acceptable thing.* His foster dad here in Sweetwater Springs used to say that to him. That man had been nothing but encouraging. He'd taught Paris more about life in six months than anyone ever had before or since.

Paris hadn't even caught his student's name, and there was no roster for this computer skills class. People had walked in and attended without any kind of formal record.

Paris watched the frowner walk with slow, shuffled steps. He was old, and his back was rounded. A hat sat on his head, casting a shadow on his leathered face. All Paris had really seen of him was his deep, disapproving frown. It'd been nearly two decades since Paris had laid eyes on Mr. Jenson, but he remembered his former foster dad being taller. Then again, Paris had been just a child.

When Paris had returned to Sweetwater Springs last year, he'd decided to call. Mrs. Jenson had been the one to answer. She'd told him she didn't remember a boy named PJ, which is the name Paris had gone by back then. "Please, please, leave us alone! Don't call here again!" she'd pleaded on the line, much to Paris's horror. "Just leave us alone."

The memory made Paris's chest ache as he watched the older man turn the corner of the library and disappear. He resisted the urge to follow him and see if it really was Mr. Jenson. But the Jensons had given Paris so much growing up that he was willing to do whatever he could to repay their kindness—even if it meant staying away.

* * *

Lacy was checking out books for the Fields girls and their nanny when Paris walked by. She watched him leave. If you flipped to the word *suave* in the dictionary, his picture was probably there.

"I plan to bring the girls to your summer reader group in a couple weeks," Mrs. Townsend said.

Of course she did. That would be a convenient nap time for her.

"I always love to see the girls." Lacy smiled down at the children. Their father, Granger Fields, and his family owned Merry Mountain Farms in town where Lacy always got her blue spruce for the holidays.

Lacy waved as the little girls collected their bags of books and skipped out with Mrs. Townsend following behind them.

For the rest of the afternoon, Lacy worked on ongoing programs and plans for the summer and fall. At six p.m., she turned off the lights to the building and headed into the parking lot.

She was involved with the Ladies' Day Out group, a gaggle of women who regularly got together to hang out and have fun. Tonight, they were meeting at Lacy's house to discuss a book that she'd chosen for everyone to read. They were in no way a book club, but since it was her turn to decide what they did, Lacy had turned it into one this time.

Excitement brimmed as she drove home. When she pulled up to her small one-bedroom house on Pine Cone Lane, she noticed two of her sisters' cars already parked in the driveway. Birdie and Rose had texted her during the day to see what they could do to help. Seeing the lights on inside Lacy's home, they'd evidently ignored Lacy's claims that she didn't need anything and had used her hideaway key under the flowerpot.

"Honey, I'm home!" Lacy called as she headed through the front door.

Birdie, her older sister by one year, turned to face her. "Hey, sis. Rose and I were just cleaning up for you."

"Great." Lacy set her purse down. "Now I don't have to."

"What is this?" Rose asked, stepping up beside Birdie. Rose was one year younger than Lacy. Their mom had been very busy those first three years of marriage.

Lacy looked at the small postcard that Rose held up.

"You were supposed to RSVP if you were going to your ten-year class reunion," Rose said. "You needed to send this postcard back."

"Only if I'm going," Lacy corrected.

"Of course you're going," Birdie said. "I went to my ten-year reunion last year, and it was amazing. I wish we had one every year. I wouldn't miss it."

Unlike Lacy, her sisters had been popular in school. They hadn't had to wear a bulky back brace that made them look like a box turtle in its shell. It had drawn nothing but negative attention during those long, tormenting years.

"It's not really a time in my life that I want to remember," Lacy pointed out as she passed them and headed into the kitchen for a glass of lemonade. Or perhaps she should go ahead and pour herself something stronger. She could tell she might need it tonight.

A knock on her front door made her turn. "Who is that?" Lacy asked. "I scheduled the book discussion for seven. It's only six." Lacy set down the glass she'd pulled from the cabinet and went to follow her sisters to the door.

"About that," Birdie said a bit sheepishly. "We changed the plan at the last minute."

Lacy didn't like the sound of that. "What do you mean?"

"No one actually read the book you chose," Birdie said as Rose let the first arrivals in. "Instead, we're playing matchmaker tonight. What goes together better than summer and love?"

Lacy frowned. "If you wanted summer love, I could've chosen a romance novel to read instead."

Birdie gave her a disapproving look. Lacy doubted anyone was more disappointed about tonight's shift in festivities than her though.

Chapter Two

Paris hadn't been able to fully concentrate for the last hour and a half as he sat in front of his computer working on a job for Peak Designs Architectural Firm. His mind was in other places. Primarily the library.

The Frowner, as he'd come to think of the old man in his class, was forefront in his mind. Was it possible that the Frowner was Mr. Jenson?

It couldn't be. Mr. Jenson had been a loving, caring guy, from what Paris remembered. Granted, loving and caring were subjective, and Paris hadn't had much to go on back then.

Mrs. Jenson had been the mother that Paris had always wished he had. She'd doted on him, offering affection and unconditional love. Even though Paris had been a boy who'd landed himself in the principal's office most afternoons, Mrs. Jenson had never raised her voice. And Mr. Jenson had always come home from his job and sat down with Paris, giving him a lecture that had proved to be more like a life lesson.

Paris had never forgotten those lessons. Or that man.

He blinked the memories away and returned his attention to the design he was working on. It was good, but he only did excellent jobs. *Your best is the only acceptable thing.*

He stared at the design for another moment and then decided to come back to it tomorrow when he wasn't so tired. Instead, he went to his Facebook page and searched Albert Jenson's name. He'd done so before, but no profiles under that name had popped up. This time, one did. The user had a profile picture of a rose instead of himself. Paris's old foster dad had loved his rose gardens. This must be him!

Paris scrolled down, reading the most recent posts. One read that Mr. Jenson had gone to the nursing home to visit his wife, Nancy.

Paris frowned at the news. The transition must have been recent because Mrs. Jenson had been home when he'd called late last year. She'd been the one to pretty much tell him to get lost.

He continued to scroll through more pictures of roses and paused at another post. This one read that Mr. Jenson had just signed up for a computer skills class at the Sweetwater Library.

So it was true. Mr. Jenson, the foster dad who'd taught him so much, was also the Frowner.

* * *

Lacy had decided to stick to just lemonade tonight since she was hosting the Ladies' Day Out group. But plans were meant to be changed, as evidenced by the fact that the book discussion she'd organized had turned into the women sitting around her living room, eyes on a laptop screen while perusing an online dating site.

"Oh, he's cute!" Alice Hampton said, sitting on the couch and leaning over Josie Kellum's shoulder as she tapped her fingers along the keys of Lacy's laptop. Not that anyone had asked to use her computer. The women had just helped themselves.

Lacy reached for the bottle of wine, poured herself a deep glass, and then headed over to see who they were looking at. "I know him," she said, standing between her sisters behind the couch. "He comes into the library all the time."

"Any interest?" Josie asked.

Lacy felt her face scrunch at the idea of anything romantic with her library patron. "Definitely not. I know what his reading interests are and frankly, they scare me. That's all I'll say on that."

She stepped away from her sisters and walked across the room to look out the window. The moon was full tonight. Her driveway was also full, with cars parked along the curb. She wasn't a social butterfly by any means, but she looked like one this evening and that made her feel strangely satisfied.

"So what are your hobbies, Lacy?" Josie asked. "Other than reading, of course."

"Well, I like to go for long walks," Lacy said, still watching out the window.

Josie tapped a few more keys. "Mmm-hmm. What's your favorite food?"

Lacy turned and looked back at the group. "Hot dogs," she said, earning her a look from the other women.

"Do you know what hot dogs are made out of?" Greta wanted to know.

"Yes, of course I do. Why do I feel like I'm being interviewed for one of your articles right now?"

"Not an article," Birdie said. "A dating profile."

"What?" Lacy nearly spilled her glass of wine as she moved to look over Josie's shoulder. "What are you doing? I don't want to be up on Fish In The Sea dot com. Stop that."

Birdie gave her a stern look. "You have a class reunion coming up, and you can't go alone."

"I'm not going period," Lacy reiterated.

"Not going to your class reunion?" Dawanda from the fudge shop asked. She was middle-aged with spiky, bright red hair. She tsked from across the room, where she sat in an old, worn recliner that Lacy had gotten from a garage sale during college.

Lacy finished off her wine and set the empty glass on the coffee table nearby. "I already told you, high school was a miserable time that I don't want to revisit."

"All the more reason you *should* go," Birdie insisted. Even though she was only a year older, Birdie acted like Lacy's mother sometimes.

"Why, so I can be traumatized all over again?" Lacy shook her head. "It took me years to get over all the pranks and ridicule. Returning to the scene of the crime could reverse all my progress."

"What progress?" Rose asked. "You never go out, and you never date."

Lacy furrowed her brow. "I go to the café all the time."

"Alone and you sit in the back," Birdie pointed out. "Your back brace is gone, but you're still hiding in the corner."

Lacy's jaw dropped. She wanted to argue but couldn't. Her sister was right.

"So we're making Lacy a dating profile," Josie continued, looking back down at the laptop's screen. "Twenty-eight years old, loves to read, and takes long walks in the park."

"I never said anything about the park," Lacy objected.

"It sounds more romantic that way." Josie didn't bother to look up. "Loves exotic fruit..."

"I said hot dogs."

This time Josie turned her head and looked at Lacy over her shoulder. "Hot dogs don't go on dating profiles...but cute, wagging dogs do." Her fingers started flying across the keyboard.

"I like cats." Lacy watched for another moment and then went to pour herself another glass of wine as the women created her profile at FishInTheSea.com.

After a few drinks, she relaxed a little and started feeding Josie more details about herself. She wasn't actually going to do this, of course. Online dating seemed so unromantic. She wanted to find Mr. Right the old-fashioned way, where fate introduced him into her life and sparks flew like a massive explosion of fireworks. Or at least like a sparkler.

* * *

An hour later, Lacy said goodbye to the group and sat on the couch. She gave the book she'd wanted to discuss a sidelong glance, and then she reached for her laptop. The dating profile stared back at her, taking her by surprise. They'd used a profile picture from when she'd been a bridesmaid at a wedding last year. Her hair was swept up and she had a dipping neckline on her dress that showed off more skin than normal. Lacy read what Josie and her sisters had written. The truth was disregarded in favor of more interesting things.

Lacy was proud of who she was, but the women were right. She wasn't acting that way by shying away from her reunion. She was acting like the girl in the back brace, quietly sitting in the far corner of the room out of fear that others might do something nasty like stick a sign on her back that read KICK ME! I WON'T FEEL IT!

"Maybe I should go to the reunion," she said out loud. "Or maybe I should delete this profile and forget all about it."

The decision hummed through her body along with the effect of one too many glasses of wine. After a moment, she shut the laptop and went to bed. She could decide her profile's fate tomorrow.

* * *

The next morning, Paris woke with the birds outside his window. After a shower and a quick bite, he grabbed his laptop to work on the deck, which served as his office these days. Before getting started on the Peak Designs logo, he scrolled through email and social media. He clicked on

Mr. Jenson's profile again, only to read a post that Paris probably didn't need first thing in the morning.

> The computer skills class was a complete waste of time. Learned nothing. Either I'm a genius or the instructor is an idiot.

The muscles along the back of his neck tightened. At least he didn't need to wonder if Mr. Jenson would be back.

He read another post.

> Went to see Nancy today. I think she misses her roses more than she misses me. She wants to come home, and this old house certainly isn't home without her.

Paris felt like he'd taken a fall from his bike, landing chest-first and having the breath knocked out of him. Why wasn't Mrs. Jenson home? What was wrong with her? And why was Mr. Jenson so different from the man he remembered?

Paris pushed those questions from his mind and began work on some graphic designs. Several hours later, he'd achieved much more than he'd expected. He shoved his laptop into its bag, grabbed his keys, and rode his motorcycle to the library. As he walked inside, his gaze immediately went to the librarian. Her hair was pulled back with some kind of stick poking through it today. He studied her as she checked books into the system on her desktop.

She glanced up and offered a shy wave, which he returned as he headed toward the computer room. He would have expected Mr. Jenson not to return to class today based on his Facebook comments, but Mr. Jenson was already waiting for him when he walked in. All the other students from the previous day filed in within the next few minutes.

"Today I'm teaching you all to use Microsoft Word," he told the group.

"Why would I use Microsoft Word?" Alice Hampton asked. Her questions were presented in a curious manner rather than the questions that Mr. Jenson posed, which felt more like an attack.

"Well, let's say you want to write a report for some reason. Then you could do one here. Or if you wanted to get creative and write a novel, then this is the program you'd use."

"I've always wanted to write a book," Greta told Alice. "It's on my bucket list, and I'm running out of time."

"Are you sick?" Alice asked with concern, their conversation hijacking the class.

"No, I'm healthy as a buzzard. Just old, and I can't live forever," Greta told her.

"Love keeps you young," Edna Baker said from a few chairs down. She was the grandmother of the local police chief, Alex Baker. "Maybe you should join one of those online dating sites."

The group got excited suddenly and turned to Paris, who had leaned back against one of the counters, arms folded over his chest as he listened.

He lifted a brow. "What?"

"A dating site," Edna reiterated. "We helped Lacy Shaw join one last night in our Ladies' Day Out group."

"The librarian?" Paris asked, his interest piquing.

"Had to do it with her dragging and screaming, but we did it. I wouldn't mind making a profile of my own," Edna continued.

"Me too." Greta nodded along with a few other women.

"I'm married," Mr. Jenson said in his usual grumpy demeanor. "I have no reason to be on a dating site."

"Then leave, Albert," Greta called out.

Mr. Jenson didn't budge.

"We're here to learn about what interests us, right?" Edna asked Paris.

He shrugged. There was no official syllabus. He was just supposed to teach computer literacy for the seniors in town. "I guess so."

"Well, majority rules. We want to get on one of those dating sites. I think the one we were on last night was called Fish In The Sea dot com."

Paris unfolded his arms, debating if he was actually going to agree to this. He somehow doubted the Sweetwater Springs librarian would approve, even if she'd apparently been on the site herself.

"Fine, I'll get you started," Paris finally relented, "but tomorrow, we're learning about Microsoft Word."

"I don't want to write a report or a novel," Mr. Jenson said, his frown so deep it joined with the fold of his double chin.

"Again, don't come if you don't want to," Greta nearly shouted. "No one is forcing you."

Paris suspected that Mr. Jenson would be back regardless of his opinions. Maybe he was lonely. Or maybe, despite his demeanor, this was his idea of a good time.

After teaching the group how to use the search bar function and get to the Fish In the Sea website, Paris walked around to make sure everyone knew how to open an account. Some started making their own profiles while others watched their neighbors' screens.

"This is Lacy's profile," Alice said when he made his way to her.

Paris leaned in to take a closer look. "That's not the librarian here."

"Oh, it is. This photo was taken when she was a bridesmaid last year. Isn't she beautiful?"

For a moment, Paris couldn't pull his gaze away from the screen. If he were on the dating site, he'd be interested in her. "Likes to hike. Loves dogs. Favorite food is a hot dog. Looking for adventure," he read. "That isn't at all what I would have pegged Lacy as enjoying."

Alice gave him a look. "Maybe there's more to her than meets the eye. Would you like to sit down and create your own profile? Then you could give her a wink or a nibble or whatever the online dating lingo is."

He blinked, pulled his gaze from the screen, and narrowed his eyes at his former landlord. "You know I'm not interested in that kind of thing." He'd told Alice all about his past when he'd rented a room from her last year. After his messy marriage, the last thing he wanted was to jump into another relationship.

"Well, what I know is, you're young, and your heart can take a few more beatings if it comes to it. Mine, on the other hand, can't, which is why I'm not creating one of these profiles."

Paris chuckled. "Hate to disappoint, but I won't be either." Even if seeing Lacy's profile tempted him to do otherwise.

* * *

At the end of the hour, Paris was the last to leave his class, following behind Mr. Jenson, who had yet to hold a personal conversation with him or say a civilized thing in his direction.

He didn't recognize Paris, and why would he? Paris had been a boy back then. His hair had been long and had often hung in his eyes. His body had been scrawny from neglect and he hadn't gotten his growth spurt until well into his teen years. He hadn't even had the same last name back then. He'd gone by PJ Drake before his parents' divorce. Then there was a custody battle, which was the opposite of what one might think. Instead of fighting *for* him, his parents had fought over who *had* to take him.

"Mr. Jenson?" Paris called.

The older man turned to look at Paris with disdain.

"How was the class?"

"An utter waste of time."

Paris liked to think he had thick skin, but his former

foster dad's words had sharp edges that penetrated deep. "Okay, well what computer skills would you like to learn?"

The skin between Mr. Jenson's eyes made a deep divot as he seemed to think. "I can't see my wife every day like I want to because I don't drive. It's hard for an old man like me to go so far. The nurses say they can set up Skype to talk to her, but I don't understand it. They didn't have that sort of thing when I was old enough to learn new tricks."

"Never too late," Paris said. "A great man once taught me that."

That great man was standing in front of him now, whether he knew it or not. And he needed his own pep talk of sorts. "Come back tomorrow, and we'll get you set up for that."

Mr. Jenson frowned back at him. "We'll see."

* * *

Lacy was trying not to panic.

A blue circle had started spinning on her laptop screen five minutes ago. Now there were pop-up boxes that she couldn't seem to get rid of. She'd restarted her computer, but the pop-up boxes were relentless. She sucked in a breath and blew it out audibly. Then another, bordering on hyperventilation.

"You okay?" a man's voice asked.

Her gaze lifted to meet Paris's. "Oh. Yeah." She shook her head.

"You're saying yes, but you're shaking your head no."

His smile was the kind that made women swoon, and for a moment, she forgot that she was in panic mode.

"My computer seems to be possessed," she told him.

This made Paris chuckle—a sound that seemed to lessen the tension inside her. "Mind if I take a look?"

She needed to say no. He was gorgeous, charming, and cool. And those three qualities made her nervous. But without her computer, she wouldn't be able to pay her bills after work. Or delete that dating profile that the Ladies' Day Out group had made for her last night. *Why didn't I delete it right away?*

"Yes, please," she finally said.

Paris headed around the counter. "Did you restart it?" he asked when he was standing right next to her. So close that she could smell the woodsy scent coming off his body. She could also feel a wave of heat radiating off him, burning the superficial layer of her skin. He was gorgeous, charming, cool, *and* he smelled divine. What woman could resist?

"I've restarted it twice already," she told him.

"Hmm." He put his bag down on the floor at his feet and stood in front of her computer. She couldn't help a closer inspection of the tattoos that covered his biceps muscles. They were colorful and artistically drawn, but she could only see parts of them. She had to resist pulling back the fabric of his shirt to admire the artwork there. What was wrong with her?

Paris turned his head to look at her. "Is it okay if I close out all the programs you currently have running?"

"Of course."

He tapped his fingers along her keys, working for

several long minutes while she drifted off in her own thoughts of his muscles and tattoos and the spicy scent of his aftershave. Then he straightened and turned back to her. "There you go, good as new."

"Wow. Really? That was fast."

He shrugged a nonchalant shoulder. "I just needed to reboot and run your virus software."

"You make it sound so easy."

"To me it is. I know computers. We have a kinship."

Lacy felt the same way about books. She reached for her cup of coffee that she'd purchased this morning, even though a jolt of caffeine was probably the last thing her nerves needed right now.

Paris pointed a finger at the cup. "That's where I know you from. You're the woman at the café. You always sit in the back with a book."

Her lips parted as she set her cup down. "You've noticed me?"

"Of course. Why wouldn't I?"

She shrugged and shook her head. "We've just never spoken." And she'd assumed she was invisible in the back corner, especially to someone like him. "Well, thank you for fixing my computer."

"Just a friend helping a friend." He met her gaze and held it for a long moment. Then he bent to pick up the strap of his bag, hung it over his shoulder, and headed around to the other side of the counter. "Be careful on those dating sites," he said, stopping as he passed in front of her. "Always meet at a safe location and don't give anyone your personal information until you know you can trust them."

"Hmm?" Lacy narrowed her eyes, and then her heart soared into her throat and her gaze dropped to her fixed computer. Up on the screen, first and foremost, was FishInTheSea.com. She giggled nervously as her body filled with mortification. "I didn't…I'm not…" Why wouldn't her mouth work? "This isn't what it looks like."

Paris grinned. "The women in my class told me about last night. Sounds like you were forced into it."

"Completely," she said with relief.

He shrugged. "I doubt you need a website to find a date. They created a really attractive profile for you though. It should get you a lot of nibbles from the fish in the sea."

She laughed because he'd made a joke, but there was no hope of making intelligible words right now. Instead she waved and watched him leave.

"See you tomorrow, Lace," he called over his shoulder.

* * *

That evening, Paris kicked his feet up on the railing of his back deck as he sat in an outdoor chair, laptop on his thighs, watching the fireflies that seemed to be sending him secret messages with their flashing lights. The message he needed right now was "get back to work."

Paris returned to looking at his laptop's screen. He'd worked on the graphic for Peak Designs Architectural Firm all evening, and he was finally happy with it. He sent it off to the owner and then began work on a new agenda for tomorrow's class. He'd be teaching his students how to Skype, and he'd make sure Mr. Jenson knew how to do it on his own before leaving.

Paris liked the thought of reuniting Mr. and Mrs. Jenson through technology. It was the least he could do for them. Technology shouldn't replace person-to-person contact, but it was a nice substitute when two people couldn't be together. Paris suspected one of the main reasons Mr. Jenson even came to the library was because it was one of the few places within walking distance from his house.

Creating an agenda for live communication technology took all of ten minutes. Then Paris gave in to his impulse to search FishInTheSea.com. He found himself looking at Lacy's profile again, staring at the beautiful picture on the screen. Her brown hair was down and spilling over one shoulder in soft curls. She had on makeup that accentuated her eyes, cheekbones, and lips. And even though she looked so different from the person he'd met, she also looked very much the same.

"Why am I on a dating site?" he muttered, his voice blending with the night sounds. And for that matter, why was he staring at Lacy's profile? Maybe he was just as lonely as Mr. Jenson.

Chapter Three

"I love the design," Pearson Matthews told Paris on Friday afternoon as Paris zipped down the gently winding mountain road on his bike. The pavement was still wet from the rain earlier this morning. Puddles splashed the legs of his jeans as he hit them.

He had earbuds in place under his helmet so he could ride hands-free and hold a conversation without the roar of the engine interfering. "I'm glad you like it, sir."

"Love. I said love," Pearson said. "And I plan to recommend you to everyone I know. I'm part of the Chamber of Commerce, so I have business connections. I'm going to make sure you have enough work to keep you in Sweetwater Springs for years to come."

Paris felt a curious kick in his heart. He loved this town and didn't like to think about leaving...but he had never been one to stick anywhere for long either. He credited the foster system for that. "Thank you."

"No need for thanks. You did a great job, and I want others to know about it. You're an asset here."

Paris resisted saying thank you a second time. "Well,

please make sure anyone you send my way tells me that you referred them. I give referral perks."

Pearson was one of the richest men in the community, so he likely didn't need any perks. "Sounds good. I'll talk to you soon."

They hung up, and Paris continued down the road, slowing at the entrance to the local library. His heart gave another curious kick at the thought of Lacy for a reason he didn't want to investigate. He parked, got off his bike, and then walked inside with his laptop bag on his shoulder.

Lacy wasn't behind the counter when he walked in. His gaze roamed the room, finding her with two little girls that he'd seen here before. She was helping them locate a book. One little girl was squirming as she stood in place, and Paris thought maybe she needed to locate a restroom first.

"Here you go. I think you girls will like this one," he heard Lacy tell them. "Abby, do you need to use the bathroom?"

The girl bobbed her head emphatically.

"You know where it is. Go ahead." Lacy pointed to the bathroom near the front entrance's double doors, and both girls took off in a sprint. Lacy watched them for a moment and then turned back to her computer. She gasped softly when she saw Paris. "You're here early. Do you need something?" she asked.

Need something? Yeah, he needed an excuse for why he'd been standing here stupidly waiting to talk to her.

"A book maybe?" Lacy stepped closer and lowered her voice.

"Yeah," he said. "I'm looking for a book."

"Okay. What exactly are you looking for?" she asked.

He scanned the surrounding shelves before his gaze landed back on her. "Actually, do you have anything on roses?"

Lacy's perfectly pink lips parted.

Paris had been trying to think of something he could do for his former foster parents, and roses had come to mind. Albert Jenson loved roses, but his wife, Nancy, adored the thorny beauties. "I was thinking about making a flower garden at the nursing home, but my thumbs are more black than green."

Lacy giggled softly. "Follow me." She led him to a wall of books in the nonfiction area and bent to inspect the titles.

Paris tried and failed not to admire her curves as she leaned forward in front of him. *Get it together, man.*

"Here you go. *The Dummie's Guide to Roses*." She straightened and held a book out to him.

"Dummie's Guide?"

Her cheeks flushed. "Don't take offense. I didn't title it."

Paris made a point of looking at the other titles that had sandwiched the book on the shelf. "No, but you didn't choose to give me the one titled *Everything There Is to Know About Roses* or *The Rose Lover's Handbook*." He returned to looking at her, fascinated by how easily he could make her blush. "Any luck on Fish In The Sea dot com?"

She looked away, pulling her hands to her midsection to fidget. "I've been meaning to cancel that. The ladies had good intentions when they signed me up, albeit misguided."

"Why did they choose you as their victim?"

Lacy shrugged. "I have this high school reunion coming up. They thought I'd be more likely to go if I had a date."

"You're not going to your own reunion?" Paris asked.

"I haven't decided yet," she said as she inched away and increased the distance between them.

Unable to help himself, Paris inched forward. He told himself it was because they had to whisper and he couldn't hear her otherwise.

"Have you gone to one of yours?" she asked.

"No." He shook his head. "I never stayed in one place long enough while I was growing up to be considered an official part of a class. If I had, I would." He looked at her. "You should go. I'm sure you could find a date, even without the dating site." Part of him was tempted to offer to take her himself. By nature, he was a helpful guy. He resisted offering though because there was another part of him that wanted to be her date for an entirely different reason.

He lifted *The Dummie's Guide to Roses*. "I'll just check this out and get set up for my class."

Lacy headed back behind the counter and held out her hand to him. "Library card, please."

"Library card?" he repeated.

"I need it to check you out."

He laid the book on the counter. "I, uh, I…"

"You don't have one?" she asked, grinning back at him.

"I do most of my reading on the computer. I guess it's been a while since I've checked a book out."

"No problem." She opened a drawer and pulled out a blank card. "I can make you one right now. Do you have a driver's license?"

He pulled out his wallet and laid his license on the counter. He watched as she grabbed it and got to work. Then she handed the card back to him, her fingers brushing his slightly in the handoff. Every nerve in his body responded to that one touch. If he wasn't mistaken, she seemed affected as well.

There was the real reason he hadn't offered to be her date for her class reunion. He was attracted to Lacy Shaw, and he *really* didn't want to be.

* * *

Lacy lifted her gaze to the computer room in the back of the library where Paris was teaching a class of unruly elders. From afar, he actually seemed to be enjoying himself. She'd called several people before Paris, trying to persuade them to teach a class here, and everyone had been too busy with their own lives. That made her wonder why a guy like Paris was able to accept her offer. Did he have any family? Close friends? A girlfriend?

She roped in her gaze and continued checking in books from the pile beside her. Paris Montgomery's personal life was none of her business.

"Ms. Shaw! Ms. Shaw!" Abigail and Willow Fields came running toward the checkout counter.

"What's wrong, girls?" Lacy sat up straighter, noting the panic in the sisters' voices.

"Mrs. Townsend won't wake up! We thought she was sleeping, but she won't wake up!"

Lacy took off running to the other side of the room where she'd known Mrs. Townsend was sleeping. Immediately, she recognized that the older woman was hunched over the table in an unnatural way. Her skin was a pale gray color that sent chills up Lacy's spine.

Panic gripped Lacy as she looked around at the small crowd of people who'd gathered. "Does anyone know CPR?" she called. There were at least a dozen books here on the subject, but she'd never learned.

Everyone gave her a blank stare. Lacy's gaze snagged on the young sisters huddled against the wall with tears spilling over their pale cheeks. If Mrs. Townsend died in front of them, they'd be devastated.

"Let's get her on the floor," a man's voice said, coming up behind Lacy.

She glanced back, surprised to find Paris in action.

He gently grabbed hold of Mrs. Townsend and laid her on the floor, taking control of the situation. She was never more thankful for help in her life.

"Call 911!" Lacy shouted to the crowd, relieved to see a young woman run toward the library counter where there was a phone. A moment later, the woman headed back. "They're on their way."

Lacy nodded as she returned to watching Paris perform chest compressions. He seemed to know exactly what to do. Several long minutes later, sirens filled the parking lot, and paramedics placed Mrs. Townsend onto a gurney. They revived her just enough for Mrs. Townsend to moan and look at the girls, her face seeming to contort with concern.

"It's okay. I'll take care of them, Mrs. Townsend," Lacy told her. "Just worry about taking care of yourself right now."

Lacy hoped Mrs. Townsend heard and understood. A second later, the paramedics loaded the older woman in the back of the ambulance and sped away, sirens screaming as they tore down the street.

Lacy stood on wobbly legs and tried to catch her breath. She pressed a hand against her chest, feeling like she might collapse or dissolve into tears.

"You all right?" Paris asked, pinning his ocean-blue gaze on hers.

She looked at him and shook her head. "Yes."

"You're contradicting yourself again," he said with a slight lift at one corner of his mouth. Then his hand went to her shoulder and squeezed softly. "Why don't you go sit down?"

"The girls," Lacy said, suddenly remembering her promise. She turned to where the sisters were still huddled and hurried over to where they were. "Mrs. Townsend is going to get help at the hospital. They'll take good care of her there, I promise."

Abby looked up. "What's wrong with her?"

Lacy shook her head. "I'm not sure, honey. I'm sure everything will be okay. Right now, I'm going to call your dad to come get you."

"He's at work," Willow said. "That's why we were with Mrs. Townsend."

"I know, honey. But he won't mind leaving the farm for a little bit. Follow me to the counter. I have some cookies up there."

The girls' eyes lit up, even as tears dripped from their eyelashes.

"I can call Granger while you take care of the girls," Paris offered.

How did Paris know that these sweet little children belonged to Granger Fields? As if hearing her thoughts, he explained, "I did some graphic design work on the Merry Mountain Farms website recently."

"Of course. That would be great," Lacy said, her voice sounding shaky. And she'd do her best to calm down in the meantime too.

* * *

Thirty minutes later, Granger Fields left the library with his little girls in tow, and Lacy plopped down on her stool behind the counter. The other patrons had emptied out of the library as well, and it was two minutes until closing time.

"Eventful afternoon," Paris said.

Lacy startled as he walked into view. She hadn't realized he was still here. "You were great with the CPR. You might have a second career as a paramedic."

He shook his head. "I took a class in college, but I'll stick to computers, thanks."

"And I'll stick to books. My entire body is still trembling."

Paris's dark brows stitched together. "I can take you home if you're not up for driving."

"On your bike?" she asked. "I'm afraid that wouldn't help my nerves at all."

Paris chuckled. "Not a fan of motorcycles, huh?"

"I've never been on one, and I don't plan to start this evening. It's time to close, and my plans include calling the hospital to check on Mrs. Townsend and then going home, changing into my PJs, and soothing my nerves with ice cream."

Paris leaned against her counter. "While you were with the girls, I called a friend I know who works at Sweetwater Memorial. She checked on things for me and just texted me an update." He held up his cell phone. "Mrs. Townsend is stable but being admitted so they can watch her over the next forty-eight hours."

Lacy blew out a breath. "That's really good news. For a moment there, she looked like she might die. If we hadn't gone over to her when we did, she might have just passed away in her sleep." Lacy wasn't sure she would've felt as safe in her little library ever again if that had happened.

"Life is fragile," Paris said. "Something like this definitely puts things into perspective, doesn't it?"

"It really does." Her worries and fears suddenly seemed so silly and so small.

Paris straightened from the counter and tugged his bag higher on his shoulder. "See you tomorrow," he said as he headed out of the library.

She watched him go and then set about to turning off all the lights. She grabbed her things and locked up behind her as she left, noticing Paris and his motorcycle beside her car in the parking lot.

"If I didn't know you were a nice guy, I might be a little scared by the fact that you're waiting beside my car in an empty parking lot."

"I'm harmless." He hugged his helmet against him. "You looked a little rattled in there. I wanted to make sure you got home safely. I'll follow you."

Lacy folded her arms over her chest. "Maybe I don't want you to know where I live."

"The end of Pine Cone Lane. This is a small town, and I get around with business."

"I see. Well, you don't need to follow me home. Really, I'm fine."

"I'd feel better if I did."

Lacy held out her arms. "Suit yourself. Good night, Paris." She stepped inside her vehicle, closed the door behind her, and cranked her engine. It rolled and flopped. She turned the key again. This time it didn't even roll. "Crap." This day just kept getting better.

After a few more attempts, Paris tapped on her driver's side window.

She opened the door. "The battery is dead. I think I left my lights on this morning." It'd been raining, and she'd had them on to navigate through the storm. She'd forgotten her umbrella, so she'd turned off her engine, gotten out of her car, and had darted toward the library. In her rush, she must've forgotten to turn off her lights.

"I'll call Jere's Shop. He can jump your battery or tow it back to your house," Paris said.

Lacy considered the plan. "I can just wait here for him and drive it back myself."

"Jere is dependable but slow. You don't need to be out here waiting for him all evening. Leave your keys in the ignition, and I'll take you home."

Lacy looked at the helmet that Paris now extended toward her, her brain searching for another option. She didn't want to be here all night. She could call one of her sisters, but they would then follow her inside, and she didn't want to deal with them after the day she'd had either.

She got out of the car and took the helmet. "Okay," she said, shaking her head no.

This made Paris laugh as he led her to his bike. "You are one big contradiction, Lacy Shaw."

* * *

Paris straddled his bike and waited for Lacy to take the seat behind him. He glanced over his shoulder as she wrung her hands nervously. She seemed to be giving herself a pep talk, and then she lunged, as if forcing herself, and straddled the seat behind him.

Paris grinned and waited for another long second. "You know, you're going to have to wrap your arms around my waist for the ride."

"Right," he heard her say in a muffled voice. Her arms embraced him, clinging more tightly as he put the motorcycle in motion. Before he was even down the road, Lacy's grasp on him was so tight that her head rested on his back. He kind of liked the feel of her body hugging his, even if it was because she was scared for her life.

He knew the way to her house, but at the last second, he decided to take a different route. Lacy didn't speak up, so he guessed her eyes were shut tightly, blocking out the streets that zipped past.

Instead of taking her home, he drove her to the park, where the hot spring was. There were hiking trails and a hot dog vendor too. On her profile, Lacy had said those were among her favorite things, and after this afternoon, she deserved a few guilty pleasures.

He pulled into the parking lot and cut the engine. Slowly, Lacy peeled her body away from him. He felt her shift as she looked around.

She removed her helmet. "Why are we at the park?"

Paris glanced back. "Surprise. I thought I'd take your mind off things before I took you home."

She stared at him, a dumbfounded expression creasing her brow. "Why the park?"

"Because you love to take long hikes. And hot dogs, so I thought we'd grab a couple afterward. I didn't wear my hiking boots, but these will work for a quick half mile down the trail. Your profile mentioned that you love the hot spring here."

Lacy blinked. "You read my dating profile?"

"Great late-night reading." He winked.

She drew her hand to her forehead and shook her head. Something told him this time the head shake wasn't a yes. "Most of the information on my profile was exaggerated by the ladies' group. Apparently, they didn't think the real Lacy Shaw was interesting enough."

"You don't like hiking?"

"I like leisurely walks."

"Dogs?" he asked.

"Cats are my preference."

Paris let his gaze roam around them briefly before looking back at her. "What *do* you like?"

"In general?" she asked.

"Let's start with food. I'm starving."

She gave him a hesitant look. "Well, the hot dog part was true, but only because I added that part after they left."

Paris grinned, finding her adorable and sexy at the same time. "I happen to love a good chili dog. And there's a stand at the far side of the park." He waited for her to get off the bike and then he climbed off as well. "Let's go eat, shall we?"

"Saving someone's life works up an appetite, I guess."

"I didn't save Mrs. Townsend's life," he said as they walked. "I just kept her alive so someone else could do that."

From the corner of his eye, he saw Lacy fidgeting.

He reached for her hand to stop the motion. "I brought you here to take your mind off that situation. Let's talk about something light."

"Like?"

"You? Why did you let the Ladies' Day Out group make you a dating profile if you don't want to be on the site?"

Lacy laughed softly as they stepped into a short line for hot dogs. "Have you met the Ladies' Day Out group? They are determined and persistent. When they want something, they don't take no for an answer."

"You're part of the LDO," he pointed out.

"Well, I don't share that same quality."

"You were persistent in getting me to agree to teach a class at the library."

"True. I guess when there's something I want, I go after it." They reached the front of the line and ordered two sodas and two hot dogs. One with chili for him and one without for her.

Lacy opened the flap of her purse, and Paris stopped her. "I brought you here. This is my treat."

"No, I couldn't—"

She started to argue, but he laid a ten-dollar bill in front of the vendor. "It's just sodas and hot dogs." He glanced over. "You can treat me next time."

Her lips parted. He was only teasing, but he saw the question in her eyes, and now it was in his mind too. Would there really be a next time? Would that be so bad?

After collecting the change, they carried their drinks and hot dogs to a nearby bench and sat down.

"I didn't think I'd like teaching, but it's actually kind of fun," Paris confessed.

"Even Mr. Jenson?" she asked before taking a huge bite of her hot dog.

"Even him. But he didn't show up today. Maybe he dropped out." Paris shrugged. "I changed the syllabus just for him. I was planning to teach the class to Skype this afternoon."

"You didn't?"

He shook his head. "I went back to the lesson on Microsoft Word just in case Mr. Jenson showed up next time."

"Maybe he didn't feel well. He's been to every other class this week, right?"

Paris shook his head. "But he's made no secret that he doesn't like my teaching. He's even blasted his opinions all over Facebook."

Lacy grimaced. "Oh my. He treats everyone that way. I wouldn't take it personally. It's just how he is."

"He wasn't always that way. He used to be really nice, if memory serves me correctly."

Lacy narrowed her eyes. "You knew him before the class?"

Paris looked down at his half-eaten hot dog. "He and Mrs. Jenson fostered me for a while, but he doesn't seem to remember me."

"You were in foster care?"

"Yep. The Jensons were my favorite family."

Her jaw dropped. "That's so interesting."

Paris angled his body toward her. "Do you know what's wrong with Mrs. Jenson?"

Lacy shrugged. "I'm not sure. All I know is she's forgetful. She gets confused a lot. I've seen her get pretty agitated with Mr. Jenson too. They used to come into the library together."

"Maybe that's why he's so bitter now," Paris said, thinking out loud. He lifted his hot dog to his mouth and took another bite.

"Perhaps Mr. Jenson just needs someone to help him."

Paris chewed and swallowed. "I'm not even sure how I could help Mr. Jenson. I've been reading up on how to make a rose garden, but that won't make his wife well again."

Lacy hummed thoughtfully. "I think Mr. Jenson just needs someone to treat him nicely, no matter how horrible he is. No matter what he says to me, I always offer him a big smile. I actually think he likes me, although he would never admit it." She giggled to herself.

Paris looked at her. "You seem to really understand people."

"I do a lot of people-watching. And I had years of being an outcast in school." She swiped at a drop of ketchup at the corner of her mouth. "When you're hiding in the back of the classroom, there's not much else to do but watch everyone else. You can learn a lot about a person when they think no one is paying attention."

"Why would you hide?" he asked, growing increasingly interested in Lacy Shaw.

She met his gaze, and he glimpsed something dark in her eyes for a moment. "Childhood scoliosis. I had to wear a back brace to straighten out my spine."

His gaze dropped to her back. It was long and smooth now.

"I don't wear it anymore," she told him. "My back is fixed. High school is when you want to be sporting the latest fashion though, not a heavy brace."

"I'm sure you were just as beautiful."

She looked away shyly, tucking a strand of brown hair behind her ear with one hand. "Anyway, I guess that's why I know human nature. Even the so-called nice kids were afraid to be associated with me. There were a handful of people who didn't care. I'm still close with them."

"Sounds like your childhood was less than desirable.

Kind of like mine," he said. "That's something we have in common."

She looked up. "Who'd have thought? The librarian and the bad boy biker."

"Bad boy?" he repeated, finding this description humorous.

Her cheeks blossomed red just like the roses he'd studied in the library book. She didn't look away, and he couldn't, even if he wanted to. Despite himself, he felt the pull between them, the sexual tension winding around its gear, cranking tighter and tighter. "Perhaps we have a lot more in common."

"Like what?" she asked softly.

"Well, we both like hot dogs."

She smiled softly.

"And I want to kiss you right now. Not sure if you want to kiss me too but..." What was he doing? It was as if something else had taken control of his mind and mouth. He was saying exactly the opposite of what he intended.

Lacy's lips parted, her pupils dilated, and unless he was reading her wrong, she wanted to kiss him too.

Leaning forward, he dropped his mouth and brushed his lips to hers. A little sigh tumbled out of her, and after a moment, she kissed him back.

Chapter Four

Sparks, tingles, the whole nine yards.

That was what this kiss with Paris was. He was an amazing kisser. He had a firm hand on her thigh and the other gently curled around the back of her neck. This was the Cadillac of kisses, not that Lacy had much experience recently. It'd been a while since she'd kissed anyone. The last guy she'd briefly dated had run the library in the town of River Oaks. They'd shared a love of books, but not much else.

Paris pulled back slightly. "I'm sorry," he said. "I didn't mean to do that."

She blinked him into focus, a dreamlike feeling hanging over her.

"All I wanted to do tonight was take your mind off the afternoon."

"The afternoon?" she repeated.

"Mrs. Townsend?"

"Oh." She straightened a touch. Was that why he'd kissed her? Was he only taking her mind off the trauma of what happened at the library? "I definitely forgot about that for a moment."

"Good." Paris looked around the park. Then he stood and offered her his hand. "Want to take a walk to the hot spring before we leave?"

She allowed him to pull her to standing. "Okay."

She followed him because he'd driven her here. Because he'd kissed her. Because she wasn't sure what to think, but one thing she knew for sure was that she liked being around Paris. He was easy to talk to, and he made her feel good about herself.

"Penny for your thoughts?" he asked a couple of minutes later, walking alongside her.

She could hear the subtle sound of water as they drew closer to the hot spring. "Oh, I was just thinking what a nice night it is."

Paris looked around. "I don't think there's a single season in this town that I don't like. The air is easier to breathe here for some reason." She watched him suck in a deep breath and shivered with her body's response.

"I've always wanted to get in a hot spring," Lacy admitted, turning her attention to the water that was now in view.

"You've never been in?" Paris asked.

Lacy shook her head. "No. That was another fabrication for the profile. I've read that a spring is supposed to help with so many things. Joint and muscle pain. Energy levels. Detoxification."

"Do you need those benefits?" he asked.

Lacy looked up at him. "Not really." All she really needed was to lean into him and press her lips to his once more.

Paris sighed as they walked. "So what should I do?"

A dozen thoughts rushed Lacy's mind. "Hmm?"

"I want to help Mr. Jenson somehow, like you suggested."

"Oh." She looked away as she swallowed. "Well, he didn't show up at today's class. Maybe you could stop by and see him. Tomorrow is Saturday, so there's no class anyway. You could check on him and make sure he's okay."

Paris stared at her. "I have to admit, that old man kind of scares me."

Lacy giggled softly. "Me too." She gasped as an idea rushed into her mind. She didn't give herself time to think before sharing it with Paris. "But I'll go with you. It's my day off."

He cocked his head. "You'd spend your day off helping me?"

"Yes, but there's a condition."

He raised a questioning brow. "What's that?"

"I'll go with you if you'll be my date to my class reunion." Seeing Mrs. Townsend at death's door this afternoon had shaken her up more than she'd realized. "I don't want to hide anymore. I want to go, have a blast, and show everyone who tried to break me that they didn't succeed." And for some reason, Paris made her feel more confident.

Paris grinned at her. "Are you asking me out, Lacy Shaw?"

She swallowed. "Yes. Kind of. I'm offering you a deal."

He shoved his hands in his pockets. "I guess Mr. Jenson might be less likely to slam the door on my face tomorrow if I have a beautiful woman by my side. You said he likes you, so…"

Her insides fluttered to life. "My old bullies might be less likely to pick on me if I have a hot graphic designer as my escort."

This made him laugh. Then Paris stuck out his hand. "Want to shake on it?"

She would prefer to kiss on it, but that first kiss had come with an apology from him. This deal wasn't romantic in nature. It was simply two people helping one another out.

* * *

Even though Paris worked for himself, he still loved a Saturday, especially this one. He and Lacy were spending the day together, and he hadn't looked forward to something like this in a while. He got out of bed with the energy of a man who'd already had his coffee and headed down the hall to brew a pot. Then he dressed in a pair of light-colored jeans and a favorite T-shirt for a local band he loved.

As he sipped his coffee, he thought about last evening and the kiss that probably had a lot to do with his mood this morning. He hadn't planned on kissing Lacy, but the feeling had engulfed him. And her signals were all a go, so he'd leaned in and gone for it.

Magic.

There'd be no kissing today though. He didn't like starting things he couldn't finish, and he wasn't in the market for a relationship. He'd traveled that path, and his marriage had been anything but the happy ending he'd envisioned. He couldn't do anything right for his ex, no matter how hard he'd tried. As soon as he'd realized she was having an affair, he'd left. He didn't stick around where he wasn't wanted.

Paris stood and grabbed his keys. Then he headed out the door to go get Lacy. He'd take his truck today so that he didn't need to torture himself with the feel of her arms around his waist.

A short drive later, he pulled into her driveway on Pine Cone Lane, walked up the steps, and knocked. She opened the door, and for a moment, he forgot to breathe. She wore her hair down, allowing it to spill softly over her shoulders just like in her profile picture. "You look, uh...well, you look nice," he finally said.

She lifted a hand and smoothed her hair on one side. "Thanks. At the library, it's easier to keep my hair pulled back," she explained. "But since I'm off today, I thought I'd let loose."

It was more than her hair. A touch of makeup accented her brown eyes, and she was wearing a soft pink top that brought out the colors in her skin. If he was a painter, he'd be running for his easel. If he was a writer, he'd grab a pen and paper, ignited by inspiration.

But he was just a guy who dabbled on computers. A guy who'd already decided he wasn't going to act on his attraction to the woman standing in front of him.

"I'm ready if you are," she said, stepping onto the porch and closing the front door behind her. She looked out into the driveway. "Oh, you drove something with four wheels today. I was ready for the bike, but I admit I'm kind of relieved."

"The bike grew on you a little bit?"

She shrugged one shoulder. "I could get used to it. My mother would probably kill you if she knew you put me on a motorcycle last night."

"I was rescuing you from being stranded in a dark parking lot," he pointed out.

"The lesser of two evils."

Paris jumped ahead to open her door, winning a curious look from her as well as a new blush on her cheeks—this one not due to makeup.

"Thanks."

He closed the door behind her and then jogged around to the driver's side. Once he was seated behind the steering wheel, he looked over. "Looks like Jere got your car back okay." He gestured toward her Honda Accord parked in front of a single-car garage.

"He left it and texted me afterward. No charge. He said he owed you." Lacy's brows subtly lifted.

"See, it pays to hang around me." Paris started the engine. "I was thinking we could stop in and check on Mrs. Townsend first."

Lacy pointed a finger at him. "I love that idea, even though I'm on to you, Paris Montgomery. You're really just procrastinating because you're scared of Mr. Jenson."

He grimaced as he drove toward the Sweetwater hospital. "That's probably true."

They chatted easily as he drove, discussing all of Lacy's plans for the library this summer. She talked excitedly about her work, which he found all kinds of attractive. Then he pulled into the hospital parking lot, and they both got out.

"We shouldn't go see Mrs. Townsend empty-handed," Lacy said as they walked toward the main entrance.

"We can swing by the gift shop before we go up," he suggested.

"Good idea. She likes magazines, so I'll get her a couple. I hope Abby and Willow are okay. It had to be confusing for them, watching their nanny being taken away in an ambulance."

"The girls only have one parent?" he asked.

"Their mother isn't around," Lacy told him.

Paris slid his gaze over. He wasn't sure he wanted to know, but he asked anyway. "What happened to their mom?" He'd heard a lot of stories from his foster siblings growing up. There were so many reasons for a parent to slip out of the picture. His story was rather boring in comparison to some. His parents didn't like abiding by the law, which left him needing supplementary care at times. Then they'd decided that another thing they didn't like was taking care of him.

"Their mother left right after Willow was born. There was speculation that maybe she had postpartum depression."

Paris swallowed as they veered into the gift shop. "It's good that they have Granger. He seems like a good dad."

"I think so too. And what kid wouldn't want to grow up on a Christmas tree farm? I mean, that's so cool." Lacy beelined toward the magazine rack in the back of the shop, picking out three. They also grabbed some chocolates at the register.

Bag of presents in hand, they left the shop and took the

elevator up to the third floor to Mrs. Townsend's room. Lacy knocked, and they waited for Mrs. Townsend's voice to answer back, telling them to "come in."

"Oh, Lacy! You didn't have to spend your Saturday coming to see me," Mrs. Townsend said as they entered her room. "And you brought a friend."

"Mrs. Townsend, this is Paris Montgomery. He did CPR on you in the library yesterday."

Mrs. Townsend's eyes widened. "I didn't even know I needed CPR. How embarrassing. But thank you," she told Paris. "I guess you were instrumental in saving my life."

"It was no big deal," he said.

"To the woman who's still alive today it is." Mrs. Townsend looked at Lacy again, her gaze dropping to the bag in her hand. "What do you have?"

"Oh, yes." Lacy pulled the magazines out and offered them to Mrs. Townsend, along with the chocolates.

Mrs. Townsend looked delighted by the gifts. "Oh my goodness. Thank you so much."

"Are you doing okay?" Lacy asked.

Mrs. Townsend waved a hand. "The doctors here have been taking good care of me. They tell me I can go home tomorrow."

Lacy smiled. "That's good news."

"Yes, it is. And I'll be caring for the girls again on Monday. A little flutter in the heart won't keep me from doing what I love."

Lacy's gaze slid to meet Paris's as worry creased her brow. He resisted reaching for her hand in a calming gesture. His intentions would be innocent, but they could also confuse things. He and Lacy were only out today as friends. Nothing more.

They stayed and chatted a while longer and then left, riding down the elevator in silence. Paris and Lacy walked side by side back to his truck. He opened the passenger side door for her again and then got into the driver's seat.

"I'm glad Mrs. Townsend is okay," Lacy said as they pulled back onto the main road and drove toward Blueberry Creek Road, where Albert Jenson lived.

"Me too," Paris told her.

"But what happens next time?"

"Hopefully there won't be a next time."

"And if there is, hopefully you'll be around," Lacy said. Something about her tone made him wonder if she wanted to keep him around for herself too.

A few minutes later, he turned onto Mr. Jenson's street and traveled alongside Blueberry Creek. His heart quickened as he pulled into Mr. Jenson's driveway.

"I can't believe he walks from here to the library," Lacy said as he cut the engine. "That has to be at least a mile."

"He's always loved to walk." Paris let his gaze roam over the house. It was smaller than he remembered and in need of new paint. The rosebushes that the Jensons loved so much were unruly and unkempt. He was in his seventies now though. The man Paris knew as a child had been middle-aged and full of energy. Things changed. He looked over. "All right. Let's get this over with. If he yells at us, we'll know he's okay. The buddy system, right?"

"Right."

Except with each passing second spent with Lacy, the harder it was for him to think of her as just a buddy.

* * *

Lacy had never been to Mr. Jenson's home before. She'd known that the Jensons kept foster children once upon a time, but it surprised her that one of them was Paris.

"Strange, but this place feels like home to me," Paris said as he stood at the front door.

"How long did you live here with the Jensons?"

"About six months, which was longer than I lived with most."

"Makes sense why you'd think of this place fondly then." She wanted to ask more about his parents, but it wasn't the time. "Are you going to ring the doorbell?" she asked instead.

"Oh. I guess that would help." Paris pushed the button for the doorbell with his index finger and let his hands clasp back together in front of him.

"If I didn't know better, I'd think Mr. Cool was nervous," she commented.

"Mr. Cool?" He glanced over. "Any relation to Mr. Clean?"

This made her giggle until the front door opened and Mr. Jenson frowned back at them.

Lacy straightened. From the corner of her eye, she saw Paris stand more upright as well.

"Mr. Jenson," Paris said. "Good morning, sir."

"What are you doing here?" the old man barked through the screen door.

"Just checking on you. You missed a class that I put together just for you."

"I hear you were trying to kill people at the library yesterday," Mr. Jenson said, his frown steadfast. "Good thing I stayed home."

"Mrs. Townsend is fine," Paris informed him. "We just checked on her at Sweetwater Memorial."

"And now you're checking on me?" Mr. Jenson shook his head, casting a suspicious glare. "Why?"

Paris held up his hands. "Like I said, I missed you in yesterday's class."

Mr. Jenson looked surprised for a moment, and maybe even a little happy with this information. Then his grumpy demeanor returned. "I decided it wasn't worth my time."

Lacy noticed Paris tense beside her. "Actually, the class is free and taught by a professional," she said, jumping in to help. "We're lucky to have Mr. Montgomery teaching at Sweetwater Library."

Mr. Jenson gave her a long, hard look. She was prepared for him to take a jab at her too, but instead he shrugged his frail shoulders. "It's a long walk, and my legs hurt yesterday, okay? You happy? I'm not a spring chicken anymore, but I'm fine, and I'll be back on Monday. If for no other reason than to keep you two off my front porch." Mr. Jenson looked between them, and then he harrumphed and promptly slammed the door in their faces.

Lacy turned to look at Paris. "Are you sure you're remembering him correctly? I can't imagine that man was ever very nice."

"Did you see him smile at me before he slammed that door though? I think he's softening up."

Lacy laughed, reaching her arm out and grabbing Paris momentarily to brace her body as it shook with amusement. Once she'd realized what she'd done, she removed her hand and cleared her throat. "Okay, our well-check visits are complete. Mrs. Townsend and Mr. Jenson are both alive and kicking."

"I guess it's time for me to keep my end of the deal now," Paris said, leading her back to his truck.

Lacy narrowed her eyes. "But my reunion isn't until next Saturday."

"Yes, but I'm guessing you need to go shopping for something new to wear, right? And I can't wear jeans and an old T-shirt." He opened the passenger door for her.

"You can wear whatever you want," she told him as she stepped inside. Then she turned to look at him as he stood in her doorway.

"I want to look my best when I'm standing beside you. And I hear that Sophie's Boutique is the place to go if you want to dress to impress." He closed the door behind her and walked around to get in the driver's seat.

"Are you seriously offering to go dress shopping with me right now?" she asked once he was seated. "Because guys usually hate that kind of thing."

Paris grinned as he cranked the truck. "Sitting back and watching you come in and out of a dressing room, modeling beautiful clothes, sounds like a fun way to spend an afternoon to me." He winked before backing out of the driveway.

For a moment, Lacy was at a complete loss for words. “I mean, I’m sure you have other things to do with your Saturday afternoon.”

He glanced over. “None as fun as hanging out with you.”

She melted into the passenger seat. No one in her life had made her feel quite as interesting as Paris had managed to do last night and today. Just the opposite, the Ladies’ Day Out group, while well-meaning, had made her feel boring by elaborating on the truth.

Paris made her feel other things as well. Things that were too soon to even contemplate.

Chapter Five

Every time Lacy walked out of the dressing room, Paris felt his heart kick a little harder. The dresses in Sophie's Boutique were gorgeous, but they paled in comparison to Lacy.

"You're staring at me," she said after twirling in a lavender knee-length dress with small navy blue polka dots. "Do you like this one or not?" She looked down. "I kind of love it. It's fun, and that's what I want for my reunion." She was grinning when she looked back up at him. "I want to dance and eat all the foods that will make this dress just a little too tight the next morning." A laugh tumbled off her lips.

Paris swallowed, looking for words, but they all got stuck in his throat. His feelings for Lacy were snowballing with every passing second—and it scared him more than Mr. Jenson did.

"Well?" she said again.

"That's the one for sure." He tore his gaze from her, pushing away all the thoughts of things he wanted to do to her in that dress. He wanted to spin her around on the dance floor, hold her close, and kiss her without apology next time.

Next time?

"Oh, wow! You look so beautiful!" Sophie Daniels, the boutique's owner, walked over and admired Lacy in the dress. "Is that the one?"

Lacy was practically glowing. "I think so, yeah."

Sophie turned to look at Paris. He'd met Sophie before, and she'd flirted mildly with him. He hadn't returned the flirting though because, beautiful as she was, he wasn't interested.

But he couldn't deny his interest in Lacy.

"Now it's your turn," Lacy said.

Sophie gestured to the other side of the store. "I have a rack of men's clothing in the back. Let's get you something that will complement what Lacy is wearing but not steal her show."

"As if I could steal the attention away from her," he said while standing.

Sophie's mouth dropped open. With a knowing look in her eyes, she tipped her head, signaling for him to follow her while Lacy returned to the dressing room to change.

"You seem like a nice guy, Paris, and Lacy deserves someone who will treat her well," Sophie said to him over her shoulder as she led the way.

"It's not like that between us." He swiped a hand through his hair. "I mean, Lacy is terrific, but the two of us don't make sense."

Sophie started sifting through the men's clothes on the rack. "Why not? You're both single and attractive.

She avoids the spotlight, and you kind of grab people's attention wherever you go."

"I do?" he asked.

Sophie stopped looking through the clothes to give him another knowing look. "Opposites attract is a real thing, and it makes perfect sense." She pulled out a dark purple button-down shirt that would match Lacy's dress. "Do you have black pants?"

"I have black jeans," he told her.

She seemed to think about this. "Yes, black jeans will work. You just need to dress up a little bit. You're a jeans and T-shirt kind of guy, so let's keep the jeans." She nodded as if making the decision. "You, but different."

"Me, but different," he agreed, taking the shirt from her. That's how he felt with Lacy. He was still him but more grounded. And Lacy was still reserved but also coming out of her shell, and he loved watching it happen. "Do you have any bathing suits?" he asked on a whim. "One for me and one for Lacy?"

Sophie's eyes lit up, a smile lifting at the corners of her mouth. "Of course I do."

"I'll take one for each of us then. And this shirt for the reunion," Paris said.

Sophie gave him a conspiratorial wink. "I'll take care of it."

* * *

Lacy felt like Julia Roberts in *Pretty Woman*. She loved the dress she'd picked out, and she'd enjoyed the way

Paris had stared at her as she'd modeled each one before it.

They left the boutique and walked back to Paris's truck. He opened her door, and she got in, tucking her bag in the floorboard at her feet. "That was so much fun. Thank you."

He stood in the open doorway of his truck, watching her. His gaze was so intense, and for a moment, her heart sped up. Was he going to kiss her again?

"I want to take you somewhere else," he said.

She furrowed her brow. They'd already spent nearly the entire day together, not that she minded. "Where?"

He placed a second bag in her lap and winked before shutting the door behind her and walking around the truck.

Lacy peeked inside the bag and gasped as he opened his own door and got behind the wheel. "This is a bathing suit."

"You said you always wanted to go to the hot spring. You and I are on one big adventure today, so I thought it'd be fitting to end our expedition by doing something on your bucket list."

"I don't actually have a bucket list," she noted, looking down at the bathing suit again, "but if I did, this would be on it. I can't believe you got me a bathing suit." Underneath her bright pink suit in the bag was a pair of men's board shorts. "Are we really going to do this?"

Paris looked over. "Only if you agree. Will you go on a date with me to the hot spring?"

A date? Had he meant that the way it'd sounded?

Because a date implied that they were more than friends, and that's the way she felt about him right now.

* * *

The night was alive with sounds of nature. In the past hour, the sun had gone down behind the mountains, and stars had begun to shimmer above as darkness fell.

Lacy came out of the changing room with her bathing suit on and a towel wrapped around her waist. Paris was waiting on a bench for her, bare chested and in a pair of swim shorts.

Her mouth went dry. This wasn't her. She didn't visit hot springs with gorgeous men. Her idea of fun on a Saturday night was curling up on her front porch swing with a good book. This was a nice change of pace though, and with Paris beside her, she didn't mind trying something new.

"Ready?" he asked, standing and walking toward her. He reached for her hand and took it. The touch zinged from her heart to her toes, bouncing back up through her body like a ball in a pinball machine.

The sound of water grew louder as they approached the hot spring. They were the only ones here so far this evening, which she found odd and exciting.

Paris stood at the steps and looked at Lacy. "You're going to have to drop that towel," he said, his gaze trailing from her face and down her body toward her hips.

"Right." She swallowed and let go of his hand. She was about to remove her towel, but he reached out for her and did the honors. There was something so intimate about the gesture that her knees weakened. The towel fell in his hand, leaving her standing there in just her suit. She felt exposed and so alive.

He met her gaze for a long moment and then folded the towel and left it on a bench. Turning back to her, he reached for her hand again. "Careful," he said quietly, leading her down the steps and into the water.

She moaned softly as the hot water lapped against her skin. "This is heavenly," she finally said once she'd taken a seat inside. He was still holding her hand, and that was heavenly as well. They leaned back against the spring's wall, and both of them looked up at the stars.

"Anywhere I've been in my life," Paris whispered after a moment, "I've always been under these same stars. I've always wished I was somewhere different when I looked up, but tonight, there's nowhere else I'd rather be." He looked over, his face dangerously close to hers.

She swallowed. "Are you going to kiss me again?"

His blue eyes narrowed. "Do you want me to kiss you again?"

"Ever since that first kiss."

His eyes dropped to her mouth. Her lips parted for him. Then he leaned just a fraction, and his lips brushed against hers. He stayed there, offering small kisses that evolved into something deeper and bigger. One of his hands slid up her thigh, anchoring midway. The touch completely undid her, and if they weren't in a public setting, she might have wiggled until his hand slid higher.

"Are you going to apologize again?" she asked once he'd pulled away.

He shook his head. "I'm not sorry."

"Me neither," she whispered. Then she leaned in and kissed him this time. Who was she these days? This wasn't like her at all.

They didn't stop kissing until voices approached the hot spring. Lacy pulled back from Paris. Another couple appeared and headed toward the spring. They stepped in and sat across from Lacy and Paris.

"We have to behave now," Paris whispered in Lacy's ear.

"Easier said than done." She grinned at him.

"And I'm not leaving until this little problem I have has gone down."

"What problem?" she asked, looking down through the clear bubbles. Then she realized what he was referring to, and her body grew impossibly hotter.

They returned to looking at the stars and talking in whispers, sharing even more details about themselves. Lacy could've stayed and talked all night, but the hot spring closed at ten p.m. When she finally stepped out of the water, the cool air was a harsh contrast.

After toweling off and changing in the dressing room, Lacy met Paris outside and got into his truck. He drove slowly as he took her home, their conversation touching various subjects. And the more she learned about Paris, the more she wanted to know.

Finally, he pulled into her driveway and looked at her.

"I'm not sure you should walk me to my door," Lacy said. "I'd probably end up asking you if you wanted to come inside." She nibbled softly on her lower lip. "And, well, that's probably not the best idea."

"I understand." He reached for her hand. "Thank you for the best day that I can remember."

She leaned toward him. "And the best night."

She gave him a brief kiss because there was still the risk that she might invite him inside. She was doing things that were surprising even herself. "The library is closed tomorrow. I can make lunch if you want to come over."

He hesitated.

"I mean, you don't have to, if you have something else to do."

He grinned. "I have work to do tomorrow, but a man has to eat, right? Lunch sounds nice. I'll be here."

"Perfect." She pushed the truck door open before her hormones took over and she climbed over to his side of the truck instead. "Good night, Paris."

"Good night, Lace."

Chapter Six

Lacy wasn't thinking straight last night. Otherwise, she would've remembered that a few members of the Ladies' Day Out group were coming over for lunch after church. No doubt they wanted to nag her about one thing or another. Today's topics were most likely the dating site and her reunion.

Then again, that was all the more reason for Paris to join them for lunch. His presence would kill two birds with one stone. She didn't need a dating site. And she and Paris were going to have an amazing time at her reunion next weekend.

She heard his motorcycle rumble into her driveway first. She waited for him to ring the doorbell, and then she went to answer. Butterflies fluttered low in her belly at the sight of him.

"Come in." She led him inside the two-bedroom house that she'd purchased a couple of years ago. "It's not much, but it's home."

"Well, sounds cliché, but I've learned that home really is where the heart is," he said.

She turned to look at him, standing close enough that she could reach out and touch him again. Maybe pull him toward her, go up on her tiptoes, and press her lips to his. "By cliché, you mean cheesy?"

Paris pretended to push a stake through his heart. "When you get comfortable with someone, your feisty side is unleashed. I like it." He leaned in just a fraction, and Lacy decided to take a step forward, giving him the not-so-subtle green light for another kiss. He was right. She was feisty when she was with him, and she liked this side of her too.

The sound of another motor pulling into her driveway got her attention. She turned toward her door.

"Are you expecting someone else?" Paris asked, following her gaze.

"Yes, sorry. I didn't remember when I invited you last night, but I have company coming over today."

"Who?" Paris asked.

"My mom."

He nodded. "Okay."

"And my two sisters, Birdie and Rose," Lacy added. "*And* my aunt Pam."

Paris started to look panicked. "Anyone else?"

"Yeah. Um, Dawanda from the fudge shop. They're all part of the Ladies' Day Out group. I got a text earlier in the week telling me they were bringing lunch."

"Well, I'll get out of your guys' hair," he said, backpedaling toward the door.

She grabbed his hand, holding it until he met her gaze. "Wait. You don't need to leave. I want you here."

Paris grimaced. "Family mealtime has never really been my strong point."

Lacy continued to hold his hand. She wanted to show the women outside that she could find a guy on her own. She didn't need FishInTheSea.com. She also wanted to show them this new side of herself that seemed to take hold when she was with Paris. "They're harmless, I promise. Please stay."

Paris shifted on his feet, and she was pretty sure he was going to turn down the invitation. "You didn't take no for an answer when you wanted me to teach the computer class at the library," he finally said. "I'm guessing the same would be true now, huh?"

She grinned. "That's right."

"You're a hard woman to resist."

"Then stop trying," she said, going to answer the door.

* * *

The spread on Lacy's table was fit for a Thanksgiving dinner by Paris's standards. Not that he had much experience with holidays and family gatherings. He'd had many a holiday meal with a fast-food bag containing a burger, fries, and a small toy.

"I would've brought Denny if I'd known that men were allowed at lunch today," Mrs. Shaw said, speaking of her husband. She seemed friendly enough, but Paris also didn't miss the scrutinizing looks she was giving him when she thought he wasn't looking. He was dressed in dark colors and had tattoos on both arms. He also had a motorcycle parked in the driveway. He probably wasn't the kind of guy Mrs. Shaw would have imagined her sweet librarian daughter with.

"Good thing you didn't bring Dad," Lacy's sister Birdie said. "He would've grilled Paris mercilessly."

"Paris and I aren't dating," Lacy reiterated for the tenth time since she'd welcomed the women into her home. She slid her gaze to look at Paris, and he saw the question in her eyes. *Are we?* When the ladies had come through the front door, they'd all immediately began calling him Lacy's secret boyfriend.

"Sounds like I'd be in trouble if you and I did get together," Paris said. "Your dad sounds strict."

Lacy laughed softly. "Notice that my sisters and I are all still single. There's a reason for that."

Lacy's other sister, Rose, snorted. "Dad crashed my high school prom when I didn't come home by curfew. Who has a curfew on prom night?" Rose slid her fork into a pile of macaroni and cheese. "I thought I'd never forgive Dad for that. I liked that guy too."

"What was his name again?" Mrs. Shaw asked.

Rose looked up, her eyes squinting as she seemed to think. "I can't remember. Brent maybe. Bryce? Could've been Bryan."

"You couldn't have liked him too much if you can't remember his name," Mrs. Shaw pointed out.

Everyone at the table laughed.

"Don't you worry, Rose," Dawanda said, seated beside Mrs. Shaw. "I've read your cappuccino, and you have someone very special coming your way. I saw it in the foam."

"Well, I'll be sure to keep him away from my dad until the wedding," Rose said sarcastically, making everyone chuckle again.

Whereas some read tea leaves, Dawanda read images formed in the foam of a cappuccino. She'd done a reading for Paris last Christmas. Oddly enough, Dawanda had told him he was the only one whose fortune she couldn't read. Dawanda had assured him it wasn't that he was going to fall off a cliff or anything. His future was just up in the air. He had shut his heart off to dreaming of a life anywhere or with anyone.

He didn't exactly believe in fortune-telling, but she was spot-on with that. Some people just weren't cut out for forever homes and families. He guessed he was one of them.

"Dad's first question any time he meets any of our dates is 'What are your intentions with my girl?' " Rose said, impersonating a man's deep voice.

"He actually said that while sharpening his pocket-knife for a date I brought home in college," Birdie said. "I didn't mind because I didn't like the guy too much, but what if I had?"

"Then you would've been out of luck," Lacy said on a laugh.

The conversation continued, and then Mrs. Shaw looked across the table at Paris. "So, Paris," she said, her eyes narrowing, "tell us about yourself. Did you grow up around here?"

Paris looked up from his lunch. "I spent a little time in Sweetwater Springs growing up. Some in Wild Blossom Bluffs. My parents moved around a lot."

"Oh? For their jobs? Military maybe?" she asked.

Paris shifted. Ex-felons weren't allowed to join the

military. "Not exactly. I was in foster care here for a while."

"Foster care?" Mrs. Shaw's lips rounded in a little O. "That must've been hard for a young child."

Paris focused his attention back on his food. "I guess I didn't really know any different. Most of the places I landed were nice enough." And there'd been somewhere he'd wished he could stay. Six months with the Jenson family was the longest amount of time he'd ever gotten to stay. It was just enough time to bond with his foster parents and to feel the loss of them to his core when he was placed back with his real parents.

He picked up his fork and stabbed at a piece of chicken.

"And what brought you back to Sweetwater Springs? If I recall, you moved here last year, right?" Dawanda asked. "You came into my shop while you were staying at the Sweetwater Bed and Breakfast."

Paris swallowed past the sudden tightness in his throat. He didn't really want to answer that question either. He looked around the table, his gaze finally landing on Lacy. "Well, I guess I decided to come back here after my divorce."

Lacy's lips parted.

Had he forgotten to mention that little detail to her? When he was with Lacy, he forgot all about those lonely years in Florida. All he could think about was the moment he was in, and the ones that would follow.

"That sounds rough as well," Mrs. Shaw said.

Paris shrugged, feeling weighed down by the truth. "Well, those things are in the rearview mirror now." He tried to offer a lighter tone of voice, but all the women looked crestfallen. Mrs. Shaw had already seemed wary of him, but now she appeared even more so.

"And since my husband isn't here to ask"—Mrs. Shaw folded her hands in front of her on the table—"what are your intentions with my daughter?"

"Mom!" Lacy set her fork down. "Paris and I aren't even dating." She looked over at him. "I mean, we went on a date last night. Two if you count that night at the park."

"Last night?" Birdie asked.

All the women's eyes widened.

"It wasn't like that." Lacy looked flustered. "We didn't spend the night together."

Mrs. Shaw's jaw dropped open, and Lacy's face turned a deep crimson.

Guilt curled in Paris's stomach. Lacy was trying her best to prove herself to everyone around her. Now her family and Dawanda were gawking at her like she'd lost her mind. It was crazy to think that she and Paris would be dating. Sophie Daniels had told him at the boutique that opposites attract, but he and Lacy had led very different lives.

"Sounds like you're dating to me. Are you going to go out again?" Rose asked.

"Well, Paris offered to go with me to my reunion," Lacy said.

Mrs. Shaw's smile returned. "Oh, I'm so glad you decided to go! That's wonderful, dear. I want all those bullies to see that you are strong and beautiful, smart and funny, interesting—"

"Mom," Lacy said, cutting her off, "you might be a little partial."

"But she's right," Paris said, unable to help himself.

Lacy turned to look at him, and something pinched in his chest. He'd tried to keep things strictly friendly with her, but he'd failed miserably. What was he going to do now? He didn't want a relationship, but if they continued to spend time together, she would.

"So, Paris, how did you get our Lacy to agree to go to this reunion of hers?" Mrs. Shaw asked. "She was so dead set on not attending."

"Actually, Lace made that decision on her own," he said.

"Lace?" Both Birdie and Rose asked in unison.

The nickname had just rolled off his tongue, but it fit. Lace was delicate and beautiful, accentuated by holes that one might think made it more fragile. It was strong, just like the woman sitting next to him. She was stronger than she even knew.

"Well, I'm glad she's changed her mind. High school was such a rough time for our Lacy," Mrs. Shaw said. "I want her to go and have a good time and show those bullies who treated her so badly that they didn't break her."

Paris glanced over at Lacy. He wanted her old classmates to see the same thing.

Mrs. Shaw pointed a finger at Paris, gaining his attention. "But if you take her, it won't be on the back of that motorcycle in the driveway. Lacy doesn't ride those things."

"Actually, Mom, I rode on the back of it with Paris two days ago."

Mrs. Shaw looked horrified.

"Maybe he'll let me drive it next time," Lacy added, making all the women at the table look surprised.

"Lacy rode on the back of your bike?" Birdie asked Paris. "This is not our sister. What have you done with the real Lacy Shaw?"

He looked over at the woman in question. The real Lacy was sitting right beside him. He saw her, even if no one else did. And the last thing he wanted to do was walk away from her, which was why he needed to do just that.

* * *

An hour later, Lacy closed her front door as her guests left and leaned against it, exhaling softly.

"Your mom and sisters are great," Paris said, standing a couple of feet away from her. "Your aunt too."

She lifted her gaze to his. "You almost sound serious about that."

"Well, I'm not going to lie. They were a little overwhelming."

"A little?" Lacy grinned. "And they were subdued today. They're usually worse."

Paris shoved his hands in his pockets. "They love you. Can't fault them for that."

The way he was looking at her made her breath catch. Was he going to kiss her again?

"I guess not."

"They want what's best for you," he continued. Then he looked away. "And, uh, I'm not sure that's me, Lace."

She straightened at the sudden shift in his tone of voice. "What?"

He ran a hand over his hair. "When we were eating just now, I realized that being your date might not be doing you any favors. Or me."

"Wait, you're not going to the reunion with me anymore?" she asked.

He shook his head. "I just think it'd be better if you went with someone else."

"I don't have anyone else," she protested, her heart beating fast. "The reunion is in less than a week. I have my dress, and you have a matching shirt. And you're the one I want to go with. I don't even care about the reunion. I just want to be with you."

He looked down for a moment. "You heard me talking to your family. I've lived a different life than you. I'm an ex-foster kid. My parents are felons." He shrugged. "I couldn't even make a marriage work."

"Those things are in the past, Paris. I don't care about any of that."

He met her gaze again. "But I do. Call me selfish, but I don't want to want you. I don't want to want things that I know I'll never have. It's not in the cappuccino for me, Lacy." His expression was pained. "I really want you to believe me when I say it's not you, it's me."

Her eyes and throat burned, and she wondered if she felt worse for herself or for him. He obviously had issues, but who didn't? One thing she'd learned since high school was that no one's life was perfect. Her flaws were just obvious back then because of the back brace.

She'd also learned that you couldn't make someone feel differently than they did. The only feelings you could control were your own. The old Lacy never stood up for herself. She let people trample on her and her feelings. But she'd changed. She was the new Lacy now.

She lifted her eyes to meet Paris's and swallowed past the growing lump in her throat. "If that's the way you feel, then I think you should go."

Chapter Seven

On Monday afternoon, Paris looked out over the roomful of students. Everyone had their eyes on their screens and were learning to Skype. But his attention was on the librarian on the other side of the building.

When he'd driven to the library, he'd lectured himself on why he needed to back away from Lacy Shaw. Sunday's lunch had made that crystal clear in his mind. She was smart and beautiful, the kind of woman who valued family. Paris had no idea what it even meant to have a family. He couldn't be the kind of guy she needed.

Luckily, Lacy hadn't even been at the counter when he'd walked in and continued toward the computer room. She was probably hell-bent on avoiding him. For the best.

"Does everyone think they can go home and Skype now?" Paris asked the class.

"I can, but no one I know will know how to Skype with me," Greta said.

Janice Murphy nodded beside her.

"Well, you could all exchange information and Skype with each other," Paris suggested.

"Can we Skype with you?" Alice asked.

Warmness spread through his chest. "Anytime, Alice."

"Can I Skype you if my wife doesn't want to talk to me?" Mr. Jenson asked. "To practice so I'm ready when she does?"

Paris felt a little sad for the older man. When Paris had been a boy in their home, they'd been the happiest of couples. "Of course. If I'm home and free, I'll always make time to Skype with any one of you," he told the group, meaning it. They'd had only a few classes, but he loved the eclectic bunch in this room.

When class was over, he walked over to Mr. Jenson. "I can give you a ride home if you want."

Mr. Jenson gave him an assessing stare. "If you think I'm climbing on the back of that bike of yours, you're crazy."

Paris chuckled. "I drove my truck today. It'll save you a walk. I have the afternoon free too. I can take you by the nursing home facility to see Mrs. Jenson if you want. I'm sure she'd be happy to see you."

Mr. Jenson continued to stare at him. "Why would you do that? I know I'm not that fun to be around."

Paris clapped a gentle hand on Mr. Jenson's back. "That's not true. I kind of like being around you." He always had. "And I could use some company today. Agreeing would actually be doing me a favor."

"I don't do favors," the older man said. "But my legs are kind of hurting, thanks to the chairs in there. So walking home would be a pain."

Paris felt relieved as Mr. Jenson relented. "What about visiting Mrs. Jenson? I'll stay in the truck while you go in, and take as long as you like." Paris patted his laptop bag. "I have my computer, so I can work while I wait."

Mr. Jenson begrudgingly agreed and even smiled a little bit. "Thank you."

Paris led Mr. Jenson into his truck and started the short drive toward Sweetwater Nursing Facility.

"She sometimes tells me to leave as soon as I get there," Mr. Jenson said as they drove.

"Why is that?"

Mr. Jenson shrugged. "She says she doesn't want me to see her that way."

Paris still wasn't quite sure what was wrong with Mrs. Jenson. "What way?"

"Oh, you know. Her emotions are as unstable as her walking these days. That's why she's not home with me. She's not the same Nancy I fell in love with, but she's still the woman I love. I'll always love her, no matter how things change."

"That's what love is, isn't it?" Paris asked.

Mr. Jenson turned to look out the passenger side window as they rode. "We never had any kids of our own. We fostered a few, and that was as close as we ever got to having a family."

Paris swallowed painfully.

"There was one boy who was different. We would've kept him. We bonded and loved him as our own."

Paris glanced over. Was Mr. Jenson talking about him? Probably not, but Paris couldn't help hoping that he was. "What happened?"

"We wanted to raise him as part of our family, but it didn't work out that way. He went back to his real parents, which I suppose is always best. I lost him, and now, most days, I've lost my wife too. That's what love is. Painful."

Paris parked and looked over. "Well, maybe today will be different. Whatever happens, I'll be in the truck waiting for you."

Mr. Jenson looked over and chuckled, but Paris could tell by the gleam in his eyes that he appreciated the sentiment. He stepped out of the truck and dipped his head to look at Paris in the driver's seat. "Some consolation prize."

* * *

Two nights later, Lacy sat in her living room with a handful of the Ladies' Day Out members. They'd been waiting for her in the driveway when she'd gotten home from the library and were here for an intervention of sorts.

"Sandwiches?" Greta asked, her face twisting with displeasure.

"Well, when you don't tell someone that you're coming, you get PB&J." Lacy plopped onto the couch beside Birdie, who had no doubt called everyone here.

"You took your online profile down," Birdie said, reaching for her own sandwich.

"Of course I did. I'm not interested in dating right now."

"You sure looked interested in Paris Montgomery,"

Dawanda said, sitting across from them. "And you two looked so good together. What happened?"

All the women turned to face Lacy.

She shrugged. "My family happened. No offense. You all behaved—mostly," she told her mom and sisters. "We just decided it'd be best to part ways sooner rather than later."

Birdie placed her sandwich down. "I thought you were the smart one in the family."

Rose raised her hand. "No, that was always me." A wide grin spread on her face. "Just kidding. It's you, Lacy."

Birdie frowned. "I was there last weekend. I saw how you two were together. There's relationship potential there," she said.

Lacy sighed. "Maybe, but he doesn't want another relationship. He's been hurt and..." She shrugged. "I guess he just doesn't think it's worth trying again." That was her old insecurities though so she stopped them all in their tracks. "Actually, something good came out of me going out with him a few times."

"Oh?" Birdie asked. "What's that?"

"I'm not afraid to go to my reunion, even if I have to go on my own."

"Maybe you'll meet someone there. Maybe you'll find 'the one,'" Rose said.

"Maybe." But Lacy was pretty sure she wouldn't find the *one* she wanted. He'd already been found and lost.

"I'll go with you if you need me to," Josie offered. She wasn't sitting on the couch with Lacy's laptop this time. Instead, she held a glass of wine tonight, looking relaxed in the recliner across the room.

"I wonder what people would think about that," Birdie said.

Lacy shrugged. "You know what, I've decided that I don't care what the people who don't know me think. I care about what I think. And what you all think, of course."

"And Paris?" Dawanda asked.

Lacy shook her head, but she meant yes. Paris was right. Her gestures often contradicted what she really meant. "Paris thinks that we should just be friends, and I have to respect that."

Even if she didn't like it.

Chapter Eight

Paris was spending his Saturday night in Mr. Jenson's rosebushes—not at Lacy's class reunion as he'd planned. He'd clipped the bushes back, pruning the dead ends so that they'd come back stronger.

Over the last couple of days, he'd kept himself super busy with work and taking Mr. Jenson to and from the nursing facility. He'd read up on how to care for rosebushes, but that hadn't been necessary because Mr. Jenson stayed on the porch barking out instructions like a drill sergeant. Paris didn't mind. He loved the old man.

"Don't clip too much off!" Mr. Jenson warned. "Just what's needed."

"Got it." Paris squeezed the clippers again and again, until the muscles of his hand were cramping.

Despite his best efforts, he hadn't kept himself busy enough to keep from thinking about Lacy. She'd waved and said hi to him when he'd gone in and out of the library, but that was all. It wasn't enough.

He missed her. A lot. Hopefully she was still going

to her reunion tonight. He hoped she danced. And maybe there'd be a nice guy there who would dance with her.

Guilt and jealousy curled around Paris's ribs like the roses on the lattice. He still wanted to be that guy who held her close tonight and watched her shine.

"Done yet?" Mr. Jenson asked gruffly.

Paris wiped his brow and straightened. "All done."

Mr. Jenson nodded approvingly. "It looks good, son."

Mr. Jenson didn't mean anything by calling him son, but it still tugged on Paris's heartstrings. "Thanks. I'll come by next week and take you to see Mrs. Jenson."

"Just don't expect me to get on that bike of yours," the older man said for the hundredth time.

"Wouldn't dream of it." As Paris started to walk away, Mr. Jenson called out to him.

"PJ?"

Paris froze. He hadn't heard that name in a long time, but it still stopped him in his tracks. He turned back to face Mr. Jenson. "You know?"

Mr. Jenson chuckled. "I'm old, not blind. I've known since that first computer class."

"But you didn't say anything." Paris took a few steps, walking back toward Mr. Jenson on the porch. "Why?"

"I could ask you the same. You didn't say anything either."

Paris held his hands out to his sides. "I called last year. Mrs. Jenson answered and told me to never call again."

Mr. Jenson shook his head as he listened. "I didn't

know that, but it sounds about right. She tells me the same thing when I call her. Don't take it personally."

Paris pulled in a deep breath and everything he'd thought about the situation shifted and became something very different. They hadn't turned him away. Mr. Jenson hadn't even known he'd tried to reconnect.

Mr. Jenson shoved his hands in the pockets of his pants. "I loved PJ. It was hard to lose him… You." Mr. Jenson cleared his throat and looked off into the distance. "It's been hard to lose Nancy, memory by memory, too. I guess some part of me didn't say anything when I realized who you were because I was just plain tired of losing. Sometimes it's easier not to feel anything. Then it doesn't hurt so much when it's gone." He looked back at Paris. "But I can't seem to lose you even if I wanted to, so maybe I'll just stop trying."

Paris's eyes burned. He blinked and looked down at his feet for a moment and then back up at the old man. He was pretty sure Mr. Jenson didn't want to be hugged, but Paris was going to anyway. He climbed the steps and wrapped his arms around his foster dad for a brief time. Then he pulled away. "Like I said, I'll be back next week, and I'll take you to go see Mrs. Jenson."

"See. Can't push you away. Might as well take you inside with me when I go see Nancy next time. She'll probably tell you to go away and never come back."

"I won't listen," Paris promised.

"Good." Mr. Jenson looked relieved somehow. His body posture was more relaxed. "Well, you best get on with your night. I'm sure you have things to do. Maybe go see that pretty librarian."

Paris's heart rate picked up. He was supposed to be at Lacy's side tonight, but while she was bravely facing her fears, he'd let his keep him away. His parents were supposed to love him and stand by him, but they hadn't. His ex-wife had abandoned him too. He guessed he'd gotten tired of losing just like Mr. Jenson. It was easier to push people away before they pushed him.

But the Jensons had never turned their back on him. They'd wanted him and he wished things had gone differently. Regardless of what happened in the past, it wasn't too late to reconnect and have what could've been now.

As he headed back to his bike, Paris pulled his cell phone out of his pocket and checked the time. Hopefully, it wasn't too late for him and Lacy either.

* * *

Lacy looked at her reflection in the long mirror in her bedroom. She loved the dress she'd found at Sophie's Boutique. She had a matching pair of shoes that complemented it perfectly. Her hair was also done up, and she'd put on just a little bit of makeup.

She flashed a confident smile. "I can do this."

She took another deep breath and then hurried to get her purse and keys. The reunion would be starting soon, and she needed to leave before she changed her mind. The nerves were temporary, but the memories from tonight would last. And despite her worries, she was sure they'd be good memories.

She grabbed her things and drove to Sweetwater

Springs High School where the class reunion was taking place. When she was parked, she sat for a moment, watching her former classmates head inside. They all had someone on their arm. No one was going in alone. Except her.

She imagined walking inside and everyone stopping to stare at her. The mean girls from her past pointing and laughing and whispering among each other. That was the worst-case scenario and probably wasn't going to happen. But if it did, she'd get through it. She wasn't a shy kid anymore. She was strong and confident, and yeah, she'd rather have Paris holding her hand, but she didn't need him to. "I can do this," she said again.

She pushed her car door open, locked it up, and headed inside. She opened the door to the gymnasium, accosted by the music and sounds of laughter. It wasn't directed at her. No one was even looking at her. She exhaled softly, scanning the room for familiar faces. When she saw Claire Donovan, the coordinator of the event, standing with Halona Locklear and Brenna McConnell, she headed in that direction. They were always nice to her.

"Lacy!" Brenna exclaimed when she saw her walking over. "It's so good to see you." She gave her a big hug, and Lacy relaxed a little more. "Even though we all see each other on a regular basis," she said once they'd pulled apart.

Lacy hugged the other women as well.

"So you came alone too?" Lacy asked Halona.

"Afraid so. My mom is watching Theo for a few hours. I told her I really didn't need to come, but she insisted."

Brenna nodded as she listened to the conversation. "Sounds familiar. Everyone told me that you can't skip your high school reunion."

"This is a small town. It's not like we don't know where everyone ended up," Halona said. "Most everyone anyway."

"Don't look now," Summer Rodriquez said, also joining the conversation, "but Carmen Daly is veering this way."

Lacy's heart sank. Carmen was the leader of her little pack of mean girls. How many times had Lacy cried in the girls' bathroom over something Carmen had said or done to make her life miserable?

Lacy subtly stood a little straighter. Her brace was gone, and whatever Carmen dished out, she intended to return.

"Hi, ladies," Carmen said, looking between them. She was just as beautiful as ever. Lacy knew Carmen didn't live in Sweetwater Springs anymore. From what Lacy had heard, Carmen had married a doctor and lived a few hours east from here. Her vibrant smile grew sheepish as she looked at Lacy. "Hi, Lacy."

Every muscle in Lacy's body tensed. "Hi, Carmen."

Then Carmen surprised her by stepping forward to give her a hug. For a moment, Lacy wondered if she was sticking a sign on her back like she'd done so long ago. KICK ME. I WON'T FEEL IT.

Carmen pulled back and looked Lacy in the eye while her friends watched. "Lacy, I've thought about you so many times over the years. I'm so glad you're here tonight."

Lacy swallowed. "Oh?"

"I want to tell you that I'm sorry. For everything. I'm ashamed of the person I was and how I acted toward you. So many times I've thought about messaging you on Facebook or emailing you, but this is something that really needs to be done in person." Carmen's eyes grew shiny. "Lacy, I'm so sorry. I mean it."

Lacy's mouth dropped open. Of all the things she'd imagined about tonight, this wasn't one of them. She turned to look at Summer, Brenna, and Halona, whose lips were also parted in shock, and then she looked back at Carmen.

"I've tried to be a better person, but the way I behaved in high school has haunted me for the last ten years."

Lacy reached for Carmen's hand and gave it a squeeze. "Thank you. Looks like we've both changed."

"We grew up." Carmen shrugged. "Can you ever forgive me?"

"Definitely."

Carmen seemed to relax. "Maybe we can be friends on Facebook," she said. "And in real life. Maybe a coffee date next time I come home."

"I'd like that." Lacy's eyes burned as she hugged Carmen again and watched her walk over to her husband. Then Lacy turned her back to her friends. "Is there a sign on my back?"

"Nope," Brenna said. "I think that was sincere."

Lacy faced them again. "Me too. It was worth coming here tonight just for that." Someone tapped her shoulder and she spun again, this time coming face-to-face with Paris.

"Sorry to interrupt," he said, looking just as sheepish as Carmen had a few minutes earlier.

She noticed that he was dressed in the shirt he purchased from Sophie's Boutique. "Paris, what are you doing here?"

"Hoping to get a dance with you?" He looked at the dance floor, where a few couples were swaying.

"I...I don't know," she said.

Summer put a hand on her back and gave her a gentle push. "No more sitting on the sidelines, Lacy. When a boy asks you to dance, you say yes."

Lacy took a few hesitant steps, following Paris. Then they stopped and turned to face each other, the music wrapping around them. "Paris"—she shook her head—"you didn't have to come. As you can see, I didn't chicken out. I'm here and actually having a great time. I don't need you to hold my hand."

He reached for her hand anyway, pulling her body toward his. The touch made her grow warm all over. "You never needed me. But I'm hoping you still want me."

Lacy swallowed. *Yeah*, she definitely still wanted him. She looked at his arms looped around her waist. They fit together so nicely. Then she looked back up at him. "I lied when I said that we could still be friends, Paris. I can't. I want things when I'm with you. Things I shouldn't want, but I can't help it."

"Such as?" he asked.

Lacy took a breath. She might as well be honest and scare him off for good. "I want a relationship. I want to fall in love. I want it all. And I just think it would be too hard—"

Paris dropped his mouth to hers and stopped her words with a soft kiss.

"What are you doing?" she asked when he pulled back away.

"I want things when I'm with you too," he said, leaning in closer so she could hear him over the music. "I want to kiss you. Hold your hand. Be the guy you want a relationship with. To be in love with."

Lacy's lips parted. Since they were being honest…"You already are that guy. I mean, not the love part. We haven't known each other very long, so it's too soon for that. That would be crazy."

"Maybe, but I understand exactly what you mean," he said.

She narrowed her eyes. "Then why are you smiling? You said you didn't want those things."

"Correction. I said I didn't *want* to want those things." He tightened his hold on her as they danced. "But it appears it's already too late, and you're worth the risk."

"So you're my date to this reunion tonight," Lacy said. "Then what?"

"Then tomorrow or the next day, I was thinking I'd go to your family's house for dinner and win over your dad."

Lacy grimaced. "That won't be easy. He'll want to know what your intentions are with his daughter."

Paris grinned. "My intention is to put you on the back of my bike and ride off into the sunset. What do you think he'll say to that?"

She grinned. "I think he'll hate that response. But if you're asking what I think…"

"Tell me," Paris whispered, continuing to sway with her, face-to-face, body-to-body.

"I love it." Then Lacy lifted up on her toes and kissed him for the entire world to see, even though in the moment, no one else existed except him and her.

About the Author

Annie Rains is a *USA Today* bestselling contemporary romance author who writes small-town love stories set in fictional places in her home state of North Carolina. When Annie isn't writing, she's living out her own happily ever after with her husband and three children.

Learn more at:

http://www.annierains.com/
Twitter @AnnieRainsBooks
http://facebook.com/annierainsbooks

Fall in love with these charming contemporary romances!

SUMMER ON MOONLIGHT BAY
by Hope Ramsay

Veterinarian Noah Cuthbert had no intention of ever moving back to the small town of Magnolia Harbor. But when his sister calls with the opportunity to run the local animal clinic as well as give her a break from caring for their ailing mom, he packs his bags and heads home. But once he meets the clinic's beautiful new manager, he questions whether his summer plans might become more permanent. Includes a bonus novel by Miranda Liasson!

WISH YOU WERE MINE
by Tara Sivec

When Everett Southerland left town five years ago, Cameron James thought it was the worst day of her life. She was wrong: It was the day he came back and told her the truth about his feelings that devastated her. Now she's having a hard time believing him, until he proves to her how much he cares. But with so many secrets between them, will they ever find the future that was always destined to be theirs?

Find more great reads on Instagram with @ReadForeverPub.

ALL I WANT FOR CHRISTMAS IS YOU
by Miranda Liasson

Just when Kaitlyn Barnes vows to get over her longtime crush on Rafe Langdon, they share a sizzling evening that delivers an epic holiday surprise: Kaitlyn is pregnant. While their off-the-charts chemistry can still melt snow, Rafe must decide if he'll keep running from love forever—or if he'll make this Christmas the one where he becomes the man Kaitlyn wants…and the one she deserves. Includes a bonus novel by Annie Rains!

SNOWFALL ON CEDAR TRAIL
by Annie Rains

Determined to give her son a good holiday season, single mom Halona Locklear signs him up for Sweetwater Springs' Mentor Match program. Little does she know that her son's mentor would be the handsome chief of police, who might know secrets about her past that she is determined to keep buried. Includes a bonus novel by Miranda Liasson!

Follow @ReadForeverPub on Twitter and join the conversation using #ReadForever.

IT STARTED WITH CHRISTMAS
by Jenny Hale

Holly McAdams loves spending the holidays at her family's cozy cabin, but she soon discovers that the gorgeous and wealthy Joseph Barnes has been renting the cabin, and it looks like he'll be staying for the holidays. Throw in Holly's charming ex, and she's got the recipe for one complicated Christmas. With unexpected guests and secrets aplenty, will Holly be able to find herself and the love she's always dreamed of this Christmas?

CHRISTMAS IN HARMONY HARBOR
by Debbie Mason

Evangeline Christmas will do anything to save her year-round Christmas store, Holiday House, including facing off against high-powered real-estate developer Caine Elliot, who's using his money and influence to push through his competing property next door. When her last desperate attempt to stop him fails, she gambles everything on a proposition she prays the handsome, blue-eyed player can't refuse. Includes a bonus novella!

Connect with us at Facebook.com/ReadForeverPub.

THE AMISH WEDDING PROMISE
by Laura V. Hilton

After a storm crashes through town, Grace Lantz is forced to postpone her wedding. All hands are needed for cleanup, but Grace doesn't know where to start—should she console her special needs sister or find her missing groom? Sparks fly when the handsome Zeke Bontrager comes to aid the community and offers to help the overwhelmed Grace in any way he can. But when her groom is found, Grace must decide if the wedding will go on…or if she'll take a chance on Zeke.

MERMAID INN
by Jenny Holiday

When Eve Abbott inherits her aunt's inn, she remembers the heartbreaking last summer she spent there, and she has no interest in returning. Unfortunately, Eve must run the inn for two years before she can sell. Town sheriff Sawyer Collins can't deny all the old feelings that come rushing back when he sees Eve. Getting her out of Matchmaker Bay when they were younger was something he did for her own good. But losing her again? He doesn't think he can survive that twice. Includes a bonus novella by Alison Bliss!